THE HANGED MAN'S TALE

GERALD JAY

THE HANGED MAN'S TALE

A NOVEL

Nan A. Talese | Doubleday
New York

All rights reserved. Published in the United States by Nan A. Talese/Doubleday, a division of Penguin Random House LLC, New York, and distributed in Canada by Penguin Random House Canada Limited, Toronto.

www.nanatalese.com

DOUBLEDAY is a registered trademark of Penguin Random House LLC. Nan A. Talese and the colophon are trademarks of Penguin Random House LLC.

Book design by Michael Collica
Jacket images: Hanged Man tarot card by Aki Horiuchi /
Getty Images; blood drops by petekarici / Getty Images
Jacket design by Michael J. Windsor

Library of Congress Cataloging-in-Publication Data

Names: Goldberg, Gerald Jay, author.
Title: The hanged man's tale : a novel / by Gerald Jay.
Description: First edition. | New York : Nan A. Talese, [2021]
Identifiers: LCCN 2021016832 (print) | LCCN 2021016833 (ebook) |
ISBN 9780385537544 (hardcover) | ISBN 9780385537551 (ebook)
Subjects: GSAFD: Mystery fiction.
Classification: LCC PS3557.O357 H36 2021 (print) |
LCC PS3557.O357 (ebook) | DDC 813/.54—dc23
LC record available at https://lccn.loc.gov/2021016832
LC ebook record available at https://lccn.loc.gov/2021016833

MANUFACTURED IN THE UNITED STATES OF AMERICA

1st Printing

For GJG

If they can get you asking the wrong questions,
they don't have to worry about answers . . .

—Thomas Pynchon

PART ONE

PROLOGUE

He told close friends about his plans. No one believed him. "Watch the TV this Sunday," he said. "I'm going to be a star." Of course they didn't take him seriously. But that's the way they were, his few close friends. No dreams bigger than banging a Deshi on the Métro or blowing up a kosher deli in the Fourth. To the rest he e-mailed, "Death to Zog (88)." Then he glanced at the calendar on his bedroom wall where the fourteenth of the month was circled in red. Only one more day.

His alarm clock on top of the bureau was set for 5 a.m. At that hour on a Sunday there shouldn't be any bottlenecks, but tomorrow was a national holiday. And driving to the center of Paris was never a picnic at any hour. His clothes were already laid out and ready to go, neat as a pin. Like Mishima, military style. The tan chinos, a crisp blue shirt, his black windbreaker with its black hood.

Naked he climbed into bed, pulled the sheet over his head, closed his eyes. Dead quiet outside. Known by the locals as wild doings in Courcouronnes, or family high life in the burbs. At least it was good to have the two of them out of the way, the house all to himself. Not to mention the old boy's big Gibson left behind. And tomorrow—he rolled over, pounding his pillow—was another day.

In the still black room the next morning, the red alarm went off like a dynamite vest. Five on the digital dot. Picking up his sheet from the floor, he tossed it back on the bed. He had urgent plans to attend to—a marquee future featuring his name in lights. One outstanding success that would redeem a life full of petty failures.

Shaved, showered, dressed, and well caffeinated, with two cups of coffee to the good, he quick-marched across the room to check himself out in the mirror.

"Ready for your close-up, Max?"

Max smiled.

"Okay! Roll 'em!"

He picked up the brown guitar case with its Gibson USA label, slammed his bedroom door closed, and strode out the front entrance into the cool gray dawn. The big case went into the trunk of his car. Before climbing in, he glanced back at the neat row of two-story buildings. They called their house the white pavilion. He called it their bourgeois dream—a bland, vanilla shoebox. Edging the property, a strip of dark green shrubs. The last thing she said before leaving on vacation was one final castrating order, "Remember, Max. This time don't forget. Water the plants or they'll die."

He'd forgotten, of course, but it made no difference. As a parting gesture, he unzipped his fly and peed all over her hedge. It looked refreshed. The damn thing flourished no matter what he did. Or didn't.

Once in Paris, everything went like clockwork. He left his car on a side street near the Parc Monceau and, case in hand, walked toward the starting point of the parade on the Champs-Élysées. Less than a stone's throw from the flag-draped Arc de Triomphe. That was the direction from which the president would make his initial appearance. Max stood behind the low metal police barricade, patiently waiting with the rest of the early birds. He could see everything from there. A perfect position.

Commandant Paul Mazarelle had always enjoyed the Bastille Day parade. The sappers of the French Foreign Legion with their orange leather aprons and shouldered axes. The caped Spahis. The glittering *casque-d'or* cavalry of the Republican Guard. And in the sky above Paris, the blue, white, and red smoke contrails of the roaring

Patrouille de France Alpha Jets. But this year he didn't think he'd have time to savor the color.

They were expecting a large crowd—perhaps one hundred thousand or more. Only two months ago President Chirac had been reelected by a landslide in a contentious runoff with the ultra-right-wing Jean-Marie Le Pen. Parisians, by and large, were glad. They didn't care for extremists. This year they cared for Americans. Ten months earlier al Qaeda terrorists had destroyed New York's Twin Towers. Today, the theme of the Bastille Day 2002 parade was Franco-American friendship. Among the honored guests in the parade reviewing stand on the Place de la Concorde were members of the FDNY. And as a special honor on the two hundredth anniversary of France's military academy, a trim contingent of West Point cadets—white summer pants, gray fitted jackets—had been invited to march beside the flamboyant young Frenchmen from the Saint-Cyr, their red and snowy white plumes fluttering.

In spite of all the frills, parade duty was no one's idea of a good time. For Mazarelle, it was a not-so-subtle hint. He might be a commandant in the elite Brigade Criminelle, but his new boss was reminding him that, whatever famous success he'd had in the Dordogne, he wasn't above crowd control in Paris. Four decades after Maigret, no one liked a celebrity detective.

Knocking on the door of the large white PC Police van, Mazarelle pushed it open and tried to step inside, but there was little room for a man his size. The intelligence unit—officers seated in shirtsleeves before their computers, telephones, LED maps, closed-circuit TV screens, shortwave radios, and other electronic gear—was a humming beehive of activity.

One of the officers glancing up recognized him. "Can I help you, chief?"

"You're busy. I'll come back."

"Just a minute." She brushed her blond hair back, picked up her pack of Gauloises, and came out to join him. "I was going for a smoke myself. Have one."

"Sure." Mazarelle liked the steady way she cupped her hands around the offered match. He took a deep drag. *Ech!* It reminded him why he'd given up cigarettes. He'd been so busy that morning when he left his office he'd forgotten to take his pipe. "Thanks," he said, and inhaling once again coughed up the smoke.

She smiled, seemed glad to see him. He didn't know why. They had barely exchanged more than a word or two at the 36 Quai des Orfèvres party.

"So you only visit on holidays?" Her eyes sparkled as she tucked her hair behind her ear. On the inside, Mazarelle was sparkling too. When a woman ran her fingers through her hair, four decades of experience told him it meant one thing.

He'd forgotten what her name was, but he'd find out. She was a woman who wore a Beretta on her hip as if she knew how to use it. Definitely worth keeping an eye on. And probably the right person to ask about threat levels and security.

She nodded. "Raised to twenty-five hundred *policiers* and gendarmes as well as the elite units GIGM and RAID. Plus air force reconnaissance planes and fighters above the parade route." She patted him on the arm. "Feel safer?"

"Sounds good—" he started, interrupted by a sudden burst of Lester Young's creamy tenor sax. "Excuse me."

Mazarelle pulled out his mobile, listened for several seconds. It was a member of his team at the Étoile with a heads-up. The parade was about to start. Mazarelle replied in a muted conspiratorial voice that he was on his way.

"Sorry," he turned to apologize, but she was gone.

He found his young aide, Lieutenant Jean Villepin, not far from the Étoile. Plainclothes Jeannot had a rocker's scalp full of long, stringy, dirty-blond hair. He wore a scruffy blue sweatshirt, grimy Nikes, and torn jeans to go with it.

Mazarelle asked, "Where's your police armband?"

"In my office."

"Looking the way you do, you'll need it. Here, take mine. The Champs-Élysées is getting jammed. But we've got a few of our men sprinkled among all the others along the route from the Arc de Triomphe to the reviewing stand at Concorde. Now get over to the rue Washington. When the president goes by, I want you shadowing the car all the way down the avenue."

"I'll handle it," Jeannot assured him.

"Above all, no matter what happens don't let him out of your sight. Can you do that?"

"I think so."

"Good. We've got the counter-sniper teams up above. But we need more bodies on the street. Besides, you've got the legs. I've seen you take the stairs three at a time at 36." Mazarelle pointed to his beat-up Nikes and winked. "Just do it."

Max heard the band in the distance. Then, coming out from behind the Arc de Triomphe as if a cloud had lifted and the sun appeared, the open-topped presidential jeep sporting small elegant French flags fluttering front and rear. The jeep moved slowly, decorously along the Champs-Élysées, preceded by a rolling wave of cheers, whistles, laughter, applause. And there he was at last! Reelected for five more years rather than seven, but five too many as far as Max was concerned. The president of France himself standing in the open jeep behind his uniformed drivers like a fuckin' god in his gleaming chariot, smiling and waving to his adoring subjects.

Max felt that he could practically touch the president as his jeep approached. How could he miss? Pulling his rifle out of the case, he snapped it up to his shoulder. "Time to die, *monsieur le président!*" Max cried. Taking careful aim, he fired. The noise of the crowd and the music of the parade were so loud few heard the shot or knew where it had come from. Those nearby who knew screamed for the police.

Mazarelle could hear from the alarm in their voices that it was serious and saw at once where they were. For a big man with a limp, he moved through the crowd with astonishing speed. Before the gunman could get off another shot, the commandant had pounced on him, tearing the rifle out of his hands. It looked like a .22. A funny low-caliber hunting gun all wrong for a serious assassin.

Other cops soon surrounded them. Captain Maurice Kalou of his homicide team materialized at his side to log the rifle for evidence. Jeannot, down on his hands and knees, had already scooped up a shell casing.

By now, two uniformed policemen had the prisoner's hands pinned behind his back and clamped in handcuffs. They each grabbed him by an arm and dragged him to the waiting van with its side door open.

"Wait a minute." Mazarelle covered the prisoner's head with his hood. "That's better. Watch his skull," he warned them. "We don't want him to get hurt." They shoved him into the van and slammed the door. As the hooded Max sat in the dark, alone with his crazy jumbled thoughts and the people outside howling for his head, the police van raced off to the Quai des Orfèvres, siren wailing.

Later that afternoon, the questioning of the suspect took place on the fourth floor of 36 Quai des Orfèvres. Commissaire Bruno Bonfils, chief of the antiterrorism unit, quickly nailed down the prisoner's identity and sent his men twenty miles south of Paris to search Max's home in Courcouronnes. They would return empty-handed.

Jeannot, checking his computer, was more successful. Max had a history of membership in various militant, extreme right, neo-Nazi organizations.

"He's on their chat rooms, their forums, every skinhead group you can think of," Jeannot whispered in Mazarelle's ear. "He threatened to attack the police, even the pope. But looking at what he wrote . . . well . . . he's kind of a loony . . ."

Meanwhile, Max had already begun answering Bonfils's questions.

Yes, he had come to shoot the president. And he was proud of it. Yes, he had come alone. His name was going into the history books.

"Are you sure no one helped you?" demanded Bonfils.

"Yes, yes, I *told* you," Max shouted, annoyed. "It was all my plan. I intended to kill him first. Then myself. But before I could get off another shot, someone knocked the weapon out of my hands."

A smile flicked at the corners of Mazarelle's mouth. Except for that, he sat motionless, a heavy plumb line beside his colleague.

"Tell me, Max," continued Bonfils, "where did you get the rifle?"

Max laughed and explained that it was hunting gear, that he'd bought it in a sporting goods store. Actually he seemed to enjoy being the center of attention for the handful of *flics* in the warm smoke-filled room. Until he suddenly realized from their demeanor that the president was still alive. He'd failed. Everything he'd planned to do. Everything he'd dreamed of achieving. It was devastating.

Now despondent, Max became increasingly withdrawn and disturbed. Noticing the change, Commissaire Bonfils abruptly signaled a halt to the proceedings and called in two of the commissariat's officers, two leathery men with their sleeves rolled up. Bonfils told Max that he would remain at 36 in *garde à vue* until they decided what to do with him.

Mazarelle turned to Bonfils and quietly said, "No, I don't think so." Pulling Bonfils outside, he shook his head.

"This guy is not part of a terror cell. He's an angry weirdo with a full basket of emotional problems. He's a *tireur isolé*, a lone wolf with a grudge."

"How can you be so sure? I think he knows more than he's saying. And given the radical organizations he belongs to, it's reasonable to assume he had help. We don't need a disaster like the Americans. No! He stays till I'm through with him!"

"Don't forget about Durn," Mazarelle insisted. Everyone at 36 knew the story of the Nanterre killer. Brought to the fourth floor for questioning, he had thrown himself out an open dormer window. "Do we need another jumper?" Mazarelle demanded. "Max is guilty as hell . . . but he's out of his mind. We're not equipped to handle someone with his emotional problems in *garde à vue*. Send him to Villejuif, the psychiatric hospital. Right?"

Bonfils had had enough. He stalked out the door, head high, and stormed down the hall, sparks shooting from his heels.

Inside the interrogation room, the two remaining cops had tipped Max's chair backward at a precarious angle. As Max struggled to stay upright, the stocky older cop laughed. The younger cop chimed in and gave Max a swift push.

"Whaa—!" yelled a startled Max, as he toppled over backward, crashing to the floor.

The older cop picked Max up and, with a violent shove, slammed him into the wall.

Max reeled backward, dazed.

The second officer put his arm around Max, letting him in on a secret.

"See that." He chuckled. "We call it 'walling.'"

The first one nodded. "Doesn't leave a mark."

The door swung open, and Mazarelle strode in. "Enough! *Ça suffit!* What kind of cops are you? Take him to Villejuif." He crossed his arms.

"All right, all right." Grabbing Max by the shackles, the young officer yanked him forward. "*Viens,* my little friend. We have a place for you."

They dragged Max out the door of the interrogation room and into the hallway. Downstairs, they pushed him through the outer doors to the courtyard, where the ambulance waited to take him to the psychiatric ward.

He would never make it there.

1

July 20 dawned brilliant and sunny in Paris. On the Quai d'Orsay, a tiny clutch of tourists was boarding the *Belle de Jour,* a small dingy canal boat under the command of Captain Marc André, whose grizzled chin and creased white officer's cap cocked over one eye were the only visible signs of his office. André was about to leave for his first trip of the day. A short journey up the Canal Saint-Martin. The canal, built by Napoleon in the nineteenth century, was designed to bring food and fresh water into the heart of the city. Now it mostly brought tourists.

Traveling east down the Seine into the blinding morning sun, the Paris Canal boat was pursued excitedly by gulls, beating their wings and screeching like hangers scraping on metal racks. The captain loved the way their white wings dazzled the air on a day like this. Circling the Île Saint-Louis, he headed north. The canal soon ran underground, disappearing below street level for some two miles, as it headed for the passage locals called "the Locks of the Dead."

The sun faded out as they descended from daylight through the entrance into the underworld. The sound of the boat's engine was magnified to a frightening roar by the tunnel's low rough-hewn stone arch and bleak shadowy darkness, the only illumination coming from the manhole-size skylights set into its roof and projected onto the water. And in the first circle of light—hard to believe it was not noticed by any of the tourists on the boat—the strange sight of a body hanging upside down.

Captain André was stunned by the suddenness of the apparition and its airborne appearance out of nowhere. He knew the Saint-

Martin well, having worked for the Paris Canal company for almost a dozen years, and had fished more than his share of homeless floaters out of the drink. Dead drunk, and usually suicides, accident sufferers, or hapless victims of violence. But never upside-down danglers like this one tethered by a rope around one ankle. If he stopped his boat now in the tunnel and was caught, he'd lose his license. André couldn't stop. But the man was clearly dead . . . and it looked like murder. He'd only a brief glimpse of the victim's face to convince him, but that was enough. Because whoever killed him had turned the dead man's face into a gargoyle of agony.

Minutes later, out of the tunnel, the shaken captain called his boss on his mobile and explained why he had to stop his boat, call the police.

"Don't you realize you've got passengers?" his boss warned him.

André knew, but he had no choice. He had to call the police at once, instantly, and report what he'd seen. It was terrifying.

2

The call, when it came, found Mazarelle shopping at the Marché Bastille, the open-air street market near his home. Once a week, the market spread out along the Boulevard Richard Lenoir, over a hundred stalls offering up stacks of local cheeses, organic meats, African prints, and cheap jewelry. And once a week, he would get up early and wander over to do some shopping before the streets filled up with bargain hunters—the foodies and the housewives with their canvas bags, fingering the cucumbers and the lettuce.

Today, he'd gotten a late start. Pushing through the crowds in front of the long green tables, he was looking for peaches, nectarines—

the best stone fruit of the season. He could see the clafoutis already, bursting with sweetness, just out of the oven. Browned that little bit on the edges. His mother's favorite recipe.

Mazarelle stood beneath the chalkboard and watched the fruit vendor writing prices on the board with a flourish, like a proud student with the winning answer.

"A bargain," the vendor said, turning toward the young mother with the stroller in front of him. "You picked the perfect time."

As she started to gather up the peaches, Mazarelle held up a cautionary finger. "Madame," he said. "Allow me." He leaned across the boxes of fruit and raised his large, black, dubious eyebrows.

"Where are the ripe ones?"

The fruit vendor looked up angrily, puffing out his cheeks. "They're all ripe," he asserted.

Mazarelle leaned forward and sniffed.

"Ripe? These are bricks." He looked in at the baby in the stroller. "You want better fruit than that, don't you?" The baby gripped his index finger and gurgled.

He thought it was the little guy making the buzzing sound at first. Reclaiming his finger, he patted down his pockets. It took him a minute or two to locate his mobile. As it got louder, it sounded as if his shorts were exploding. He pulled out the phone.

"*Allô!*"

"Mazarelle—"

It was Daniel Coudert, the head of the Brigade Criminelle. Since the success of the Reiner case, Mazarelle had been staffed to his division. The *Crim*. The elite. The top one hundred detectives in France. But Coudert wasn't sure Mazarelle was such a good fit.

"Mazarelle!" Coudert seemed to be yelling out the window of his office. "Where are you?"

Mazarelle said, "In the Marché Bastille."

"What the hell are you doing there?"

"One minute, *patron*. Hold on . . ."

The fruit vendor was back, more aggressive than ever. "These peaches *are* ripe. Here, feel them."

Mazarelle sniffed again. "I don't have to feel. I can see the color. I can smell." Mazarelle waved the vendor off.

"Peaches?! Mazarelle . . ." shouted the voice in his ear.

"Just a minute, boss."

Mazarelle held the fruit up to the peach man's nose. "You picked the whole tree at the same time, didn't you? Too early. Smell them."

The vendor took a sniff, puzzled. "What's wrong with that? There's no smell at all."

"Exactly!" He flashed a wide-open smile at the mother and her baby. "Try the stand down the street."

Turning away, Mazarelle strode down the aisle between the stalls and answered Coudert.

"Sorry, boss, what's going on?"

Though still relatively new to *la Crim,* Mazarelle could read the storm clouds in his *patron's* voice like a barometer. Coudert was summoning him in. He was about to be called on the carpet. Coudert had heard about the argument with Commissaire Bonfils after the parade.

Mazarelle crossed the bridge onto the Île de la Cité, heading toward the monumental building that stretched along the river Seine, its gray-white stone a throwback to the palaces of an earlier time. His destination, 36 Quai des Orfèvres, was a palace of a different kind—of racketeering, organized crime, homicide. The home of the Police Judiciaire for nearly a century.

Climbing the stairs to the office, Mazarelle stuffed his pipe into his jacket pocket. A soothing bowl to ease the stress. The black linoleum on the staircase leading to bureau 315 creaked with each step. On the third floor the plaque on the wall announced La Brigade Criminelle with its thistle emblem and motto: *"Qui s'y frotte s'y pique."* Meaning, as they say, "If you play with fire, you might get burned." A warning . . . and on days like today, Mazarelle thought, one pointed directly at him.

Outside the *patron's* office, it was as quiet as if his small staff had suddenly been called away. No one left behind guarding the throne room. Nothing but the smell of stale cigarette smoke and burned coffee. Mazarelle glanced down at the worn floor in front of Coudert's closed door. It was littered with old cigarette butts of petitioners who'd been waiting to see him. Pulling out his pipe, Mazarelle went from pocket to pocket searching for his tobacco.

"*Bordel de merde!*" he simmered. Shoving his pipe back into his jacket, he straightened his shoulders, clenched his fist, and knocked.

"*Entrez! Entrez!*"

Coudert was on the phone, listening intently. With his custom-made navy jacket off and in his blue shirtsleeves and suspenders, his shirt collar unbuttoned, Mazarelle's usually dapper boss was looking a little wrinkled, as if he'd already put in a tough morning. He motioned for Mazarelle to sit down. Mazarelle still didn't know the name of the Impressionist artist who'd done the original of the reproduction on the wall behind Coudert, but he liked it. A rower wearing a straw hat, a clay pipe in his mouth. Once again Mazarelle searched his pockets and had the same sorry results.

Coudert hung up the phone and sat back in his chair as if considering how to begin. He leaned forward.

It was then Mazarelle noticed his tie. Covered with the colorful red, white, black, and blue pattern of the Brigade Criminelle seal. He himself hated ties. In fact never wore one if he could avoid it.

"Nice tie," he said.

Coudert looked down and seemed surprised by what he was wearing. "My wife. A birthday present. She likes it."

"She has good taste."

The boss was clearly tired of chitchat. "I've news for you."

Mazarelle thought, Uh-oh. Here it comes.

"You and your men did a good job last weekend at the parade."

"Thanks." He wasn't expecting that. "Anything else?"

"Yes. A new case. A hanger . . . A body found an hour ago in one of the tunnels on the Canal Saint-Martin."

"A suicide?" asked Mazarelle.

"Oh no, this is murder. He was hanging upside down."

He took in Mazarelle's expression, and nodded.

"*Mais oui,* it's strange. And the press is on it already. The mayor has been calling. It's upsetting tourists. First the attack on the president, then this. It looks political. It's bad for the city, and bad for everyone."

"Some kind of terror thing?"

"That's what we're worried about. No one knows. No one seems to have any leads at all." Coudert gave Mazarelle an uneasy glance. "You're supposed to be good at this kind of thing. The unusual. The twisted."

He waved off Mazarelle's sputtered response.

"You're the one with the reputation. So . . . we need an answer on this. And fast. I'm tired of hearing from the mayor already. You can check in with the Commissariat Central in the Fourth. You'll be taking over from them. Since that's where you used to work, I wanted you and your team to handle it. Fabriani was your old commissaire there, wasn't he?"

"Yes, of course." Mazarelle was a bit surprised by the assignment.

"That should make for a smooth transition."

"The body upside down?"

"Odd, n'est-ce pas? Well, he's all yours. Call Fabriani. He'll fill you in on the details. Then pull your team together and get started. And don't forget. Keep me posted on developments."

Mazarelle hesitated. "Anything else?"

"Oh yes, one thing more. I heard about what happened between you and Bonfils. According to the psychiatrists you may have been right about not keeping the prisoner in garde à vue given his frail mental state—"

"Exactly—look what happened when he tried to escape."

"Yes—but Bonfils was the superior officer on the scene. It was his call. Mazarelle, I know your men think you're a supercop, but do me a favor. You're new here. Try to make an effort to get along with your brother officers. And your old boss Fabriani as well."

"What about him?"

"What I mean is I want you to focus solely on your murder case. Nothing else."

Mazarelle shot him a quizzical glance.

"Look." Coudert paused and sighed. "There's a rumor that Internal Affairs is checking into something going on in a few commissariats in the city." Coudert rubbed his chin, irritated.

"You know them," he went on. "Always on the hunt for something. They need to justify their existence. All I ask is stay out of the way. Leave it alone, okay?"

"*D'accord.*"

"We're all getting a lot of heat on this. We need to make it go away. Remember, Mazarelle, Fabriani is in charge over there. It's his shop. So do me a big favor and don't trample on any toes. Clear?"

"I'm on my way."

3

The sun was rising higher over the Quai d'Orsay, when Mazarelle and his team headed down toward the Seine. The river shimmered in the late morning light.

Waiting for them on the stone embankment were Captain André, who'd discovered the hanged man, plus members of the Brigade Fluviale. Everyone climbed aboard *la fluv*'s high-speed patrol boat, and in a matter of minutes, they were headed upstream.

Leaning back in his seat, Mazarelle glanced around at his team. The shaggy young Jeannot. The earnest Maurice. The men other commandants might not want to work with. But Mazarelle counted himself lucky.

Even here on the boat, Maurice Kalou, their *procédurier,* or detail man, was already busy making notes for his records. He might grumble, but he was perfect for his role on the team. He'd been a police desk man ever since his arrival in Paris from the Ivory Coast. Meticulous, formal, conscientious to a fault, he had worked twice as hard to get where he was and in time would probably rise to the top at the BC—if the bureaucrats didn't hold his dark brown skin against him. Mazarelle admired him and hoped he might one day succeed. He knew that Maurice had the sort of personality that would refuse to give up anything without a struggle.

"Ah, boss," he sighed. "You see how high profile this one is. Everyone's going to be watching." The only married man in the group, Maurice sometimes felt that he was spending more time with the team than with his own family. He shot Mazarelle a cautioning look. "The paperwork alone is going to eat up the next month."

"*Oh la vache*, Maurice, don't complain. This is gonna be fun." Jeannot brushed his long stringy hair back and jammed his sunglasses on top of his head, beaming at both of them. "A *putain* of a case, right, *chef*?" Jeannot had more energy than any three other detectives combined. Mazarelle hoped he could learn how to control it.

The boat shot forward, heading toward the Canal Saint-Martin, its huge outboard Yamaha engine revving high.

"The body's right up here," Captain André told them as they came around the bend. "Just inside the entrance to the first tunnel." But when they pulled up to the spot—despite the impressive speed of their boat—it was already too late. All trace of the body seemed to be gone. Except the familiar smell of death which, as usual, made Mazarelle wince.

"It was here"—the captain pointed. He looked frantically up and down the tunnel. "Right here."

The disappearance seemed to shake him more than the hanging itself. What strange new world was this, where dead bodies suddenly awoke and vanished?

Mazarelle, however, knew better. This was no zombie apocalypse. Some overeager cop had started in early, taking the body down before he arrived.

Heading up with Maurice to the small park at the street level above the tunnel, he stopped at the edge of the grass.

"Ah shit!" he muttered.

A tall, dark figure with razor-thin sideburns ambled over toward them, chuckling as he came.

"Still detecting, Mazarelle?" He smirked. "I thought you had quit."

"Théo." Mazarelle didn't intend to waste an extra syllable on his former colleague.

But Detective Théo Legardère, from Mazarelle's old commissariat in the Fourth, was happy to carry on the dialogue for both of them. "Oh right. Promoted to the famed Brigade Criminelle." He looked over at Maurice and spread out his palms with incredulity. "For what?"

Mazarelle sighed. "The body, Théo?"

Legardère jabbed his thumb at the tent on the far side of the park. "And why was it moved?"

Legardère's eyes narrowed, but the smile never left his face. "This was our case. Our arrondissement. Before we got turfed out of it. So now it's yours, Mazarelle. Well, lucky you! Looks like it's going to be a bitch." He looked the big man up and down. "Of course, if you don't want it . . ."

Mazarelle waved him away with the back of his hand. Legardère's grin hardened.

"You know, Mazo, you really should stick to your profiteroles." He gave Mazarelle a not so gentle poke in the stomach. "But I guess you already have."

Laughing, he strolled away.

Watching him go, Mazarelle blew out a steady stream of air, and shook his head. "Envious bastard," he said softly.

Maurice nodded to himself. He knew what his boss meant. After the Reiner case, Mazarelle's name and face had been plastered onto front pages nationwide. *Libération* had labeled him the "Swiss Army knife of detectives." The headlines hadn't gone down too well with certain colleagues. Mazarelle might not care much about the coverage, but everyone else sure seemed to.

Mazarelle headed over to the tentlike arrangement on the edge of the park. Three white-clad forensic technicians from the Police Scientifique were gathered around the makeshift table, going through the evidence to confirm the identity of the murder victim. Head to toe, they were wrapped in white plastic suits, like scientists in a bioterror lab. What appeared to make their job much easier in this case was that in the victim's inside jacket pocket they'd found an expensive leather wallet with his driver's license and a French *carte d'identité*.

"Who said you could cut him down?" Mazarelle asked.

"I did," said Fabriani. The head of the station gave a curt nod as he approached. "When I heard you'd be taking over the case, Mazarelle, knowing you as I do, I didn't think you'd want to waste any time getting started. Okay?"

"I suppose it will have to be."

"Good. Let me show you something." Fabriani brushed Mazarelle's annoyance aside and bent down over the body to open the collar of the victim's jacket.

The man's face was twisted into an almost unrecognizable mask of agony. Remarkably, his lambent blue eyes were opened wide. Who was he staring at when he died?

"Doesn't look happy to be here," offered Fabriani.

Mazarelle grunted, not really listening. He had no time for cop banter. For him, homicide investigations always began and ended with the victim. Others might triangulate the scene, starting on the perimeter and working their way in. But not Mazarelle. He gently eased the hanged man's collar wider, looking again at the dried dark-red marks he'd noted around the Adam's apple. He had to remind himself—the body wasn't hung by his neck. So how did he die? Mazarelle wondered. The smell of the cadaver was momentarily oppressive. Fabriani showed him the documents found on the body—the small print, the tiny photo.

"Alain Berthaud." Mazarelle nodded, though he had to look at the photo more than once to make sure. "The private investigator. I've heard the name."

"He's all yours. Good luck!"

The men in white of the Police Scientifique were just finishing up, collecting their photos, nail clippings, animal hairs. They reported that in this murder, robbery probably wasn't the motive. The victim's wallet was stuffed with cash and thick enough to choke a crocodile. Maybe more than a thousand euros.

Mazarelle put on gloves and bent over the body. That close to the dead man, the smell of alcohol helped. Knowing that the technicians sometimes missed things, he went through the victim's clothes. And sure enough, tucked inside the breast pocket of his jacket, Mazarelle found a small card they'd overlooked. A card bearing the inverted image of a dead man—the Hanged Man from a tarot deck. Strange, Mazarelle thought. Fumbling a glassine envelope out of his back pocket, he picked the card up by the edges, and placed it inside.

He handed the envelope to Maurice.

"Look like a clue to you?"

4

hat afternoon, Mazarelle cranked up the lyrical sax of Coleman Hawkins and drove his battered Renault over to L'Agence AB. It was his least favorite part of the job. He had to tell Alain Berthaud's partner the bad news—his associate was dead.

Half a flight up the stairs, Mazarelle eyed the two names on the door, the dusty dieffenbachia, the file cabinets, and faded wingback chairs. Berthaud had opened his private investigation agency in the early nineties. Luc Fournel, then a lieutenant at the Commissariat Central in the Fourth Arrondissement, had taken a very early retirement in 1998 and joined Berthaud at the agency. They soon became partners.

Fournel's secretary, an attractive woman named Laure, told Mazarelle to wait. "I'll see if he's in."

She sounded as if she were covering for him. Mazarelle thought it was probably a toss-up whether Luc was in the office or not. Mazarelle had known Luc for years at the old commissariat. He was somebody who had always loved a day off and could pack more into one than most cops he knew. But always griping about the limits of his wallet when it was probably his imagination that was the problem. Which was most likely the reason he had never made captain. Mazarelle heard that he'd been doing well financially since hooking up with his partner. He was curious to see how he'd take the news.

"Well, look what just blew in!" Fournel said, when he finally came out of his office. He eyed his visitor like a gift he didn't trust. Then turning to his secretary, "Why didn't you tell me who was waiting, sweetheart? This *is* unexpected. How can I help you, Mazarelle?"

Fournel looked better than Mazarelle remembered. Surprisingly fresh, even healthy, given his decadent ways.

"You think so?" Fournel readily admitted he was still smoking too much, drinking too much, eating too much. "So if nevertheless I'm looking passable, I don't know why. Maybe it's the short haircut. My barber Joseph's idea. A new *coupe en brosse* image for the 'can-do gumshoe.' What do you think?"

His clipped spiky steel gray hair heightened the cut of his jaw, the hard edge of his entire face.

"I think your barber was right."

"On the other hand I've been doing some jogging lately. Maybe that's it."

"Couldn't hurt."

The former member of Fabriani's commissariat was clearly not expecting a visit from his old colleague. Or seemed not to be. Fournel's eyes opened a little wider when Mazarelle asked about the last time he had seen his partner. He said he didn't know where Alain was. Supposed he was running a little late this morning. "Why?" he demanded. "What's going on?" Mazarelle explained that he was sorry to be the bearer of bad news, but Alain Berthaud was dead.

Fournel seemed genuinely stricken by his partner's death. He couldn't believe it.

"We were just having drinks last night. Over at Café Arielle. By the Canal Saint-Martin?"

Mazarelle nodded sympathetically.

"We were there with Guy. Remember Guy Danglars? Still on the job. He was helping us with some information for a client."

Fournel sat down abruptly, as if the weight of the moment had finally become too much. He wanted to know how Alain died. He knew he'd been drinking heavily. "Car crash?" he asked.

"No. He was found hanging."

"Hanging?" Luc seemed shocked. "Alain would never kill himself."

"Murder, most likely," Mazarelle reported.

"What? How did it happen?"

Mazarelle ignored the query. He had questions of his own. "What time did you leave the café? Did you all go together?"

Fournel had a story to tell. He explained that he left early, before midnight. He wasn't feeling well. "Stomach cramps and pains in my chest. I left Alain and Guy drinking and decided to go home. On the way I felt worse and drove instead to the emergency room of the Hôtel-Dieu. The ER doctor didn't like what he saw and wanted more tests. He insisted I remain in the hospital overnight under observation," Luc explained. "He didn't release me till late this morning. By and large no worse for my ordeal. Except now my veins are black and blue, and I still have stomach cramps."

Mazarelle asked if it was his heart.

Fournel shrugged. "Probably the *moules* I had for lunch."

Taking out his meerschaum, Mazarelle filled its large bowl with a nice new blend of Small's Philosophe and lighted up, tossing the wooden match into the empty wastebasket.

"So tell me, Luc, how did you like working with Alain?"

"We were old friends," Fournel said. "Like brothers."

Cain and Abel? mused Mazarelle, watching the stream of smoke pour out of his pipe.

"What about clients?" he asked.

"You know, the usual. Matrimonial bust-ups, business crimes, missing persons, missing money, missing property."

"Any unhappy customers?"

Fournel shot him a look. "You know I can't do that. If I hand my clients to the police, I won't have any more clients."

Mazarelle nodded. "Then again . . . he's your partner. I would think you'd want to help." He paused to puff again, and let the thought sink in. "So what *can* you tell me about the cases he was working on?"

"Okay, well just between us . . ." Fournel ran his hand thoughtfully through his brush-cut hair. "I will tell you this. Had a wife in here last week. Her husband was connected. In one of those Gypsy mobs. She thought he was fooling around, had a girlfriend. Thought she could take him for big money. Wanted Alain to follow him and find out."

Mazarelle lifted an eyebrow. "Really? Cheating husbands?"

Luc pulled himself up stiffly.

"Got to make ends meet. Easy to be all snooty when you're on a salary." He shook his head. "Anyway, Alain got the goods on him all right. Up to his Speedos with some hot little girl. Got it all on video."

"How did that go down?"

"How do you think? Man that guy is capable of anything . . ."

He looked up at Mazarelle, an idea dawning in his eyes.

"You know, he came storming in here. And he was mad. Threatened all sorts of damage. Said if Alain didn't back off, he would gut him like the squealing pig he was. Said he'd be begging for mercy."

Mazarelle, jotting notes in his small pad, looked up, astonished. "The week before he died? And that didn't spring to mind?"

"There were so many threats . . . Alain was always running into trouble."

Mazarelle scribbled furiously.

"What was the name?"

"It wasn't my case. Babo something or other."

"Okay. Where did he live?"

"He was one of those Gypsies. Where do any of them live?"

Mazarelle opened his mouth for a quick retort and stopped himself. Finally he flipped his notebook shut. "So where are Berthaud's notes on the case?" he asked. "Any records?"

Fournel opened his partner's door and pointed inside. A haphazard stack of papers piled high on the desk. The crooked lampshade. The calendar with model photos that looked like it belonged on a garage wall.

"Alain was a great guy," he said, "but not exactly a demon for records." He tilted his head at the stacks of paper. "He was always saying he was going to start getting organized."

Mazarelle looked in and nodded. "Probably thought he had more time."

5

Alain Berthaud's desk yielded stacks of magazines, and ten pounds of paperwork for Maurice to sort through. Most of it looked like chicken scratches. But when it came to angry husbands, with only a first name to go on, Mazarelle figured he might need some extra help.

His physical therapist, Angelique Vasseure, was a wonder. With her small acupuncture needles, she could relieve more of his aches and pains than anyone else he knew. But that wasn't why Mazarelle needed her now. When it came to odd bits of information—a recommendation about the occult world, for example—Angelique was a great source. She was full of stories, seemed to know everyone in Paris. And when he asked about the Romani, she gave him the fortune teller—Madame Mireille.

Her *cabinet* was located in an RV parked behind a modest grove of trees on the edge of the Nineteenth Arrondissement. He knocked on her door; and she was waiting for him, the television blaring, a fuzzy gray terrier barking furiously at his approach.

"Shhh, Tezia." She settled the little dog at her feet. "She watches out for me. She's just a little overprotective."

Behind her desk, madame flicked off the singer in midchorus and leaned back in her black leather chair. A long ebony cigarette holder dangled between bright red lips. They matched the crimson on the drapes covering her walls. She studied him through her watchful kohl-rimmed eyes and said, "I've been looking forward to your visit, monsieur, ever since your call. How can I help you?" She had a low voice that comforted, a hint of raspiness that perhaps spoke of mysteries in her own life.

Mazarelle had long ago learned the value of starting small—easing his way in. He let the little dog sniff his fingers, then reached into his jacket. Removing the tarot card that he'd found on the body of Alain Berthaud, he pushed it across the tabletop toward the three lighted candles in the red, green, and yellow glass jars in front of her.

Madame Mireille leaned forward, turned over the card, and studied it. The Hanged Man dangling upside down from the tree of life by one ankle, hands hidden behind his back, face staring straight ahead, his head glorified by a nimbus. Red pants, blue coat, yellow shoes. She nodded in silence and muttered one word: "*Classique.*"

Mazarelle moved more closely to the edge of his seat, not wanting to miss anything else she might say. He shifted his weight, and the wooden chair groaned under him. He glanced around for a window to open, but assumed if windows existed at all, they were behind the drapes. The smell of her perfume was dizzying.

She lifted a well-polished red nail and slowly tapped the card, her ringed finger coming down heavily like a metronome. "This card"— she tapped it again—"is a key to the Major Arcana. Card twelve. One of the most mysterious in the entire tarot deck. It's simple, though subtly complex. It attracts, but simultaneously repels. And in countless ways, yes, it contradicts itself." She paused, to make certain he had grasped what she was getting at before moving on. "Let me put it this way," she said. "At the very heart of the role it plays in our lives is paradox." She scratched the terrier's ears. "*N'est-ce pas, mon amour?*"

Mazarelle stared at her, stroking his mustache and disclosing with a smile that he was at a loss. "Forgive me, madame," he had to admit, "I don't understand."

She nodded. "It's not always easy to grasp the wisdom of the Hanged Man's contradictions. He tells us that we control by letting go, we win by losing, we see more by looking at less. In short, if we're to see at all, we must—like the Hanged Man—learn to see things differently."

"Interesting." The commandant picked up the card he'd given her and pocketed it. "But then again"—Mazarelle laughed—"maybe not." He leaned back. "What I mean, *chère madame,* is this. If someone I knew received such a card, and assuming of course that it wasn't too late, what could I tell him? Is the Hanged Man an omen? What might his future hold?"

"A good question. A period of waiting, yes, indecision, perhaps."

"And danger?" Mazarelle smiled. "Does he face any danger?"

Madame weighed her answer carefully before replying. "The man who got this card?" She shook her head. "No, I think not. It's too late for him now. His time has come and gone." Madame Mireille got up and seemed shorter than he'd expected. "The danger, *monsieur le commandant,* is for *you.* Grave danger. I can tell you think this is all a game. Some big joke. But let me assure you that the danger I see for you is *quite* real. *Au revoir, monsieur.*"

Mazarelle couldn't wait to get out of the place. It seemed creepy as a casket. He felt suffocated. But heading for the door, he had one last question. "Ever hear of a Gypsy—a guy named Babo?"

Madame Mireille stopped on her way through the curtains. "You think I know all of the Romani in Paris?" she scoffed.

"Well," Mazarelle pressed, "where would be a good place to start?"

"You might try out by the Petite Ceinture"—she shrugged—"if you last that long."

6

The color of the sky above Paris was a crystal blue, a beautiful, clear French blue dotted with radiant white clouds. As Mazarelle made his way along the shining streets, the city looked lovely, the café windows newly washed and sparkling, the trees green and leafed out.

But around the corner, up ahead, sat a completely different kind of city . . . a town built of rubbish and scrap. Housing some twenty thousand immigrants who had come from Romania and Bulgaria in recent years in search of a better future. They had found themselves trapped in a new kind of slum, like this Romani urban camp that rose before him, near the abandoned railway tracks. "La Petite Ceinture," as it was called by the locals, stretched the size of five football fields, a quarter mile of danger and decay.

Mazarelle opened his jacket, unbuttoned his shirt collar. Frisking himself to make certain that he'd remembered to take his pistol out of his desk. It probably wouldn't be necessary for the job he might have to do, but out on the edge of the city, the police weren't always welcome visitors. His colleagues had reported run-ins out here more than once.

Making his way along a muddy road lined with a caravan of dented old cars parked bumper to rusty bumper, he entered the half-demolished shantytown. Plywood shacks, little bigger than outhouses, wobbled uncertainly. The tarpaulin on their roofs was held down by rocks against the gusting wind. On top of the rubble, exhaust pipes thrust their necks up like U-boat conning towers. On the ground, piles of debris and a splattered child's doll, her body stuffed with straw and buttons for eyes partially blinded by drying mud. Behind this chaos, a cinder block wall with a graffito warning—I SPY.

In the middle of a tropical splash of sunlight sat a burly Romani, crouched down on the torn knees of his purple pants, washing his laundry in a Pepto Bismol–pink rubber tub. He gave Mazarelle the barest hint of a nod and kept scrubbing, his swollen beer belly straining against his striped shirt. Behind, his wife and kids crowded into the doorway of a corrugated box with no running water and little power. Through the open door Mazarelle could see the long, thin extension cord they used for their electricity and the juice flickering. The thick rubber band holding the big guy's hair in a braid down his back was much more dependable. Mazarelle came closer as the man held up the Real Madrid T-shirt he'd been washing to check for holes and stains. The commandant noted the guy's white teeth jammed into the brown face, his flashy gold incisor, his razor scar, and his sneer when Mazarelle asked about Babo.

"Never heard of him!" growled the Romani. "Ask *them*." He nodded in the direction of the two old-timers playing dominos. Mazarelle was surprised that he hadn't noted them close by, sitting bent and motionless on their rickety chairs and quietly smoking.

The mob of scruffy kids who had seemed to come out of nowhere now surged around their visitor, curious to see who he was. Mazarelle noticed with a twinge just how painfully thin they were, their legs little more than sticks poking out of their short pants, their dark eyes big as saucers. When it came to government aid, the Romani of Paris were rarely first in line. The last time they had important visitors, it was their mayor himself, who had looked around the shabby encampment and was overheard to say, "I guess Hitler didn't kill enough of them in the last century." Which was followed by the Ministry of the Interior's inspectors, and then an army of cops and bulldozers, tearing through the shacks, demolishing the only tiny homes they had. A half of the Petite Ceinture camp was now gone, the other half waiting to be torn down in the near future but still sheltering its disheveled human cargo. And Paris wasn't alone. He had seen the paperwork. More forced evictions were coming all across the country.

Mazarelle offered up an ID and a smile. Kids like these had faced their share of bad luck over the years. Ever since the Romani people first arrived in Europe from India in the twelfth century, they'd been singled out as a plague on society, as if they had some sort of genetic predisposition to petty crime. Turned into slaves in Romania and England; locked up in Serbia and Austria; expelled and deported in Spain, Venice, and Rome, they were the target of forced schooling and imprisonment all across Europe. Even in twenty-first-century France, Mazarelle knew, his force still kept clandestine files on them.

When the kids realized that this official visitor was from the police, they drew back instinctively. Pulling themselves together, shoulder to shoulder, they formed a defensive wall, shouting at the top of their lungs, *"Flic! Flic! Flic!"* They chanted the word as an incantatory curse, thrusting their hands stiff armed and cross fingered like red-hot pokers at Mazarelle, attempting to keep this officer away. As they yelled, they thronged around him, whipping themselves into a frenzy.

Mazarelle eased his way through the surly group as if they weren't even there. Walking away free and clear until all of a sudden he felt what seemed a fatal tugging on his bad leg. It was the smallest guy in the gang. He was attached to the commandant like a suction cup. A guy named Sami.

"Psst!" he called in a whisper with his finger to his lips, looking up at Mazarelle. "I know Babo," Sami said.

Mazarelle took out a pen and a thick pad. Riffling through the pages, he was reminded of what lousy records Alain kept. Halfway through, he found a blank page. "Last name?" he demanded.

"Banderas."

"Address?"

"Who knows?" Sami shrugged.

"Where can I find him?" Mazarelle asked.

"He moves around a lot. But mostly in Montmartre. Not far from where the old Cirque Medrano was.

"And if you've got any stuff to sell," Sami added, "he'll give you a good price. I should know. He's got my girlfriend."

Her name was Flor, and little Sami loved her dearly. He wished he could tell this big guy how much he missed his fifteen-year-old sweetheart, her fiery eyes, her jet-black hair. He totally rejected her dumb notion that her new forty-two-year-old boyfriend was a dreamboat, and that their relationship was a match made in heaven. Before Babo stole Flor away, Sami had thought of him as a cool guy who always paid well. But now Sami hated him. He thought Babo was an old lech preying on a teenager half his age. Sami didn't expect their relationship to last, but he had to face facts. Though he planned to hang around a while, within easy hailing distance of Flor, hoping they'd break up soon, he was no longer one hundred percent sure how long that might take.

Mazarelle looked impatient, and was already on his way, so Sami didn't even try to tell him what he thought about Babo. But he did have a question for him.

As Mazarelle was leaving, he heard Sami calling after him. "Tell me 'Stache"—he winked—"are you *really* a *flic*?" For whatever reason, the kid had tried to be helpful, so Mazarelle had no wish to be cruel. He bent down to short pants's ear and whispered, "I've been called worse things in my life."

7

Outside the shantytown, Mazarelle was on the phone with Maurice. Mazarelle needed the facts on Babo Banderas—his address, his contacts, his priors. It didn't take Maurice long to find the file. It was big enough.

"He's a fence. Word is, he's tied in to some of those Mafia Romani clans like the Casamonicas. These guys are infamous. People are too scared to testify against them. Listen to this. One informant said: 'They are animals. They cut off fingers.'" As for the address, Maurice told him it was near the Place des Abbesses Métro stop. The way things turned out, it was and it wasn't.

When Mazarelle finally arrived at Abbesses, he found that he was at the bottom of one of the deepest stations of the Métro system. The good news was that they had two elevators. And in fact they both were actually there waiting for him when he arrived. The bad news was that *both* of these *ascenseurs* had handwritten signs taped to their doors with the message *Hors de service*.

Mazarelle steeled himself to walk up the eight steep flights of the staircase. Or rather limp. Fortunately, he'd been going to his gym lately a couple of times a week in preparation for the Bastille Day security assignment. When he finally got to the top of the stairs, he congratulated himself. Coming out the iconic art nouveau entrance, with its flowering green Guimard-style vines, his pulse was steady, his breathing untroubled.

Mazarelle soon found the number he wanted, a not particularly stylish, unpretentious apartment building on a quiet block. The concierge's residence was well marked and well lighted. Her name was Madame Lulu. "Lulu B.," she clarified, to make certain there was no confusion in the commandant's mind with the many other Lulus on her block. How many were there? he wondered. The petite Lulu ran her hand through her bushy blond hair and shook it in his face, raising herself up closer to the big guy's nose to give him the full sensory 3D impact of her latest coiffure—like Ingres's Thetis, flirting with the giant Jupiter.

Mazarelle smiled and asked about Babo. He confided, "Don't worry, *chère madame*. I'm an old friend of his."

"Mademoiselle," she replied coolly, looking him over cap-a-pie. "Monsieur Banderas is out for the day."

"I'll wait here," Mazarelle said firmly, as if putting down an anchor. His mind was made up. He showed her his police card to help her along.

She raised her eyebrows, put the key in his smooth warm palm without a word, sensing perhaps that he could be trusted or else that her morning was full of enough chores. She shrugged, then spun away smartly on her heels. No sooner had she gone than Mazarelle slipped the key into the lock and strode inside. He didn't quite know what to expect, or what to make of it when he saw what was there.

The open door revealed a brilliantly lit Weegee scene, as if captured candidly by the reporter's flash camera and scandalous unblinking eye. The fence's relatively small three-room apartment was jam-packed with stuff acquired slowly over time by getting and spending and more than occasionally stealing.

Under the large Air France travel posters from Paris to Dubai on the red velvet walls were countless cartons of contraband cigarettes. Gaming consoles were stacked high in the corners of the room, surrounding a trio of life-sized marble leopards.

Nearby sat a stunning set of red satin chairs with solid gold frames. To Mazarelle's professional police eye, they looked as if they had been stolen from a reception room at the Vatican.

The commandant had done his share of apartment searches over the years. He had a methodical approach that served him well, working his way around the bathrooms, the bedrooms, the living room. But here, the sheer volume was overwhelming. There were clues everywhere. Only not to the right crime.

As he poked around the toilet, the vents, under the sink—the most common hideaway spots for the average criminal—Mazarelle felt his spirits sink, and his stomach started to grumble, a reminder of the breakfast that he had missed. Peeking inside the refrigerator he found the moldy remains of a half-eaten goulash. Mostly, the shelves were crammed full of contraband wristwatches, from Timexes, Casios, and cheap Oulm army timepieces to an Omega Seamaster and a half-dozen top-end Rolexes with cases of rose gold, the favorite of all the Mafia Gypsy clans. The refrigerator motor had been turned off, the plug pulled out as well. Nothing useful there. And nothing will come of nothing, he thought. Poetry cheered him up a little bit and especially Shakespeare when he felt glum, but it did nothing to lessen his appetite.

Madame Lulu, who only once before had been inside this apartment, knew little about what went on there. All she cared about was getting her rent every month on the dot, and staying on the right side of the authorities. When monsieur returned, it was good that she hit the buzzer because Mazarelle had grown drowsy going through the immense secret trove he'd found in the apartment. When the sleeping bear heard her buzz from downstairs and jumped up, he had barely enough time to race inside to the bathroom to splash some water on his cheeks.

Then, suddenly, Babo was there, a box under his arm, his girlfriend Flor in tow. And his temper filled the room. "I don't know you!" Babo screamed. "Who the hell are you? Who let you in? Get the fuck out of here!"

Mazarelle drew himself up. "Allow me to introduce myself," he announced in a deep resonant voice. "Commandant Mazarelle, of the Brigade Criminelle. I'm investigating a homicide that occurred a few days ago."

"A murder? What's that have to do with me?" Babo fumed.

"The victim was a private investigator by the name of Alain Berthaud. Do you know him?"

Babo put the box down on the table. Quieter now. He gave Mazarelle a long, squint-eyed stare.

"Know him?" he said flatly. "That prick made a mess of my life." Babo caught himself and abruptly stopped.

Mazarelle nodded slowly, sympathetically.

"I understand you threatened him."

"Hell, yeah," Babo snapped. "Messing around in my private life. Taking pictures. Sneaking into my bedroom."

Once again he had worked himself from a simmer to a full-throated boil. Clearly Babo was a volatile guy. Mazarelle filed it away.

"So it seems you have a criminal record. A connection to the Casamonica family in Rome. The Gypsy Mafia."

"Oh, sure." Babo looked over to Flor. "It's easy to blame the Gypsies. We're all criminals, right? There's a crime—find a Gypsy!"

He threw his hands out to underscore the injustice.

Mazarelle thought it was a good performance. Not quite Olivier or Johnny Depp, but still, full of emotion. On the other hand, there was that big stack of TVs piled against the wall.

Taking in Babo's outstretched palms, he spotted something else. A raw, blistered welt cutting across the flesh of both hands. It looked painful. It looked like a rope burn. The kind of cut you might have from hanging a heavy body.

"How'd you get those?"

"That?" scoffed Babo. "That's nothing."

"Right. And you came by them . . ."

Babo sighed, aggrieved with the world. "I have an import business. All right? We're always boxing up things and sending them out. One of the boxes got away from me."

Mazarelle wasn't convinced. "Okay," he said. "So tell me. Where were you on the night of July nineteenth?"

"The same place I am every night. Between the legs of my sweetheart."

Babo turned to his *chouchou*. On cue, Flor replied, "Of course he was here with me! Where else would he be?"

It was an alibi, but only the slimmest. With that temper, those rope burns—and the threat against Berthaud—Mazarelle thought he might have his suspect.

"All right, Babo. I understand what you're saying. But we have to check all this out."

"Go ahead." The suspect smirked.

"I mean down at headquarters. You're going to have to come with me until we can get a little more information. A few more questions answered."

Mazarelle put in the call for a police car, and sat down to wait.

Now Babo paled. "I am *not* a murderer," he insisted. "This is just crap."

An hour later, even as the commandant pushed Babo into the police car downstairs, the thief continued to protest. It was the way he swore to his innocence that would come to haunt Mazarelle.

8

Out in front of 36 Quai des Orfèvres, a crowd was already gathering as Mazarelle and Babo pulled up in the police car. Dozens of angry faces, shouting, chanting. Maybe a hundred or more.

Send them home! read a sign. France for the French.

Mazarelle sighed. How had word already leaked out into the chat rooms? He asked the driver to pull up closer, but this was as close as he was going to get today.

No barricade. No officers out front. They weren't making it easy for him.

"Here we go," he said. "Keep your head down." He opened the door. An ugly sound rippled through the crowd.

"That's him," someone yelled. "*Gitan!* Murderer!" Other voices chimed in. A college student waving his fist. An old woman waving a sign. A man in a dark gray sweater. The crowd started to surge forward.

In his snapshot-like scan of that moment, Mazarelle took in the frantic faces. He recognized the expressions. The agitation. The fury. A lot of dark clouds on such a sunny day. And they were so convinced of the rightness of their cause. That's what made them scary.

Mazarelle put an arm around Babo and hustled his suspect toward the front door of the building.

Even as he pushed forward, an image came to him. A memory, straight off the rugby fields of his youth. A ball carrier had gone to ground. His friend Khalil, fresh from Algeria, holding on to the leather ball for all he was worth. In the ruck, players from both teams pushing and shoving. And then things turning really nasty. As if the anonymity of the pack unleashed an inner violence. Stomping, digging in their elbows, raking toward his face and eyes with their fingernails. "You dirty Arab," they hissed. "Go on home. We don't need your kind here." Young Mazarelle couldn't believe what he was hearing at first. And then he did. Reaching down, he threw bodies off right and left, put the young Khalil under his arm like the ball, and plowed through them all.

And here he was again, his shoulder into the crowd, parting the bodies in front of him.

Up ahead, the demonstrators seemed to be redoubling their efforts. "Kidnappers!" came the shouts. A red-faced woman in a blue coat, screaming, "They kidnap little kids!" As if shouting the old wives' tale made it more true.

Out of the corner of his eye, he caught the man in the gray sweater again, tracking along on the far side of the crowd. Mazarelle noticed the odd expression. The faces all around were full of heat and anger, but his was curiously cold and expressionless . . .

The crowd pressed forward, closing in. A wave of bodies crashed around him. Now there were sticks waving in the air . . . and then the flash of metal.

Out of nowhere, a blade came slicing out.

Mazarelle barely had time to swing Babo behind him. The point snicked forward. He caught it on his forearm. The edge slashed through his jacket. It cut fabric and flesh.

The man in the gray sweater, the blade jutting out of his hand.

With a yell of pain, Mazarelle rolled his arm forward and snagged a wrist. Twisting until he heard a snap and a shout. The clank of metal on the ground.

Babo had stopped, staring at him openmouthed.

All around, the crowd was still shoving, still yelling as if nothing had happened.

"Thieves! Killers. String them up. Send them home."

Mazarelle ignored the blood trickling down his arm. He kept his hand clamped on Babo's shoulder.

"You coming?"

9

As the door slammed behind him, Mazarelle pushed Babo forward. *"Putain,"* he said to the sergeant inside. "They are out of control."

"They're worried. Can you blame them?"

Dabbing at the blood on his forearm, he pushed Babo toward the officers on duty. "Put him in *garde à vue.*"

He ripped off the sleeve of his shirt and wrapped it tightly around the wound, tying the knot with his teeth.

Babo kept staring at him. For such a loudmouth, he didn't seem to have much to say.

Coudert had heard the commotion. Coming down the stairs, he took in the scene by the door, his detective, the officers clustered around the Romani.

"Babo," he said with a little smirk, "what trouble are you in now?"

"You know him?"

"This guy? You bet. If you'd been here longer instead of vacationing in the Dordogne, you'd know him too."

Watching the officers take Babo away, Mazarelle stifled his first response. Coudert was his boss, after all.

"So what's his story?" he asked.

"Old Babo?" Coudert gave a grim smile. "He's one of the usual suspects. Find a crime anywhere around Montmartre. Pickpockets. Breaking and entering. His gang is probably in on it. He's got a record as long as"—Coudert stopped midsentence—"as . . ." The comparison seemed to defeat him. He waved a dismissive hand. "You know those guys. It was only a matter of time before he went down for something bigger."

"Hang on," said Mazarelle. "He's only in for questioning. We haven't even—"

"Sure, sure. Don't worry," said Coudert. "He did it all right."

He headed back up the stairs to his office. Over his shoulder, he tossed back a bouquet of praise.

"Nice work, Mazarelle. Didn't know you had it in you."

10

The camera flashes were already going off as Mazarelle entered the conference room.

Up front, behind a hive of microphones, Coudert and Fabriani wore self-satisfied smiles, basking in the warm glow of the camera lights. The room was packed, and loud. It was surprisingly crowded with print journalists, wire service stringers, video shooters—the whole motley collection of the fourth estate. Now they were all focused on Coudert as he rolled through his statement.

". . . to announce the arrest of Babo Banderas."

Scanning the room, Coudert spotted Mazarelle by the side wall.

"And here's the detective who made it all possible. Commandant

Paul Mazarelle. The ace who solved the Dordogne murders. The man who's brought the tarot card murderer to justice."

The flashes grew more intense, more insistent, as they turned toward him—an explosion of light and heat.

"Wait," said Mazarelle. "What?"

"No need for modesty, Mazarelle. This strange killing is cleared, off the books. Paris can sleep well at night again. Thanks to you."

Mazarelle was baffled.

"What are you talking . . ." he said quietly, almost to himself. "It's not . . ."

The reporters had no time for hesitations. They had already pivoted back toward the two bureaucrats. They had questions.

"Is this a crime wave?"

"Is this a trend?"

"Is France safe?"

Fabriani stepped up to the microphones. He held out his hands for quiet. "We understand. It's been an upsetting time here in Paris. A dangerous time."

He looked around the room, giving the cameras time to focus in on him.

"We've had an attempted assassination. A strange murder. No wonder our citizens are concerned. It feels as if things may be slipping out of control."

He drew himself up to his full six foot one inch frame. Tall, and he knew how to wear a suit. The charcoal pinstripe. The burgundy tie.

"But we are here today to tell you that your national police are on the job."

He slammed his palm down on the lectern.

"We stand guard at the gates. We are here to protect you. We're here to enforce the law. And we will not fail."

The staccato rhythms set off a new crescendo of flashes.

Mazarelle had seen enough. Walking out of the conference room, shaking his head, he spotted Maurice coming from the other side of the hall.

"Is he running for something?" Mazarelle asked.

The captain nodded sagely. "Some people bloom under the

lights . . . like a tulip in the sun. Have you ever seen the tulip tree of West Africa? The Nandi flame?"

"If only they spent that energy on the investigation," said Mazarelle.

Maurice had something for his boss. He was carrying a computer printout, several pages long. It was Babo's record.

Mazarelle stood still as he read it.

Leafing through the pages, he saw no shortage of arrests. And convictions. Robbery. Breaking and entering. Multiple counts of receiving and selling stolen property. Confirming Coudert's comments.

But with each turn of the page, Mazarelle seemed less and less content.

"Look at this. What do you see?"

He handed the printout back to Maurice.

"A lot of time in jail?"

"Sure, sure. His record is long. But in all that time, Babo has no record of violent crimes. Look . . ." His index finger jabbed the page. "No weapons charges. Never used a gun or a knife. Not even an assault."

"So?"

Mazarelle shook his head. "He's got a temper, but he's never even been booked for a fistfight. He's an easy target. He just doesn't feel right for this."

Maurice looked back at the conference room. His eyebrows slowly raising. His mouth opening.

"But . . ."

Maurice pointed back over his shoulder.

"They just . . ." His voice trailed off.

Mazarelle said nothing. He was focused on the printout.

"Are you *sure* you want to do this?" asked Maurice.

Still no answer.

"But if it's not him, then . . ."

Mazarelle looked up.

"Exactly," he nodded. "That's the job."

PART TWO

11

The headlights sliced through the thick sheets of rain hurtling down from the sky, the all-terrain tires gripping the cracked pavement of the one-lane road, sliding out on the curves. Behind the wheel, the driver stared into the downpour. His beat-up Jeep had seen better days. It could use a new paint job as well. If he ever got back home.

Paris had gone well—a mission accomplished on the backstreets of the capital. Just a few scratches to show for it. But now, here in the south, under the unseasonable rainstorm battering Provence, the tension was slowly building in his nerves.

He was not a religious man, choosing to put his faith in his own skills rather than robed prophets. But on this miserable night, he had to admit there was a certain wisdom in the actions of Noah. Here was a man who knew the way of the world—that land could be shaped, beasts could be tamed, but when the heavens opened, there was little else to do but sit in a wooden box and wait it out. Yes, life was formed from water, but to go back to it, to be consumed by it—that meant an icy darkness one was unlikely to return from. He'd done it once before and survived, but had no desire for an encore performance.

He hammered his foot against the accelerator, his car negotiating the serpentine road, as the four-wheel drive Jeep rocketed onward. On nights like this, the narrow country road between Marseille and Avignon, low on lights and overgrown with vegetation, was usually deserted, but tonight was different—tonight the universe seemed intent on testing him.

Blocking his way, the yellow Bentley's bloated body dominated the road ahead, cruising along at what, in the most generous of terms, could be described as a crawl. These yuppie fucks! Ever since the age of the internet had begun, his most treasured routes, his most prized hideaways were quickly becoming tainted with money and privilege—and worst of all, the people that came with it.

The Jeep driver thumped his horn with a clenched fist. If this jackass dawdling in front of him would learn how to drive or simply get the hell out of the way, he might get back home some time before the Rhône, flooded and roaring alongside the road, carried him off. Closing the gap between the cars, he brought his Jeep up behind the Bentley Arnage, practically brushing bumpers, and laid on the horn again, this time flashing his high beams for good measure.

Up ahead, the driver was silhouetted in the light. Some sort of Saudi type. A dishrag on his head. Foreign plates on the back of the car. Moving at a snail's pace. This was what money did. It made you feel superior, as if the rest of the world was playing by your rules and not the other way around. He beat his horn like a drum, the staccato rhythm exploding through the air like the rifle volley of the FAMAS he had carried for so many years.

An arm shot out the Bentley's driver side window, middle finger raised skyward and jabbed high into the low-hanging black clouds overhead. The Arab's sausage-shaped finger adorned with a thick golden ring, emerald fixed in the middle, taunted the Jeep driver. It was a dare: Do something.

You want to play games, huh? His anger boiling over, the Jeep driver yanked his steering wheel to the left onto the muddy shoulder, throttling the engine to life and pulling up next to the Bentley's driver's side. He could feel the skidding of his back wheels, sliding closer and closer to the roaring banks of the river.

With a sudden violent jerking turn, he threw the Jeep's steering wheel to the right, slamming into the driver's side door of the Bentley, replacing the snooty Arab's smirk with a look of true alarm. The cars skittered and swerved alongside each other, zooming down the road.

He drew his front tires even with the Bentley's rear axle, delivering the fatal blow, smashing the Jeep's nose into the Bentley's back tires.

The Bentley's tires screeched and lost all traction, careening into a nearby ditch.

The rain was still coming down hard. The Jeep driver pulled off the road, and lifted the hood of his black sweatshirt over his head. It was time to send this towelhead back home.

The hooded man reached the Bentley's driver's side door and bent his head down to eye level with the heavyset Saudi, who sat shaking, quivering in his seat. He fumbled in his pockets, bringing out his wallet and thrusting it in the Jeep driver's face.

"Please! I have money! Take my money!"

The hooded man stared back coldly, his hatchet features unmoving, taking in the wood grain, the beige leather, the Tintin comic on the passenger seat—a gift no doubt for Saudi Junior—as the rain beat out a rhythm of chaotic fury on the roof of the beached Bentley.

Then, from the Jeep driver's lips, a slow, nasty grin.

12

On Monday morning, when Mazarelle lumbered up the 148 steps to the fourth floor at 36 Quai des Orfèvres, Maurice and Jeannot were already in the office. Serge, the department's young part-time intern, had arrived earlier and was busy at one of the file cabinets. Up here, where the work got done, their space looked like some forgotten corner of an attic—desks jammed together, dingy off-white walls, cardboard boxes of files heaped in the corners, all under a sloping mansard roof.

Maurice had the sports pages spread across his desk, and he was wagging his finger at Jeannot.

"You watch for him," Maurice insisted. "Didier Drogba. He's majestic on the field. He only plays for Guingamp now, but Olympique de Marseille will surely sign him soon."

"Come on!" Jeannot smiled. "The Ivory Coast?" The only thing cops liked more than solving cases was giving each other a little grief. And when it came to his team, Maurice was such an easy target for teasing.

"You don't know, Jeannot. We are the best. The best in all of Africa. The mighty Elephants."

Jeannot couldn't resist. "And what exactly have you won, again?"

"Aha. My young friend, you reveal your ignorance. We won the African Cup in 1992. A glorious day in Abidjan."

"One time in fifty years. Okay. But even then . . . didn't it go to penalty kicks?"

Maurice slammed the sports section shut. "Perhaps we should focus on our work."

Mazarelle, meanwhile, had been staring at the front page. Chewing on the end of his pipe. Annoyed. Something was bugging him.

"Look at this . . ."

He flipped the page around toward his men. The headline read: "Arrest in Bizarre Tarot Murder Case."

Mazarelle began reading aloud: "'Police announced an arrest in the strange killing of Alain Berthaud, sixty-one, co-owner of the private investigation agency L'Agence AB, found dead last week in the Canal Saint-Martin. Babo Banderas, forty-two, a Romani with a history of petty crime, was charged in the murder that has shocked Paris—'"

Mazarelle broke off. "They have the card. They even have its history. Listen to this . . . 'Another remarkable feature of this unusual case: the tarot card Berthaud had in his jacket. It bore the sign of the Hanged Man. According to an anonymous police source, it was likely meant as a warning.'"

He shook his head, and went on to the sidebar: "'The hanged man image predates even the invention of tarot cards in the fifteen hundreds. In Italy, this type of image was called a *pittura infamante*. It was a picture of someone guilty of betrayal—shown hung for it from a gallows upside down—'"

"Seriously?" Jeannot broke in. "They really used to hang people upside down?"

"That's what it says. They thought it was even slower and more painful than a regular hanging."

Mazarelle tossed aside the paper. "A Gypsy. A tarot card. They're all done." He shook his head. "The reporters like him for it. The crowds in the street like him for it. Our boss likes him for it. Everyone just wants to string the Gypsy up and move on."

Jeannot shrugged. "It's hard to feel sorry for him. What about that fifteen-year-old girlfriend?"

"This isn't a popularity contest. There's a lynch mob inside and outside. And if we don't do something fast, they're gonna convict him of a murder he may not have committed."

"Is he not guilty?" asked Maurice. "The *patron* certainly thinks so."

"He's guilty of all sorts of things. But this?" Mazarelle offered up his palms. "Hard to tell. He's a jerk. But that's not illegal. If it was, half of this building would be in jail."

"Still, why push so hard?" asked Jeannot. "Especially when no one else wants us to?"

Mazarelle rapped his knuckles on the table. "That's when you have to push."

"After all"—Maurice still wasn't convinced—"didn't the *patron* say to wrap up the case?"

Mazarelle smiled. "Of course we will. The right way. We've got at least a few weeks to pull together the evidence for the trial. Let's see what else we can find."

The morning meeting was a daily ritual—a chance for all of them to get up to speed. Mazarelle ran them through the details of his interview with Berthaud's partner, Luc Fournel, and Luc's claim that on the night of the murder he'd gone to the emergency room at the Hôtel-Dieu. Said he'd spent the night there.

"Convenient," exclaimed Jeannot.

"True," said Mazarelle. "The guy always was a slacker and sleazy on the job. And there's still something off about him. But his story checked out. The docs said he came in sick, threw up, and slept it off all night in the hospital. That's a pretty good alibi."

Jeannot said he'd visited Alain Berthaud's bachelor apartment in the Marais and revisited his office at the Agence AB. It seemed to him that neither the apartment nor the office had ever been lived in. Or worked in, for that matter.

"The apartment was like an anonymous hotel room." He sounded amazed as he described it. "No dirty dishes or clothes. Nothing. It was bizarre. The office had only that one messy pile of papers on top of the desk that we initially picked up—all useless. Nothing in the desk drawers."

Maurice nodded. He was the one who'd gone through that pile of unsorted papers.

Mazarelle glanced down at his aide's densely written pad of notes. Maurice had the sort of neat, tight, crabbed handwriting that could put more words on a page legibly than almost anyone else he'd ever met. Mazarelle's own penmanship was inkblot prone and stain splattered since elementary school. His thick fingers and large hands couldn't make his letters toe the line.

Maurice, always less comfortable talking than writing, wet his lips, took a deep breath, and straightened out his tight blue sport jacket.

"First, the cash. I'm only getting started. We cannot be sure where it's coming from yet, but there seems to be a lot of it floating through the Agence AB."

"That could be a motive right there." Jeannot jumped in. "Right boss?" Mazarelle waved Maurice to keep going.

"Second, I pulled Berthaud's phone records. One thing is clear. He was making—and receiving—multiple calls from one number in the days just before he died. It wasn't a listed number. Looks like some kind of burner phone."

Mazarelle nodded thoughtfully.

"A lot to consider . . ." His voice trailed off. "Time to get going."

13

Mazarelle's appointment was with a locksmith, up in the narrow park that ran above the first Saint-Martin Canal tunnel. The old man was grumbling as he came walking up, munching on half a baguette. A worker for decades on the edge of retirement, as crusty as the bread he chewed.

"*Et pour ça,* I had to give up my breakfast?" He shook his head as Mazarelle showed him the police ID.

The commandant wasn't worried about the grousing. He pulled out his sunniest smile. "Let's look at the scene," he said.

Staring down through the wire-cage skylight, he tried to get a glimpse of the steel beam from which the dead body of Alain Berthaud had been hung. The protective metal cage was bolted in place with an impressively solid H-shaped lock.

"Bfffff," the locksmith sighed. "The Fichet 480. Ten wafers. Two sidebars. Used to be state of the art."

"So you can't do it?"

"I didn't say that."

He pulled open his shapeless, gray worker's coat and reached inside the pocket. He drew out an enormous ring of keys—long skinny keys, short squat keys, keys of every shape and dimension. Double siders, dimples, Abloys and paracentrics. Flipping through them, he stopped at the two H-shaped keys he had. He held them up to the light, twisting them slowly in front of his eyes as if appraising a gem. And shaking his head once more, flipped right on past.

Finally, he came to a small featureless shaft of metal, not really a key at all—no shoulder, no cuts, no tip. Jamming it into the tumblers, he gave a quick, strong snap of the wrist . . . and the lock came free.

He spread his palms out, as if offering up a gift.

"Any blank key of hardened material can be used to forcibly rotate and unlock the 480." He gave a small, modest smile. "That's why they discontinued this model."

With the locksmith's help, Mazarelle removed the protective metal wire-cage skylight. He knew that the body had been taken down from below by the white-clad Police Scientifique, who'd reached it by standing in a rubber raft on the water. It still griped Mazarelle that they'd done it before he arrived on the scene. He'd had to get their description afterward. The men in white told him how they'd struggled to bring the body down. It was a slow, difficult task. Fortunately they were two strong men.

Mazarelle dropped onto his stomach. Sticking his head through the skylight, he looked down on the scene below, trying to re-create in his mind's eye how it must have looked.

"*Incroyable!*" he exclaimed to himself.

Dangling from the steel beam, the dead body must have appeared as an eerie vision. Hanging upside down. The ankle swaying at the end of a rope. And closer to the water, the brilliant blue eyes glittering in the shaft of light that poured down through the skylight.

Seen from above, the dimensions of the steel beam and the canal below made it clear to Mazarelle how challenging it must have been to string up the body there. It couldn't have been Babo acting alone. At a minimum, it would have taken two accomplices to hang the heavy corpse from the steel beam—at least one above and one below.

From the beginning, a single question had nagged at Mazarelle— why was this strange location chosen for the body? If the murder was Babo's revenge, he could have left the corpse anywhere. By the side of the road. In a dumpster behind a café. Instead, the murderers had chosen a placement that took real effort. And they'd made no attempt to hide the crime. The whole point was to call attention to it. This murder scene had been staged. Like a movie set. It was too theatrical, right down to the small shaft of light focusing on the body, like a spotlight shining in the blackness of the tunnel. No question—it was a warning. And a very public one at that.

"Now"—the locksmith sighed—"can I go home and have my *café crème?*"

By the time Maurice returned from lunch, holding a cup of hot black coffee in each hand, Mazarelle was already back at his desk.

"In the nick of time. Thanks," said Mazarelle, taking one of the cups. "I'd just hit the bottom of my eye opener. I'm ready for a second."

Maurice accepted the fact that once they started on a new case, they rarely had time for real meals, like normal people. Sipping his coffee, Maurice watched as his chief, using a magnifying glass, examined some of the photographs sent to him by the Police Scientifique. Black-and-white close-ups of the victim's hands tied behind his back.

Mazarelle passed the magnifier to Maurice. "Do you know what kind of knot that is?"

Maurice gave his boss a puzzled look.

"What's the matter? They don't have knots in West Africa?" Scowling in annoyance, Mazarelle explained that the knot tying Berthaud's hands behind his back was one of the simplest in the book—a half hitch. And none too dependable unless secured by an additional half hitch. Which made Mazarelle think that it was probably tied postmortem. The work of an amateur. It wouldn't keep anyone captive.

"But *this* one—" Sounding impressed, he pointed to the knot around Berthaud's ankle that had bound him to the beam above. "This one was most likely tied by someone who knew a thing or two about knots. It's known as a constrictor, a secure weight-bearing knot. Difficult to untie and once tightened a real bitch to release."

"Sorry, boss. Not my area of expertise—"

"Forget it," Mazarelle said. "The point is . . . two different knots—two different suspects. At least two people working together. Which is borne out by the scene at the canal. I'll double-check the knots with Jeannot when he gets in. All those years of scouting have to be good for something. So where the hell is he?" Mazarelle checked his watch. "We're already late . . ."

14

The Alain Berthaud autopsy was scheduled to begin at 3 p.m. sharp. By the time Mazarelle and Jeannot showed up, it was already underway.

One of the advantages of being head of his own homicide team was that these days Mazarelle didn't have to attend most autopsies himself. Usually he could avoid their suffocating mix of chemicals and death in the air—a foul cocktail of formaldehyde, ammonia, and gastric acid. He was glad to delegate the assignment to younger, less sensitive noses like Maurice's. But this time the case was simply too big, the pressure from above too great.

Cracking two tiny pieces of clove—one for each nostril—he pushed open the door to the morgue's autopsy room and strode inside, with the hesitant Jeannot in his wake.

The medical examiner looked up, his scalpel raised mid-incision.

"Ah, the great man himself." The examiner beamed, waving the bloody knife in Mazarelle's direction.

Though Gilles Chardon was short, middle-aged, balding, with a black comic stub of a mustache and Mazarelle a great bear of a man with a hairy horseshoe under his nose, the two men spoke the same language. They were friends. They liked each other's independence, the confident way each did his job. And inasmuch as Chardon's mingy 'stache seemed to be temporary—a mere placeholder waiting to be shaved off in favor of something more substantial—Mazarelle didn't hold it against him. He gestured over to introduce his young colleague Jeannot.

"It's his first time . . ."

"A neophyte? We'll be gentle."

"So." Mazarelle jumped right in. "Time of death?"

"Well, you brought me a body that was hanging underground. In a tunnel. Cold and moist—right?" He started to make the incision in the chest. "I can't give you much more than you already know. It's some time yesterday morning, between one a.m. and nine a.m., when the body was found."

Jeannot wasn't really listening. He was staring down at the knife as it cut its Y across the victim's ribs. Chardon followed his riveted gaze.

"Don't worry about the chest," he said. "Look at the eyes." He pointed his scalpel down at the victim's face. "See the red dots?"

Jeannot was trying hard to stay focused. But his chalky pallor was getting closer and closer to the color of the body on the slab. Mazarelle gave him a little poke in the side.

"This is interesting. Pay attention."

He and Chardon exchanged small conspiratorial grins.

"They're burst blood vessels," said the medical examiner.

Jeannot brought his hand up to his mouth.

Mazarelle had started nodding vigorously. "Petechial hemorrhaging. Right?"

"Telltale sign. All those red dots. Some sort of choking. Supply of oxygen gets cut off. The blood vessels in the eyes start to burst."

"Cause of death, then?"

"Well, we won't be sure till the tox screen comes back later this week. But it looks good for it."

"Wait a minute." Jeannot was trying hard to rally. He turned to Mazarelle. "I thought you said that death wasn't by hanging."

Chardon nodded. "That's where it gets really fascinating." He slashed the rest of the incision into the stomach lining to reveal the intestines. "Our subject here was hanged, not by his neck but by his left ankle. But that's not what killed him. The hanging happened after he was already dead—and before rigor mortis set in. You can tell by the way the blood pools in the body."

He pointed to the dark purple shoulders. "See? Lividity. Gravity pulls the blood down to the lowest point."

"So not a death by hanging, but what then?" asked Mazarelle.

"Some sort of choking. Look at those marks around his neck."

Circling Berthaud's neck was an angry dark red band. A thick line just under the Adam's apple—maybe a couple of thin ones merged together.

Chardon went on: "But he wasn't choked by hand either. My best guess is death by ligature strangulation."

"A rope?"

"Well, if it was a rope, it's like no rope I've ever seen." He pointed back at the neck. "A normal rope digs into the skin. Leaves all sorts of abrasions. This was something smooth."

Chardon poked at the skin around the neck.

"Whatever the weapon was," he said, "it was applied with great force by a killer of formidable strength. It looks as if he came from behind. He crushed the victim's larynx and fractured his hyoid bone."

Even before the body wall had been sewn up with thick twine and big stitches and hosed down by the diener, and the morgue attendant had gone for his mop and pail to clean up the autopsy suite's bloody floor, Mazarelle and Jeannot started heading out of the room. Jeannot needed some fresh air. Before leaving, Mazarelle told Chardon that he was expecting the autopsy report no later than tomorrow.

"I'll try," Chardon muttered. "That's all I can promise."

"You'll *try*?" Mazarelle's face broke into a huge smile. He waved his finger in Chardon's direction. "That's just like you. Such a crafty bastard. Always making sure you've left plenty of wiggle room. That can mean anything from we'll get it tomorrow to maybe next year!"

Chardon grinned back.

"But this one has juice, right from the top." Mazarelle's index finger underscored the point. "We have to work fast . . . By the way, did you find any evidence to suggest where the murder might have occurred?"

"Not really. But there was very little blood on the body, including from the lethal wound. And I'm told there was no blood at all at the canal site. In my opinion, the victim must have been murdered elsewhere. Perhaps in his home . . . The dead body then driven to the canal, and hung there."

"Which reminds me, where is his car?" Mazarelle turned to Jeannot. "He's supposed to have had some sort of fancy new Mercedes, right?"

Jeannot nodded. "According to Fournel. We know Berthaud drove it to the Café Arielle. But it's not in the lot over there, that's for sure."

They emerged from the autopsy room with Jeannot still looking a little dazed, as if he were exiting from the darkness of a movie matinee into bright sunlight.

"Was it the smell? Did the stink bother you?" Mazarelle inquired.

Jeannot said that it did, "a little."

"Me too. You didn't know Berthaud did you?"

"No, it's not that. I didn't know him, but I suppose it was his face as much as anything else."

"Look, Jeannot." Mazarelle wrapped his big protective arm around the young man's shoulders and said, "Cheer up! I know that place can be depressing—a Grand Guignol horror show. They used to come to the old morgue right over there behind Notre Dame by the busload to see the homicides, suicides, and accident victims fished out of the Seine. The dark underside of the City of Light. The stuff we deal with every day. But you have to embrace all of it—every little piece of the puzzle—if you want to put those pieces together. That's the job."

"Hard to believe," Jeannot said. He was thinking about the cadaver's organs—heart, kidneys, liver, lungs—spread all around the autopsy tables like meat in a butcher shop.

15

Rhythm. It was all a matter of rhythm when it came to breaking down the animal. Each process had its own tempo. The scraping staccato cuts to separate hide from carcass, the legato slices to part fat from flesh. The lean man in the black hoodie did not fancy himself a musician, but with each slice, he could feel his audience mesmerized by his movements.

Wiping his hands on the sides of his black sweatshirt, he hefted the blade again. A nasty looking number, the Camillus combat knife, with a seven-inch bowie blade ending in a vicious clip-point. In the twenty-odd years he had owned the knife, the Camillus had yet to let him down. You could soak the compressed leather hilt in water, blood, it didn't matter—and still keep a vise-tight grip on the handle. Best of all, it was not flimsy. Where other knives would bend or crack when cranked around inside a body, the carbonized-steel bowie blade of the Camillus made the body do the cracking instead.

It had been many years since the knife had seen any true action, but once sharpened it would not forget its purpose. Picking up the ceramic rod he set to work.

Shhhhhing. From the linoleum-covered floor the black and brown German shepherd looked up, eagerly tracking the man's precise movements.

Shhhhing. Ceramic on metal, grinding away the dull layers of carbon steel that had already done their job, revealing the vicious gleam of a sharpened edge.

A familiar rhythm beat its way into his head, one he had not thought of in years, not since the days he first used the Camillus. The rigid lockstep march of his unit, the blinding brightness of their *képi blancs* against the dark green hues of the jungle, their regimental chant.

With each sharpening stroke, he hummed to himself: "For this knight destiny, / honor, fidelity, / We are proud to belong." He worked his way up to a crescendo. "The Devil is marching with us!"

He turned to the German shepherd, grinning, gesturing with the Camillus. "The Devil marches with us! Right, Teufel?" The dog wagged his tail jovially in response.

Spinning back to the counter, the man began to carve. Long, deliberate strokes, placing the meat into a bowl beside him. "See this? If you truly respect the hunt, nothing goes to waste." The dog sniffed the air approvingly, as if admiring the man's frugality.

As he finished, the man turned to face his German shepherd. "We eat everything! Isn't that right, Teufel? Good dog."

Teufel wagged his tail enthusiastically as the man approached with the bowl, giving it a final stir before placing it in front of the animal. The dog didn't delay, sticking his snout right into the bowl. The dog's owner watched his canine companion with a look of fascination. Until something caught his eye.

Clicking his tongue against the roof of his mouth, he reached down into the bowl. How could he have missed that? He shook his head, and tugged at the ring on the small hunk of meat, allowing the light to catch the gold band—the bright green emerald fixed in its center refracting streaks of blue and green around the kitchen.

"Well, *almost* everything. Right, boy?"

He scratched the dog behind the ears. Pocketing the ring, he tossed the finger back into the bowl.

A minute later, Teufel licked the bowl clean.

16

The message sat on Mazarelle's desk—a pink summons from the powers that be. It was Coudert, wanting to know the status of the investigation. Calling to make sure the prosecution was on track and all the details lined up as the case headed toward trial. Mazarelle hadn't quite gotten around to mentioning his misgivings about their suspect, Babo, in the jail, or his latest findings. In his experience, bosses were like pets. You didn't want to confuse them with too much information, too many words. They were skittish and easily rattled.

In the meantime, he was pushing hard for new facts. And his team was retracing Alain Berthaud's final steps, trying to figure out who saw the victim last.

Maurice had just come back from the Café Arielle. The owner had recognized Alain Berthaud from the blown-up photo Maurice had shown him. "Yes, that one. He was here Friday night."

"You're sure?" Maurice asked.

The owner examined the photo again. "I'm sure. There were three of them," he recalled. "Never seen them in here before. Friends celebrating. Having a good time. The only odd thing I remember is that the one with short gray hair suddenly left early. When I asked him about paying, he said, 'They'll pay.'"

"What time did his friends leave?"

"About one a.m. They were laughing, telling each other jokes. Stayed on drinking until closing. By the time they left arm in arm—holding each other up—that one, Berthaud, was completely sloshed."

The owner thought one of them had a car, but he had no idea who drove, or where the car was now. It seemed to have disappeared from the lot. Like Berthaud.

Mazarelle was only modestly encouraged by Maurice's report. "So we know where he was up until around one a.m. or so. The last few hours are a blank. Which doesn't help us much."

It was sounding less and less likely that Babo was involved. Unless he and his men had stood around outside the café, unseen, waiting all night for Alain to emerge. Babo was the kind of man who might explode and get into an argument. But a carefully planned ambush with a weapon? That seemed beyond him. Mazarelle just wished he knew where Berthaud had spent the missing hours.

As if on cue, the phone jangled on the desk. It was Jeannot, all enthusiasm, like a golden retriever with a ball in his sights.

"Chief, we've got it!"

With car horns blaring in the background, Jeannot was calling in from the streets of the Twentieth Arrondissement. He described how Maurice had come up with the license plate number for Alain Berthaud's car, and then put the information about the victim's missing automobile out on the police internet circuit. In less than two hours, the 2002 Mercedes-Benz C-class sedan was spotted, parked in a glum, graffiti-marked stretch of town near the Porte de Vincennes. A local aubergine—the meter maids not so affectionately known as "eggplants"—had seen a vehicle answering the description on the rue des Maraîchers, between the Hôtel Beauséjour and Le Moderne, two fleabags where guests didn't stay long and the sheets were rarely changed. Jeannot had already raced over to check it out.

"It's the car for sure," enthused Jeannot. "Perfect match on the ID." There was a pause as he walked around to the driver's side window.

"I think there's something on the headrest. It looks like . . . it looks like a little blood. Whoa . . . I'm gonna take a closer look."

"Stop!" Mazarelle's voice cut through like a foghorn. "Do not move. Do not touch anything."

"But, chief . . ."

"You know the drill. The Police Scientifique. Call them in now. Get them over there right away to check it out. Ask them to see if there's any usable DNA."

"Okay, okay . . ."

Jeannot sounded so glum, Mazarelle took pity on him.

"So, without touching anything . . . tell me what you see."

"Well." Jeannot started to rally. "There's not a lot of blood. Surprisingly little in fact. Doesn't look like it's from the driver. Maybe a little on the seat. But it's definitely there behind the headrest and a little on the backseat."

"Any signs of a struggle?"

"Not really boss, sorry." He paused. "The car is pretty much empty. Only a bottle of water and a box in the driver's side door. It says 'balles' on it. No, 'balles à blanc.' Blanks. That's strange. Hard to tell from this angle."

There was a silence as Mazarelle thought and stroked his mustache.

"The driver's seat, where is it?"

"What do you mean? It's in front of the wheel."

"No, no. Is it even with the passenger seat?"

Jeannot peered in through the side window.

"Actually, it's much farther back than the other one."

"Ahhh." From Mazarelle, a slow contented sigh.

"What? What does it mean?"

"Think about it, detective. How tall was Berthaud?"

"Average, I guess. Why?"

"And the distance from the seat to the pedals?"

"It's kind of far . . . Oh, *putain*!" The light finally went on for Jeannot. "It would never have been there normally. It must have been shoved back."

"And why, Jeannot?"

"Because maybe there was some kind of struggle. Like someone was choking him, and slammed the seat back."

"And so that means . . . ?"

There was an awe-inspired silence, as all the pieces began to click into place for Jeannot just as they had for his boss minutes before.

"This is definitely the crime scene."

"Okay." Mazarelle punched a button on the phone. "I'm putting you on speaker so Maurice can hear."

"There's nothing ordinary about this one." Mazarelle jabbed his finger down at the sepia file on his desk. "This murderer. Whoever he was, he knew his trade. Played his weapon the way Heifetz played his fiddle. He must have been hiding behind the driver's seat, waiting for Berthaud to return to his car. And then, without warning, killed him from behind."

There was no sound at all from Jeannot and Maurice. They knew their boss well enough not to interrupt when he got on a roll.

"Imagine . . ." Mazarelle continued. "Berthaud climbs into the car, and slips in behind the wheel. And suddenly—the rope, or cord, whatever, out of nowhere. He never sees it. It comes from the back seat, around his neck. Before he knows it, he's yanked backward. He struggles to get away. Manages to scrape his attacker, perhaps with the keys he's holding. But he's pulled up and back—halfway out of his seat. The rope bites into his neck."

Jeannot couldn't help himself. "But he must have tried to get away."

"Of course. He's struggling like crazy. He's almost standing in his seat. His face is pushed up against the moonroof. He's looking out at the night sky—out into the infinite darkness—as the last breath leaves his body." Mazarelle shakes his head.

"*Putain, chef.* That's amazing."

"It's a theory for now, Jeannot. Get PS over there right away. And get them to send us a full report. The only lead this guy seems to have left behind was those few drops of blood."

"All right," Mazarelle told Maurice as he hung up, "I've got to go downstairs in a little while. I'm about to be squeezed by Coudert. See what else you can come up with. The *patron* wants progress. And I need to stall him. *Allons-y!*"

17

Later that afternoon, Mazarelle walked over to his old commissariat in the Fourth Arrondissement to interview Guy Danglars. According to the eyewitnesses, he was one of the last people to see Alain Berthaud alive.

The offices had been rehabbed recently, but the fluorescent lights still made everyone look pale. Striding down the old hallways, Mazarelle was struck by how much he had changed since he was stationed here, while for all the renovation, the buildings basically stayed the same.

Peering inside offices up and down the hall, Mazarelle found no sign of Danglars. He sighed. It seemed as if Guy hadn't come to work again. He must have called in sick. Mazarelle supposed he'd done too much celebrating like his pal Fournel.

Looking in the doorway of one last office, he was surprised to see Émile Coluche—a familiar face but not necessarily a friendly one, or one he cared to see. Coluche appeared equally as startled to see him. And even a little annoyed. They had a history together.

When Coluche first joined the commissariat, he'd quickly gained a reputation for being a cocksman. Though married, he was always seen with some woman other than his wife. At first Mazarelle was amused by his frequent meetings with Coluche and his different lady friends, until one day he ran into him with Martine, Mazarelle's own wife. It had only been a meeting at a bar, but Mazarelle became angry, said nothing, and kept his distance. Then, after Martine's death from cancer, Coluche hadn't even sent a card with a word of sympathy.

On this occasion, the past was like a mephitic smell in the room. But Coluche was too much of a smoothie to let it interfere with his social face and glib tongue. There weren't many men his age who looked as good as Émile Coluche. Even his hair—the thick glistening blond waves that had long ago started to thin out—seemed to have undergone a renaissance. It was as if Coluche knew the sort of thing calculated to tick Mazarelle off. And, as for Danglars, Coluche had no idea where he was.

"I thought you were all through with us, Maz. What are you doing back here?"

Mazarelle explained that his new case involved a murder in the neighborhood.

"Oh, right," Coluche acknowledged. He'd read about it in *Le Monde.* "Sometime, when you get a minute, I'd like to talk to you about that."

Taking out his pipe, Mazarelle lighted up and exhaled contentedly. "Sure. No time like the present. Let's talk."

Coluche hesitated, licked his lips. Not so eager after all.

What the hell, Mazarelle decided. It might be fun to push.

"So—you saw that article in *Le Monde*? What was that about betrayal? A warning? Do you have any idea who's being warned? Any sense what that's all about?"

Coluche nodded. Then lowering his voice to a funeral-home murmur, he whispered one word, *"Ripoux."*

That wasn't what Mazarelle had been expecting. "What are you talking about?"

Inside the world of the police, *ripoux* meant one thing. Crooked cops—the dangerous, twisted kind every real policeman hated. The slang term came from flipping *pourri,* the word for "rotten." And there was nothing as rotten as a dirty cop.

Coluche looked up and down the hallway.

"Listen, Mazarelle—there's things . . . something a little strange going on here. And, with Berthaud's murder, they may have gone too far. Who knows who might be next?"

Not what Mazarelle was expecting at all. It was like kicking over a rock and finding a den of snakes.

Clearly on edge, Coluche said, "I'm no *mouchard,* Mazarelle—" Even for a smooth talker like him, the code wasn't anything to play around with. The blue wall of silence. First year recruits, fresh out of the national police college, knew—you keep your mouth shut. You messed with that at your peril.

"Come on, Émile," interrupted Mazarelle. "What the hell's going on here? What does it have to do with the murder of Berthaud?"

"I'm not sure."

But now Mazarelle had his teeth into it, and he wasn't letting go.

"How about a guess . . . ?"

Coluche had folded his arms across his chest, holding on to his sides, as if to keep himself intact. And quiet.

"Money?" asked Mazarelle.

A long sigh . . . And then . . . "*Big* money. Among other things."

"How so?"

"Look—it's still a rumor as far as I'm concerned, but they're saying that there are people at a few commissariats who are working the deal. Selling out to the highest bidder. Not that many, but you don't want to mess with them. Word is there's a lot of cash on the line. Maybe something political too. There are folks here with a lot to lose."

"Which folks?"

Coluche's eyebrows went up as if the sky was the limit. "I don't know exactly. I can't say. I'd only be guessing."

"But the rumors . . ." Mazarelle prompted.

"The rumor . . ." Coluche paused, and sighed again. "The rumor is there are people here who have a business that's thriving. And it seems they intend to keep it going no matter the cost—even Alain Berthaud's life for one."

Tantalized, Mazarelle wanted to know more. "Where did Berthaud fit in? Can you give me any specifics? Who's buying what? Who's selling?"

Coluche had reached the end of the line. "No." He was emphatic. He shifted uneasily in his seat. "I don't really know anything useful. And even if I did I've got zip to tell. I've kept my nose clean and out of other folks' business. That's the way I intend to keep it. Not to mention my pension. I'm not greedy like some people around here."

"Like who, for example?"

Coluche stood. "Another time."

As he left, Mazarelle thought, I'll be back. He wondered if Coluche would in fact be able to stay clear of Internal Affairs—the *boeuf-*

carottes. No surprise that most cops didn't like them—but especially dirty cops.

As for himself, Mazarelle saw trouble. When Coudert gave him the hanged man case and warned him about stepping on toes, Mazarelle had thought it was a no-brainer to keep away from his old colleagues. Now, after what he'd heard from Coluche, Mazarelle wasn't so sure.

18

Mazarelle was still chewing over Coluche's last words as he headed for the doorway. On his way out, he almost ran into a figure hurrying in. Looking up, he was startled to see Guy Danglars. Guy's face when he saw Mazarelle was anything but welcoming.

"I heard you were here looking for me."

"Good to see you too, Guy. I could use a little help," Mazarelle offered confidingly. He steered his old colleague down the hall into the open break room. Pouring a couple of cups of coffee, he offered one to Guy, and took a sip. His face puckered up.

"Ooh . . . still industrial strength," he said. But Guy didn't seem to notice. He was on to his third mouthful.

Looking down at the liquid as he swirled it around in the cup, Mazarelle asked gently, "What can you tell me about the other night . . . two nights ago . . . at the Café Arielle with Luc and Alain Berthaud? What were you doing?"

"Working on my headache." He grimaced. "I heard you were handling Alain's murder for 36."

Mazarelle said, "That's why I'm here. Anything you can tell me?"

"When you come right down to it," Guy had to admit, "there isn't much." Guy took a couple more chugs and finished off the rest of his coffee.

"It all started out well," Guy told him. The three of them having a good time. The wine drinkable and flowing nonstop, like the chatter and the jokes, and the talk about the old days. Guy admitted that he always liked a party. Plus the two partners seemed to have worked out some business differences before he arrived. So Athos, Porthos, and Aramis, *les trois amis,* celebrated with their glasses high and swords sheathed just in case. The noise and festivity making it almost impossible to distinguish between pinchbeck smiles and the real thing. Even after Luc's sudden departure when he began feeling lousy, the two of them were still carrying on as if there'd be no tomorrow until the café finally emptied out. Maybe 12:30 or 1:00 a.m.

"By then," Guy said, "there were only a few cars left outside, including Berthaud's new black Mercedes. I asked Alain whether he was going to drive that monster in his condition and he laughed. He was plainly potted. I explained that I'd left my car parked near the commissariat and could use a ride back to pick it up. Alain said, 'Now you're talking,' threw open his car door, and shoehorned me into the passenger seat. Then he jumped into the driver's seat and drove me back. That's it!"

Asked by Mazarelle what time he got home, Guy placed it roughly at somewhere before 2 a.m.

"Interesting," the commandant said. "Anyone see you come in?"

"Really?" Guy's eyes flared. "So you're checking up on me now?"

Mazarelle shook his head.

"Talk to my concierge. She never sleeps."

"Look"—Mazarelle tried to placate his old colleague—"my guess is that you were probably the last one to see Alain Berthaud alive. What do you think?"

"How the hell do I know?" Guy's face appeared to have broken out in an angry raspberry rash. He didn't care for the conclusive way Mazarelle was tracking "his murder suspect" right up to Guy's doorstep. Guy had no idea where Alain went after he dropped him off. "Probably sitting in on an all-night poker game in Little Asia," he offered. "Or maybe he went to visit a girlfriend there. Who knows where the hell he went? You tell me."

Mazarelle knew when he was being stonewalled. He headed for the door. But on the way out, he stopped for one last question.

"Which reminds me," Mazarelle said, "was Alain ever married?"

Guy, like any Frenchman, seemed to have been born knowing how to blow out his cheeks when putting absurdity in its place. "*Was,* yes. But that's a long story."

"Go ahead. I'm listening."

"It ended about a year ago. A wedding full of dreams and promises. Followed by a bitter divorce. The word *'acide'* doesn't do it justice. Olga, his wife, a pediatrician, actually charged him with molesting their only child—Danielle, a sweet ten-year-old kid. But child abuse was only the beginning. For his part, Alain charged her with being *une droguée.* Cocaine. They loathed each other."

"Which one got custody of the child?"

"Neither. The maternal grandmother has Danielle."

Guy wagged a finger at Mazarelle.

"If you're looking for a motive . . ."

He didn't need to finish the sentence.

19

hen Jeannot had tried to visit Madame Berthaud's office, he was told the doctor was too busy to see him. Too many runny noses and broken arms. Jeannot, being much too nice, let that stand. So Mazarelle decided to make the appointment himself. Either Berthaud's ex would free up some time, or she could spend the day with him at the police headquarters. She promptly booked an hour for him in Neuilly.

For a high-class neighborhood, the doctor's waiting room looked as if it had been ransacked. Framed pictures from *Beauty and the Beast* dangled from the chipped and shabby walls. Brightly colored Lego pieces were sprinkled all over the floor like Chinese firecrackers. Torn Tintin comic books covered the end tables.

Madame le médecin was a tight little package. Although she claimed not to have seen her former husband in ages, she was still primed to go off at the mere mention of his name. He had been ducking his alimony payments for months. She was furious that her lawyer couldn't find his money. So none of it would be going to their daughter, Danielle. The only legacy he left her was a lifetime of suffering from his abusive treatment.

"That's why I hate him so!" the doctor exclaimed. When she heard he'd been murdered, she didn't blink. The only thing she couldn't believe was that she hadn't been the one who did it. She said, "I've no idea who killed him, but whoever it was I owe him a serious debt of gratitude."

Mazarelle wondered if she might owe the killer some money as well. She certainly wasn't big enough to have killed her husband all by herself—let alone to have hung him upside down. And under Mazarelle's prodding, she retrieved the paperwork that showed she had been at the hospital with a ten-year-old patient that evening.

But looking the seething Olga up and down, Mazarelle had to wonder, could she have recruited someone to do it? There was too much anger there, no matter the alibi. Had Berthaud's life offered too big a jackpot for his family to ignore at the end? Did Olga or her daughter stand to inherit the agency cash from his death? There was more than one way to make a deadbeat dad pay up.

"But I'll tell you the last straw." Olga was still fuming. "It was half a year he hadn't been paying us. I got my lawyer to check where the money was going. And he found out that asshole had been giving cash to some political organization. Lots of cash."

"Really? No one else mentioned he was into politics."

"Oh yes," she said. "Not conservatives or socialists. It was one of those fringe groups."

"Fringe?"

"Although these days, who can say? They're all sort of fringe."

Olga couldn't remember the name. "But I remember reading about them beating people up. Disgusting."

Like everyone in France, Mazarelle had been tracking the rise of the new nationalistic groups, angry populists with a grudge to stoke. Recently, it seemed they were becoming more and more active, riding fear and outrage into the hearts of their countrymen.

"When was this?"

But Olga had run out of facts. She had no more information to share. Just a lifetime of resentment. "Why should I be surprised? Nothing about that man is too reprehensible."

Mazarelle thanked her for the information. "I'll have my team check in with your lawyer." He headed for the door.

But she was still raging.

"Giving his money to some right-wing *salauds* instead of his own flesh and blood. What kind of a man does that?"

20

The banner was fluttering in the afternoon breeze. A white flag emblazoned with a black symbol—a cross with a ring around it. A Celtic cross. It looked like a bull's-eye.

Coming down the quiet side street in the Thirteenth Arrondissement, Mazarelle and Maurice turned through the imposing entryway into a modern gray cement bunker. Inside, the sign on the wall bore a name in large block letters—Défense Nationale.

In the corner, on a small video screen running on a loop, an impassioned speaker was pounding on a lectern. "Everywhere violence . . . fear and anarchy. People don't dare to mention it . . . They look on in stupefaction. But the real answer . . ."

Mazarelle shot Maurice a look. "I can't wait to hear."

The main hall was filled with rows of folding chairs, battered plastic seats that had seen a lot of use. The rest of the furniture was scraped and scuffed. Stacks of flyers sat on the card tables along the wall.

Onscreen, the speaker was working up to a fiery finale. "We will bring the glory back to France . . ." he droned on. "The destiny of this great country . . ." Maurice sighed.

"Over there," said Mazarelle. "In the corner."

A polished thirty-five-year-old in a navy suit, his hair slicked back in a full Gordon Gekko, was talking animatedly with two young men. Their hair was shorn to sharp buzz cuts, their black windbreakers stretched taut across their muscled backs. Maurice and Mazarelle made their way over.

"Mazarelle. Brigade Criminelle." Mazarelle was no-nonsense. "Who's in charge?"

"That's me. François Macquart."

The voice was icy.

Mazarelle gave him a slow, thoughtful once-over. Macquart had a hard-edged face that seemed all silhouette. His eyes were a cold, dark gray. Not a man you'd want to share a pastis with any place or time.

"We're here to talk to you about an investigation."

The two thugs stepped forward, but Macquart stretched out an arm.

"No no, gentlemen, it's fine. I'm happy to talk. We have nothing to hide. Why don't you come on in."

He shot a look at Maurice.

"You—it might be better if you wait out here."

Mazarelle started to object, but Macquart was already walking away. Maurice rolled his eyes, and waved Mazarelle inside.

The office at the back was surprisingly well furnished. An immense wood desk, all cherry and walnut, sat front and center. Framed posters in primary colors adorned the walls. Portrait of an extremist as a public relations executive. He pointed Mazarelle toward a slick metallic chair. It wasn't comfortable for a man of Mazarelle's bulk. He wasn't sure it would have been comfortable for anyone.

Macquart didn't even wait for Mazarelle to get settled in. He was a self-starter.

"I assume you're here to talk to me about Max Vidal? We know him, of course. He's always writing into our online forums—but understand, he's not a real member—"

"No no," interrupted Mazarelle, surprised that Macquart didn't even seem to know that Max was dead. "That's not it. Not at all. I'm investigating a murder—"

"A murder? Well—I love to talk to the police. You know the facts better than anyone. In the past few decades, we've had more unemployment . . . more urban violence. And why? Migrants. Refugees. Ever since we started letting more of them in . . ."

Mazarelle held up a hand. "Sounds like racism to me."

Macquart's eyes narrowed. "Ha! Typical," he sneered. "It's not racism," he said. "It's patriotism. We're here to protect our country. The way Charlemagne did. To stop an invasion. There's too many of them. They're all over the streets."

"According to who?"

"Look around. Anyone with eyes can see. They need to be taken care of."

Mazarelle shook his head. "Who's putting you in charge?"

Macquart drew himself up. "My ancestors fought under Napoleon. My namesake was a brigadier general. We know a little bit about fighting for our country."

Mazarelle cleared his throat to change the subject. But the hard-bitten young man had a message to deliver. And he was just getting warmed up.

"It's not only us. You saw this latest election. The country is finally waking up. They're finally ready to step forward. It's an inspiring moment. Truly inspiring."

For Mazarelle, there was an investigation to run. But he wasn't going to let some things slide. Some things didn't deserve a free pass.

"So why all the violence?"

"We're not violent. We're passionate. But we let our ideas speak for themselves."

A bushy eyebrow shot up. "Really? What about Lyon and Rennes?"

"Those Moroccans?"

"Yeah, the beatings in the town square. What about the Jewish kids shot outside their school? And that attack on the mosque in the middle of prayers. Four people dead."

"We had nothing to do with any of that."

"Not what we heard." Mazarelle let the silence open up. Macquart shifted uncomfortably.

"So why are you here?" he asked at last.

Mazarelle nodded, as if he'd been staring at a chessboard, waiting for that move.

"Alain Berthaud. He was one of yours?"

"I'm sorry. We have lots of members. I don't know them all."

"The one who was found strung up in the Canal Saint-Martin?"

Macquart nodded slowly. "Sure, sure I remember now. That was sad."

"We have evidence that he had been donating money to you over the past few years. What's his connection to your group?"

"Wait a minute. Why are you digging around in this? Don't you already have the killer in custody?"

Macquart began to nod vigorously.

"Sure you do. A Gypsy, right?"

"Alain Berthaud. What—"

"Of course." Macquart broke in. "The police would rather find a less sympathetic killer. Why won't you convict these lowlifes when the evidence is against them? The ones who make our country poorer, dirtier, more divided."

Mazarelle's face tightened. He leaned forward. "Can you answer the question? Did Alain have any enemies in the group?"

"Enemies? No way."

"Anyone who'd wish him harm?"

"Of course. You're looking for a killer . . . here."

Macquart shook his head.

"You see someone whose politics you don't agree with and you assume—"

He broke off, frowning. And picked up again.

"Commandant, why in the world would we have any reason to kill him? He was a member in good standing. A contributor to the cause. It doesn't make any sense."

Mazarelle had a pretty good idea exactly who Macquart was underneath his suit and the hair gel. But his logic was hard to argue with.

And now, through the door, the commandant became aware of a commotion outside. A noise getting louder. Voices raised.

"Right!" came a shout. "As if they'd make a macaque like you a detective."

"Ragheads and jigaboos invading our homeland."

Mazarelle could hear Maurice trying to stay calm. "I was raised right here in Paris. Now step back."

But the two men with him were getting themselves worked up.

"The fourteen words. You know the fourteen words? 'We must secure the existence of our people and a future for white children.'"

"Sir, no one wants to take your future away. Quiet down."

"We're being swallowed alive by immigrants like you. Invaders. Trying to replace us. Well we have a tradition. An identity. A culture."

"You need to take a step back, sir." Maurice squared his shoulders and drew himself up, working to keep control.

"You're not going to replace us."

"Back off!"

As Mazarelle opened the office door, he saw Maurice reach for his gun.

But the two men flanking him didn't flinch. The shorter one took a step forward.

"You think that scares us?" he said. "You have no idea what you're dealing with . . ."

The tall lanky one reached inside his jacket.

The situation was going downhill fast.

Quicker than anyone realized, two huge muscled arms flashed out, as Mazarelle strode forward and wrapped the lanky man in a great bear hug. Lifting him up. Shaking him. Floundering off-balance, the gunman clawed at the arms around him.

Everyone else froze, openmouthed.

Almost nonchalantly, like a housewife tossing out the trash, Mazarelle threw the gunman across onto his compatriot.

The two men went sprawling into the corner, their guns skittering across the floor. In one deft motion, Maurice swept up their weapons.

"I think we'll let everyone cool down," said Mazarelle.

"All right with you, Monsieur Macquart?" Maurice added.

He and Mazarelle shared a grin.

The two men on the ground looked up, battered and bruised. There was a lump forming on the forehead of the tall one. Blood trickled out of the short one's nose.

Mazarelle turned for the door.

"Have a nice day," he said.

Out on the street, Mazarelle adjusted his jacket, and the two of them set off toward the boulevard.

"That was unpleasant, wasn't it?" Mazarelle said. "You think they were covering something up?"

Maurice reached out a hand to stop him. "You don't realize." He paused. This wasn't the kind of thing he liked to talk about. "Of course, that was bad. But this kind of thing. This isn't . . . It happens all the time."

"Oh come on. This is 2002. A new millennium."

"Yeah—like the old one."

Mazarelle didn't have much to add to that. He shook his head and put an arm around Maurice's shoulder.

21

Inside the cluttered office, Mazarelle's feet were up on his desk, clearing a space among the stacks of papers, notes, small piles of ash. In his hands, he fiddled with a small plexiglass box. It was a gift from Jeannot, presented with a flourish—the shell from the Chirac shooting, framed as a memento the day the case was closed.

Not exactly by the book, but it still made Mazarelle smile to think of Jeannot's beaming grin.

At least most of the time. But now, he'd had yet another call from Coudert. There was nothing like a high-profile case to get the phones ringing—the mayor calling the head of the Police Judiciaire, calling his boss Coudert, calling him. But today, after Mazarelle's depressing experience with those neo-Nazi thugs, the nonstop pressure from the top felt especially griping.

He wished he could wrap things up, but very little about this case made sense. If Alain Berthaud's death was a message, who was that message meant for?

Mazarelle sighed. At least Alain's Mercedes was a good lead—potentially their best. Jeannot had called in the forensic team from the Police Scientifique, but they hadn't heard anything back so far. Which was strange.

"Hey, Maurice," he called. "Any word on the forensics? Any blood work from the car? Any prints or DNA?"

He could hear Maurice flipping through the case file, scanning down his neat, orderly lists of evidence in a binder that was growing thicker and thicker.

"Nothing so far."

"What's taking so long? Has everyone forgotten how to do police work?"

"Well, the DNA takes a while. But they must have something back on the rest. They promised us something by today."

Mazarelle decided it was time to be proactive. He swung his feet down from his desk, picked up his phone, and called the office of the Police Scientifique. He pressed the speakerphone button so that everyone could hear.

"What can I do for you?" The PS official's voice came booming out like a cement mixer, its rumbling barrel spinning seemingly out of control.

"This is Mazarelle. Your team was doing a workup on a Mercedes for us. A C-300."

"What case?" The voice was abrupt, no-nonsense.

Mazarelle turned to Maurice, who passed him the case file number in his tiny, precise handwriting.

"Zero two thirty-three seventy-four. We haven't gotten anything back from your forensic work at all."

There was a pause as numbers were typed into a computer on the other end of the line.

"Right. Of course not. Your man said not to worry about it."

"What?"

"Your guy—he called and canceled a couple days back."

"Canceled? What the hell are you talking about?"

"Zero two thirty-three seventy-four, right? I've got it right here." Mazarelle could hear him shuffling through a stack of papers. "He said forget about it. So I forgot about it."

"Who said that? Who would ever say something like that?"

Mazarelle turned to Maurice. "Cap—did anyone here call them?"

"No way," said Maurice. "What do you think this is? We're organized here."

Mazarelle turned back to the speakerphone. "Who called you?" he demanded. "Who put in that cancellation?"

"How should I know? What am I, a secretary? Someone called and said not to run the tests. I didn't run the tests. That's what I know."

Mazarelle took in a deep breath and tried to keep his cool. The lab techs were a precious resource—always overworked. Too many tests to run, too many unsolved cases, not enough techs.

"Well," he said, "no matter what anyone else told you, this is Commandant Mazarelle saying you had better get out there and start doing the forensic work on that C-300."

"Mercedes C-300." Another pause. "We don't have it."

"Wait." Mazarelle couldn't help himself now. He was definitely starting to lose his cool. "You don't even know where the car is?"

"Probably sent over to one of the impound lots."

"Well then, *mon ami*," Mazarelle's temper began the slow boil, "you had better get your PS asses the hell over to that impound lot and run those forensics. Now!"

"Right now, it's lunch. Enjoy your afternoon, Commandant."

The dial tone filled the room.

Only a seasoned bureaucrat could make such politesse sound like a giant "screw you." Mazarelle slammed the speakerphone off with his palm.

No forensics. Another wait.

Was it just a mistake? Or was somebody trying to interfere with his investigation?

22

t was nearly 10 o'clock as the sun went down over the silvery streets of Paris. Summer nights started late here, farther north than Toronto or Montreal. And in the twilight, as the streetlamps lit up at the end of a long workday, Claire Girard, editor in chief of *Paris-Flash,* was crossing the rue Delambre, her Louboutin heels clicking along the pavement as she darted through the traffic. If she was moving fast, there was a reason. Ever since she'd read the news of Alain Berthaud's murder in *Le Monde,* she'd been worried. Her sources had told her it was only a matter of time before the Brigade Criminelle would want to question her. And a couple of hours ago, she'd gotten the call.

Claire was pretty certain the coming summons had something to do with Berthaud's death. The relationship between her magazine and the dead private investigator was a little too close for comfort. She was well aware that his company, Agence AB, had worked for the magazine on such stories as pedophile priests (entitled "Bad Habits"), movie stars in trouble (Gérard Depardieu, Jean-Paul Belmondo, Catherine Deneuve), and, most recently, on *PF'*s upcoming story involving the four-time consecutive winner of the Tour de France, Lance Armstrong, and drugs. But all that was out on the table.

What worried her was the other work. She assumed somebody had leaked to the Brigade Criminelle, or even to Internal Affairs, that *Paris-Flash,* and perhaps other publications too, had been paying *flics* big money for access to confidential case files. And there were one or two other jobs off the books she was concerned about, as well as the handful of cops who had no problems bending the rules and a desire to cash in while they could. But what did the investigators know? And whom would they target? The murder of Berthaud was obviously a warning: keep your mouths shut or turn up as a tarot card the way he did.

That's why Claire was heading to this emergency evening meeting at the Rosebud, across the street from the *Paris-Flash* offices. She needed to see Berthaud's partner, Luc Fournel, herself. She had to find out if he too had been contacted by the commandant. And what Mazarelle wanted to know. Even if tomorrow proved to be only a fishing expedition on the part of the commandant, she'd have a better idea what to expect after talking to Fournel. She was taking along Philippe Riche, her deputy editor and bagman. Philippe knew Luc. He knew the retired cop well.

The Rosebud was a dimly lit *intime* scene with a long zinc bar and jazz music from the last century in the background. Right now Django Reinhart, the great Romani jazz guitarist, and the Hot Club de France were gliding through "Moonglow." It was the sort of place Man Ray or André Breton or perhaps even Paul Gauguin, all of whom earlier lived on Delambre, might have enjoyed. Or if not there, then across the street, at the old Dingo Bar, which was where Hemingway went in 1925, and where he met Scott Fitzgerald to celebrate the publication of his latest novel, *The Great Gatsby*.

On this night, a thick-necked guy with short, steel-gray hair was holding down one of Rosebud's few large tables in the rear. He was not the sort of customer you'd ask to move to a smaller table. Especially since most were occupied already, and especially since he was one tough-looking ex-*flic*. Luc Fournel had never been inside Rosebud before, one of the few bars anywhere in Paris that could make that claim.

He spotted the two of them as soon as they came in the door because the striking woman with Riche was young, chic—and as Riche had told him on the phone—looked as if she had something to do with money. Fournel knew little about fashion but a lot about money. While still on the force, he'd seen the trail of cash flowing from *Paris-Flash* to L'Agence AB. That was one of the reasons he'd decided to take early retirement and join the agency himself.

Luc Fournel waved. Riche led their way to the corner table. At that hour there were mostly men in the bar, and a number of them turned to watch Claire as she went by. Luc could see that the silk black-and-white Hermès scarf she wore was expensive. He enjoyed the fact that the table she was heading toward was his.

Philippe introduced Claire to Fournel, and he was pretty much what she was expecting. Only more so. His face looked as if it had been chipped out of stone. Only his hands surprised her. When they shook, she noticed that his musician-like fingers were long and expressive. But the private detective's voice was tuneless, and he wielded it like a club. The white-jacketed waiter came over to ask what they were drinking. Claire said she'd take a glass of port. Philippe asked for a Bloody Mary.

"And for you, monsieur, another scotch and soda?" the waiter asked, whisking his empty away. "A double," Fournel ordered.

Even before their drinks arrived, Claire had no time for small talk, and that seemed to suit Fournel perfectly. When she asked if Mazarelle had wanted to see him too, he replied, "Naturally! The day I came back from the hospital he was in my office waiting for me. Mazarelle may seem slow and plodding, but he's not as dumb as he looks. The questions he asks are probably the ones he already knows the answers to. So my advice to you is watch your step."

"Did he ask about your clients?"

"He did."

"Did he ask if you worked for *Paris-Flash*?" Claire probed.

"Not that I recall. But then I don't recall everything he asked. I do recall that if he didn't ask, I didn't answer. And I certainly didn't volunteer anything. But I assume he'll be back. If so, that's what a lawyer is for."

"Who do you think killed your partner?"

"Oh, I've got a few people in mind. Either they hated Alain or felt their world would be better off without him. *If* you know what I mean?" Fournel gave her an in-your-face look that could curdle sweet cream, and a mocking laugh. "Maybe you had some reason to keep him quiet?" He smirked.

Claire didn't care for bullies, but the cynical way he spoke made the private investigator seem like he might know more than he said. She pulled out the article in *Le Monde* about his partner's dead body hanging upside down with a tarot card in his pocket.

"So what did the card mean?"

"Must be what the newspaper said. It was clearly a warning. Berthaud should have kept his damn mouth shut. Not become a *mouchard* for the cops." He gave her a pointed look. "Right?"

Claire stood up abruptly. "I've got to go. I've got a busy day tomorrow." The waiter hurried over with a check for the table. Claire snatched it up. "I'll take care of that. Let's go, Philippe."

"Hold on." Fournel had something to tell them. "I've got that material you wanted about Chris Sarganis and his teenage models. Some great stuff. And pictures too. Why don't you drop by my office tomorrow and pick it up?"

Business as usual, Claire thought. His partner dead, and he's still looking to cash in. She couldn't get over his sangfroid. Cold-blooded as a viper. Before Philippe could reply, she told Fournel, "We'll think about it."

Startled, Philippe glanced at his boss to see if she meant it. She did.

Fournel glowered at Claire, not caring for her tone. He wasn't good at surprises. "Don't think too long. Trust me, you're not the only ones in the market."

"Are you coming, Philippe?"

23

The next morning, Claire Girard strolled into 36 Quai des Orfèvres at 10:50 a.m., climbed the endless stairs to the fourth floor without having to stop to catch her breath, and at 11:00 *précises* was ushered into Commandant Mazarelle's office. The commandant ran a tight ship. Obviously he had a thing about that. Claire was glad she decided to arrive on time rather than tease him about punctuality.

"Madame Girard." Mazarelle rose from his desk. Frankly she was amazed at how much of him there was when he leaned forward to shake her hand. Even Mazarelle's horseshoe mustache was on a grand scale. He looked ferocious. But what she liked best about him were his manners, at least where women were concerned, and the warm way he made her feel welcome rather than a criminal in this legendary, sinful building. She supposed somebody that size could easily be intimidating. Would probably have to be in a place where for almost a century some of the most hardened killers in all of France passed within its walls. Fournel had said that he wasn't as dumb as he looked. As far as Claire was concerned, there wasn't anything about the commandant that was dumb looking.

As for Mazarelle, he couldn't take his eyes off her. He'd no idea Claire Girard would turn out to be so young and lovely. This warm day her face glowed. She had on a cool dark-blue silk jacket and white pleated skirt. She wore her black shoulder-length curls casually uncombed. On her lapel, a stunning gold sunburst of a pin with a turquoise core, her earrings gold and turquoise.

Claire gazed at him with her big dark eyes. Claimed that she was alarmed to find herself in the Brigade Criminelle office. What was this all about? Was it possible he'd made a mistake? Girard, after all, wasn't an uncommon name in France. Or had she perhaps inadvertently done something wrong? That was possible. Could the commandant please explain? If only she could help him straighten this out . . .

Mazarelle could see she was upset. He asked if she'd care for a glass of water. Apologized for all the steps that she had to climb. He held up his pipe and hoped she wouldn't mind if he smoked. Madame Girard was most appreciative. She had to admit that she found the smell of tobacco on a man's clothes almost as appealing as that of certain perfumes on a woman's.

As he lighted up, Mazarelle squinted across to the far end of the office. He was pleased to see Jeannot busy on the telephone. Leaning across his desk, Mazarelle asked in a low, soft voice if she knew about the body found hanging on the Canal Saint-Martin.

She'd heard. "It sounded awful."

"The victim's name was Alain Berthaud. Did you happen to know him?"

"No. Not personally." The way she averted her eyes made him doubt she was telling the truth. "But still shocking. I knew the name."

"He was a private investigator."

"Is that so?" she said, and nodded. "That's what I thought."

Mazarelle was pleased to hear this. "Why was it that you thought so?"

Claire explained that in her line of work, *Paris-Flash,* accurate information was the difference between success and failure, what she called the "coin of the realm." Her magazine used many sources, among them his agency—L'Agence AB—to help verify their facts every week. He asked if she found them reliable.

"If they weren't reliable, we wouldn't use them. Our readers must be able to depend on what we say. If not, we'd be out of business. And so far, *Paris-Flash* has been a very successful publication." Claire wanted the commandant to understand that a *hebdomadaire* magazine with a circulation as large as hers used more than one private investigator, more than one agency.

"Do you know Berthaud's partner, Luc Fournel?"

"Not well. I was introduced to him once."

Mazarelle gave her an incredulous look. The smoke seemed to

gush out of his mouth, his nose. She appeared to be talking about a complete stranger. "You realize, madame, that Monsieur Fournel works for you?"

"Yes—yes, I know that." She seemed flustered to appear not to know. "Of course he does. But not as a regular employee on our payroll. Monsieur Fournel is a contract worker. That's *totally* different."

Mazarelle, somewhat chastened, mulled over her distinction. "I see. What does he do for you, this former police officer?"

"I'm not in charge of Monsieur Fournel's particular assignments. Ours is a very large, specialized, complex operation, Commandant. Perhaps one day, if you have the time, and you're still interested in *Paris-Flash,* I'd be more than happy to take you around and show you how my magazine works."

"I'd love that!" Mazarelle said, jumping at the chance. His eagerness made her almost regret her offer.

Mazarelle asked what she thought about the hanged-man tarot card found on Berthaud's body. Claire replied that the newspaper article she'd read said it was probably some sort of a warning.

"Who did you think was being warned?"

Claire supposed that was anyone who might betray the murderer. Reveal his identity. Or anything about the crime.

"As the editor of *Paris-Flash,*" he asked her, "and having bought information from the victim's agency, do you feel frightened? Are you worried about being in danger?"

She thought over his questions as if they had never occurred to her and then looked at him anxiously. "No, not really. Should I be?"

Mazarelle put down his pipe in the ashtray on his desk. "Let me be frank, Madame Girard. I'm surprised that you as the editor in chief of *Paris-Flash* seem not to know what's going on in your organization. If not you, then who does know? Surely not every job in your shop is delegated or subcontracted. Can you tell me where the buck stops?"

Claire held her temper. This was no time for self-indulgence. "We've done nothing irregular that I know about," she insisted. "And certainly nothing that other magazines such as ours aren't also doing." She leaned toward him and pressed his hand. The warmth of her touch held out the promise of more. "I'll try to help you all I can,

Commandant, but believe me when I tell you I know nothing about your murder."

"I'm sure you will help us."

He sprung up, shook Claire's hand, and said he was delighted to have met her. His final words of advice were, "Please, be cautious. These are dangerous people with whom you're dealing. Not to be trifled with. Do I make myself clear?"

She smiled at him. Taking her by the arm, he said, "Not everyone finds it easy to locate the exit here. Let me show you the way out."

At the top of the staircase, she thanked him for being so *gentil*. He stood there watching her quickly disappear down the stairs. Who knows? he thought. This might turn out to be one of those rare cases where business could mix with pleasure.

PART THREE

24

The alarm shattered the silence at 3:15 a.m. on a sweltering summer night.

Inside the Montrouge *préfecture de police,* the two young officers on duty startled awake. Their midnight espressos worn off hours before, they had been dozing in their chairs, their feet up on their gray metal desks. Jolted by the dispatch call, they hustled outside. Throwing their police car into gear, they headed off down the street, as the call came in again:

"Twenty-one rue Louis Lejeune. Break-in in progress."

There's something about the stillness of a French suburb in the dead of night—a stillness on the verge of exploding into one crime or another. For the two young officers inside the white Renault police car, in the darkness of this oppressive July evening, the silent blandness of the streets of Montrouge seemed to hold all sorts of dangerous potential. Just two and a half miles from the center of Paris, Montrouge sat on the southern edge of the metropolis, plain and featureless. With the lights out, it seemed as if the buildings had unloaded all their residents, sending them off *en vacances* into the sweaty heart of the summer.

The empty streets flew by as the white police car raced up the rue Louis Lejeune, its two-tone klaxon blaring. The car slammed to a stop along the curb.

The spacious modern structure at *numéro* 21 seemed to take up an entire city block—a squat, low-slung horizontal office building clad in a modern veneer of metal and glass. What its salmon and steel façade lacked in elegance, it seemed to make up in security. Like some modern-day fortress shielded by a mesh of metal slats. The logo out front read UNHCR—the UN High Commissioner for Refugees.

The young officers dashed around the corner to the entryway of the office building to find they weren't the first on the scene. They had responded to the alarm in an admirable five minutes. Almost a record. But another police car had beaten them to it. The car was already in place, neatly parked on the side of the block where no residential parking was permitted.

Two cops were stationed out front of the building, leaning up against the white metal barricades, trying to keep cool on a hot night. Placed as they were in the shadows, around the corner from the streetlights, it was hard to make out their faces at first, but they wore the distinctive navy uniforms of the Police Nationale, with the classic insignia of the blue sailing ship carving the waters of a red background.

The taller one, with the ice pick sideburns, took a long pull on his cigarette. He didn't seem too concerned with the alarm or the threat the clanging bell seemed to indicate.

The young Montrouge policemen slowed to a halt in front of their colleagues. They knew all their own officers and these two were not familiar. They assumed the cops had to be from across the line in Paris, paying the kind of visit their neighbors sometimes made.

"What the hell's going on here? What's that siren all about?"

The Paris cop looked up, and puffing out his cheeks, blew out an insouciant stream of smoke. "Nothing to worry about. False alarm. *Pas de panique.*"

The young Montrouge officer looked around, taking in the scene—the four-story headquarters, the two Paris cops.

"False alarm?" he asked.

The bell hadn't stopped ringing. The young officer didn't seem convinced.

The cop with the sideburns sighed and waved them away with the back of his hand, his fingers flicking at them like unwanted crumbs on a dinner table.

"Everything's under control, junior. We called it in. Why don't you head on back to bed before your wives come looking for you."

Reluctantly, still looking over their shoulders, the young Montrouge officers got back in their patrol car and slowly pulled away from the curb, heading off down the rue Louis Lejeune, the same way they had come.

As the Renault disappeared around the corner, the two Paris cops leaned back into the shadows. Up above them, on the third floor, a shadowy figure passed across the glass of the large window—silently gliding back and forth like some large exotic tropical fish hunting for its prey. The muted glimmer of a flashlight, playing over the file cabinets, framed the scene.

Looking up, the policeman on the street below placed two fingers to his lips, and gave a short, sharp whistle.

Upstairs, the flashlight clicked off.

25

The summons from Coudert came right in the middle of his lousy lunch. Mazarelle wolfed down the rest of his cold club, which had taken forever to arrive from the bistro downstairs, and hurried into the *patron*'s office. Grunting as he planted himself heavily down opposite his boss.

Coudert glanced pointedly at the watch on his wrist—the gleaming dials of the Audemars Piguet Royal Oak. The *patron* was a man who admired elegance, and hated wasting time.

"What's the matter?" He eyed his visitor. "Aren't you wrapping up your case?"

A couple of days in and Coudert was already pressing him to move on.

"No, no . . ." Mazarelle waved his question aside. "Nothing like that. It's the baba au rhum waiting for me upstairs in my desk drawer."

The *patron* could barely suppress a smile.

"Well, don't want to spoil the digestion. But the *directeur* is getting impatient. What have you got for me?"

"Okay." Mazarelle took a breath. This is where things got delicate.

It was hard enough solving a crime. But doing it within an office bureaucracy required a whole other set of skills. With Coudert totally convinced that they had the right man in jail, Mazarelle couldn't express his doubts without suggesting a plausible alternative. Until he had one, he had to keep things vague and stall for time. Deflection and tap dancing. Luckily, for a big man, he was light on his feet.

"So we've confirmed the identity of the victim. Alain Berthaud. Killed by strangulation. Some kind of rope. But not the one he was hanging from. And he was most likely killed somewhere else. And moved to the canal afterward."

Mazarelle explained that Berthaud's new 2002 Mercedes had been tracked down by his men in a gritty section of the Twentieth Arrondissement. First indications were that it was very likely the scene of the crime. No one else knew that, or that the murder probably took place shortly after Berthaud left the Café Arielle at 1 a.m. on July 20.

"So, I can tell you that we already know the what, where, and when—approximately—this murder occurred. How it was done, I have a possible idea. But we have no eyewitnesses, nothing linking our killer to the scene of the crime. We're working on it."

"Anything else?"

"Yes—there's the tarot card that I found in Berthaud's jacket. The Hanged Man."

Mazarelle told the *patron* that some experts had suggested more than one meaning to the card. Others believed that the grim image of a body dangling upside down was clearly meant as a warning: "You rat us out, fink, and you're next."

Coudert, suddenly and without warning, seemed to become very unhappy. "Look Mazarelle, where the hell are you going with this warning of yours? Who's being warned? About what? Is this something political?"

"I'll let you know that as soon as we do." Mazarelle appeared as calm as if he knew all the answers, which seemed to infuriate the *patron* even more. Coudert made it clear that he did not want Mazarelle wandering all over the place. That would be a mistake for a lot of reasons, especially if it led to suspecting people unconnected to the murder.

"Keep focused on the evidence against Babo Banderas, dammit. We don't need to know about some cockamamie warning. Forget this bogus tarot bullshit. Don't turn your investigation into a carnival sideshow. You've got one job, and instead you seem to be sticking your nose into everything else. My advice to you, Commandant, is get us what we need to convict a killer. Do I make myself crystal?"

Mazarelle, thus far, had found Coudert a good man to work for as long as the problems were small and few in number. He hadn't seen him under stress till now. He didn't like the view. How the hell did the *patron* want him to wrap up a case without gathering all the pieces in the puzzle?

As Mazarelle got up and headed toward the door, Coudert called after him. "Have you seen your old boss?"

"Fabriani? Yeah, briefly."

"Good. Keep it that way. Stay out of trouble."

Mazarelle told him nothing about Fabriani inviting him to a fundraiser dinner for old time's sake. Or of Coluche's suspicions about the *ripoux* group and the dangers they posed. He wanted to give no hint of stepping on anyone's toes.

26

The Beauséjour, on the rue des Maraîchers, was near the Père Lachaise cemetery in a run-down, impoverished, poorly lighted neighborhood of shabby buildings and cheesy third-class hotels. Before going in, Mazarelle glanced around, smelling the air as if it might be a clue. Inside the small cheerless lobby, he asked the clerk at the front desk whether he was on duty Friday night and early Saturday morning. "No," he said. "I'm the day clerk." But, yes, he did see the black Mercedes parked out front. He also saw the cops come and tow it away. Anything else—Mazarelle should ask the night clerk, who luckily was still gathering his things together and about to leave.

The night clerk, whose name was Jules, did indeed remember the black Mercedes. It was a quiet night out front and he was busy working on his stamp album, which he was now taking home with him.

Jules was a lifelong stamp collector, an enthusiast about all aspects of his collecting. The importance of using a good magnifying glass to keep them in mint condition, the right hinges to prevent discoloration, and most important of all, he claimed, clipped fingernails to keep the stamps' edges clean and crisp. Mazarelle listened patiently. He had to admire Jules. In a neighborhood like this—the Dempster-Dumpster of Paris—it must have been a full-time job to keep his edges clean and crisp rather than buried under the shit. Which was more than a little like Mazarelle's own profession. Mazarelle asked him whether he saw anything unusual about the Mercedes or knew whose vehicle it was.

The night clerk did see somebody inside the car. "I couldn't tell who it was," Jules said, "because some of the lights from the hotel sign in front had burned out." At first, he thought, maybe it was somebody who'd pulled over for a breather and was sleeping. Then the car began bouncing around. It was like a lifeboat caught in a heavy chop, and he realized there were two people inside. Whatever it was they were doing, they weren't sleeping.

Now that wasn't the first time he'd seen something *comme ça* in this neighborhood.

"I mean a gentleman suddenly attracted to a young lady from the milieu who decides to take her for a test run before laying out any serious *fric* for a room. You see it all the time. But this looked like two guys."

He caught Mazarelle's sudden look and misread it. "Not that there's anything wrong with that," he hurried to add.

"So what happened next?" Mazarelle tried to get him back on track.

"So I went back to my stamps," he recalled, "and twenty minutes later, they were still out there. So finally I come out of the hotel to see what's going on. That's when the guys in the car saw me. And they jumped out of the car like it was on fire."

"Two guys? And was anyone still in the driver's seat?"

"No, no, just those two guys. Must have been dumping the car. They sprinted down the block. Then I saw them climb into this little supermini at the end of the block and drive off."

Mazarelle wanted to know what they looked like.

"Hard to tell from here. I'd say two good-looking guys—who knows? In this neighborhood we make allowances. But there is one thing. The strangest thing—they seemed to have rubber gloves on. Like one of those late-night cleaning crews."

"Like they were cleaning the car?"

"Right. Rubber gloves, paper towels. Clearly, I interrupted them."

"Uh-huh . . . What did you say they looked like?" Mazarelle asked again.

"One, I think, was medium height. A little chunky. The other pretty tall, wearing a black hoodie. That's it. I gotta go."

For Mazarelle, the hotel manager's story was just what he needed. The first real descriptions of his suspects. Neither of them sounded like Babo. And now, he was more convinced than ever—the car was the key to the case. He needed to check out what PS had found in its analysis. He felt sure that whatever they had found, the car would lead him to Alain's killer or killers. Especially if Jeannot was right and what he saw in the car were indeed flecks of blood.

With continuing pressure from Coudert, Mazarelle decided he had no time to waste. He had no love of his new office-issued mobile phone. But at times like this, he had to roll with the new century.

"Maurice," he shouted into the phone.

"Boss. I can hear you fine. No need to yell."

"Oh, sorry. Look, what do we have from PS on the car?"

There was a clattering of keys as Maurice clicked through to the evidence spreadsheet.

"Ah, well . . . nothing."

"What—nothing yet?"

"No, sorry."

"All right, listen, I'm not going to wait around for them to get their thumbs out of their asses. What do you have on its location?"

More clattering.

"Well it says here that the police had the car under surveillance there in front of the hotel in the Twentieth. Jeannot called it in to PS. It was left there overnight. Spotted by the team making their rounds about four in the morning. The cops brought a tow truck around later in the a.m. and impounded the car."

"And which *fourrière* was it sent to?"

"There are six in Paris, plus the Impound Chevaleret for cars held long-term. You should probably check with the commissariat of the Twentieth Arrondissement."

At the commissariat, the answer was prompt—the suspicious Mercedes had been sent to the Impound de Pantin in the Nineteenth Arrondissement. Right on the other side of the Périphérique, explained the cop at the *préfecture*. Not too far. Mazarelle jumped in his car and drove over.

The impound lot spread out under the midday sun like a giant cemetery of battered metal.

Mazarelle strolled down the row upon row of parked cars within the barbed wire. The lot manager's office was a shanty. It was manned by a sullen bruiser whose forearms were dripping with tattoos, including a death's head and a Celtic cross.

Mazarelle flashed his credentials at the manager, and asked to see Alain Berthaud's car. The black Mercedes-Benz. Series C.

"Who are you?" the manager muttered.

Mazarelle pulled out his ID and showed it to him again.

"And the car? Got a license number?"

Mazarelle gave him the information.

The manager eyed Mazarelle's badge sharply, sighed, and started typing Berthaud's car info into his computer.

"Nope. Not here."

Mazarelle tilted his head to the side, confused. "I've got the paperwork from the commissariat right here. It says the car was towed to your lot."

The manager typed some more, and shook his head.

"No Mercedes belonging to Alain Berthaud. No Mercedes at all on this lot."

"What are you talking about? Who moved it?"

"Nobody. Nobody *moved* the car. We have no record of the car. It was never here. Period."

Mazarelle took a step back, stunned.

"Well, where is it then?"

"No idea."

"Well look in the damn machine. That's key evidence in a murder case."

The manager waved a tattoo-covered hand at the screen.

"Doesn't matter what it is, it's not here."

Mazarelle was getting mad. "Well, check again!" he yelled.

The lot manager looked outraged that anyone would call his expertise into question—his expression a mix of anger and incredulity . . . as if a chicken bone the size of a harpoon had been impaled in his throat by Captain Ahab.

"Listen, pal. The computer says the car isn't here, so that's it, it's not here. Go bother someone else."

Mazarelle's eyebrows lowered and meshed.

"See what your computer says about this!" With one swift swing of his arm, he swept the monitor off the desk onto the ground, smashing it.

Ignoring the lot manager's purple face and screams of anger, Mazarelle stormed out.

Driving off, Mazarelle was angry and confused, the wheels turning in his head. Maybe he had gone a little too far on that car lot. Still, it was becoming clear—someone was messing with his investigation. Definitely.

But who? And why?

27

On the second floor of a five-story building in the tony Eighth Arrondissement, not far from the Champs-Élysées, sat a small, nondescript office, nowhere near as posh as might have been expected from the Michelin-starred restaurants and hotels that lined the nearby streets. This cramped space, with its peeling wallpaper and beat-up desks shoehorned together, was the headquarters of the one department cops and crooks hated with as much venom—Internal Affairs.

On this sunny afternoon, Michel Clay and Gérard Alembert were sitting quietly at those adjoining desks, waiting. The younger Clay absentmindedly sketched pictures on his legal pad, images of parachutes. From time to time, he glanced over at the big mirror on the side wall and adjusted his tie. Alembert turned on the electric fan and checked his watch. Waiting didn't bother them. They were used to waiting. In fact, they were famous for it. Internal Affairs had long ago been nicknamed *"les boeuf-carottes,"* after the ingredients of a good stew. When it came to interviewing suspects, the *boeuf* knew how to let them simmer.

And a case was simmering now. A case that seemed to involve cops scattered throughout Paris. Behind the famed blue wall of silence, something rotten was clearly going on. For the *boeuf-carottes,* that stench of corruption was a call to arms.

Of course, Clay and Alembert had been running into all sorts of resistance ever since they started their new round of questioning. But what did they care about the snide remarks? Why worry if some cops said the reason the *boeuf* worked in pairs was because they didn't even trust each other? These two—Alembert and Clay—had been named peepers and snoops and even traitors. And those were the nicer names. So what? They liked their work. They were sure it made a difference.

Outside they heard the old elevator grind to a halt on their floor.

Suddenly, the door slammed open and smacked against the wall. A tall, brooding figure strode in—Detective Théo Legardère, waving a letter in his hand.

"Okay—I'm here," he growled.

He tossed the summoning letter down on the desk, and looked from Clay to Alembert.

"Glad you could make it," said Alembert. As if the departmental summons was an invite to a dinner party.

"So what the hell is this all about?"

"It's really nothing. Nothing important," said Alembert, patting the air gently with both palms to placate the detective. "We're trying to figure a few things out. Just hoping you can help us clear it all up."

"Take a seat." Clay gestured at the empty chair across from them.

Legardère hesitated a moment. Trying to keep some sort of control in the balance of power in the room.

"This won't take long, you said."

"Right, so let's get started." Clay gestured again.

Legardère pulled the dented chair forward and sat down.

"I can't believe you're wasting my time like this. Making me come in here when I've got a full load of cases I should be working."

"Just a few simple questions for you to answer," said Alembert.

"Let's start with this one," Clay jumped in. "Do you remember where you were around three a.m. two weeks ago this past Sunday?"

"You must be joking."

"No," said Clay dubiously, as if humor were an ancient art form he'd heard of once but never actually encountered.

"I was probably asleep. I don't know," Legardère snapped.

"Of course," said Alembert. "Who remembers that kind of thing? Say, have you ever been to Montrouge? You ever spend any time there?"

"Montrouge? What kind of fishing expedition is this?"

"Maybe you could answer the question."

"I have no idea. It's outside the Périphérique, right? I must have driven through it a million times."

"Well, here's the thing," said Alembert, in his deep, soothing voice. "We've got this tricky problem. There was a break-in at the UNHCR—you know, the immigration headquarters. It looks as if some files went missing. We're trying to figure out what happened."

"Immigrants? Really? You should be talking to the Montrouge cops, not me."

"*Bien sûr.*" Alembert nodded. "Well, you see . . ." He paused.

And Clay jumped in. "We have a witness who says you might have been in the neighborhood."

Legardère drew himself up in his chair and slowly stared from Alembert to Clay and back.

"Oh, it's like that? Right . . ."

He nodded slowly, carefully, as if the muscles in his neck hurt, as if they were tensed and twisted, and barely managing to keep his head attached to his body.

"Do you know how long I've been a cop? Nineteen years. Nineteen fucking years!"

He slammed his hand down on the metal desk in a single explosive movement.

"My father was a cop. His father was a cop. I've got more commendations than all of you put together."

Legardère jabbed his fingers in their direction.

"It's not enough that I've never been promoted to the BC. Which I've more than earned, let me tell you. And now you're gonna hassle me with this chickenshit."

He stood up suddenly and looked around as if seeing the dingy office for the first time.

"No wonder you're stuck in this shit heap. It's the perfect place for you."

"Now, detective," said Alembert, holding up his hand gently. "No need to get excited—"

"*Allez au diable!* I'm outta here."

Legardère stormed out of the room.

Clay and Alembert exchanged glances and nodded at each other. Gathering their notes together, they too left the room. In the hall they opened a nondescript door, revealing a small side room. Inside the darkened chamber, the young Montrouge cop had been watching the entire exchange through the two-way mirror.

"Was that him?" Clay asked.

The cop hesitated. "Look, I don't want to make any trouble . . ."

Alembert looked at him, nodding his head slowly, nonjudgmentally. Seconds ticked by. More seconds. The silence seemed to gather weight. It seemed to be almost palpable, an object hanging in the air between them.

The young officer made a grimace and sighed.

"Maybe . . . It was definitely an officer from the Police Nationale. I saw the uniform. But the face . . . it was in the shadows."

"Didn't you mention the sideburns?" urged Clay. "Those long thin ones. Ice picks, I think they're called? He had those, right?"

"It was so dark," the cop said. "I can't say for sure . . ."

At the end of a long and not particularly satisfying afternoon, Alembert emerged from his offices, and found a familiar shape leaning up against a plane tree on the street outside. Impossible to miss the rugged dimensions of Paul Mazarelle.

"Gérard. You have a minute?"

Alembert walked over, his hand outstretched.

"Paul. I heard you were back from the Dordogne. And all about the arrest you made at the parade. Couldn't stay away from the big city?"

"You get all the best cases. Have a minute for a quick coffee?"

Perched on the wicker chairs at the zinc-topped tables of a nearby café, Mazarelle took a sip of his *café express* and sighed appreciatively.

"Look, I've been hearing rumors. You're working on something. An investigation into some dirty cops. *Ripoux.*"

Alembert stared at the traffic on the busy intersection nearby. He nodded slowly, thoughtfully. It was hard to tell if he was confirming Mazarelle's hunch. Or just nodding. "We can't help you on that. You know department policy. We can't comment."

Mazarelle added a little more sugar and gave the cup a quick stir. The tiny spoon seemed lost in his big hand.

"I tell you why I'm asking. The Berthaud case? It feels as if someone is messing around in my investigation. Evidence is going missing."

"Sounds careless."

"Unless it's on purpose."

Alembert swirled the last of the *café express*. His eyes seemed fixed on the bottom of the cup. Out on the street, a taxi raced by, honking its horn.

Mazarelle pushed back the demitasse. "There's something odd going on," he said. "You must have some thoughts."

Alembert finished off his coffee in one swallow.

"Only one," he said. "Be careful."

He stood up and stuck out his hand.

"Paul, it was great to see you."

Mazarelle held onto the hand for a moment. "Anything at all?" he asked.

"Sorry," said Alembert. "You're on your own."

28

t was a little after 11:00 a.m., and at the Lutetia, the legendary Left Bank luxury hotel, the art deco lobby was bustling with new arrivals.

Standing beside the giant vase of flowers by the front desk, the skinny bellboy watched wide-eyed as a stunning young woman in a midnight blue suit came through the front doors, gliding across the lobby, heading directly to him. He blanched when he heard what she wanted.

"Oh, we're not allowed . . ."

Her smile shimmered like a promissory note. "It's a small favor. Who has to know? It would be so sweet if you could help me out."

Poking his head behind the front desk, he came back with the information.

"Five fourteen," he stammered. "The Arman Suite."

Claire Girard gave the bellboy a wink and slipped him one of the brand-new twenty euro notes.

"À la prochaine," she whispered.

Upstairs on the fifth floor, Claire stopped in the hallway for a quick moment, ran both hands through her hair, and gave the waistband of her skirt a quick roll, lifting the hemline an extra inch.

Down the hall, inside a tastefully decorated suite, junior congressman Frank Nash was just stepping out of the shower, when there was a knock at his door. Toweling himself off, Frank dried his trim chestnut hair. This time the knock was louder, more insistent. Opening the bathroom door, Frank called out irritably, "Come in, dammit!

Leave the food. I'll sign the check when you come back to pick up the dishes."

More knocking. Whoever was at the door, there was no quit in him. He wasn't going away. It was then Frank realized he'd been speaking English. The staff at the Lutetia in the past always understood English. That was the least he could expect at those prices. *"Un moment, s'il vous plaît. J'arrive! J'arrive!"* He wrapped the towel around his waist and headed for the door.

The self-possessed young woman standing there sized him up with calm eyes. She seemed to approve of his style, his chiseled chest. "Frank Nash?" she inquired, her voice soft and uncomplicated.

He was completely taken by her high cheekbones and her gleaming cascade of black velvet curls. One of the things he'd always found so delicious about Paris was that when somebody who looked like this knocked on your hotel door you knew it was no mistake. Frank nodded.

She held out her hand and said, "I'm Claire Girard."

He took in the delicate fingers, the exquisite profile.

"You're with the hotel?"

"May I come in?"

He wasn't going to stand in her way. He held the door wide open and watched her stride into the room.

Claire was used to the looks. Men were so predictable. Show a little skin and it was amazing how malleable they got.

Fresh off Tom Ford's latest runway, her new Saint Laurent suit was all business, with a hint of after hours. At first glance, it was tailored, demure, but the sides of the skirt were slashed with a tantalizing one-inch gap. Black satin ribbons were inserted to hold together the seams. Like everything about Claire, her outfit was precisely calibrated to exploit the fine line between elegant and provocative. It looked stylish; it looked as if it might simply fall off at the slightest pull of a ribbon.

Nash couldn't figure out what she was doing there. "Who sent you?" he asked.

Claire brushed the question aside. "Mr. Nash, I think we can help each other."

Frank's smile was all teeth.

"I'm sure of it," he said.

As Nash closed the door, she launched right in without hesitating. "So you've been having some trouble lately." It wasn't a question.

"Trouble?"

Her expression was carefully neutral. But she smiled inwardly to see how she'd unsettled him. "You thought it might be a good thing to come here to get away from the scandals."

Again, not a question. This time he bristled.

"Not at all. What the hell is that supposed to mean?"

Not a very convincing denial, she noted to herself.

"Have you heard of the magazine *Paris-Flash*?"

"The French tabloid? The one that did that article about Hitler's spy service here at this hotel?"

"You're thinking about *Paris Match*," Claire corrected him, her voice pure steel. "So what? We've done celebrities and scandal. But we've done lots of serious stories about de Gaulle, Picasso, Tom Cruise. And we're read all over France, all over Europe."

He paused to gaze at her, amused now by her spirited defense.

"You're a reporter for them?"

"I'm the editor in chief. That's why I'm here, Frank."

"A journalist. I should have known." He walked back toward the door. "What a waste. I've got a PR person who handles that."

She stared at him for a long moment.

"Not very well from the look of it," she said.

Reaching into her jacket pocket, she pulled out a couple of xeroxed articles and slammed them down on the desk. Lurid headlines, paparazzi pictures. The reason he had left the States in the first place and come here on this fact-finding mission, to let it all cool down.

"Here's the thing," she said, taking a step toward him. "There are some nasty details out there that could be used against you. You don't want that."

Was she threatening him? He moved back a step.

She closed the distance, right up on him now. He shifted nervously.

And suddenly an earnest, sweet smile of understanding lit up her face.

"Frank . . . you don't need more gossip pieces about your latest romantic conquest. You need someone who takes you seriously."

He was surprised at how much Claire seemed to know about

him. That he was a Desert Storm war hero from Minnesota, that he was the so-called golden boy of the Democratic Party and that he had recently been reelected to his third term in the U.S. House of Representatives.

"You need to remind them of that. You need to change the story." She trailed her fingers down his chest, and pointed to the towel. "And I can wait for you to change."

Nash looked down, grinned—and for the first time in five minutes, relaxed. Now this was his kind of conversation. Slowly, he sank back into the overstuffed chair, the rippling muscles of his abdomen flexing. "Oh no, don't worry," he said. "I'm fine like this."

Her eyebrows rose, but her response was interrupted by the knock at the door announcing room service finally arriving—a rolling table with white linen and ivory china.

"I'll take care of it." Claire shooed the waiter out of the room, and with a practiced twist of the wrist, opened the champagne, pouring the mimosas for herself and for Frank. The two of them sat down opposite each other at the room-service table.

Okay, she thought. Now for round two. She took another sip, and went in for the kill.

"I've been told that you're the new head of the House Immigration Subcommittee—that you're here to study France's *centres de rétention administrative*—the detention centers for immigrants and refugees. I've done an article or two about them myself in the past couple of years," she said, conveniently leaving out a couple of facts—for example, that her exposés had now made her less than welcome at all twenty-four of them. Even before rumors of recent suspicious deaths inside the centers had made them a hot-button issue.

"I'm sure you might need someone to help you with the French."

Not for the first time in his life did Frank get the feeling he was being manipulated. As a congressman, it happened all the time.

"Ah, it's so sad," he said. "Actually, I have a translator assigned."

"Someone who knows the story? Someone as useful as me?" She gave him a shy smile, and fingered one of the black satin ribbons. "We could have an amusing time."

Nash's smile broadened. In the jujitsu of seduction, he wasn't sure who was winning. But the sparring was fun.

She might be a little edgy . . . but she had a point about his PR. She could be of some use to him on this trip to France. And, besides, with a body like that she'd be a pleasure to have around. Perhaps he'd let her tag along. Keep a record of his work for the House committee. After a few days, what woman could resist him?

"Why not?" he said.

"So—we'll be in touch?"

She got up, and heading for the door, offered her hand.

Nash accepted, and inspected the digits. Grinning, he gave her a tug, and pulled her in close to him. He ran the fingers of his other hand along the lapel of her jacket, toward her breast.

Claire looked up, serious. She put her hand on top of his. Frank's smile broadened. But then, somehow, he couldn't tell quite how, she'd slipped right under his arm and was walking away down the hall, the flash of skin glowing through the slits on the side of her skirt.

"I'll see you in a few days." She waved over her shoulder.

On the elevator down, she nodded to herself. He would do nicely for what she had in mind.

29

The *Paris-Flash* office on rue Delambre was only a few doors away from the Boulevard du Montparnasse. Mazarelle wondered why, since returning to Paris, he hadn't been back to this neighborhood before now. There were a number of excellent restaurants within easy strolling distance. But it was the prospect of seeing Claire Girard once again that drew him in.

The top three stories in the narrow building housing the offices of her magazine were full of activity. Mazarelle got off the elevator at

Reception, identified himself, and asked to see the editor in chief. He was told to have a seat. She'd be with him shortly.

Above his head, the illuminated *"Flash"* of the magazine's name on the wall blinked continuously at the elevators. He picked up a copy of the week's *Paris-Flash* with its cover pictures of the singer Vanessa Paradis and the American actor Johnny Depp. A nice-looking young couple. Mazarelle liked her big hit "Joe le Taxi." As he flipped through the pages, he began to hum the tune. He almost missed the article with Fabriani's smiling face. "Mr. Law and Order," it proclaimed. "Claude Fabriani has been touted by many as the next minister of the interior, perhaps even prime minister." Mazarelle shook his head, and flipped on to an article about *Amélie*. Now that was more upbeat.

When told he could go into her office, Mazarelle was surprised to find that Claire was not alone. The smartly dressed young man sitting on her desk looked like an American. Claire was bent over, adjusting a thin delicate gold chain around her ankle. Her visitor nodded his head in approval. She glanced up as Mazarelle entered.

"Oh, how very nice to see you again, Commandant." She introduced Frank Nash. "Look at the lovely gift I received from Monsieur Nash." Claire extended her tan leg, turned it this way and that. The gold glowed against her sun-kissed skin. Her skirt was well above her knee.

Mazarelle cleared his throat. "Very nice." He wasn't sorry that he'd come unannounced, but far from glad. He didn't care about jewelry. He was there to talk about murder. He told her he needed to find out about Berthaud's connection to the magazine and the articles in which *Paris-Flash* used information from his Agence AB. Claire took him down the hall to see her deputy editor, Philippe Riche, who had dealt with both Luc and Alain.

The office was cluttered, stacked high with article proofs and old copies of the magazine. Pushing aside some folders to clear a space to perch, the commandant didn't waste any time.

"How long has Luc Fournel been working for you?" he asked. "Did he start when he was still on the police force?"

"Non, non, jamais." Riche brushed aside the idea. But he added

that recently L'Agence AB had been helping *Paris-Flash* with material for a number of articles. They were just one of many absolutely legitimate sources. He mentioned "Life in the Fast Lane" (Nico Manfredi's tell-all account of what it was like to be a Ferrari Formula 1 race car driver, on and off the track), and the magazine's upcoming cover story about the secret love affair between two members of the president's inner circle.

"Do you have any articles assigned right now on the police? Officers breaking the rules?" Mazarelle peered at Riche curiously from under his bushy eyebrows. "I understand there have been some rumors about dirty cops. And maybe a connection to the right wing? White nationalists?"

He tapped his finger on the cover near Riche's elbow. An image of Macquart's sneering face was emblazoned with the headline "Rising Tide of Anger."

The deputy editor grew pale. "Nothing like that. I would know. The only one who does that kind of article is Madame Girard herself. And she is usually much too busy editing the magazine."

Back in her office, alone now, Claire flipped off the intercom on her speakerphone as the conversation ended. Lost in thought, she fiddled with a silver pen on her desk.

On his way out, Mazarelle stopped by Claire's office to thank her and say goodbye.

On the spur of the moment, he offered to meet her for lunch the next day.

Her face filled with regret. "Ah, *monsieur le commandant*. I'm so sorry. But things are so hectic here at the magazine." She spread her hands apologetically. She had seen this film before.

Of course, he understood—he understood completely. Heading for the door, he stopped suddenly as if struck by a thought. "You must be busy preparing for the Internal Affairs investigation as well."

He thought he saw her eyes widen for a microsecond. But she shook her head.

"Never really had the pleasure of talking with any of those gentlemen. What exactly are they investigating again?"

"Oh, it's boring. Crooked cops selling information."

"Hmm." She nodded, recalculating, trying to find a way back.

"That might be an interesting story. We probably *should* talk a little more."

Then, as if the idea were hers and had only now occurred to her, she offered to meet him for lunch in an hour. Mazarelle agreed. He knew the perfect place to go. She smiled in a way that made him think the lunch might not be just a business appointment.

30

An hour later found Mazarelle and Claire seated face-to-face across a lunch table at one of his favorite small neighborhood places, Monsieur Lapin. Though she'd heard of the restaurant she'd never actually eaten there. Claire, as he'd hoped, was completely taken by its quaint intimacy, but frankly she was surprised by his choice of a place with its froufrou pastel decor and the "precious" porcelain rabbit figurines in every nook and cranny.

Standing behind the small bar near the front door when they came in was the owner, Monsieur Lapin himself, who as Mazarelle recalled had a wonderful dry sense of humor and a mustache that, of its kind—pencil thin and really quite elegant—rivaled his own. Lapin was pleased to see the commandant once again. It had been a while. He checked his reservations and led them to a small table in the corner, moving the chair back for madame with a flourish, as if the show were about to begin. Mazarelle glanced at the amused Claire, fearing that perhaps Lapin was overdoing it.

But the quality of Monsieur Lapin's food lived up to his theater. It was outstanding. Especially the flavor of the wild rabbit marinated in red vinegar, herbs, and spices, and stewed in a good red. They both congratulated the owner, who seemed pleased but restrained. It was as if he were waiting to see whether the commandant had noticed the soupçon of unsweetened chocolate in his sauce. Only then did he raise their bottle of Côtes du Rhône, refilling their crystalline glasses.

As they ate, Claire and Mazarelle watched each other over their wine. Mazarelle noticed the way she brushed her dark hair back from her eyes, the subtle curves of her crisp navy business suit. The editor was looking carefully at him as well, trying to read Mazarelle, like a footnote in a foreign language. Everything about this lunch was concerning. This detective seemed tenacious. The kind who would never give up. And while she might not have anything to do with his murder case, some of his inquiries might be headed toward dark and dangerous places. Risky places for her. How should she navigate this? Could he be useful?

She put down her wineglass and tucked a loose lock of hair behind her ear. "So tell me about the death of the investigator Alain Berthaud. Are you getting closer to finding out who killed him?"

Mazarelle took a thoughtful sip. "It's not that easy to tell how much longer a case will take. I've found that in murder cases each has a unique rhythm all its own. This case, for example, leaped from the starting gate, but now"—he shook his head—"I'm afraid it's a dogtrot. We're getting closer in one sense, but I suspect that things may be much more complex than we initially thought. We'll see."

"Don't worry," she consoled him. Her fingers reached out to delicately trace the top of his hand. "Things will pick up. All you need is a little patience. You'll see."

At that very instant it seemed to him they had already begun to improve.

Recalling how upset she was when she first came to his office, Mazarelle asked if the Internal Affairs officers had spoken to her yet about their corruption case. Had they contacted her? Asked her any questions? "Not yet," she said. But he noted the way she flicked her eyes—up and to the right. A sign, he thought, that she wasn't telling him the whole truth. Mazarelle smiled and filed it away for future reference.

Her eyes glistening from the wine, Claire changed the topic. What she enjoyed talking about was her magazine—telling stories about the scoops, the exclusive interviews they had wangled. Mazarelle was fascinated, and Claire clearly loved a good listener. Especially one with such a powerful physique. He looked like a granite boulder in a linen suit. She liked power, always had. And knowledge too. There was nothing a journalist appreciated more than information.

Mazarelle mentioned that when he was in her office, she said she'd be going out of town in a few days with the American politician he'd met there.

"I'm sorry to see you go just when we're getting on so well," Mazarelle glumly mumbled.

Claire's eyes darted up from her wineglass. She nodded slowly and smiled. Leaning forward, she confided, "It's only a short work trip. We won't be gone long." She had to admit she was a little charmed by his jealousy. She wondered how deep it might run.

The messenger arrived as they were pushing back from the table. One of the interns from *Paris-Flash*, with an envelope in his hand.

"Someone dropped it off at the front desk," he said. "They told us it was important." His expression was all modest efficiency, trying to please the boss. "So I ran it right over here."

Claire moved a few steps away from the table and opened the envelope.

Inside, a flash of color. It was a tarot card. The Hanged Man.

There was no note, nothing else inside.

She turned the envelope over, looking for a return address. There was none. The color drained from her face.

Mazarelle saw her expression. "What's the matter?" he asked.

The matter? Claire stiffly smiled at Mazarelle, as her brain churned furiously. The matter, she thought, is that someone, I don't know who, has threatened my life. Someone who knows that Internal Affairs has called me in. If I don't keep my mouth shut, they're going to kill me. That's the matter.

"Oh, it's nothing," Claire said, tucking the envelope away in her purse.

———

Outside on the street, Claire stopped and asked if perhaps he had a few moments more to spend with her. She'd enjoyed their lunch and didn't feel like going back to work quite yet. They were having so much fun that she felt like a schoolgirl on a blissful spring day who'd decided to play hooky.

"Plus," she said with a shy grin, "I'd love to hear more about your investigation. It sounds so exciting."

What she wouldn't—she clearly couldn't—tell Mazarelle was how rattled she was feeling. She wanted the comfort of his powerful presence a little longer. Like a mastiff at her side. At least until she decided how to deal with that frightening warning.

The Château Saint-Germain was also on the Left Bank but closer to the river on the rue de l'Université. Despite its name, the small hotel was anything but palatial. That was one of the reasons, ironically, Claire had chosen it for her pied-à-terre. Given the kind of high-pressure job she held, it was important for her to get away from the telephones, noise, and confusion. Few were aware of its existence. Even though Armand Lavoisier, her husband, thought he knew all about her private life, he'd never seen this lodging. Or if he had, perhaps chose not to mention it. Theirs was an open marriage. She didn't want to know about his private life and, as for him, he thought he knew all about hers.

As they came in, the well-groomed clerk at the front desk greeted Madame Girard warmly. The three-story hotel's modest drawing rooms were intimate, cozy, snug rather than grand, and though the Château had no restaurant its quiet bar was a treasure. Mazarelle headed toward the dark walnut interior of the bar. But breezing right by, Claire pointed toward the elevator. Her small two-room suite was on the top floor. She kept it reserved for her private life. She needed a place like that.

Though Mazarelle was never one to hesitate, he was uneasy. Such a lovely young woman. And most likely not a suspect in the case. Most likely. Still, this was not exactly by the book. By any book, in fact.

The elevator in the lobby was no bigger than a telephone booth. Claire got in. Seeing there was little space left for him, Mazarelle said, "I'll take the stairs."

"Don't be silly." Grabbing his arm, she pulled him into the elevator after her. "It's the third floor!"

Upstairs, in her private rooms, he watched her shrug off her navy blazer and toss it onto a chair. He felt uncertain what to do next. She was gorgeous. She was a decade and a half younger than him. He really shouldn't be there.

"So tell me about these *boeuf-carottes,*" she said, brushing the breadstick crumbs from his jacket. "Here, let me get you a little wine."

As she opened the Saint-Émilion, she was still trying to calculate how deep her trouble was. If she played it right, she could get him to help. Even if there were things she couldn't talk about. Her hand shook as she poured.

She recharged her smile, and came back into the room with the two glasses and a big grin. "Is their investigation getting in the way of yours?"

"Not at all," said Mazarelle. "Are you worried about them?"

"No, no." Claire's words rushed out. "Unless . . ." She gave him a teasing smile.

"Are you here to lock me up?" She held out her wrists.

She was trying to be seductive. But to Mazarelle, she seemed on edge, jittery.

He put down his wine, trying to read her eyes.

"Are you okay?"

"Fine. Why?"

She slid next to him on the sofa. He stopped her, gently. And gave her a long, appraising glance.

"What's going on?"

In a lifetime of romance and seduction, it was the last thing she expected. Someone who was actually paying attention to what she was feeling.

Her eyes started to glisten. She took a deep breath. Got herself under control.

"It's nothing."

"Nothing?" he asked, brushing her bangs out of her eyes.

"Just some bad news at work."

He's really kind of sweet, she thought.

She kissed him once softly, and poured some more wine. Outside, the sun disappeared on the back of the drapes as the afternoon glided into dusk.

When they parted, it was almost dinnertime.

31

"*M erde de merde!*" Mazarelle groaned. He'd had a lovely afternoon and his spirits were still soaring, but his head ached. The penalty paid by the old boy for his teenage high jinks with the beautiful Claire. Who knew where this was headed?

And now Mazarelle was caught in traffic. He glanced at his rearview mirror and noticed that he hadn't even put on a tie. He was going to show up at this black-tie event minus any kind of cravat. Serves them right, he thought. That's what they get for inviting somebody like me.

If his boss knew where he was going for dinner, he'd shit a brick. A command performance at the Fabrianis'. A fundraiser for the policemen's union. The Fabrianis lived in a sumptuous apartment on the rue Champfleury overlooking the Champ de Mars in the fashionable Seventh. He was glad to have been invited. It was a good cause. But coming in the door, it was soon clear to him that this was also a launch pad of sorts for Fabriani's political aspirations. The mix was half cops, half politicians.

Since Mazarelle had never been there before, the Fabrianis gave him the grand tour. In the kitchen, there were two stoves—one electric, one gas. Mazarelle had heard that the wife liked to cook. In the bathroom, there was a whirlpool tub which Mazarelle's aching muscles yearned to soak in. The oriental rug in their living room, he dimly recalled, was one that Martine had described as *"classique."*

And the view of the Eiffel Tower—*superbe!* Monsieur Eiffel's gift to its visitors, a lavish promise of all Paris had to offer its admirers. Looking out, Mazarelle felt his heart beat a little faster. The tower so close it filled all the windows. Their apartment—and Mazarelle wasn't even sure he'd seen it all—could have been a palace. Dozens of guests here, and still so much room. He supposed that Fabriani would probably sum up Mazarelle's own place as a *triste* little box.

In short, the Fabrianis were living in luxury. The money belonged to his wife, Juliette, who came from a wealthy family. Actually, she was probably the reason Mazarelle had been invited to dinner. She'd been a friend of his wife, Martine. There was nothing snobbish about Juliette, who apparently didn't care about money. Not unheard of, Mazarelle thought, among people who had more of it than they could ever spend. And there were more than a few of them here tonight, ready to open their wallets.

The dinner was excellent, the cognac afterward smooth and elegant, a Delamain XO. Fabriani held it appreciatively at arm's length. "I visited the *maison* a few months ago. This is how they test it—by smell. Not too close, where the nose gets overwhelmed with the alcohol. Just here—*la bonne distance.*"

Juliette rolled her eyes, and smiled at Mazarelle. The assembled guests murmured appreciatively as Fabriani got to his feet. This was the moment they had come for.

"Thank you so much for being here." He opened his arms wide to welcome them all in. "It's an important night. We all know how crucial our policemen are. The first responders. The first ones on the scene. And tonight we get to show that appreciation. Tonight we're not just giving money. We're making a statement about what's important. The safety of a nation. Security in our streets and our towns. In these uncertain times, we stand behind our police. They understand what it means to stand tall. To stand firm. To stand up for our national values. And we will stand behind them. We will not fail them. Thanks again for coming and making your presence felt."

A bit dramatic for Mazarelle's taste, but the crowd loved it. They were on their feet, cheering and whistling as if the Rolling Stones had wrapped up a two-hour set. An excited buzz filled the room, as the guests broke into small groups to chat.

Mazarelle was soon surprised to find himself in the middle of a gathering of invited politicians. "You're that detective?" one national assemblyman asked, incredulous. "The one who caught Reiner?"

"Well, it was a team eff—"

"Nonsense." Juliette had come over to join the group. "It was him. And did you hear about the parade? Bastille Day?"

"Chirac?"

The group had gotten bigger. And like an MC, Juliette was working the room.

Her husband had told her all about what Mazarelle and his men had done to capture the president's would-be assassin.

"That was you?"

Mazarelle shrugged. "Right place, wrong time."

He looked around for a way out. But the group wasn't going to let him go.

"What was the story with that shooter—the crazy guy, Max? Was he some kind of terrorist?"

"They never found out." The assemblyman knew the whole story. "He died trying to escape."

Wandering over, Fabriani clapped Mazarelle on the shoulder. "Very impressive, this one. Just the sort of quick thinking we need in times like these. Right, Paul?"

Except for that *horreur,* Juliette thought it had been a wonderful parade. "Especially the Foreign Legion. With their orange aprons, their huge axes, oh là là!"

Mazarelle nodded, glad for the subject change. "The sappers."

"Yes, yes," she agreed. "Those fierce beards. They looked like the murderers and cutthroats they all used to be. Criminals hiding out from the law."

Fabriani said that was a long time ago. "You all remember Luc Fournel, don't you? Before he was in our commissariat he was in the Legion. Can you imagine Luc with a beard growing like a jungle all over his face?"

The sound of Juliette's laughter was so infectious that Mazarelle almost wanted to join in, but he only smiled, as Fabriani went on.

"Luc in the Legion was no desperado. In fact, he saved a comrade's life. Won a medal. He was a hero. And frankly, when he took early retirement from our office, I was sorry to see him go. We lost a plum."

Mazarelle asked his host if the medal was for something Fournel had done in battle. Fabriani wasn't sure.

"I think the incident occurred in North Africa. But he never talked about it. Luc's not one to blow his own horn."

Mazarelle was struck by the Fabrianis' good opinion of Luc Fournel. It wasn't something that he shared with them. Could he be wrong? Perhaps. He had no real basis for his feelings except some rumors and intuition.

But as the Fabrianis continued to talk about Luc's great qualities, their enthusiasm had the curious effect of souring Mazarelle's opinion of the former legionnaire even more. He was tempted to turn their image of Fournel around like a trompe l'oeil painting. To see their former hero in a different light. And instead of confirming what he'd heard from Fournel himself—the seemingly rock-solid alibi he had as a patient in the hospital on the night of the murder—Mazarelle was now inclined to consider another scenario.

Sitting here in the Fabrianis' elegant apartment, he suddenly remembered one of his favorite martial arts films—the great Wong Kar-wai's *Ashes of Time*. The Chinese wuxia classic dealt with the theme of murder for hire. A surrogate. Mazarelle sipped his brandy and considered this new prospect. It would certainly offer a different view of his case.

Getting up, he apologized for having to leave a little early. He had an appointment the next morning that he couldn't afford to miss. *"Le boulot,"* he said to Fabriani, throwing up his hands helplessly. "You know?"

Mazarelle thanked Juliette for her wonderful dinner. The time had flown by.

She had one small question to ask him. Glass in hand, she pulled him aside into what must have been Fabriani's home office.

"Listen, Paul, I know my husband wouldn't want me to mention this, but I'm a little worried."

Mazarelle took in the ornate moldings and medallions . . . the vast dimensions of the room. "Not enough square footage?" he asked.

She waved the joke aside. "Ever since he's become more visible, he's been getting letters. Hate mail. They're really terrible."

She walked around behind the mahogany and rosewood desk, with its intricate detailing, its ormolu mounts, and its engraved leather top, and picked up a stack of papers.

"Look, Juliette. That goes with the territory. Once your name is known, people think they can write anything to you."

"No, but it's more than that." She sighed. "Will you do me a favor? Take a look. If I'm wrong, tell me. I need to know."

Mazarelle was proud the encouraging smile never left his face. He knew there was no way out of this one.

"Well. It's the least I can do for such a lovely evening." Mazarelle reached out his hand and, folding up the stack of letters, tucked them away in his jacket pocket.

On her way out she asked, "Tell me. How's the beautiful Michou? Does she enjoy being back in Paris?"

His wife's cat had loved curling up in his overstuffed armchair. She had clawed and chewed enough of it to make her feel right at home. But not enough to make her stay. One day he'd returned from 36 and she was gone. Despite being warned, his cleaning lady had left the apartment door open after throwing out the garbage. They had posted reward signs with his telephone number, but so far no one had called.

It only took Mazarelle a moment to decide. "I haven't heard any complaints."

Juliette sipped the end of her wine. She'd never forgotten how Martine used to dote on that sleek gray cat of hers.

Fabriani came in and took their guest under his arm. Talking nonstop, he led him out of the long hall covered with photos of their family and friends, the Fabrianis' nearest and dearest. Mazarelle nodded, impressed by how many important political figures he recognized among them. And how many had been there that night. At the front door, his host asked, "And what about Luc's partner?" It was as if the murder of Alain Berthaud had just occurred to him. "Any progress with that Gypsy?"

"Some. I wish there was more. We're working around the clock as it is."

"Is it true what I hear"—his old boss cut to the chase—"that you've been hanging around with the press, Mazarelle? What's that all about?"

Startled, Mazarelle wondered how the hell he knew about Claire. A stoolie, he supposed. Fabriani probably had an army of them working for him *au noir*.

His host locked eyes with him. "My advice to you, my friend, is take care of business. You've got your own case to look after. Not somebody else's. Be smart."

Mazarelle was tempted to ask him what the hell that meant. But why bother? Rather than wait for the elevator and risk more of Fabriani's bullshit, Mazarelle decided on the stairs.

32

To Laure, Mazarelle filled the entrance to L'Agence AB with the odor of bad news. He wasn't expected. She glanced up at him through hooded eyes and said, "It's good to see you again, Commandant. Should I tell Luc you're here?"

"*S'il vous plaît, mademoiselle.*"

Luc Fournel had been told who was waiting for him and thought he knew why. Fournel appeared perfectly calm, poised, even elegant, with one hand in the jacket pocket of his bespoke glen plaid suit, a lighted cigarette hanging negligently in the other. He reminded Mazarelle of a self-portrait by the German artist Max Beckmann. Painted in a tuxedo and black tie as the well-heeled roué. Though Luc had to leave shortly, he said he was glad to see Mazarelle.

"In that case," Mazarelle said, "you can help me on one point. Did your agency ever do any work for the magazine *Paris-Flash*?"

Fournel thought that was possible. But it was the sort of work that Alain would have done, and the magazine's deputy editor, Philippe Riche, would have commissioned. The sort that made the agency profitable.

"A long way from the old precinct." Mazarelle nodded.

"I don't miss it." Luc's laugh reminded the commandant of an automatic weapon going off. "Especially the mingy money."

"Fabriani, on the other hand, misses you in his unit." Mazarelle described the dinner party that he was invited to the night before by their old boss. "He certainly spoke highly of you."

"That was nice of him."

"He called you a hero."

"Full of compliments, wasn't he? He never invited *me* for dinner."

"He said you even got a medal. Saved someone's life," he said, "while in the Foreign Legion."

"Oh that! Ancient history. What a memory! That was years ago, during basic training."

Mazarelle took out his pipe and began filling it with Philosophe. He lighted up. "What happened?" he asked.

"Who remembers? We were kids then. Short pants." Fournel, ambling down memory lane for the moment, was simply pleased to be asked about the past, pleased to have a sympathetic ear. He supposed that it must have happened on their long hike. The trek that all the new recruits had to take before graduation. "We called it the ballbuster."

Mazarelle asked, "How long?"

Searching through his past for a number, Fournel shrugged. "*Very* long. Endless . . . and soon we were all feeling like dead men walking. All of us traveling full kit. Toting weight over distance on the marshy trail because it had been raining nonstop all along the Bouches-du-Rhône. And the guy next to me—almost as large as you are, Mazarelle—slips down the muddy riverbank, and falls into the fast-moving ice-cold water. His backpack caught by a fallen tree limb, he was pinned beneath it."

Fournel recounted diving into the muddy glacial water, catching hold of the drowning legionnaire, and very nearly drowning himself. Freeing the guy's backpack, Fournel dragged him to shore.

"No wonder you got a medal." Mazarelle was impressed. The

smoke streamed out of his lighted pipe as if from a rising rocket. "Was he a friend of yours?"

"Never saw him before in my life."

"You didn't even know his name?"

"*Copain.* That's all I needed. 'Hang on, *copain!*'"

Mazarelle rolled his eyes in disbelief. Did Fournel take him for a fool?

"You're joking? You mean you risked your life for a stranger?"

"We were comrades, Mazarelle. You know what the corps' motto is? *Legio Patria Nostra.*"

"Meaning?"

"Forgotten your Latin, Mazarelle?" he mocked. "That's one for the confession box the next time you're in church."

"Don't hold your breath."

33

The call from an unfamiliar number came into the office at the Brigade Criminelle the next morning. Transferred by the Préfecture Centrale. Jeannot had picked up the ringing phone, and listening, his eyes widened.

"Ah, *chef* . . ." Jeannot hesitated.

"Spit it out."

"Ah, well, I have some bad news."

The missing Mercedes-Benz—the crime scene itself—had surfaced. Someone had spotted it on the rue Heurtault in Aubervilliers, a commune outside Paris. A baker, driving by on the Périphérique, on his way to make the dinner tarts.

The only problem—the car was on fire.

According to the baker, he had seen the black C-300 starting to smoke, the first flames licking at the edges.

Mazarelle grabbed the phone from Jeannot.

"What's the condition of the car?" he shouted into the receiver.

"*Sais pas,*" the baker replied. "How should I know the condition of the car?"

Mazarelle growled. "The usual way? You've got eyes?"

"I'm trying to help you out, buddy. All I know is, that fire was just getting going when I drove by. If you put any dough in there, it wouldn't last long."

Mazarelle slammed down the phone and turned to Jeannot.

"Let's go. We've got to see that Mercedes."

With the sirens blaring, they made it in minutes.

Slamming their doors shut, Mazarelle and Jeannot hurried over to the car. Flames were shooting skyward as they tried to peer in the windows. The glass was already darkened by the smoke and soot.

Taking off his jacket, Mazarelle smashed it down, trying to beat back the flames.

Sparks flew.

He slammed the coat against the car again and again. Ignoring the temperature, he kept going, his arm windmilling against the blaze. The heat was brutal.

On the other side, Jeannot was doing the same, faster if anything.

But the fire kept growing. Minutes went by. Finally, overcome by the heat, they stepped back to rest.

The explosion was eardrum shattering. Pieces of the car went rocketing skyward. Like a volcano throwing up lava, shooting balls of fire flew off in all directions. Not quite sure how it happened, Mazarelle and Jeannot found themselves flat on their backs. They did their best to curl up and avoid the flying debris. A fender came hurtling over and slammed off Jeannot's hip.

Mazarelle wrapped his burly forearms around the dazed young man and dragged him away from the flames.

In the distance, they could hear the sirens of the *pompiers*. Arriving too late.

Mazarelle wanted to keep looking. Maybe some small clue, something useful, could have survived in the rubble.

Seated, rubbing his hip, Jeannot gave a sad smile.

"Honestly, boss. It's fried like bacon. Whatever evidence there was is long gone."

34

t was barely dawn when the pounding started. Whomp. Whomp. Whomp. The wooden slats sliding back and forth. The cord bending around the pulley.

On the first floor of a stylish small home in the heart of Paris, in the center of a gleaming wood parquet floor, a figure was up on a NordicTrack machine, his legs grinding, his breath ragged.

Even this early in the morning, sweating hard, Armand Lavoisier was impeccable—his distinguished salt-and-pepper coiffure, his buffed nails, the rich maroon velour of his YSL tracksuit. For a man in his sixties, the Canal+ executive was well tended. He had to be to keep up with his wife.

Two and a half decades separated them, the studio executive and the young editor. They had recently been called the power couple of the French media. It was no secret that he had bankrolled her magazine.

Showered and changed into an immaculate linen suit, with a burgundy breast pocket square, he strolled into the dining room to give his wife a kiss. He wondered where she was going and why she looked so radiant. He wondered where breakfast was.

Even at this early hour, Claire Girard too was impeccable. The sun streaming in through the dining room windows lent her a halo that limned her long black curls. Her glowing tan was heightened by her cream-colored jacket, her black T-shirt, a gold necklace that sparkled in the morning light.

Claire was at the dining room table, gathering up copies of *Paris-Flash*, when their housekeeper, Emily, came hurrying in the door. She had been to the *boulangerie* on the rue Coquillière. The croissants and brioches were still warm from the oven, and they smelled heavenly. Emily bustled about pouring their coffee.

As soon as Claire saw her husband come in, she waved a dummy copy of her magazine's upcoming issue at him and tossed it over. The cover lines in red caps read:

THE WINNER: LANCE ARMSTRONG
THE CHARGE: DOPING
THE LOSER: TOUR DE FRANCE

Mopping a few drops of sweat off his forehead, Armand congratulated her. They'd sell tons of copies. "Wasn't your writer the one who called Armstrong 'a cancer on cycling'?" he asked. "That's gotten a lot of play."

"Yes." Claire smiled. "No one else got inside his U.S. Postal team the way we did." As a result, all the last day she'd been hassled by their lawyer threatening to sue the magazine.

"That's the price you pay. Here I am trying to make this scandal sheet into something we can be proud of. A journal with real investigative pieces."

Armand nodded sympathetically.

"It's not easy. Especially when we keep getting ignored. Remember that piece we did last year. The detention centers—all those refugees behind bars—a tragedy waiting to happen. But no one was interested."

"It didn't change much, did it?"

"No, it didn't. But this summer, there are protests planned all over France. Left wing, right wing. They all want to shut those centers down."

"Really?"

Claire wagged her finger at him.

"You'll see."

He tilted his head to the side inquiringly.

"You remember the American politician I mentioned, Frank Nash? I'm picking him up at the Lutetia in an hour. We're driving up to the Sangatte camp near Calais. They've been having all sorts of trouble there."

"You really think they'll let you in after that last article?"

"The American Embassy arranged it all. I'm along for the ride. A quick overnight."

"You have a plan?"

Claire's smile broadened.

"Just wait."

Armand spread out his hands in surrender to her charm. "You're even more delightful when you're mysterious."

On the whole, he wasn't inclined to be jealous. And since there was such a difference in their ages, he wanted to make sure that she had all the freedom she needed. Armand understood that a woman her age married to an older man might need more than her husband provided. However, what Armand knew, and Claire soon discovered, was that if there was any lopsidedness in their relationship it had long been on his side of the marriage bed, not hers. Often away on business, Armand had a fondness for other women that seemed almost insatiable. Still, on that morning, as Claire drove off to meet the charming young Nash in her gleaming black Porsche 911 Carrera with the top down and a dazzling red scarf over her head, he felt something new—a twinge of vulnerability perhaps. Was he getting old?

Inside his study, Armand closed the door and, picking up his mobile, began to tap.

35

Mazarelle hadn't needed an alarm clock to wake up since he was a schoolkid. But the morning after the fire, he could have used one. It had been a terrible night. He thought he had gotten off unscathed, but when his feet hit the floor, he felt like the foul rag-and-bone shop of the universe. Limping over to the bathroom, he dragged himself under the shower—not so much to clean up as to wake up. The hot water unlocking his muscles. The mustache in his bathroom mirror one or two gray hairs older. Later, in the half-empty refrigerator, he found breakfast—a box of succulent black Turkish apricots and, on the stove, a double shot of jet-black espresso. A curtain-raiser for his day.

He didn't get into the office until after 10 a.m.

Jeannot was very glad to see him. "Where've you been, boss? I've been trying to reach you everywhere."

"Here I am," Mazarelle said, presenting himself palms up and totally available. "What's going on? Not another discovery?" Mazarelle didn't smile, but Jeannot had come to appreciate his chief's little jokes.

"Maybe. But this time I think we may have a live one."

"Sounds good. Let's hear it."

"Didn't you say that Guy Danglars told you he left the Café Arielle with the murder victim when it closed? And that he was home in bed about two?"

"That was it, more or less. Luc Fournel left earlier. And after all the partying, Guy was pretty much wiped out himself. Why do you ask?"

"Look here." Jeannot called the boss over to his desk and pointed at the computer screen where he'd been working. He'd been examining the digitized police *fichier* for traffic violations across the different arrondissements in Paris. Cited in the Twelfth on the early morning of July 20, 2002, was a fender bender in front of the Gare de Lyon. The driver of the car was Guy Danglars. "If that's *our* Guy Danglars," Jeannot said, "he wasn't home at all. He was stopped, questioned, and nearly arrested that morning at four thirteen a.m. for '*conduite sous l'influence de l'alcool*.'"

"Good catch!" said Mazarelle. Turning to Maurice, who'd been standing at his side, he said, "See if you can track down the owner of the car that Danglars damaged. And find out who else saw the accident that morning—anything that might be helpful."

In what seemed no time, Maurice was back with the names of two eyewitnesses, and he'd already arranged for them to talk with the commandant.

The first witness was Jean-Pierre Bonnaire. Mazarelle thanked him for coming in so promptly. Bonnaire had been waiting for his train at the Gare de Lyon that night after spending the holiday in Paris, but there had been a delay due to equipment failure.

"I was standing out front, smoking a cigarette, watching the police rounding up these homeless guys. Must've been from one of those immigrant camps they shut down. Anyway, that's when the yellow Renault came along. A supermini. It pulled into the space between the two cars parked at the curb, and a tall guy with his hood up leaped out. Yelling something to the driver and racing through the rain into the station. I caught a glimpse of him as he hurried by—a tanned, leathery-skinned skyscraper *mec* with fierce black eyes. Well—you don't see one of those every day. So I wondered who he was and why in such a hurry.

"When I looked inside the terminal, he was standing in front of the information board of arrivals and departures. Then I saw these three dark teenage kids come up behind him. Gyppos scrounging for money. I'll never forget the look on his face. Pure contempt. I wondered if maybe he knew them. Or if not, was there something about them that he recognized and loathed?

"Then I heard him shouting at them. I couldn't tell what the hell it was, but it was loud and it wasn't French. Whatever it was they were scared. I mean, you know, *really,* shitting-in-your-pants scared. Slowly they began backing away from him, and then all at once the three of them bolted toward the door."

"How about the accident?" Mazarelle asked.

"It was when I turned that I saw the collision. The one I told the cops about. The little yellow supermini that the hoodie had just gotten out of was being bumped into by this big classy car behind him as he tried to park. Two! Three times! Either the guy behind had lost control or didn't care. I think the driver of the mini must have eventually gotten pissed at having his sporty little car turned into a piñata. Suddenly he shoved his clutch into reverse, floored the gas, and went roaring back into the Renault Laguna Estate behind him. It made quite a thunderclap."

The second witness, Etienne Regnard, was an older man—the driver of the Laguna Estate.

The commandant thanked him for taking his valuable time. Could he provide them with information about the incident that involved his vehicle, a Renault Laguna, and a yellow Renault Clio hatchback, an incident that occurred early on the morning of July 20 in front of the Gare de Lyon?

"Certainly. I'll try my best," said Monsieur Regnard. "My wife and I had pulled up in front of the station. We had dropped off her brother who was planning to catch a four fifty a.m. train home. We were about to leave when this little canary-colored sports car cut in front of our Laguna Estate, blocking our way. Without warning, he slammed back into us. It seemed as if he'd wanted to pull out and by mistake put his car in reverse."

Mazarelle asked if there had been much damage to his vehicle.

"*Alors*—it sounded pretty serious. So I got out to see what had happened. My wife did too. Fortunately it wasn't as bad as we thought. Only my side mirror had been seriously damaged—cracked and broken off. I was thinking that guy was going to have seven years of bad luck. That was his first mistake. But then he got out and began complaining to me. That was his second. His third was the way he smelled. It was as if he'd spent the last twenty-four hours marinated in whiskey. No sooner did my wife notice the alcohol on his breath, than she began to scream, '*Vous êtes bourré alors?*'"

"Yes," said Mazarelle. "And what happened then?"

"You wouldn't believe—the drunken fool jumped up and down and shouted back, '*Taisez-vous, salope!*' By then a small crowd had gathered. I grabbed my wife, pulled her into our car before things got violent. It was then I saw him dive into his car and start to drive away, but someone had called the police. Luckily there were cops nearby who arrived just in time and stopped him."

"Anything else?" asked Mazarelle.

"Well—after the police had examined his identification, they came over to us and said, 'He's an off-duty cop. Don't worry. We'll take good care of him.'"

When the two witnesses had left, Mazarelle shook his head. That was what he liked about Parisians. They didn't always see things the same way, but they almost always had a story to tell you. The inconsistencies between their accounts were pretty normal for eyewitnesses. But it didn't really matter to him. What did was that early on the morning of July 20—at a time when Guy Danglars was supposedly at home sound asleep—he was involved in a minor auto accident in front of the Gare de Lyon. Then there was the curious passenger who got out of Guy's car. Who was he—that tall hooded character with striking dark eyes and a remarkable temper? The one who seemed able to put the fear of Jesus into three hustling teenage *Gitanes*. No wonder the street-smart Jean-Pierre Bonnaire thought it was probably just as well you didn't slam into one of those strange types every day.

36

Returning to his old commissariat in the Fourth Arrondissement, Mazarelle was eager to question Guy Danglars about the accident report. He found the disheveled detective heading out the door on a burglary call. Mazarelle slammed it shut before he could go.

"What the hell were you doing at four thirteen in the morning in front of the Gare de Lyon when you were supposed to be tucked in bed with an ice bag on your head?"

Flustered, Guy said he couldn't sleep. He said he went out despite the changeable weather and met someone he knew from the neighborhood who needed a ride to the station. So he did him a favor. Ran him over to the Gare de Lyon. Got stuck in traffic behind some roundup of refugees, shuffling along with their tattered duffels on their shoulders. Who knew where they were going? When asked the name of his friend, Guy became unusually worked up, jittery. "No, no, no, no! You've got the wrong idea. He wasn't a friend."

"I thought that's what you said. You met someone you knew in the middle of the night and gave him a ride to the station."

"Just a passing acquaintance," Guy insisted. "You know what I mean? A favor. It was raining, for Chrissakes!"

Mazarelle knew. Guy was full of shit. With a phony alibi. But he wasn't going to get much more from him today. Mazarelle told Danglars the next time he saw his pal, get a phone number for him.

Back in his office, Mazarelle decided to have Guy's supermini impounded and gone over from stem to stern by the Police Scientifique. And this one wasn't going to get lost. If there really had been a mystery pal inside that mini of his, Mazarelle told his men, they needed to see if he left behind any traceable fingerprints in the car. Things might be escalating, but with a fellow cop they could get dicey. They had to play this carefully.

Guy sensed that his flimsy story had sprung a serious leak. In fact, after thinking it over, he realized that he didn't care for Mazarelle's reaction at all. He knew he'd have to touch base with Luc and soon. Get some advice.

"I think we've got a little trouble," Guy said when he reached Luc at the agency. "I need to talk to you, but not on the phone."

"Exactly," Luc agreed. Especially now, he thought, when the *boeuf-carottes* were all over and they couldn't be certain what landlines were being hacked. Luc knew that Guy didn't just fall off the turnip cart. Knew, more or less, he could be trusted.

37

They arranged to meet in the agency office late that afternoon after Laure left to do her shopping. That way, the two of them would be alone.

When Guy told Luc what had happened at the Gare de Lyon, Luc blew a fuse.

"Tell me," Luc confronted his friend, "because I can't figure you out. How could you be such a schmuck? All you had left to do was go home, climb into bed, and pull the covers over your head. Were you still drunk?"

"Don't be silly. You saw what I drank. I just had a few . . ."

Luc stared at him, then shook his head as if he couldn't bring himself to say the obvious. "And after the cop car showed and stopped you for questioning, why didn't you immediately call me at home? Or here? Or on my mobile? You might at least have left a message, for crying out loud! Why did you wait so long? It was an emergency, goddamn it!"

Guy shrugged uncomfortably and said, "Get off my back." Sucking the air into his lungs as if it might be his last breath, he gasped, "Give me a break, will ya? Stuff happens—"

"Okay, okay." Luc tried to calm him down. But why was he such a slob? Why couldn't he pay more attention to detail? Guy seemed to be unraveling right before his eyes.

"Listen," Luc said. "I hate to tell you this, old buddy, but I kid you not. You look lousy. Like you're falling apart. Why don't you try to get yourself back in shape? Maybe start exercising again."

"Yeah—you're right. I need something."

The two were quiet for a few seconds.

"Tell me—" Luc blurted. "Did Mazarelle have anything else to say? Anything about Max?"

"Not really. He asks a lot of questions, but he doesn't let on much, does he?"

"That's a virtue others might consider practicing."

"Don't worry," said Guy. "He's dogged, but he's not a genius. Plus there's nothing for him to find. Nothing connecting us."

Luc wasn't so sure. In fact, he wasn't sure at all. There were unanswered questions. And once on the trail, Mazarelle was a bloodhound. Luc remembered how relentless he was in the old days when they were together in the Fourth. He'd cracked some of their toughest cases. Maybe he wasn't breathing down their necks yet, but how many mistakes like this one could they afford? Right now the real problem they faced was becoming increasingly apparent to Luc.

He looked at his chain-smoking pal slouching in the office chair. His belly over his belt, his shirt hanging almost out of his pants. A fuckin' slob. He didn't like to think so, but it was Guy himself who was the problem. No question he was a weak link, but was he the kind who would all of a sudden crack under pressure, or the less high-strung variety who under Mazarelle's nonstop blowtorch questioning might eventually be reduced to Jell-O? Maybe Luc would have to stop kidding himself. Maybe it didn't make a goddamn bit of difference. Either way, Guy was trouble.

Fidgeting in his chair, Guy shook out another cigarette, lit it up, and took a long drag. With a cig in his mouth, he felt smarter, cooler, and didn't have to say a word to Luc. On the other hand, Luc never seemed to have trouble keeping his own mouth shut.

Both were quiet for a few moments. "Why is it, Luc," Guy suddenly broke out, "that you always think you're in charge of everything?"

Luc shook his head and smiled in pain as if faced with an impossible task. "I've got a lot on my mind, old buddy. Like people who create messes that I've got to clean up."

Guy thought he knew what Luc had in mind. It sounded very much as if he was being dumped. "You're not about to give me the shaft, are you, Luc?"

Luc laughed. "Don't be a jerk. Of course not."

"Especially since there's one thing you can count on. If I go down, you're going down too!"

PART FOUR

38

On a beautiful summer morning like this he was glad to be out of doors getting his rays. Taking Luc's advice, Guy was trying to get back in shape. Clear his mind of the cobwebs. Less alcohol and more fresh air. As promised, he'd gone back to his old routine of jogging at sunrise in the Parc des Buttes-Chaumont. Before it became a park in the mid-nineteenth century, it had been a *chauve mont* on the outskirts of the city—a sinister bald hill where nothing grew except huge mounds of horse carcasses and dead human flesh. The city hung its murderers there and left them to rot.

What was once a foul garbage dump was now an attractive park—one of the five largest in Paris. With its exotic trees, rich bird life, sunny lush lawns, dense grottos, cliffs, belvederes, and lake, all in the romantic English style, the Buttes-Chaumont was currently considered by many to be the most picturesque of the city's parks. There were more than three miles of paths that wound through its heavily wooded areas. Ideal for jogging or walking your puppy. Best of all, the park was never crowded this early. He was the only runner out here this morning.

Perhaps that was why Guy paid little attention to the two approaching figures in the distance—a tall fellow out walking his dog. Nothing unusual about that as long as the animal was safely leashed, as required by all the park signs, and wasn't going to get in his way.

In fact, distracted by the dog, Guy barely noticed the man's face. Shielding his identity were oversize dark sunglasses and a large floppy straw hat with its wide brim tilted down to keep the glare out of his eyes and provide sun protection. No, Guy barely noticed him. His eyes were fixed on the oncoming German shepherd, a large handsome athletic brute of an animal with its alert chiseled face and pointed ears locked on the approaching jogger. Guy kept running toward them as the man and his dog drew closer and closer. If it were a French Beauceron, the detective might have been more confident he'd recognize a fellow cop. He tried to give the dog a wide berth as he went by.

As the German shepherd passed Guy, the tall man in the straw hat let the leash play out. It made a high-pitched whistling sound like a high-end reel on an expensive fishing rod. Then, abruptly, the tall man locked the leash in place. It was at this point that he did something extraordinary. As he walked past Guy, the tall fellow looped the leash over and around the jogger's neck in one smooth move, dragging him backward. He then gave the leash a vicious yank. Before Guy—unable to breathe—could flee in some futile, wild, desperate attempt to elude death, as if that were even remotely possible, he fell crashing to the ground, his windpipe crushed. Rushing over to the fallen body, his attacker placed two fingers on Guy's carotid, feeling for a pulse. Nothing. There was nothing. Not the slightest blip. Satisfied with his results, he unwound the leash from around his victim's neck, snapped it up to its normal length, and glanced across at his patiently waiting dog. His master patted him on the head.

"Come, Teufel," he called. *"En route!"*

The old Jeep was hurtling south. He was glad to be going home, pleased with the way his work had turned out. These days everything he did felt more and more gratifying. He couldn't recall ever having had such a strong sense of satisfaction before. Not even years ago when he was a young guard in the town of Milesia in Ceaușescu's Romania. He'd worked there in a political prison for women run by the notorious Commander Vasilescu, the head warden known as "Ivan the Terrible." Though there were other tyros also working under the commander, Vasilescu seemed to single him out—calling him "Young Ivan." He was seen as a rising star of the secret police. As for his real name, it was so long since he'd used it he only rarely thought of it. Dako Lupei—Dako the wolf.

He glanced across at his black-and-tan dog. "Did I ever tell you about that?"

The dog's eyes popped open. On the passenger seat, Teufel stared at him—his eyes big and black as umbrellas. He looked as if he'd be glad to hear all about it. Eager to learn whatever it was. Anything. Tell me, the dog seemed to be saying. And motionless waited for his master's voice.

He began with her name. It was Valentin, Valentin Nicolescu. He remembered that she was fifteen when she was arrested—not much younger at the time than he was. But he didn't remember the charge. It had to be political or she wouldn't have been there. Some anti-government demonstration. She was very pretty, though that didn't last more than a few months. Nor did her teeth. What did was how tough she was. No matter how she was treated, she remained unbreakable. Her will, but not the other parts—the fingers, the arms. That was why she was sent to him.

To his face, she called him the Beast. According to his spies, she called him a lot worse. He had to laugh. He enjoyed sending inmates to what they named the "black hole," a damp windowless concrete tomb in the basement used for beatings and psychological torture. "For you," she told him, "we're all just animals." She was right—he did think they were animals. It was probably the last thing he could recall her saying.

What he never forgot was the uniform he wore. He'd always had a special fondness for uniforms, and what they represented. Back there in Romania, and even when he had fled to France. It was why he had joined the Legion. A brotherhood. A bond. A spirit that glued men together. He took one hand off the wheel and stroked Teufel's head, his back. His boss had had a dog too. He loved having one of his own.

39

Coudert couldn't get over the death of Guy Danglars. Though not one of his own men, Danglars was an officer in the Fourth—one of Fabriani's people. Coudert was fuming. Absolutely irate about the killing of a cop. And this was no ordinary murder. An innocent jogger running in the park to keep himself physically fit, one step ahead of the bad guys, and then . . . *zap*! It was goddamn scary! He'd already sent a team out to the crime scene in the Parc des Buttes-Chaumont.

Nicolas, the *patron's* assistant, knocked on his office door and walked in without waiting. He was tired of waiting. It was clear he didn't know what to do. The commandant was giving him a hard time.

"Sir, I just had a *third* call from Commandant Mazarelle. He wants to know about the Danglars murder case. Should he and his men get over to the Buttes-Chaumont? What do I tell him, sir? He's waiting for your answer."

"*No, goddamn it!*" Coudert shouted. "Tell him no. How many times do I have to say the same thing? Tell him to stop calling and to investigate his own damn case. His job is to wrap up the evidence on Babo. The hanged man trial is coming. Guy Danglars's murder has nothing to do with Alain Berthaud. This was a cop killing, dammit! Tell him that Alice Duhamel and her team are already on the scene. The case is theirs. Is that clear?"

Upstairs in his office, Mazarelle waited for news. Despite the absence of any tarot card (at least so far), Mazarelle knew with an eerie certainty that these killings were linked. He felt it in his bones. Wasn't

Guy one of the last people to have seen Alain Berthaud alive? Weren't he and Alain and Luc Fournel all there together, drinking and carrying on in the Café Arielle? And now two of those three men were dead. Mazarelle couldn't understand why Coudert had assigned the case to Duhamel. It was ridiculous! Outrageous! She wasn't even tuned in to developments in the hanged man investigation. Was Mazarelle the only one who'd noticed what had been happening to people all around Luc? Oh yeah, okay, maybe they weren't dropping like flies, but enough were sure as hell getting murdered. It should have been his case. Why didn't Coudert trust him?

40

The pale glow of the computer monitor illuminated Maurice's tired face. His gaze wandered to the small clock in the corner of the screen. 9:26 p.m. Maurice let out a sigh, leaning back in his chair and rubbing his weary eyes. His wife would have his hide. It was his turn to read the bedtime story. Tintin. *L'Étoile Mystérieuse*. He had promised. But he had been in the weeds and time had slipped, as it so often did. It had still been light out when Mazarelle first sauntered over to his desk, the commandant's eyes sparkling with a fresh burst of post-lunch energy.

"Maurice, I've been thinking," exclaimed Mazarelle. "Have we gone back through Berthaud's financials? We know the man loved money. Maybe it got him into trouble. Go at it again. See what you can dig up. You always find something."

And with that Maurice was plunged into the depths of spreadsheets. Accounts and routing numbers. Tabulating and cross-referencing. The world was chaos, but at least it seemed manageable when laid out in a table. You could find patterns. That's what Maurice was really looking for. Patterns. Berthaud could no longer speak for himself, but his habits could.

At least that was Maurice's hypothesis; the reality of the situation was turning out to be much more convoluted. Sure, Alain liked money, but he liked to spend it much more—and indiscriminately, it seemed. Every night a different restaurant, all Michelin starred no doubt, because each bill was large enough to raise both eyebrows. Luxury spa days here, designer shirts and triple-digit bar bills there. The records read more like that of an heiress than a private investigator.

Maurice scrolled farther down the spreadsheet to the next line item. Something purchased for thirty-two euros. He paused and scanned across to the business. Armurerie Austerlitz. Maurice smiled.

Early the next morning, he was already waiting, two coffees in hand, when Mazarelle arrived at the office. He passed one over to the chief, who gladly accepted. As Mazarelle took a sip, Maurice reported his find.

"Berthaud's financials were a lot of nothing, except this." He pointed to the spreadsheet on his screen. "You see what I highlighted?"

Mazarelle nodded, scratching his chin. "So our man bought something at a gun store . . . Strange."

"In his line of work I'll bet he had no shortage of enemies. Maybe he was scared for his life?" suggested Maurice.

"True, but why now? Alain worked as an investigator for decades. And this amount of money . . . Thirty-two euros? The only gun you can buy with that is a water pistol." Mazarelle shook his head, trying to put together the pieces.

"There's something else." Maurice broke the silence. "Berthaud didn't have a license for a firearm. He never got one."

Mazarelle's gaze shifted from the spreadsheet to Maurice, his eyes lighting up with excitement. "So what you're saying is, whatever he was doing here, it was on the q.t."

Maurice nodded. "That's the idea."

Mazarelle affectionately smacked Maurice on the back, sending shock waves reverberating through his bones. "Excellent sleuthing, Maurice. Let's go get some answers."

The sun was just beginning to shine over the tops of the buildings in the Twentieth Arrondissement when the two of them arrived at the Armurerie Austerlitz. The local shopkeepers were still trickling into their shops. The metal gate stood resolutely covering the gun shop's front entrance, but that didn't deter Mazarelle. He pounded against the metal barrier with his huge mitts, the clang echoing through the urban canyon. Maurice scanned the area uneasily. He never saw the point in causing a scene, even when it was on official business. Better to keep your head down and focus on the work. As if by consensus, the neighboring merchants had suddenly decided the sidewalk outside their shops needed tidying. They pretended to sweep as they stole suspicious sidelong glances at the African and his companion outside the *armurerie*.

Mazarelle caught the looks. "Don't worry." He smiled at Maurice. "They've probably never seen anyone so handsome before." He turned back to the store.

"Allllô!" boomed Mazarelle, shaking the barrier with both hands. Maurice finally joined in, pushing an open palm against the gate.

Then, a stir of movement. Or at least there seemed to be. It was still dark inside the store, but the feeling of being watched from within the inky blackness chilled Mazarelle like a winter gust. He smacked the gate once more, and hard.

The shop door behind the grate flew open, revealing a long and lean man with graying hair, his body all sinew and bone.

"Can't you idiots take a hint? We're closed. Closed. Fuck off!"

Maurice stepped back. Confrontation was not his strong suit. Mazarelle, on the other hand, lived for moments like this. He calmly reached into his pocket to retrieve the small leather wallet where his ID was housed.

"You know, my friend, I sincerely wish we could fuck off." Mazarelle's tone was cordial. "After all, the farmer's market is open. But as you can see, we are here on official business."

The shopkeeper's face softened, taking on a shade of embarrassment.

"Why didn't you say you were police?" he mumbled as he hastily unlocked and lifted the metal fence.

"Just trying to be discreet," said Mazarelle, throwing Maurice a wink.

The skinny shopkeeper gestured for the pair to follow him into the store. Inside, under the posters of bin Laden in the crosshairs, the space was crowded with all manner of weaponry. Crossbows, knives, truncheons, ropes, and of course guns. Lots of guns. New ones, antiques. Personal defense, hunting. The sheer amount of stopping power on display boggled Maurice's mind. The shopkeeper settled down on the stool behind the counter.

"So what can I do for you two? I take it you're not here to purchase."

Mazarelle grinned. "Not unless you're selling information."

The shopkeeper's face twisted in confusion. He shook his head.

"Listen, I already told you guys everything I know."

Now it was the commandant's turn to be confused.

"What does that mean?"

"I don't know—I thought you all worked together."

Staring at the shopkeeper, Mazarelle waited for an explanation that made sense.

"Some cop was here a few days ago, looking through the security footage."

Mazarelle turned to Maurice, who shook his head. Other cops? As far as Mazarelle knew, his unit was the only one pursuing this case. Maybe something federal? Or was someone inside the BC trying to mess with him again? He turned back to the shopkeeper.

"Do you remember the name?"

The shopkeeper's blank expression told him. He'd have more luck if he'd asked for the names of the prime ministers of France's Fourth Republic. The only answers he was going to get were on the security tape.

"I'm going to need to see that footage."

The shopkeeper nodded.

"One more thing." Maurice pulled out his printout of the spreadsheet, and pointed to the highlighted item. This was his turf now.

"Can you tell us what this purchase was?"

"Sure, huh . . . That's funny . . ."

The shopkeeper paused.

"What?" urged Mazarelle.

"No, it's just, this purchase happened on July ninth . . . Same day your buddy was asking about."

Energy coursed through Mazarelle's veins like liquid fire. This was not a coincidence. Coincidences didn't exist. He recognized the distant scent of truth and locked on to it, like a great white sensing blood in the water a mile off.

But Maurice was even faster. "The purchase records, if you don't mind."

The shopkeeper nodded, and began clicking around on the desktop computer by the register. He grunted a few times as he scoured the records, finally singling out the desired line item.

"Okay, for thirty-two euros? It says here a box of twenty-two caliber blanks."

The shopkeeper looked up to Mazarelle inquisitively. Maurice furiously scribbled the new details in his notepad. Mazarelle nodded, trying not to let his face betray his surprise. Blanks? What the hell was Berthaud doing with blanks? Especially if he didn't have a gun.

He was hoping for clarity from this visit, but instead he seemed to be going down a rabbit hole. Maybe Madame Mireille was right. The more he learned, the less he understood. Maurice brought Mazarelle back to earth.

"And the tape. Can we see that now?"

"Right, of course!"

The shopkeeper turned to the cabinet behind him, revealing a wall of labeled VHS tapes. He scanned the tapes, then stopped, squinting and shaking his head. He double-checked, thumbing through them again before letting out a low whistle.

"I don't know where it is, but it's not here."

"Well, it didn't just walk off, did it?" Mazarelle snapped back.

The shopkeeper shrugged. "I don't know what to tell you. Looks like it did."

The lead was so close that Mazarelle could almost feel it in his hand. And now he was being told that it didn't exist. No. That was not going to fly.

"Fine, then we're confiscating all the tapes. Official evidence in a murder."

"A murder?! What murder? You can't do that!"

Maurice could see the situation deteriorating as Mazarelle's temper began to flare. Usually the *chef* was immensely patient, but in the face of a perceived slight or injustice? His cool vanished faster than an ice cube in the Sahara.

"We most certainly can!"

"It's private property!"

The two men were face-to-face now.

Maurice stepped in, gently inserting himself between them. It wasn't always easy to keep Mazarelle focused, especially in moments like these.

"What about backups?" he interrupted. "Is that something you do?"

"Backups?!" the shopkeeper spat back reflexively. And then his sour expression suddenly changed.

"Backups . . ."

After getting past the initial embarrassment of the incident, the three men now sat shoulder to shoulder in front of a VCR and small TV in the back room of the *armurerie,* scrubbing through the footage in question. On-screen, the customers moved through the store in hyperspeed, picking things up, putting them down, walking in, and walking out. Overall, it seemed to be a fairly quiet day with only five or so interactions. Finally the tape arrived at the time stamp corresponding to the time of Berthaud's purchase. And sure enough, there he was, in grainy black-and-white. Alain Berthaud, still alive, buying a box of blank rifle rounds for a gun that he didn't own. The hanged man, back from the grave. There had to be more.

"Happy?" asked the shopkeeper.

"Can we rewind or fast-forward a bit? I want to see what else he was doing in the store."

The shopkeeper sighed and scrubbed backward. On-screen Berthaud moved in reverse, a sort of jerky moonwalk, as he browsed the *armurerie*'s wares. Nothing there. Then zooming forward, past the purchase at the counter, he was suddenly in another corner of the store, examining hunting apparel . . . with another man. This other man looked familiar too . . . but from where? The two seemed to be talking, but both men kept their gaze fixed down on the clothing. Then something seemed to pass from Berthaud's hand to the stranger's, and then into the stranger's pocket.

"Wait! Press play here."

The shopkeeper did as requested. Now playing at normal speed, the context of the situation crystallized for Mazarelle. A clandestine meeting of some sort. It was clear Berthaud had been waiting for the stranger, but what were they talking about? There was no audio. Both men wore grim, masklike expressions. Then the handoff. Something from Berthaud's pocket went to the stranger, but it was too grainy to make out.

"Do you have any other angles?"

The shopkeeper let out another sigh.

"You know this is a business, right? I need to open at some point . . ."

"The sooner you show us the footage, the sooner we're gone, *mon frère*," replied Mazarelle.

The shopkeeper grabbed a VHS sitting next to him and swapped it with the one in the VCR, fast-forwarding to the time code in question, and pressing play. From this angle Berthaud's face was in almost complete profile. Mazarelle shook his head. This was going to be pointless. But then the stranger entered frame and Mazarelle's jaw dropped. He looked over to Maurice, who had the same stunned expression.

"That's that guy . . ." stammered Maurice.

Mazarelle nodded.

"That's . . . what's his name?"

The commandant took a deep breath.

"Max."

The tape kept playing on-screen. From this angle you could see the exchange more clearly. Money. A wad of bills passed from Berthaud to Max. Maybe something else too. More muted discussion, and then Berthaud was gone from the camera.

Max stood still in frame, counting the bills that had been passed along. And then he turned to the aisle with the hunting rifles.

Mazarelle turned to face the shopkeeper. "You know who that is, right?"

The shopkeeper shrugged. "Yes, of course."

"The Chirac shooter. Here in your shop. What did he buy?"

The shopkeeper looked squeamish, a grown-up caught with his hand in a nasty cookie jar. Finally he said, "Ehh, a rifle, what else?"

Mazarelle stood and abruptly ejected the tape from the VCR, being sure to grab both VHSs. "We're keeping these," said Mazarelle as he passed the tapes to Maurice and strode out the door. His mind was spinning. He needed fresh air.

The narrative Mazarelle had been building—the timeline of Berthaud's last days—had just been blown apart. A veritable humpty-fucking-dumpty of a situation.

What did Alain Berthaud have to do with Max? It didn't make any sense. Max was a nut—a loony who tried to kill the president. Maybe Berthaud leaned pretty conservative when it came to his views on immigration. Maybe he had right-wing friends, but he was nothing like this neo-Nazi fruitcake.

Still, Alain had clearly funded the purchase of Max's rifle. They had the tapes to prove it. The question was why? And who was trying to make it all disappear?

41

The trip back to the station was long and silent. As Maurice drove, Mazarelle looked out the window at the passing trees—lindens, chestnuts, honey locusts flashing by. Maurice knew his boss's rhythms. Best to keep quiet and keep out of the way.

The new lead was a lot to absorb. At first it seemed overwhelming, but slowly, gradually, Mazarelle sensed that it was reinvigorating him. Until the visit to the *armurerie,* he'd been feeling as though he were wandering in a dark hallway, groping around for an exit. Now suddenly things looked different. He could see the start of a path. And some trapdoors as well.

He had been thinking this case was about the *ripoux.* Magazine payoffs. Rumored beatings. The warnings. From Luc to Guy to his mystery passenger, everything seemed to tie back to the dirty cops. But now this.

Twelve days before his death, Alain Berthaud had met Max at the gun shop. What was the link? Unfortunately neither one could tell him anymore. But maybe the evidence could.

Back at his office, Mazarelle's first call was to the Archives Nationales. A most urgent affair, he said. He needed access to any remaining evidence from the Chirac assassination attempt. Of course he didn't mention his own name. He used Coudert's.

The official on the other end of the line knew the answer without hesitating.

"No, not possible."

Everything was already classified. The case was closed. The suspect was dead.

Mazarelle hesitated. Then thought he'd try another approach.

"Even for Commissaire Fabriani's office?" he asked. There was silence on the other end of the phone as the man weighed his options. He could nip this in the bud himself, but he knew better than to annoy one of Fabriani's friends. He asked for a number where his caller could be reached, curtly informed him that he would see what he could do a little later, then abruptly hung up. But when later came, it was not the news Mazarelle was hoping for.

This time it was a *conservateur* on the phone. He hemmed and hawed, trying to let this assistant of Fabriani down softly. However the bottom line was that not even a chain saw was going to cut through all the layers of bureaucratic red tape required to gain access to the materials from the Chirac incident. It was "*tout simplement impossible.*"

As far as Mazarelle was concerned, the situation was ludicrous. They had in their possession evidence that could help solve a homicide, *his homicide,* and they were stonewalling him. Stonewalling justice. Why? Was something in the Chirac file top secret—too classified for his eyes to behold? It was such a ridiculous idea that Mazarelle laughed. If not for him France would be talking about Chirac in the past tense.

Now, as Mazarelle sat at his desk stewing over the file, he could not help feeling as if Berthaud himself were mocking him. This entire case was upside down. Starting with the hanging. The tarot card. A botched assassination attempt. And to top it off, an innocent man was sitting in jail.

The commandant hunted around in his desk, finally retrieving his meerschaum pipe and tobacco. He opened the bag of Philosophe and took a deep whiff of its smooth blend. A nice puff would help get the juices flowing. He could feel it. Taking a kumquat-sized pinch of tobacco, he stuffed it into his pipe and lighted it, inhaling deeply. The smoke flooded into the deepest nooks and crannies of his respiratory system, the murky tendrils poking and prodding around his innards, doing its own investigation. Mazarelle wondered what secrets lay within his body. On second thought, given his years of smoking, drinking, and eating well, he probably didn't want to know. He exhaled in a prolonged dragon's puff, the smoke hanging over his desk like a thick fog.

As he brooded, Mazarelle's gaze settled on the shell suspended in its

Lucite case sitting on the edge of his desk. Good to be reminded—he was the one who had foiled that assassination attempt! He was still at the top of his game. So what if he was in the mud right now? It wasn't as if he hadn't unstuck himself before. And right there was the proof. He put his pipe down and picked up the framed cartridge.

Spinning it around, side to side, he watched the light dance off the Lucite. He gave it a half twist.

Max the shooter. Alain the detective. Both at that store. Both dead now.

He gave it another twist. A new direction. The Lucite gleamed.

What was the connection?

He knew about Alain Berthaud's link to the Défense National group. And here was Max with Alain. It wasn't a huge leap to assume they all shared the same extremist views. Anti-immigration. Anti-Moslem. Anti-Semitic. Anti-everything. And pro-violence. It was disgusting. But it didn't make them all assassins.

As he examined the framed cartridge, his mind wandered back to the other question that had been bothering him. Why had Alain decided to meet Max in the gun store to begin with? He could have given him the money anywhere else. Somewhere more private. Unless there was something he needed there. But all he himself had purchased was . . .

Unless . . . Mazarelle shook his head. The idea was too crazy.

He put the framed cartridge down and sat back in his chair, turning the thought over in his mind. And as he did, he remembered the Hanged Man card. With this case in particular, the craziest leads seemed to be the most fruitful. If only he could get his hands on the Chirac evidence. He just needed . . .

He looked back to the framed memento of his heroic act, and the gears clicked.

He caught his breath. He potentially had the only piece of evidence he needed.

42

azarelle sprang up from his chair, grabbed the framed cartridge, and strode away from his desk, calling as he came.

"Maurice! Jeannot!" Brandishing the Lucite frame for the two to see, he exclaimed, "We need to get this thing out of here ASAP!"

Maurice and Jeannot looked at each other.

"The cartridge!"

Jeannot was the one to answer.

"Boss, I thought you liked our present. You don't need to make excuses to get rid of it. You can just tell us."

Mazarelle shook his head. "What? No! We need to send it to ballistics."

"For what?" asked Jeannot, his head cocked to the side.

Mazarelle tried for patience.

"For testing. The shell."

He handed the plexiglass frame to Maurice.

"It's the same casing we picked up that day, right? The one from the parade? It never left our hands?"

"Absolutely." Maurice knew his bullets—the nine mils and the .357s, the wadcutters, the hollow points, and the full metal jackets. He also prided himself on chain of evidence, even when the case was over. This one was a .22 LR, the same one Jeannot had found back on Bastille Day.

"So how can we test to see if . . ."

Mazarelle looked lost in thought, on to the next idea.

"To see . . ." Jeannot prompted him.

The commandant's attention snapped back.

"To see if this thing is a blank."

Maurice look startled.

"No testing required. You can tell by the casing itself. But why do you want to do that?"

"Remember what we saw on that tape? And what Jeannot saw in Berthaud's car? Now if you can figure out whether this cartridge is from a blank, you better damn well tell me."

Mazarelle passed the Lucite frame over to Maurice who held the shell up to his face. He turned the frame over, inspecting all sides of the spent cartridge.

Finally, Maurice looked up. He nodded.

"You see the crimping at the top of the casing? That's normally where the bullet would be. But this shell never had a bullet."

Jeannot was having a hard time keeping up.

"Wait. What?"

Maurice pointed to the fanlike folding pattern at the top of the cartridge.

"On blanks they crimp it like this to keep the powder in."

"Are you sure?"

"No question. It's a blank."

"So . . . at the parade . . . Max was shooting blanks?" asked Jeannot, his face creased in a mask of concentration. "What the hell does that mean?"

"It means, my dear Jeannot, that we may now have a new lead. A reason why someone might want Berthaud out of the picture," said Mazarelle, eyes twinkling.

43

When Mazarelle awoke early the next morning, he was still thinking about Jeannot's question. A puzzle he needed to solve. And he was getting closer. Just a little more time . . .

It was then that he noticed the message from Claire on his mobile.

"Hello, *chéri*, I'm back in town," she said. "See you at noon. Missed you."

He caught himself grinning. She must have sent it at the crack of dawn. His smile widened. He hadn't felt this way since Martine. Just a friend, but who knew what came next? He'd have to cancel several meetings he'd scheduled for the morning. Easily done, but it all took longer than he expected.

He was already a little late as he hurried into the hotel. The desk clerk was busy—talking to guests. The lobby seemed to be festively decked out in yellow roses as if to welcome Claire's return. Mazarelle simply had no patience to wait for the elevator. Ignoring his limp, he took the stairs three at a time to the top floor. But as he approached Claire's landing, Mazarelle felt his legs cramp up, pressure on his chest, a shortness of breath. What the hell was the matter with him? It was then he realized that her door was slightly ajar. Suddenly he had a very bad feeling. Without knocking, he pushed the door open and went inside. Only the smell of her marvelous perfume seemed familiar.

Claire, on the other hand, appeared eerily still. She was sprawled out naked on top of the bed, motionless, her black curls splayed around her zinc-white face. With not a care in the world except for her tightly clenched fist. Opening her fingers, one by one, he found

the tarot card in her hand. It was the Hanged Man. She'd been strangled. Her head lolled to the side. The marks on her neck were livid.
As if whoever did this wanted to wrench her head off in a frenzy.

Turning away, he went over to the windows. Mazarelle stood
there for a few moments, not moving. There were tears in his eyes.
He opened the door onto the balcony to get some air. A police car
went by below in the street, siren blaring. Pulling himself together,
he walked back to the bed, bent down, and kissed her lovely lips.
They were cool. Whoever did this was probably long gone by now.
He felt he was losing his grip. He couldn't bear to look at her this
way, and yet he couldn't bring himself to look anywhere else, as if
somehow he was to blame for what happened. If he'd just been more
attentive to the threat she faced, warned her what she was up against.
But he did warn her, even stressed the fact that she was dealing with
dangerous people—killers. Whatever he'd done, it wasn't enough. A
wonderful woman like Claire to have ended like this. It made him
feel empty inside, as if something crucial had been cut out of him,
leaving nothing but a painful sense of loss. She'd clearly been playing
with fire. Whoever did this, Mazarelle swore that he'd find them and
make them suffer.

He bent over to examine the Hanged Man's card in Claire's hand.
It was very much like the one that he'd found on the body of Alain
Berthaud—but given the way he was feeling, he couldn't be sure.
Mazarelle hadn't believed Claire for a second when she'd told him
she knew nothing about his murder victim. Any more than when she
said, "I'll try to help you all I can, Commandant." Actually she was
almost convincing. It was her direct look combined with a knowing
but innocent face that made her irresistible. Initially he'd assumed
she was trying to keep him distracted and herself informed about
what he was up to. But love does peculiar things to a man, and soon
he didn't give a damn what she was doing, or why for that matter, as
long as it included him.

The ringing phone on her desk startled him. He picked it up, and
stayed silent. Almost anything might be a lead.

But the caller wasn't talking either. That was strange. It was like a
game of chicken. Who would crack first?

Suddenly, on the other end of the line . . .

"Claire? Claire?"

Mazarelle didn't recognize the voice. He kept his silence.

"Are we still good to go?" More urgent now.

Finally Mazarelle had to ask: "Who is this?"

The click on the other end of the line was the only answer he got. That and the phone number that popped up on the screen. The area code 04 for the South of France.

Mazarelle stayed for a long few seconds staring down at Claire's phone. And then the detective in him finally took over. He started with 36 and the BC, reaching out to Maurice first. He wanted their *procédurier* for the record. He told Maurice to trace the number, and to round up Jeannot and Serge immediately.

"All of you should meet me here at the Hôtel Château Saint-Germain. There's been a murder. When you arrive, don't stop at the front desk. Say nothing to anyone. Come right upstairs. Top floor."

Next he called the Police Scientifique and told them where to send the men in white. The one victim: a woman, adult, in her thirties, Caucasian—murdered. The crime scene a room on the top floor of the Hôtel Château Saint-German. Identifying himself as Commandant Mazarelle of *la Crim,* he said he and his men would be waiting for them.

On his first visit, Mazarelle had noticed the small office Claire had set up in an adjoining alcove. She'd said it was where she did her real work. Looking around the little room, he didn't have the patience to rummage through her desk drawers. That would come later. The computer on top of her desk would probably be more interesting. As for that, he'd let Jeannot handle it when he arrived. There were other calls he had to make first, but he was too depressed to make them right away.

Mazarelle had always thought of himself as an optimist, but life seemed to be making the challenge harder and harder for him. And the older he got, the higher life raised the bar. Now, with the death of Claire, perhaps he wasn't up to it anymore. The angel of optimism seemed to have deserted him. One after another, the women of his life had died on him.

No matter what problems he had with those he loved, he'd always come back for more. That was the way he'd felt about Martine, his young wife, even on those occasions when she went away without a word, and then returned to fill his life as if she'd never left. With the secretive Claire, it was hard to understand what was on her mind other than ambition. That was the only way he could make sense of her marriage to the wealthy Armand Lavoisier.

When he eased open Claire's bureau drawer, he found a rainbow of pink, red, yellow, orange, and blue bikini panties floating on a pleasant cloud of lavender sachet. No surprise there. It was what he found underneath that was unexpected. When he opened the black leather business notebook and saw the familiar names of Alain Berthaud, Luc Fournel, Guy Danglars, Théo Legardère, and Philippe Riche, and the enormous amounts of money that each of them had been paid, Mazarelle realized how deeply Claire had been involved with the *ripoux*. He closed Claire's notebook and put it away in his jacket. He wanted to think about what came next before throwing her name to *les boeuf*. Even dead, he wanted to protect her reputation.

Under the black notebook sat a handful of file folders. Opening the first, Mazarelle smiled. Inside, he saw Frank's picture, and several scrawled pages of notes. He knew it! She was doing an article on that American playboy the whole time. That made more sense now. What dirt had she found on the congressman? Was it a motive for murder? The second file was more of a shock. It had Mazarelle's own picture in it. He slammed it shut.

With the folders in his hands, Mazarelle almost missed the sound of the doorknob turning, it was so quiet. But the handle was rotating slowly, almost imperceptibly. Mazarelle was startled. This was way too fast for his team to have gotten there. Jamming the files into his jacket, he hurried toward the balcony, moving with surprising speed for a man his size. If this was Claire's killer, coming back to clean up the scene, he would be ready.

But the men entering the apartment were not killers. They were cops, pulling on gloves. Not Mazarelle's team though. He didn't recognize them. How had they gotten there so fast? He was about to step back into the apartment to greet them, when the words he heard stopped him cold.

"Where is it?" the stocky one was asking. He and his partner, the cop with a buzz cut, had walked right by the dead body on the bed. They didn't seem to be interested in the murder. They were looking for something else.

"He said it would be here."

From the balcony, Mazarelle watched both men as they went through the drawers in the apartment. Both seemed to be wearing the uniforms of the National Police. Mazarelle was sure he didn't know them, but they seemed familiar somehow. Who the fuck were they?

"Black, right? I don't see the damn thing."

"Keep looking. We're screwed if it gets out."

Mazarelle could hear more rummaging around in the drawers, just beyond his eyeline, and then the low buzz of a mobile phone.

"*Oui? Oui. Merde alors.*" The cop jammed the phone back into his pocket. "That was Théo. They're almost here. We've got to go."

Mazarelle emerged from the balcony to see the apartment door closing. And now he had a decision to make. He could follow the dirty cops. They were clearly up to something illegal. But it didn't seem to be murder. And with every fiber of his six-foot-three-inch frame, Mazarelle wanted the killer.

Staring grimly at Claire's lifeless body, he did the thing he knew a detective is never supposed to do. He blew past the evidence, the meticulous review of data, and went right to the list of suspects. The tarot card clearly put Alain Berthaud's murderer at the top. Frank Nash was on the list. And, frankly, he had to admit that, to others in the department, he would soon be on the list as well.

Mazarelle tried to take a breath. Angelique, his physical therapist, was always talking to him about breathing. As if he didn't breathe all the time. A deep cleansing breath she called it. This one felt soiled all the way down. But he couldn't duck his next call anymore.

The *patron* was astonished when he learned that Claire Girard, the editor in chief of the popular *Paris-Flash*, had been murdered.

"What the hell is going on in this city anyhow!" Coudert exploded. "How was she killed?"

Mazarelle said that it looked like she'd been strangled. Visible bruises around her neck. A violent murder.

"Who discovered the body?" asked Coudert.

There was a momentary pause before Mazarelle told him that he'd discovered the corpse. "Madame Girard"—he volunteered, to avoid interruptions—"has a pied-à-terre. A small private office on the top floor of the Hôtel Château Saint-Germain. It's far from the brouhaha of her magazine's editorial offices."

She'd called him early that morning, Mazarelle explained. She had something to tell him about the case of the Canal Saint-Martin's hanged man. And considering the sensational nature of that story, she preferred to give it to him in her private office. Mazarelle understood that completely.

"Yes, yes, of course," Coudert acknowledged. "Go on."

"That's it."

"You mean she was dead when you got there? She left nothing?"

"I didn't say that. I haven't begun my investigation yet. But I can tell you this. Madame Girard had clutched in her hand a tarot card of the Hanged Man that appears to be identical with the one we found on the body of Alain Berthaud."

"Aha! I see. Do we have a goddamn serial killer on the loose?"

"Much too early to tell."

"What else?"

"Nothing. Except that I've informed the PS to set up a crime scene, notified my team to meet me here, and before doing anything else called you to learn if this will be part of my case too."

"Of course it will. Don't be ridiculous. Now get started and keep me fully informed of your progress. Understood?"

"I'll do my best, chief."

Before looking over Claire's room, Mazarelle had one more call to make. He tried to reach her husband at home. Somebody by the name of Emily answered. It was Claire's housekeeper. Madame Girard wasn't home. "Can I take a message?" she asked.

Mazarelle identified himself and asked for Monsieur Lavoisier. He had some news for him. Could he stop by? Emily said that monsieur had left early that morning on the TGV to Lyon and would be back tomorrow. Mazarelle asked if she had a phone number where he could be reached, and she did.

It was a Lyon number. A secretary said that Armand Lavoisier was just getting out of a meeting about a new Canal+ project. "I'll call him. Hold on."

"Yes? What is this about?" Lavoisier had a velvet voice, patient, curious, reeking of culture. "Who is this?"

Commandant Mazarelle explained why he was calling. He had some bad news. He reported that Monsieur Lavoisier's wife had had a serious accident. In fact, she was dead. That sounded so cold, so unkind to Mazarelle, that he added, "I'm truly sorry." He wanted Lavoisier to know that there would have to be an autopsy and promptly. Mazarelle pointed out that his wife had been murdered. In this sort of case they tried to have as little delay as possible. Lavoisier objected, couldn't understand his need for such haste, insisted that they wait until he got back to Paris. The commandant coolly suggested that Monsieur Lavoisier return home as soon as possible. Lavoisier said that he planned to be back in Paris tomorrow on the TGV.

"That'll do," Mazarelle said.

"Just a minute. Hold on. Where was Claire killed?"

"I'll tell you all about that when I see you here."

Lavoisier paused. "I'm changing my reservation. I'll be leaving later this afternoon at three p.m. I'll call when I arrive. Give me your number and address." He jotted them down. "I should be in your office by six p.m."

"Better," the commandant assured him.

44

The knocking was coming from the door. Despite the Paris traffic, his team had made good time.

"*Oh, la vache!*" Jeannot cried. He couldn't take his eyes off the naked woman on the bed. "That's one beautiful lady, boss. Do you know who she is?"

Mazarelle strode to the bed and covered Claire with a sheet. "Yes, I do."

Maurice told the *chef de groupe* that as they entered the Château Saint-Germain he'd noticed a few of the vultures from the press gathering outside like storm clouds.

"Already!" Mazarelle said.

Jeannot wondered how the paparazzi got on it so fast.

"Probably an informant at the hotel's front desk," said Maurice.

Mazarelle slapped his forehead. "*Imbécile!*" he cried, annoyed with himself. How could he be so stupid? Using the phone on her desk rather than taking his mobile outside. So flustered by Claire's death that he'd no idea his brains had seeped out. He guessed that the hotel management downstairs had listened in to all his calls. "That's what they do these days. Even small hotels like this. For some reason they think they're entitled to know what's going on."

The men in white arrived and shooed Mazarelle and his team out of the room into the hotel hallway. Standing there, Mazarelle organized his men. He wanted Jeannot and Serge to go to *Paris-Flash* on the rue Delambre. "Speak to Philippe Riche, Madame Girard's deputy editor, and tell him what happened. Say I sent you. Then go through her desk. Get me her calendar, her files, her address book, her Rolodex, and anything else you can find of potential importance to us."

Then turning to Maurice, Mazarelle said, "You know what to do. I want a record of everything that went on here to add to the report. After that arrange for the removal of the body to Dr. Chardon and schedule the autopsy. And I want the uniforms downstairs to keep the paparazzi outside where they belong. Remember *outside*. Let's go."

At the front desk, the clerk was a runty little guy. His prize possession seemed to be the *clefs d'or* he wore, the symbol of the hotel's concierge, on his jacket's blue lapels. He was anxious about what was going on upstairs. But before he could ask the two of them any questions, Mazarelle had some questions of his own.

"Did anyone come to see Madame Girard before I arrived?"

"I wasn't aware of anyone. But I was called away from the desk for a short time. No, I don't think she had any visitors until you arrived, Commandant."

Mazarelle asked if she was there yesterday.

"Not as far as I know. She was gone all day. I didn't even see her last night when I closed up. But she has her own keys. She could have come in late. I know she was up early this morning because she called for her *petit déjeuner* at seven a.m."

"Thanks. That's helpful. Now, please don't let anyone go up to the third floor unless they have police identification."

The desk clerk's face clouded over. "What's going on, Commandant?"

"It's a crime scene. Only police are allowed."

Mazarelle headed toward the door, and stopped suddenly. Turning back, he offered a warning: "And if I find out that someone here's been talking to the paparazzi again, you can come visit me at police headquarters at the Quai des Orfèvres."

Outside the hotel there were already half a dozen reporters milling about. He recognized a few of them from the years when he and Martine had lived in Paris. Hervé Stein was an old acquaintance who covered crime stories freelance for *L'Express* and all the major weeklies. Mazarelle nodded at him. They all wanted to know what had happened. They'd heard that the editor of *Paris-Flash*, Claire Girard, had died.

Mazarelle made a quick decision. The victim was one of their own. He had to give the press something. But he needed to keep the scene contained. Drawing himself up, Mazarelle gave them his ninety-second presser. In short declarative sentences, he explained that as yet he'd very little information for them. All he could confirm was that Madame Claire Girard, who'd been staying at the hotel, was dead. She had been murdered. The investigation was underway. Anyone with any information could contact the Brigade Criminelle. After that, their questions followed thick and fast. Holding up his hand, Mazarelle said that as soon as he had any answers, he'd tell them.

Stein shouted, "Does this case have anything to do with the hanged man who was found on the Canal Saint-Martin?"

Mazarelle shot him the fish-eye.

"It's too early to tell who may or may not be involved. That's all we've got for you right now."

As Mazarelle hurried away, Stein caught up with him in front of the bar on the next block. He suggested they go in for a drink. Though Mazarelle, gray-faced and exhausted, wanted to get back to his office, he had a second thought. Perhaps it was an idea whose time had come. "Okay," he said. "One."

When the waiter appeared and asked what they wanted, Mazarelle said, "Cognac—okay by you?"

"Perfect." Stein smiled at the prospect.

"Two glasses of Delamain," Mazarelle ordered. "And bring us some olives too." He was about to take out his pipe but changed his mind. He'd no intention of staying that long.

As soon as the cognac arrived, Stein raised his glass in a toast to the new commandant at the BC.

"Thanks," Mazarelle said. "These are busy days lately."

The commandant picked up a gleaming black olive stuffed with feta cheese and popped it into his mouth. "Kalamatas?" he asked the waiter.

"*Mais, oui.*"

"Delicious." He took another, and passed the plate to Stein.

"I never told you how sorry I was to hear about Martine," said Stein. "Such a lovely woman, and so young . . ."

Mazarelle nodded gloomily. Rubbed his eyes.

"You look as if you've been working hard."

"Yes, I have," said Mazarelle, thinking that's the least of it.

"How do you like your guys at the BC?"

"No complaints. Young, eager, and some pretty sharp."

"Hah! Sounds better than some of your former pals at the Fourth, as I remember."

"You've got a good memory, Stein," Mazarelle cut in. "So tell me—you knew Claire pretty well, didn't you? You wrote for her enough. How much was she using our cops for information?"

Stein stopped mid-olive. He had intended to work Mazarelle for background on the investigation. He hadn't expected to find himself on the receiving end of awkward questions.

"Information?" he stalled.

Mazarelle nodded. "The kind you pay for."

Stein took a long sip of his cognac. Mazarelle's eyes never left his.

Finally, the reporter put down his glass with a sigh. "Off the record?"

Even on this grim day, Mazarelle had to smile. "You think I'm going to print it somewhere?"

"Okay, okay." Stein pushed the glass away. "Sure, *Paris-Flash* used some of those *ripoux* guys. Everyone does it."

Mazarelle knew that Stein wrote for most of the major periodicals.

"Look, it's a few euros here, a few euros there. And we get tips on stories that might stay buried otherwise. It's almost a public service."

Mazarelle wasn't about to buy that one. But as much as any reporter, he knew you didn't want to interrupt the flow once someone was talking.

"Any idea who?"

"No, I never got into it that much."

That was another lie Mazarelle was going to let go.

"But Claire, did she have a falling out with any of them? Did it sound as if someone might be gunning for her? Any dirty cops?"

Stein was shaking his head even before Mazarelle finished.

"No, no, nothing like that. Everybody really liked Claire. If anything, a little too much maybe. They were all trying to get into her pants."

Stein paused for another sip.

"She was such an attractive woman. And bright, too."

"Yes, she was," Mazarelle said wistfully. The preterite clearly depressed him. He'd seen more than his share of murdered women before, but seldom one he cared for so much. He drank his cognac in silence.

"No, Claire never really mentioned the *ripoux*," said Stein. "That was just a fact of business."

Sipping his woodsy, honey-colored brandy, Mazarelle began to feel that he'd had enough socializing. He swallowed what was left in his glass in a gulp.

But Stein was still talking. "Last time I saw her," he said, "must have been about a week ago. She was hinting about something else— some dirt she had dug up on an American big shot. A senator maybe? It sounded important. Of course, she wouldn't tell me any details."

Stein didn't know Mazarelle well enough to see the quickening of the glance, the sudden focus of the eyes. He rambled right on.

"And speaking of scoops," Stein said, "what can you tell me about . . ."

But Mazarelle was already in motion. He pulled out a few bills, dropped them down on the small round marble-topped table, and said, "Thanks for the chitchat. Got to go."

45

Despite the gloom of Claire's death weighing him down, Mazarelle, fueled by the cognac, pushed the ton on his back up the black linoleum staircase at 36. He climbed to the third floor and went into the main office to pick up his mail. But even distracted, how could he not be intrigued by the white-haired *zazou* sitting on the bench? Could that be—? The thought that he might be Claire's husband amazed him. It wasn't that he didn't know she was married. After all, he'd spoken to the man a short time ago. But he never imagined what he looked like. Certainly not wearing a *sportif* blue blazer, white pants, white sneakers, and a blue and white striped shirt. He seemed as out of place here as if he were waiting pier side at Cannes for a sleek white speedboat to ferry him out to his yacht.

"Monsieur Lavoisier?"

"Ah, at last!" He was up on his feet. "Commandant Mazarelle. I've been waiting for you."

"Thanks for coming so soon."

"I couldn't believe what you told me on the phone. Claire dead! I can't wrap my head around it. How did it happen? Are you sure it's definitely her?"

The commandant waved Lavoisier's breathless questions aside. "Not here. Let's go upstairs to my office. Follow me."

Upstairs on the fourth floor—sitting opposite his visitor—Mazarelle noticed Claire's husband's tired bloodshot eyes. He wondered if the old boy had been crying. He decided to let the excited Lavoisier ask as many questions as he wanted while providing not much in return.

"Yes. It's definitely her. She was just in our offices, so we could identify her. And, no, nothing yet. It's still early days in our investigation."

But Mazarelle had his own queries. "When did you last see your wife? Do you know what she planned to do today?"

"Claire was away for the past two days in the South of France with the American politician, Frank Nash. They were working together on an article . . ." He paused. Suddenly bursting out—"I don't know why she had to use him. From what I've learned about Monsieur Nash, he didn't come to Paris from Washington without baggage."

"What do you mean? Politics?"

"No." Lavoisier shook his head emphatically. "*Not* politics."

It was clear that he wasn't about to say what he meant. Mazarelle moved on. "Do you know when she planned to return to Paris?"

He expected Claire back late that day or the next. "In any event, she would have been back tomorrow. We planned on having dinner together at home."

Mazarelle thought he knew very well what Claire had in mind.

The extra day . . . she had set it aside for him. He wondered, uncomfortably, how her husband would feel if he sensed that.

Lavoisier wanted to know if the commandant had already spoken to Nash.

Mazarelle indicated that he hadn't but intended to. He thought maybe he should push Lavoisier again. "Why do you ask?"

"I guess there's something about him that makes me nervous—"

"Do you mean suspicious?" Mazarelle interrupted.

"No, I didn't say that. I said 'nervous.' And that's what I meant."

"O-kay," said Mazarelle coolly, as if he couldn't care less. "Have it your way." Then he turned toward the door.

Maurice was back. He apologized for interrupting them. The men in white were still taking photos of the crime scene when he left them, but Maurice thought Mazarelle would want the list of what they found as soon as possible.

"Yes. Let me see it."

Maurice had crammed four pages full of details. Even at a hurried glance, Mazarelle could see that all of it was neatly laid out in the Ivorian's tiny handwriting.

"Thanks. I'll check it out later."

But something had caught Mazarelle's eye.

"I see that Madame Girard had some jewelry with her. Did she always wear expensive jewelry?"

"Claire had expensive taste. She liked good jewelry, and so do I." He glanced down at the gold watch he wore. "Why bother with any other kind? Whatever I bought for her was the best."

"Do you know what jewelry she took with her?"

He didn't. But he assumed she had her diamond ring, gold wedding band, her pearl earrings, a watch, a necklace, a pin or two. He really didn't know what else, but recently he'd given her a present that she seemed quite fond of. A pendant he bought from Van Cleef & Arpels. It was called *Oiseau de Paradis.*

Mazarelle again scanned Maurice's list. "I don't see any pendant here."

"Maybe she didn't take it. I'll check at home," her husband said.

"What about this gold ankle bracelet?" Mazarelle asked, looking at the list.

"Gold!" The color drained from Lavoisier's lips. "She took that damn thing with her? I'd never buy Claire a piece of cheap crap like that. More like gold-plated tin. The kind that turns your skin green overnight. I warned her about that guy."

In a way, oddly enough, that was how Mazarelle himself felt. He'd certainly seen the way Claire looked at the handsome young Yank. The truth was he couldn't get it out of his head.

Lavoisier got up. "Can I see her?"

"Are you sure you want to?"

He thought about it. "Why?" he asked. "Has she had the autopsy already?"

"It's not scheduled yet, but we'll let you know."

"Where will it be done? I'd like to see her before then."

Mazarelle gave him the address of the morgue in the Twelfth and said he'd meet him there.

Lavoisier was firm. "I'll go by myself."

"No, I'm afraid not. This isn't a funeral home." Though Mazarelle would have much preferred not to join him, that wasn't the way the medical examiner did his job. Especially not a stickler like Chardon.

As Lavoisier left, a messenger arrived at the door and handed Mazarelle a package. It had an unfamiliar return address—Sofitel Boutique de Cadeaux, Marseille. Mazarelle opened the package and inside found a gift-wrapped tobacco pouch with a note. "*À monsieur le commandant, ton amie,* Claire." He ran his fingers lightly over it. The pouch was almost as soft as her skin. For a moment, Mazarelle was stunned. Then really quite moved. Touched to learn that, in a way, she was still looking out for him.

46

Whenever Fabriani had a problem that he couldn't share with his wife, he'd often try to unravel it at No. 6 on the rue de Ponthieu—a short, narrow street with a variety of small shops and an entrance to an arcade that led to the Champs-Élysées. The only identifying mark on the door was the number. Outside bright sunlight, loud street noises, stalled traffic, honking delivery trucks, motos, but passing through the double doors of *numéro 6* was like entering an air lock into a decompression chamber. Inside, the lighting was soft, indirect, the music on the sound system an elegant piano piece by Satie. The small sign on the wall whispered in lowercase letters—the aristo club.

Jérome, the club's host, greeted Commissaire Fabriani warmly. Fabriani alerted him that he was expecting a guest and then went on to the club's inner room—a cozy area full of leather chairs and the quiet buzz of civilized conversation. Sitting down on the soft chamois cushion of his familiar chair, in his usual corner, he scanned the day's headlines. The Défense Nationale were in the streets of Calais, mixing it up with immigrants and refugees.

Fabriani opened his private humidor and chose his first cigar—a Romeo y Julieta, which he enjoyed not only because it bore his wife's name, but because it was a Reserva Real Maduro. He'd barely lit up when Jérome brought over his guest. He put down the newspaper with a contented sigh and tapped a finger on the front page.

"Our right-wing friends. So eager. So easy to . . ." He offered his hand and gestured to the dark leather seat next to him. "How do you like the jacket I picked out for you?"

As he sat down, Luc Fournel ran his fingers over the sleeves. They may have been too long but he'd never worn a silk jacket before.

"Very nice."

Luc was impressed with the Aristo Club. Pleased by the sound of his heels on the gleaming parquet and the smell of money—the one thing he was good at sniffing out.

"I like the decor," he said, pointing to the framed paintings on the wall.

Fabriani smiled, wondering if his old lieutenant could tell that Manet's Portrait of Mallarmé with a Cigar, Frida Kahlo's Portrait with a Cigar, Picasso's Cigar on a Sword, and Larry Rivers's Dutch Masters with Cigars were all weak variations of famous paintings and not the real things.

Jérome brought over a flute of Henriot Blanc de Blanc and an assortment of cigars for the new arrival. From the way he hesitated, it was obvious to Fabriani that Luc wasn't much of a cigar smoker, but also that he enjoyed being catered to. Fabriani watched the care he exercised, amused at the cigar he selected. An Arturo Fuente God of Fire Robusto. It fit his big craggy face to a tee. Fabriani handed Luc his cigar cutter, then ignited the Xikar that Juliette had bought him.

Luc settled back to smoke in his leather chair as if he were a regular member. "So who did you think did it?" he asked. "Not that I'll miss her—but I wonder . . ."

The question surprised Fabriani. Made him pause. Did Luc really intend to keep him in the dark about his latest piece of violence? Fabriani had understood why Berthaud had to be eliminated. Even Guy, he supposed. But why did Luc need to have Claire killed? Suddenly, it occurred to him—was she perhaps planning to cut his Agence AB out of the money chain? But if so, weren't there other ways to deal with such difficulties?

"Really?!" exclaimed Fabriani. "If you don't know, then who does?"

Luc looked puzzled. "Écoute, Claude—I can name you half a dozen victims of the Paris-Flash scandal treatment who would have paid handsomely to have Claire eliminated."

Fabriani concluded that Luc simply had no intention of revealing anything he knew about the murder. So he went on to what really bothered him most.

"It's the timing of what happened, Luc—with the boeuf-carottes and Mazarelle both sniffing around. I especially don't like it that anyone who ever had any connection to us might be suspected. Especially now. Well, there's not much we can do about that anymore, but if we put our heads together, it may be possible to keep Mazarelle's investigation of Claire's murder from spreading. Don't you see?"

"Sure. I agree—Mazarelle has to go, or it might be us next—but what do you imagine we can do about it?"

"*D'accord!* Mazarelle has to be stopped—but no more of the strong-arm stuff, Luc. The important thing is that you don't behave like a loose cannon. We've had enough violence already."

Putting down his cigar in the huge ashtray, Fabriani leaned forward. "Listen to me, Luc. I've given the Mazarelle matter a lot of thought recently and I think I've come up with a fairly simple way to handle him."

"I don't see how . . ."

"Leave it to me. I'll do it myself . . ."

"I'll believe that when I see it. But if you can pull it off, *chapeau*, my friend. You have my hat."

Fabriani looked at his watch and turned to Luc. "I've got to go. I have an important meeting at the Ministry of Interior. You can stay here as long as you want. Put it on my bill."

To Luc, Fabriani presenting himself as the voice of reason was a new one. He found the idea laughable, almost bizarre. The commissaire was so ambitious. He'd do almost anything. On the other hand . . . Luc raised his flute of champagne to the departing commissaire as he left. "Thanks, Claude—and I wish you well."

Outside, Fabriani walked down the block and got into his glittering silver-birch Aston Martin. It had been a special present from his wife—a James Bond fan—for her husband's last birthday. Slipping down behind the wheel on the ultrasmooth hand-stitched tuxedo-black leather seat, he was still delighted by its new-car smell. Before turning on the ignition, he pulled out his mobile and tapped in the phone number of Coudert's office at 36.

Coudert's assistant, Nicolas, answered. "Yes, Commissaire. He's in a meeting. Can I take a message?"

"Ask him to call me as soon as he's free. It's very important!"

"Don't worry, sir. I'll tell him," he promised.

Fabriani switched on the car's engine and it growled as if its cage had been unlocked. Passersby on the street froze in their tracks. Waiting to see what came next. On Ponthieu, the traffic that had been stalled on and off all afternoon parted like the Red Sea, and Fabriani, roaring into line, neatly filled the gap. He was on his way.

By the time he'd gotten back to the Fourth, Fabriani had heard from Coudert.

47

ou can go right in," Coudert's assistant said. "He's waiting for you."

Mazarelle glanced at the bald eagle with glasses seated outside Coudert's office.

"No-no," said Nicolas. "He can wait." He waved Mazarelle in.

Coudert was standing at one of the two large windows—his hands clasped behind his back—gazing at the river traffic below.

"Shut the door," he said. Coudert turned and saw what his visitor was about to do. "No please . . . Don't sit down."

Mazarelle noted the florid multicolored ascot he was wearing. It was inescapable. "Nice neckwear. Another present from your wife?"

Coudert brushed his question aside. "This is not going to take us very long."

Mazarelle glanced at him quizzically.

"I just received a call that I found quite disturbing. To be frank, Commandant, I'm very disappointed in you. I had high hopes in the beginning about your coming here to *la Crim*. And, as you know, we've given you some of our most important cases. We're still waiting on your evidence for Babo. And now this . . ."

"If you're talking about the hanged man, it hasn't been easy. It's

taken us longer than I'd hoped. We've had some distractions, awkward detours. That sort of thing. But I think now—"

"No! That's not it," Coudert broke in. "That's not what this is about.
I'm talking about the murder of Claire Girard."

"What? You must be joking. That just happened. You just gave
that case to me."

The *patron* drew himself up and, folding his arms, stared at Mazarelle. His tone of voice was dark, chilling. "I'm far from joking,
Commandant Mazarelle." There were things about the big guy that
Coudert had managed to put up with until now . . . but barely. For
one thing, he didn't at all care for his ironic style. His irreverence.
His overdone mustache that covered half his face, and all of his intu-
itions. The primary reason he'd put up with a lot from Mazarelle was
that he was definitely useful as a detective. That, however, no longer
seemed to balance the books as far as Coudert was concerned.

"What do you mean? I don't understand."

"Is it true, Commandant, that you were carrying on an affair with
Madame Girard, a person of interest who was being investigated by
Internal Affairs in connection with police corruption?"

"We were friends. But that's it. So what?"

"*More* than friends." Coudert winced, as if from a stench. "Don't
take me for a fool. You were lovers."

A series of thoughts went cascading through Mazarelle's brain.
How the hell did Coudert know about his private life in the first
place? And why should he feel guilty? He decided to play it right up
the middle.

"She was never a suspect in my case. She alibied out early on."
Mazarelle shook his head. "So, yes, we were friendly. But we never
slept together. Much to my regret," he finished with a sigh.

Coudert looked as if he were undergoing a major stress attack.
Eyes bulging, back ramrod stiff, his rapid breathing in stertorous
gasps. It was Coudert rampant, and he appeared about to explode.
He was furious.

"Don't you realize what you've done is a flagrant conflict of interest? The rumor is everywhere that you were lovers. What if word
about this gets out? We'll all be on the carpet. The minister will trot
over here from Interior and give us holy hell. Not to mention what

the media will do. We'll be the laughingstock of every TV newscast and comedy show in all of France. And that's even before they send you away to serve Capital One for murdering your girlfriend. You seem to have forgotten that *you* found her dead body—which, when this gets out, makes you the number one suspect."

"What are you talking about? Are you nuts?"

"She was dead and you were there with her."

"Of course I was there. We had an appointment. I found her. I called you, remember?"

"Well, it won't be much of a leap when you get named one of the prime suspects in her murder."

"That's ridiculous! Her body was already cold when I arrived."

"Tell it to the *juge d'instruction*."

Mazarelle stepped back and shook his head. "I think you may be a little over-the-top, *patron*."

Coudert found it especially galling to endure Mazarelle's attempt at being reasonable.

"Listen, Mazarelle, even aside from the murder case, and your clear conflict of interest, there's another issue here as well. The one thing I asked you to do for me—the *only* thing really, other than solve the crimes you were assigned—was keep away from Fabriani and your old commissariat in the Fourth. I asked you, *please* not to step on his toes. Didn't I say that?"

"Yes, you did," Mazarelle readily acknowledged. He hoped even a born administrator like Coudert might understand that he was trying to cooperate with him and not be a blister on the heel of progress. "But as such things often are," he explained, "it was more complicated than that. You see, Fabriani and his wife invited me to dinner. They seemed to be making a special effort to be friendly to the widower. They had known my wife, Martine. So what was I supposed to do—kick him in the balls?"

The *patron* was running out of patience with him. "Your problem, Mazarelle, is that you simply don't give a damn about police protocol. The way we do things here. I'm afraid that I have no choice. With all this put together, I'm going to have to suspend you. I think you probably need a breather. Either you'll learn what it means to follow orders or you're out of here. That's official, Mazarelle. And if you don't believe me and ignore what I'm saying, I can assure you it will be terminal."

Mazarelle looked him in the eye. "Am I fired? Is that what you mean?"

"I think that even you should understand what I mean. I said 'suspended.' Now get out of here before I change my mind."

"What about my team and the two cases they're working on? Who's going to handle them?"

"Captain Kalou will take over. I've already notified him. Do you have any doubts that he can do the job?"

Mazarelle thought it over. "No . . . no. Maurice would have been my choice too."

"Well at least we can agree on that. Now give me a break, will you? Get the hell out of my sight. I don't want to see you anywhere in the vicinity of my office for a long time."

Mazarelle started to the door then turned back to his boss. "How long did you say?"

"Don't push me, Commandant." Coudert pointed to the door.

Mazarelle yanked it open. He was about to slam the door closed behind him but thought better of it.

At the staircase, he decided not to go back upstairs to his office. The way he felt now he couldn't bear to see any of the men on his team. Knowing them, they'd probably try to cheer him up and that would stick in his throat like broken glass.

Gravity took him down and out onto the sidewalk. In front of the building a young woman was trying to push a wheelchair-bound invalid into a white van and not doing it very well. Mazarelle went over, lifted the wheelchair and its elderly passenger, and put both inside. You might say almost threw them in. Mazarelle was so pissed with what had gone on upstairs, he felt as if he'd been squeezed through a wringer.

That asshole Coudert, thought Mazarelle. Couldn't get rid of me permanently no matter how much he huffed and puffed. I must still have some friends at the Ministry of the Interior's office. Coudert thinks that if he pushes me closer to the edge of the volcano, I'll either jump or fall in. Fat chance. Don't hold your breath, *patron*.

PART FIVE

48

For Maurice Kalou, the fresh air near the river was a reprieve after a day of formaldehyde and dead flesh. Depressing anytime, but even more so when the flesh was once as lovely as Claire Girard's. The autopsy had taken longer than expected. Dr. Chardon, the medical examiner, had almost smoked his entire pack of Gauloises by the time he was finished. Now Maurice was walking across the Pont Saint-Michel to the Left Bank with a lot on his mind.

The last twenty-four hours had been sheer upheaval for Maurice. For the first time since arriving in Paris from his hometown of Abidjan, the large port city of the Ivory Coast, he had finally realized his dream. After decades on the force working homicides, now, at last, he was in charge, leading his own team at the famed Brigade Criminelle. Even if it was only temporary. For a buttoned-down, meticulous man, his pride threatened to burst his jacket. But at the same time, he felt terrible for his *chef*. He knew Mazarelle was no more capable of murder than he himself was. Still, the commandant was guilty of a mistake with Claire. The whole situation drove home the code Maurice had always lived by: Follow the rules. Stick with the rules. Bad things happen when you break the rules.

Donovan's Irish Pub was like a familiar face after wandering among strangers for what seemed eons. Opening Donovan's celebrated gleaming red door, he was met by the friendly brouhaha of music and voices, the alcoholic smell of Guinness, the festive clink of glasses. As usual the happy hour that had started at 4 p.m. was now in full swing and growing wilder by the minute.

The fair-skinned Caitlin with her beamish Irish smile came

rushing over—sure-footed on the sawdust covered floor—and met his questioning look with a wave of her green-painted fingernails. "You're late. He's back there with the friends. They've been waiting for you for hours."

Seated in the room at the rear, Mazarelle sat bookended by Jeannot and Serge, who were hard at work attempting to cheer him up. Their arms draped convivially around their depressed, deposed *chef*. All three equally sloshed.

Gathering up their empty glasses, Caitlin asked, "Fresh pints all around?"

"D'accord!" they cried in unison.

As they waited, Jeannot filled them in about a surprising phone call he'd had early that morning from Lucien Klabakov.

"Who?" Mazarelle asked.

"The owner-publisher of *Paris-Flash*," Jeannot explained. "Claire's boss." Klabakov was extremely wrought up. He wanted to know if they had any news for him about her killer. He'd asked if there was anything he could do to help. Apparently, he'd gone on a bit about Claire—called her a brilliant editor. A terrific writer. A wellspring of exciting new ideas. A real innovator in magazine publishing. And she was fearless too.

Klabakov told Jeannot that he was the one who thought she'd be great as *Paris-Flash*'s first woman editor in chief. And she was. After finding the *nid d'amour* where Princess Diana and Dodi were hiding in Saint-Tropez, she'd hired the helicopter pilot and photographer who captured the lovers' early romantic story for their readers. *PF* had been a small, little-known *hebdo* when Claire first took over the reins of his magazine. Claire made it into an important, must-read, moneymaker. A *succès fou*. And she was beautiful—too beautiful for any words that he could think of.

"He called her a golden girl," Jeannot said. "When he spoke about her, he sounded more like her sweetheart than her boss."

Mazarelle sighed. Yet another one, he thought gloomily. "Okay, okay, enough. Add him to our persons of interest. Now let's move on. We know the victim was strangled. But what actually killed her?"

Maurice, lifting his Guinness stout, looked up slowly as all eyes turned to him. He paused, and took a long swallow, stalling for time.

He was all for supporting his old boss. But Mazarelle was supposed to be suspended. And here they were, all working the case together, just the same as ever.

"C'mon, Cap," Jeannot urged. "What did Chardon say?"

It wasn't what Chardon had said that Maurice was remembering. It was the two aides in the corner of the room, whispering to each other. *"Boucaque,"* the tall one had said to the other, and stifled a laugh. They thought he hadn't heard. But he had been hearing those whispers since he came to Paris as an eight-year-old. From the lycée to the butcher shop on the corner, they wouldn't say anything to his face. But, when they thought he wasn't looking, his classmates would still wave the bananas behind his back and snicker.

He had come to the Quai des Orfèvres to join a police force that prided itself on being enlightened. But over a drink at the end of the day, in a bar like this one, he knew they saw him as an outsider—a visitor from some dusty African plateau who would fit in better with the wildebeest than here in the force. And running his own team? Almost no one believed he would ever merit that. Even if his forensic accounting alone had cracked several recent cases—following the money until it gave up the killer—still, only a handful understood his real worth. One of the few was sitting right across the table.

Maurice took one more sip, then made his decision as his glass went down. Mazarelle was still the best investigator he had ever seen. Might as well use his brains while he could.

"The ME claimed it was asphyxiation. Manual strangulation. According to him, the most singular aspect of this murder was its violence. He found bruise marks all over the victim's upper body, especially her neck. In fact, her hyoid bone had been fractured. To him, that all indicated both strength and some kind of raw emotion. There were bruise marks but no fingerprints. Meaning the killer was probably wearing vinyl gloves and the crime probably premeditated. What the killer left behind were bits of his skin under her fingernails. And if we're lucky, some usable DNA."

Mazarelle said, "So she was trying to fight him off."

Maurice nodded. "That's what the ME said."

There was a silence as they all thought about the victim's last moments.

Then Jeannot pulled out his notes. He reported that the last meal she'd eaten that morning was *un petit déjeuner* that was brought up by a maid around 8:30. Mazarelle asked if they had checked with the desk clerk as to the time he arrived.

Jeannot said, "It was shortly before noon."

That seemed about right to Mazarelle. He confirmed that the first call he made back to the office was not long after arriving; by their records it came in just after 12. Jeannot concluded, "So that all lines up. And whoever killed her did so within those three morning hours or so, say between eight thirty and eleven forty-five. Right?"

Mazarelle nodded. "That's my guess." He scanned the attentive faces of his team. "When I arrived, I noticed there were no signs of a break-in, not on the door or in her room. So most likely it was someone she knew. Let's talk suspects."

Tracking Claire's movements, Serge and Jeannot had gone to *Paris-Flash* and loaded up her files, desk calendar, address books, boxes of papers, and the hard drive from her computer. Her legendary Rolodex was enormous. It contained her contacts among royalty; celebrities from the worlds of politics, entertainment, sports, business, fashion, the arts, and the sciences; as well as names of the rich and famous. It was so big it had to be double-bagged. Her secretary became alarmed when he saw how much they were taking. Here, at the pub, they laid out some of their trove for their eager boss's inspection.

Leafing through Claire's calendar, Mazarelle ran over the names. Frank Nash, the visiting American politician. No doubt a lover too. Was he the jealous type? Philippe Riche, her deputy. Claire's intermediary, her bagman, the one who insulated her from the dangers she faced as an editor. Had he gotten in over his head? It was Riche who now would most likely be under the most pressure from Internal Affairs to inform them about contacts with *les ripoux*.

Then there was Luc Fournel. Alain Berthaud's partner at L'Agence AB. Mazarelle had seen enough of Claire's notebook to realize it was dynamite. Perhaps Luc was worried about it too. All their off-the-books financial dealings laid out in black-and-white. Claire might well have represented a serious threat to Luc and his friends.

Mazarelle watched Maurice and Jeannot's eyes as he went down the list. Clearly Claire had led a complicated life, their expressions seemed to say. Why had he made it so much more complicated? If they'd asked, he couldn't have justified himself to them. Nor could he have explained the role of the Hanged Man tarot card found at the site—either the work of a copycat or the same killer. Which was it? Without Mazarelle it would now be their job to find out.

Downing what was left in his glass of beer, Mazarelle held up his empty for a refill as Caitlin came by.

"Anyone else?" she asked, gazing around the table. She enjoyed having the attention of the group of good-looking French cops. Especially the young cute ones.

Mazarelle smiled up at her, a twinkle in his eye. *"Pour tous,"* he ordered, spreading good will. The team cheered, and Caitlin laughed at the way they watched her as she walked off with their order.

"Okay, okay," said Jeannot. "What about the husband? Isn't he always a suspect?"

"*Always* in my house," said Maurice.

The others chuckled, enjoying cap's joke at his own expense.

"But in this case," Mazarelle continued, "probably not. We know that Lavoisier was in Lyon at the time we estimate the murder occurred. And when I met him in my office after he returned to Paris, he seemed strung together by gossamer."

Maurice nodded. "At the autopsy," he said, "he took one quick look at his wife's body and burst out crying. He couldn't stay. I saw him run out. His eyes filled with tears that could break your heart. I suppose he couldn't face what came next. That doesn't strike me as likely behavior of the violent killer we're after."

Jeannot asked, "What do you think, boss?"

"It's not what *I* think anymore. Now it's what Coudert thinks. And he thinks I'm your man. Don't forget, I'm the guy who discovered the body. And I happen to be big enough, and strong enough, and violent enough—don't forget that—to have done the deed."

Jeannot groaned. "Come on. Sure you've got the testosterone. Not to mention *la force à l'état brut*—but you'd never—"

Serge interrupted, "We know you couldn't have done anything like that, Commandant."

"Merci, mon petit," Mazarelle said, patting the young intern on the back. "Tell that to our *patron.*"

Later, as they walked out the door of the pub, saying good night to each other, Jeannot turned to Mazarelle. "So, boss," he said, "what are the next steps?"

Maurice interrupted the young lieutenant. "Now, Jeannot," he said. "We know that with the suspension the commandant has a lot on his mind. We can't ask him to do our jobs for us."

"But, Maurice," said Jeannot, "it's Mazarelle."

Maurice gave Jeannot a firm look. "We'll meet at the office in the morning and talk over our plan." And with that, he headed off down the street toward the Seine.

Jeannot and Mazarelle watched him go.

"Boss," the young detective said, "the shit is raining down from the top. And you can't count on him for an umbrella."

He gave Mazarelle a bittersweet smile.

"You know Maurice. He's a good guy. He admires you, but he's by the book. He'll do his best, but he's not gonna go out on a limb, especially with his family and all. If you want to be sure of clearing your name, you'll need to find the killer yourself."

49

The last thing Mazarelle remembered from the night before was Jeannot dropping him off in front of his building. He thanked him and told him to get back in the car. Next, he'd want to come upstairs to Mazarelle's apartment and tuck him in bed.

The morning after, Mazarelle's mouth was a wasteland. He had a pounding head and couldn't shake the memory of the strange dream he'd had. It began with a knock on the door. And then the clairvoyant had emerged from his sleeping mind. He'd barely thought of Madame Mireille since he'd first met her. Now she had a message for him—straight from his subconscious.

She said, "Just one word."

"Plastics?" he asked.

"Don't be foolish," she snapped. "I mean 'paradox.'"

Mazarelle was about to say "I'm sorry. I don't understand." But she was gone like the ghost of Christmas Past. He wondered if her wisdom might apply to the three murders he'd been thinking about lately, all three by strangulation, and two marked by the tarot card of the Hanged Man. Was paradox relevant to the lives of all three? Mazarelle wondered if it would be relevant to himself. Would he win by losing? He'd certainly lost by being suspended. Maybe next came the good news. With any luck and a change of direction, he hoped at least to see differently.

Despite the strange messages from his alcohol-soaked brain, this morning he seemed to be in one piece. Especially after a very large mug of very black coffee that not only opened his eyes but kept them cocked that way. It also helped that he had "Blue Train" on the phonograph. He enjoyed hearing Coltrane revving up a cascading wall of tenor notes backed by an all-star group. Reaching for his pipe, Mazarelle lighted up. Though there were storm clouds outside, he hoped it wouldn't rain. Not that it mattered. Whatever the weather, and whatever Coudert expected, Mazarelle was determined to begin his pursuit of Claire's killer. And if he wanted to avoid being hassled by his boss's stooges, he would have to leave Paris.

Following his instincts, he knew exactly where to go. But first he would ask Jeannot to get him the information he needed.

50

Hurrying through the Gare de Lyon, Mazarelle barely looked up at the early morning commuters who edged out of the way as he strode across the main concourse. He was in no mood for obstacles. There were enough in his life already.

Around him, the train station glittered and hummed. The third busiest station in all of France. Ninety million travelers a year came through here. And still the station glowed like a Tiffany lamp. Rebuilt for the world exposition of 1900, its sweeping arches, glass and steel ceilings were a monument to the beautiful people and beautiful architecture of the belle epoque.

Mazarelle had no patience for the station. He couldn't wait to leave. Was it possible that Claire had already been dead for three days? Three whole days gone by and no leads. And now that he was suspended from the Brigade Criminelle, he had even less time to waste. Especially with Coudert turning the focus of the investigation his way. There was something odd about that. Well—now that he had to leave town, there was only one way out of this mess. Before he became an official suspect, he had to solve this case himself.

Mazarelle checked the schedule in his hand. He had time before his train left the station to catch a quick café au lait. Sipping the scalding liquid, he thought about making a call back to the office to check in with Maurice, and decided against it. He loved Maurice like a brother. But with him running the case, Mazarelle didn't have high hopes for a quick conclusion.

Maurice was dogged, methodical. He could add columns like no one else on the Quai des Orfèvres. And evidence—Maurice could inventory evidence like a champ, all of it on spreadsheets, tabulated and color coded. Something that eluded Mazarelle. But when it came to inventiveness, deduction—to finding the flash of inspiration buried in that evidence—that wasn't his strength. Maurice's only real vision was for his mighty Elephants, and their World Cup chances. And unless the killer had an amazing first touch on the ball and a rocket right foot, Mazarelle was afraid that Maurice might take years to find him. Not that he himself, he thought ironically, had been doing so remarkably well . . .

It was time to get going. Mazarelle headed down to the end of the platform, and boarded the sleek TGV.

Minutes out of the station, the high-speed train began to move beyond the city. All smooth speed and fire, it sped away and veered into its true glide path. A lovely thing to see. Free from the ground, from everything holding it back, the train raced onward, faster and faster, gaining momentum at over a hundred miles an hour. With its angled nose and its sleek metal fuselage, it flew forward like a great steel blade stabbing into the heart of the French countryside.

Outside the train's windows, the scenery seemed to blur. The rundown, grimy exurbs outside Paris had given way to the landscape of central France—the golden wheat fields shimmering under the sun. Yet for Mazarelle, the whole thing seemed to run together into one beige streak, free of human figures. For all its loveliness, it was the sort of landscape that had solitude built into it—open and empty.

Heading toward Marseille, the miles flew by, a seven-hour ride shrinking down to less than four, as the train hurtled across the countryside, now at over one hundred and eighty miles an hour. And at the quiet, still center of it, Mazarelle sank down into the cushions that supported his lower back.

In the seat next to him were three or four crumpled coffee cups. He sat looking out the window glassy-eyed, the remnants of a half cup in his hand. He took a sip and grimaced. The coffee was terrible. His stomach felt like a knotted knitting bag. What he needed was a good espresso rather than the mud that came out of the SNCF machine in the TGV hallway. It was a penalty for this ridiculous life he was leading. An ace investigator who couldn't even prevent his own girlfriend from getting murdered.

It seemed as if it was raining. It couldn't be raining. The sun was out.

In the window's reflection, all he could see were Claire's sparkling eyes, her lovely profile, her face turning toward him, lit up from within . . .

And still the train rocketed south. It was remarkable how fast you could go, and still be lonely.

For the first time since he'd discovered her strangled body, Mazarelle finally had the time to think about the meaning of Claire's death. The way it had happened, what she had meant to him. The kind of hours they had spent together. The kind of future they might have had. After a half hour lost in painful thoughts, he finally told himself to stop. That sort of thinking wasn't cathartic. It didn't help. Actually, self-reflection, in his experience, never did anyone any good. It hurt too much.

No, forget introspection. It was time to make someone pay. He just needed to make sure that the person who seemed to be responsible for her murder was in fact the one who had actually done it. He looked down at the dark blue folder sitting in his lap. The edges worn down and crumpled from handling. It was a copy of the dossier he had taken from Claire's apartment. He had been studying it a lot over the past two days.

He flipped it open to look inside.

"*Salaud,*" he muttered.

Frank Nash's handsome visage smiled up at him. It was the press picture from a PR package for the U.S. House of Representatives. A three-term congressman. Chairman of the Immigration Subcommittee.

But underneath was where things got interesting. Claire's notes described Nash's past—the scandal that almost derailed his political aspirations. Nash had gone through plenty of girlfriends before. In some articles she'd gathered, he was compared favorably to the young Jack Kennedy—a drive for power and a libido to match. But then there were the unsavory rumors about a cute young teen. Nash had claimed to friends that he was *sure* she was eighteen. She was so pretty. Plus she seemed to know more about sex than anyone he had ever met. He had never seen a body quite so flexible before. And my god, those pierced nipples!

Nash's supporters had called the pregnancy an accident, but it was almost preordained, given all the time the two had spent in the sack. She claimed it was true love. He said nothing at all. It was his father's money—the fortune in furniture—that made the whole mess go away and guaranteed no bumps on Frank's anticipated glide toward the Senate, and who knew what beyond. The entire untidy problem had simply disappeared. And the girl too.

In the media, there had been no mention of the incident beyond rumors. Maybe a few unattributed quotes—less a young Kennedy and more a young Polanski. But no one went too far in that direction, with the threat of libel hanging out there from the entire Nash clan. And so, according to press reports, there was nothing to report.

Except that now, as Mazarelle looked down at the folder in his lap, it was all laid out in Claire's elegant handwriting. The story that everyone had guessed, but no one had known for sure. And Claire had the damaging details—the teenager's name, the number of zeros in the check.

Flipping through the pages, Mazarelle couldn't help smiling. He really missed her. Even if the ambitious Claire had used him—and he had little doubt that was what she had been up to—Mazarelle felt closer to her than at any time since her death. She understood the hunt for facts. She had chased down the details on Nash when no one else could. All brains and charm—such a woman! Sure, she had created a folder on him as well. That had hurt, but he had to respect a good investigative job. Besides, there was nothing really in his file, beyond the way his father had abandoned him and his mother—an almost standard story for a self-absorbed actor. Nothing in that at all. Nothing. Not anything worth talking about. Unlike this . . .

Glancing back down at the folder on his lap, Mazarelle tapped his finger on the photo, right between the eyes of the wealthy American politician. Nash must have caught on. Mazarelle thought the American had probably found out about her digging into his past. He must have been worried. He was a rising star in Congress. The last thing Nash needed was for this old baggage to resurface.

Mazarelle knew motives. To him, this was a gold-plated one—money and power, and the fear of a nasty revelation. In his experience, that was enough to make someone do almost anything. Poor

Claire, all that passion and energy, and she had no idea what she was walking into.

He could still see her naked body spread out across the hotel bed, the terrible bruises around her lovely neck.

Couldn't this damn train go any faster?

51

Just before lunch, the TGV pulled into Marseille's Gare Saint-Charles. Unlike the Paris station, this one was entirely business. A big industrial stone bunker with a shed roof. But that was fine by Mazarelle. He had business to take care of.

Hopping off the train, Mazarelle waved aside the red caps who offered assistance. He threw the overnight bag over his shoulder and headed into the Saint-Charles terminal, following the crowds as they hurried down to the end of the platform. Families and kids, and women dressed for the coming *vacances* in big straw hats and sheer flowery tops. Normally he would have stopped to enjoy the view. Now he had no time.

He decided not to get another coffee as he headed for the doors. He had been through almost a half dozen since leaving Paris, and he was getting tired of burning his tongue. But maybe a quick *chocolat*? The smooth whipped cream that makes the lips feel as if they'd been sent out to the spa. The smell from the snack bar with its stack of freshly baked brioches was enough to lure him over.

He was halfway to the snack bar, when the nearby kiosk stopped him dead in his tracks. Hanging on the front of the kiosk, a magazine cover blown up. With a photograph. *His* photograph. The rugged nose. The craggy cheeks. He was happy to say, he was looking good.

He ran his forefinger and thumb over his proboscis, almost without thinking. Like that TGV locomotive—up front, cutting nobly through space. Maybe not beautiful, but carving a good figure.

The rest of the magazine cover was much less of a treat. His photo and Claire's photo were side by side. And the headline read: "Senior Police Officer Wanted for Questioning in Editor's Murder." What the hell was that? Worst of all, it was Claire's own magazine, *Paris-Flash*.

He grabbed a copy of the magazine, ripped it open, and started to skim through the article quickly. There was not much new there: the strange murder in the pied-à-terre at the Hôtel Château Saint-Germain. The body sprawled across the bed. They did their editor the courtesy of not mentioning her naked final pose. But the conclusion the reporter drew was something else entirely. "Reports have it that the Brigade Criminelle are now interested in talking with one of their own—Commandant Paul Mazarelle—in regard to the murder that has shocked all of Paris in the past week."

Mazarelle took a deep breath as his fingers started to crush the edges of the magazine. This was something *la Crim* never did— hanging one of their own out to dry. Airing the dirty laundry. Whatever the damn metaphor was. He slammed the crumpled magazine back down on the rack. Something was going on here. Someone was screwing with him.

As he turned away, out of the corner of his eye, he caught one final detail—one last sprig of parsley to top off this shit sandwich. The byline. "Hervé Stein is a crime reporter who often writes for *L'Express* and *Paris-Flash*." How about Hervé Stein is a traitor who will turn on his friends when he gets wind of what he thinks is a good story? That son of a bitch now seemed to be accusing him of being Claire's murderer.

And the bastard never even told him that he had an article about Mazarelle himself in the oven. He never even called to ask him for a comment. All that talk about joining an old friend for a quick cognac for old times' sake across the street from the crime scene. All BS. He should have known.

Now, Mazarelle realized, the heat was really on. Once the press got a hold of a story like this, everyone's life at the Quai des Orfèvres would be miserable until they came up with an answer. As for Coudert, he was just the kind of brownnosing bureaucrat who would see the headlines and start worrying about what his bosses were think-ing. That is—if he wasn't feeding the papers the headlines himself.

Mazarelle knew that once the wheels of police bureaucracy started turning, you'd better get out of the way or you'd get caught in the gears. He had to make progress on the case, and he had to do it fast. He owed it to Claire. He owed it to himself. He needed to find her murderer and to clear his name. And that was what he'd come to Marseille to do.

It was time to see Frank Nash.

Out the door of the station, he winced as he made his way down the interminable steps to street level. So many damn steps. His knee twinged—the least favorite souvenir from his days on the rugby field. But he still remembered the shock on that tackler's face when he ran right through him—the gaping arms, the stunned expression. And as he limped forward and dove across the line, grounding the ball, the cheers going up. He'd paid no attention to the wrenching ache in his knee. If there was one thing Mazarelle was good at when pain came in his direction, it was endurance.

He strode down the last steps, and set off on his way.

There was a crowd at the car rental agency. When Mazarelle got to the head of the line they didn't have many cars left. But they did have a deal for him. A brand-new two-door Renault Mégane with stick shift and diesel turbocharger engine.

"How much?"

The clerk looked at the big guy with the impressive mustache and smiled. "I think you'll be pleased."

"What gives you that idea?" asked Mazarelle, ever the skeptic.

"I'm an optimist. Here." He handed him the papers and keys for the car and pointed to the door. "Right out there. It's waiting for you. Hawaiian blue."

"You mean the peewee?" Mazarelle had been expecting a small car, but this was ridiculous.

"Go ahead, try it. You'll love it. It'll fit you like a glove."

"Bullshit! I need one the size of a Hispano-Suiza."

The clerk shook his head. "You're large, but the Suiza is as big as a hotel. We don't handle them. Only Picasso could afford a car like that. And for what this one costs you to rent you've got a bargain. Made in France. Trust me."

"I'll bet."

Outside, Mazarelle opened the car door and gave it a once-over. Cute, he thought, and pushed the driver's seat as far back as it went. Then shoehorning himself behind the wheel of the little Renault, he glanced at the gas gauge, saw that it registered full, and he was on his way.

Mazarelle soon discovered he was lost in the maze of the Quartier Belsunce by Marseille's old port. Turning onto the rue de la Prison, he found himself on one of those streets in Marseille that still retained their earthy names—unlike those Paris roads such as the Headless Woman and the Boulevard of Thieves that had been cleaned up by Haussmann in the nineteenth century. In many other ways as well, Marseille seemed not to have been sanitized. The city still had its dark reputation for drugs, gangs, organized crime, and official corruption. And, Mazarelle thought, maybe a murderer too.

He pulled the little Renault over to the curb. On a stoop nearby, a small group of Senegalese refugees huddled together, watching the traffic, waiting for offers of day jobs. Levering himself out of the driver's seat, Mazarelle stopped a young student with a satchel on his back, hurrying back to his lycée after the lunch break. The young man stared at the inspector and the little car with a worried look.

"Le Sofitel?" he sounded surprised. *"Très cher, monsieur!"*

"No, no." Mazarelle laughed. "Just visiting a friend."

"A friend?" The teenager took in Mazarelle's rumpled jacket with a doubtful expression. "Well, see if they let you in. Head down to the quai, and follow it all the way around the port. You can't miss it."

52

The Sofitel was a sleek, modern, curvilinear building with succulent plants circling its entrance. Mazarelle considered the warm greeting he received at the front desk as five-star pricey. Fortunately he wasn't staying there. The one thing he regretted not sharing was their "Magnifique Spa," which offered their guests the dream of deep tissue massage. But he did have one souvenir from the Sofitel already. He rubbed the tobacco pouch in his pocket. Even in death, Claire had sent him in the right direction.

"May I speak to the manager?" he asked.

The manager's office was dotted with photographs of the hotel's facilities, its grounds, its pool and palm trees, the boats in the harbor. The flower on his desk was an elegant white orchid. The name on his plaque was Kenneth Jarnier, his tan a radiant promise of what Marseille held for their guests. He made it clear that he was there to be of service. Mazarelle pulled out his wallet and, with a nonchalance that suggested he'd been through this sort of drill before, flipped it open. No need to worry anyone about the suspension.

Jarnier scrutinized his photo. "Ah, Commandant Mazarelle! A pleasure. How can I help you?"

"I'd like some information about one of your recent guests. However, I'm not sure what name she may have used." Mazarelle explained that madame was the editor of the well-known magazine *Paris-Flash*.

The manager smiled. "No problem. Many of our guests are celebrities using other names. Do you happen to know if she was traveling alone?"

"No, not with any certainty. But as far as I know, she was here for her work. Anyhow she almost always used her professional name—

Claire Girard. I should explain that I'm investigating her murder. It happened in Paris last week."

"Murder? How terrible!" Jarnier's tan suddenly seemed to have fled. Mazarelle nodded.

"Well . . . let me see . . . I'll check our register."

Though he was obviously flustered, it took him only a second or two.

"Yes, indeed, Commandant—Madame Claire Girard did stay with us for two days last week. I see that madame left us quite early in the morning after her second night at the hotel. In fact, I see that we made the arrangements for her predawn flight back to Paris—"

"Did you also have a Monsieur Frank Nash registered here at the hotel?"

"Nash? Hmmm . . . Yes! We did. They apparently checked in at the same time."

"Can you tell me whether they shared a room?"

"No, they did not—they had separate rooms, but on the same floor."

"One more question. Did they leave together?"

"Let me see . . ." The manager turned a page. "Monsieur Frank Nash is still registered here. Top floor. Opéra Suite."

Mazarelle nodded. Exactly what Jeannot had found out.

As Mazarelle turned in the direction of the elevators, the manager cleared his throat.

"Commandant—did you say she was murdered in Paris?"

"Yes, I did."

"Terrible. Terrible. Well—at least it didn't happen here at the Sofitel—"

"Right!" Mazarelle snapped. "Not the sort of thing that's good for business, is it?"

The elevator was made of glass and chrome, and it moved with the speed and smoothness of an electronic deposit. But that wasn't fast enough for Mazarelle.

He had thought about calling up ahead to Nash. But why give him an advance warning?

As the elevator opened, he shot off down the hall toward the Opéra Suite. Banging on the hardwood door.

"Wait a minute. Wait a minute. *J'arrive!*"

The door to the suite opened. And there was Frank Nash. They'd met once before, in Claire's office, but this time was different.

Mazarelle stared at him for a long moment. Claire had been attracted to this? The slicked-back hair? Even the smile seemed plastic. And based on that smile, Nash clearly had absolutely no recollection of their meeting.

Mazarelle started to reach into his pocket for his badge, and stopped, remembering his suspension once again. But the pause was only a heartbeat. He figured Nash would have no way of knowing about his status. And suspended or not, he had work to do here.

"Commandant Mazarelle. Paris. Brigade Criminelle," he introduced himself. Sternly. Formally.

"Commander. What brings you here?"

To Mazarelle it was all fake American charm. He had no time for charm.

"I'm here on a murder investigation."

"Murder?" Nash looked down the hallway. "You'd better come in."

Seated on the sofa of the opulent suite, a thousand-dollar view of Marseille's Old Port stretching out from the window, Nash opened his arms in his best constituent-greeting style.

"So what's this about a murder?"

Mazarelle had done dozens of friends and family notification visits in his time. But this time out, he was as blunt as a forearm to the chest.

"You knew the victim. Claire Girard."

"Claire." The smile slid off Frank Nash's face. "Claire? Are you sure?"

Mazarelle nodded.

Nash shook his head. "No, that can't be right. I just saw her a couple of days ago." The tears started to well up in his eyes. "That must be a mistake."

To Mazarelle, the emotion seemed a little suspect.

"You haven't heard? It's been in the papers."

Nash gestured forlornly at the *New York Times,* open on the living room table. "I—I guess I haven't been reading the French papers."

He walked over and poured himself some coffee. And turned back to his visitor.

"I'm sorry. I'm forgetting my manners. Would you like some?"

In this already long day, the silver carafe in Nash's hand would no doubt offer the best coffee he would have. But Mazarelle didn't want anything from Frank Nash. He was focused now.

"So what were you doing here?"

"Well, we were researching some of the incidents at the immigrant detention centers. But to be honest"—Nash spread his palms out, all American candor—"I also saw it as the beginning of a relationship. Something special."

"Okay, okay—" interrupted Mazarelle, who didn't especially want to hear about Frank and Claire's love life. "Where were you at the time of the murder?"

"Well," Nash started, then stopped. "What happened to her? When was it? You never told me."

"Three days ago. In Paris. Between eight thirty and noon." That was all the detail Mazarelle was going to offer a suspect.

"Three days ago?" Nash narrowed his eyes, trying to calculate back. "She left for Paris very early that morning. She said she was catching the six a.m. flight. She must have just gotten in."

"And you didn't go with her?"

"No, I was here."

"Can you prove that?"

"Well, I was driving to another center that afternoon. The one at Toulouse-Cornebarrieu. I was meeting people there."

"So no one saw you that morning?" Mazarelle nodded to himself, almost satisfied. "Hmmm."

"Well, I told you, I was driving."

"No one at all?"

"I went alone. I met them, it must have been around two or three."

"Hmmmm." Mazarelle seemed more intent now. "So what you're really saying is that you have no alibi then for that morning."

Even the smooth-talking Nash stopped at that one. "Alibi? But I would never." Finally, he shook his head. "No, I guess not."

He looked out over the Old Port, his thousand-dollar view.

"I did stop for gas. On the highway before Montpellier."

———

A quick phone call to the gas station confirmed it. An American with movie-star looks, driving a sleek BMW? Hard to miss him. He was there at noon. Which meant there was no way he could have been in Paris during any part of that time window.

Dejected, Mazarelle was out of ideas. He'd been almost certain that Nash was his man. Now he wasn't sure what to do next.

There was only one idea he knew that, from past history, was a surefire winner—he could bury his sadness in food.

The manager at his hotel's front desk had a suggestion. Chez Rémy. A great restaurant. And a stunning view of the harbor if you didn't mind walking to get there. It was a nice early evening for a stroll. Warm, but not humid. One of the three hundred or so perfect days every year according to Mazarelle's Marseille guide book.

The manager called ahead for a reservation. Chez Rémy special-ized in bouillabaisse, but they needed a twenty-four-hour heads-up for preparation. At least for most visitors. However, Mazarelle wasn't a detective for nothing. He got on the phone and officially intro-duced himself. The restaurant was happy to oblige an important visi-tor from the famous Brigade Criminelle in Paris.

Mazarelle gathered that it was the sort of high-price place that called for a clean shirt. Which was about as far as he was willing to go by way of presentation. So, a couple of hours later, refreshed and feeling much better at the prospect of food, Mazarelle started out for the restaurant. The luxury yachts and sailboats in the marina seemed to be all tied down and tucked in for the night already.

No sooner did he walk in the door than the host—wearing a merchant officer's peaked black hat—greeted him like an old friend. "Monsieur Mazarelle, of course." He was a party of one, but it made no difference. His mustache was more than welcome here. Mazarelle was led to his table like visiting royalty. The view from the front win-dow even at this hour was spectacular, with a forest of sailing masts spread across the harbor, and, crowning the city at the illuminated top of the hill, Marseille's dazzling Basilique Notre-Dame de la Garde.

His waiter brought a surprise gift from the kitchen, an *amuse-bouche* that actually lived up to its name. Slices of warm toast covered by a thick truffle cream and paper-thin leaves of white truffles. Next came Rémy's *spécialité*. The bouillabaisse. The waiter brought out a huge platter of seafood with some extraordinary looking fish. One orange-colored, big-headed, bony creature with large side fins and sly evil eyes.

Mazarelle laughed, pointing out, "That's the ugliest fish I've ever seen."

"*Pas de panique*," the chatty waiter reassured him. "It's a gurnard. Not pretty but the flavor is quite good. And this one, with the big eye? We call it *jaune d'oré*. John Dory, right? But its real name is Saint Pierre. The rock of the Church."

Mazarelle felt a frisson as he recalled the fisherman who betrayed Christ by denying knowledge of him three times. That same fisherman who would soon after be crucified upside down—just like the Hanged Man. Was this another warning like Berthaud's tarot card, only this time for him? Madame Mireille would say: of course.

Did anyone know that he was down here asking questions about the Paris murders, and still on the case? Well, he thought—until further notice, I am, goddamn it!

When the waiter finally returned with a tureen in which some of the fish had been boiled down to a hot saffron-colored, anise-flavored soup with assorted Provençal herbs and spices—Mazarelle marveled at how the fish had been transmogrified into a broth so smooth and rich and rare, it was like molten gold. A magical sea change.

"How do they do that?" the inspector asked. "What's the secret?"

The waiter smiled. "Julia Child said you have to be born in Marseille to make the authentic bouillabaisse."

And when the sommelier brought the bottle of wine he'd ordered—a Côtes du Rhône grenache blanc—and poured it, Mazarelle drank the glass down in a single swallow. The dinner, proving to be so memorable, was topped off by one of Rémy's exquisite desserts—la tartelette aux framboises.

Mazarelle suddenly felt his stomach rumble, his eyes darken as if a rain cloud had passed overhead. He sat back in his chair, loosened his belt, took a deep breath. That was better. Getting up, he paid the bill and shook hands all around. Rémy walked him to the exit. As he approached the *pharmacie* next door, Mazarelle smiled. The light from the green bulbs outlining the cross in the window bathed his face. It occurred to him that in a pinch they might have a stomach pump inside or at least an *émétique*.

53

On the walk back along the harbor, Mazarelle took out his mobile phone and dialed, prepared for the worst.

Jeannot was glad to hear from him.

"Boss, how are you? Where are you?"

He filled Jeannot in on the details of his trip south. "Nash was a dead end. He alibied out. There's no way he could have made it to Paris in the time frame."

Telling Jeannot to hold on for a minute, Mazarelle pulled out his pipe and tobacco. Perhaps it was the feel of the pouch that unsettled him. Though it had been a wonderful dinner, the only thing missing was Claire herself, and she was so much missed. As he strolled along, phone to his ear, listening to Jeannot talking about the team's doings, the metal rings clinking against one another on the sails in the harbor sounded incredibly lonely to Mazarelle. He wanted to fly back home as soon as possible.

"I guess that's it, Jeannot. I'll be heading back to Paris tomorrow."

"Ah, boss—maybe not."

Jeannot didn't want to ruin his mood. But Mazarelle's mood was now beyond saving already.

"Okay, spit it out."

"It's not looking good." Jeannot sighed. "The PS found your fingerprints all over the apartment."

"Of course, I was there. I told everyone."

"Right, but that's not the way it's playing up the line. They're looking at you as a suspect."

"That's ridiculous."

"Of course it is. But, boss, you'd better find the killer. As soon as you come back here, you're going to be caught up in their questions."

"Well," Mazarelle had to admit, "right now all I've got are questions. I'm not sure what the next move is."

"*Chef*, there is this one thing—something that Maurice came up with—"

"And?"

"He was going through the bank records of the Agence AB, and there were a lot of suspicious deposits. It looks as if they came from magazines."

"Hmm . . ." Mazarelle tried not to sound too disappointed. He had been so focused on Claire, he had lost track of the Babo/Berthaud case. Besides, he knew all about those deposits and their connections to the line items in Claire's little black ledger. Alain Berthaud was clearly the conduit for that money from the magazines to the police. But that didn't get them any closer to the killer. He continued to listen with half an ear, until Jeannot said, "and it looks as if Luc is going to inherit all of Alain's stake in the business. It was in the will, all to him."

And that was a lot of money. Which should put Luc back in the frame as a suspect again. Except that he was in the hospital that night with a perfect alibi. But could there have been . . . ?

The idea came to Mazarelle from out of nowhere.

"Thanks, Jeannot," he said abruptly. "Gotta go."

Luc was a suspicious guy. The only people he might trust were those with whom his bond went a long way back.

54

The next morning, Mazarelle's destination was only about ten miles from Marseille, but in his tiny rental car it felt a lot longer than that. The road sign read Aubagne. After France's exit from its colonial outpost in Algeria, the famed *Légion étrangère* had been headquartered there. Since he'd spoken to Luc Fournel about his experience in the Foreign Legion, Mazarelle had been wanting to make this trip. As he drove up to the entrance gate of the museum, he was struck by the tightness of security. Probably because of 9/11 last year, he supposed. But this barracks town still kept its legendary military museum open to the public.

He parked his car and followed the signs to the museum. On the wall before the entrance was the Legion's motto in huge block letters: LEGIO PATRIA NOSTRA. Staring at the words, Mazarelle finally got the point—the Legion was their fatherland. To would-be legionnaires who'd given up their homeland to come here, it was important to identify with something new. The Legion from its beginning had attracted foreigners with checkered pasts eager to wipe their slates clean with a new name, a new identity, and the possibility of French citizenship. The new recruit was trained in loyalty to the group, pride in being a member of an elite military team. On every side, that tradition of esprit de corps was drilled into the newcomer's head. They came from 140 countries, but now they shared a new bond—a new country—with each other.

Captain Seznec, the young-looking curator of the museum, stressed that fact in his introduction to the pamphlet Mazarelle had picked up on his way in. Not only had Seznec studied for his position at the Museum of the Army but also at the Louvre. Mazarelle sat down to scan the rest of his short intro before going in to see the curator. "The most prized relic that we have," the curator wrote, "is kept in a glass reliquary in our crypt."

Mazarelle was amused. Seznec sounded to him more like Cardinal Richelieu than a military officer.

"The reliquary contains the articulated wooden prosthetic hand that belonged to Captain Jean Danjou. He'd been leading a company of sixty-four men that had run out of ammunition and was defending the Mexican city of Puebla with only bayonets when he lost his hand. Besieged by two thousand revolutionaries in their legendary battle at hacienda Camarón, Danjou and his vastly outnumbered legionnaires took an oath on April 30, 1863, never to surrender. Only three legionnaires survived. Once every year on Camarón Day in Aubagne, the captain's wooden hand is displayed on the parade grounds."

Mazarelle knocked on Captain Seznec's door. When the captain jumped up to meet his visitor, he seemed as young and trim as his picture. Perhaps it was his voice. He stood ramrod straight, his shoulders back, his tan military shirt open at the neck, his epaulettes as flat as if sewn in place with a carpenter's level.

"How can I help you, monsieur?"

Mazarelle explained who he was and why he was there. "Yes, that's right. I'm a reporter. Paul Mazarelle. I'm working on a freelance article about the Legion today. Everyone knows about your heroes of the past. Danjou and the others. But what about the young legionnaires in our time? Are they still as self-sacrificing as they once were?"

"*Bien sûr!* Our training is more demanding now than ever. If you look at *Képi blanc*, our magazine, you'll see what I mean."

Mazarelle asked, "Are you familiar with the name Luc Fournel?"

Seznec thought a moment. "No. I don't think so."

"He was a recruit here not long ago. Maybe ten, fifteen years."

The captain made a dismissive gesture. "Before my time. Why do you ask?"

"I was told this story at a dinner party in Paris. Someone there thought it might interest me. About a young, and extremely brave legionnaire. It was the last day of his four-month training program. The final hurdle before receiving his sealed envelope. Would he be in or out?"

"What did you say his name was?"

"Fournel. Luc Fournel."

Mazarelle repeated the name. This time it seemed to strike a chord in the captain's mind. "And what did he do?"

"He saved someone's life. Won a medal for bravery. And did it while still only a recruit."

The captain was impressed. "How long ago did you say?"

"About fifteen years."

"Definitely before my time, I'm afraid." Seznec sighed. He was sorry not to be of more help, but he had a suggestion.

"Have you been up to our annex yet in the village of Puyloubier? It's not far. Less than thirty miles. We have our Hall of Heroes there. Original portraits and early uniforms in fabulous condition. Strange weapons from all over the world. And a wall of medals as well. I suggest you speak to Staff Sergeant Jacques Delapierre who's in charge of our collection there. He's been with us a long time. And if there's any legionnaire who knows what happened to your man Fournel, it would be the sergeant. Though he's only got one eye, he's seen more than most folks with two."

Standing up, they shook hands. Seznec could feel the granite in the reporter's grip. This guy, he thought, must have broken more than a few pencils in his time. A few bones, too. The captain smiled. "Tell him I sent you."

The legionnaires had an Hôpital des Invalides and a veterans cemetery in Puyloubier that Mazarelle had read about. He planned to skip them. But, time permitting, their vineyard, though relatively small, might be worth a tasting or two. As for the captain's tip about Sergeant Delapierre, that was the lead he thought most promising. And when he actually met the sergeant and introduced himself, there was even more that grabbed Mazarelle's interest. With a patch over one eye and a livid scar below, Delapierre was a most remarkable-looking man. He'd been a sapper and still had the engineers' cool steady gaze, long black whiskers streaked with gray, and the upright bearing of someone who knew how to shoulder an ax. What also pleased Mazarelle was the small red tattoo on the underside of Delapierre's wrist. But when he told Delapierre that he was writing about Luc Fournel, asked if he knew him, and saw the sergeant smile, it was then Mazarelle sensed he'd struck gold.

After they'd moved to the sergeant's office and were sharing a bottle of the Legion's own Côtes de Provence, one bearing their label "Domaine Capitaine Danjou," Delapierre began telling him the tale—riveting to Mazarelle—of his recruits' final march, the last test they always took to qualify for the Legion. Those who finished and were still on their feet would probably graduate. Those who didn't were dumped. It was a forced march. Three days of high-energy, nonstop agony. Carrying full kit over distance.

"The time that Fournel did the march," Delapierre said, "the group started out close-knit and looking as if they might go the distance trekking together along the banks of the Rhône, which was almost at flood stage. But by the end of the second day, the weather had turned so foul they were strung out all along the marshy trail like camel shit. Then came the last day. They woke to a cold high wind, ratcheting up to a full-blown mistral that snapped at them from behind. And the needle-sharp drizzle became a mist that became a fog all along the muddy bank."

Sergeant Delapierre described how he'd turned to Fournel and said, " 'Get up to the front of the line, Luc, and tell those jackasses to slow down and wait for us. I don't want to lose any of those beauties of mine in this soup. We're on our way.' I myself arrived in time to see one of my men knocked into the water by a falling tree. Pinned beneath it, he screamed for help. Fournel dove head first into the icy Rhône. Grabbing the legionnaire's heavy backpack, Fournel yanked it off his shoulders and dragged him out from under the branches of the fallen tree. Then, in one desperate maneuver, Fournel lifted him up toward the bank. He saved his life."

Stomping his foot as if to mark where it happened, Delapierre asked his visitor, "How about that?"

Mazarelle took out a pad and said, "The recruit who was rescued— what was his name?" The sergeant's face clouded over, a worried look. His tongue scurried across his lips as if searching for leftovers. Swallowing what remained in his wineglass, he shrugged and shook his head. "It's my memory. Let me think about it for a bit. These things sometimes take me time now."

"Right. Of course. And Fournel, for his courage? What did he get?" Mazarelle asked.

"A five-year service contract. And for his selfless act of heroism, the Legion's Medal of Honor. I'll show you one downstairs." And when they went downstairs, Delapierre remembered to show Mazarelle a medal like the one Fournel received, but not the name of the recruit he rescued.

The sergeant was better about the legionnaires' uniforms, their weapons, the battles in which they were used. As for Mazarelle, he was curious about everything, even the captured weapons like the Zulu's assegai, which was used for murdering enemies noiselessly at a distance. And when Delapierre showed him a glass case containing one of their own unconventional weapons and how it was used, Mazarelle was positively thrilled. There were two mannequins in the case, one in back of the other. And like all those in the exhibition, these two were extremely lifelike, their cheeks ruddy, their poses so flexible that they lifted the entire exhibition to a level of high drama. But it was their weapon that especially fascinated Mazarelle.

The sergeant brightened when he noticed the reporter's interest, and he was eager to talk about the weapon. "This one we still carry on commando raids. We've labeled it 'sentry removal.' The weapon we call 'la loupe.' The silent killer. It's a double-looped garrote. And works just the way you see it there in the glass case. The attack is from behind, and in close quarters it's deadly. The attacker drops his double loop over his enemy's head. And no sooner does the victim feel the garrote tightening around his neck—and frantically pulls on it to loosen it, to tear it away—than he ends up tightening the second loop. There is no escape."

"Clever," said Mazarelle.

The sergeant agreed. "All my men were trained in its use. And some of them were absolute wonders. Which reminds me . . ." His face broke out in a smile from ear to ear. "I'll be damned! No, it's not the name of the recruit who Luc saved. That'll probably come to me sooner or later. It's something else about him. He was amazing with *la loupe*. Could have been an instructor. He was great with survivalist skills. One of our best. Leave me your phone number in Paris, and if I can help with a name I'll get back to you."

It was on the way out that they passed the boutique for visitors to the veterans hospital. On the sound system, Edith Piaf was finishing "Mon Légionnaire."

"What a voice! But I get tired of hearing the same goddamn song all the time," griped Delapierre.

Mazarelle noticed that a couple walking away from the counter with purchased gifts was speaking German.

"We get a lot of *boches* here," Delapierre told him.

Mazarelle pointed to the *képi blanc* on the shelf behind the sales clerk. He asked if they had a small one that might fit a child.

"How old?"

"Small."

"We have small."

As Delapierre waited, Mazarelle arranged for the *képi blanc* to be sent to Maurice and his wife as a present for their young son. A *képi* for the little captain. Maurice had a lot on his shoulders these days. That might make him smile.

Then eyeing the display of rouge, blanc, and rosé wines, Mazarelle bought a bottle of rouge for the sergeant and one for himself. Taking a card, Mazarelle put down his home address and, handing it to Delapierre along with one of the bottles, he said, *"Merci mille fois, mon frère."*

55

Not long after Mazarelle had left, the sergeant opened his small personal address book, dialed Paris, and soon recognized the familiar hard, flat sound of Luc Fournel at the other end of the line.

"Good to hear your voice, Luc. It's been a while."

"How you been, Sarge? What do I owe my good luck to?"

"I've just had a visit from a guy who was very interested in you."

"That so? Do I know him? Some old friend of ours?"

"Never saw him before. A big guy. With the largest goddamn horseshoe under his nose I've ever seen. And I've seen my share of 'staches. You might say I've seen them all." His laugh ended in a wheeze that sounded like emphysema. "But—but—that's not why I called. He wanted to know all about you. All about the forced march the lot of you were on as recruits and how you won your medal."

"What! I don't believe this. That was ages ago. Who was this guy?"

"A free-lance reporter doing a story about the Legion today. Do our recruits still have the right stuff? He'd heard about you. How your buddy had fallen in the river and you dove in to save his life. He loved what I had to tell him. Couldn't get enough of it."

"This reporter. Did you get his name?"

"Mazarelle," Sarge said. "Paul Mazarelle. A good guy. I liked him." There was a pause. "You don't know him, do you?"

Luc said, "No. I don't. But if you hear from him again, do let me know. And thanks, Sarge."

Luc felt as if he'd swallowed something that had gone down the wrong tube. But he needed only a few seconds to recover.

Picking up his phone again, he called a familiar number.

"Glad I got you in. I just heard from our friend Delapierre. He had an exciting visitor at the Legion's Hall of Heroes in Puyloubier. Said he was a reporter. Interested in our old rescue story. And guess what his name was?"

"Please—no games."

"It was Paul Mazarelle."

The response at the other end of the line was explosive.

"Yeah, right," Luc sneered. "Of course, it was him. He's supposed to be suspended. But he's still working the case."

Only a hissed intake of breath.

"Listen, you're as much at risk as I am. Maybe even more."

The voice at the other end was calm now. No hesitation.

"Great," Luc said. "Do it!"

56

It was still early in the morning when Mazarelle got off the plane and grabbed a taxi into the city. Though he hadn't been gone long from Paris and his team, it seemed forever. He'd made some progress in Marseille, but any longer he'd be wasting his time. If there was a penalty to pay for going back now, he thought, the hell with it. He had a lead—a possible tie-in for all three killings. It was time to get moving. He was tired of sitting around gathering rust. He'd risk it.

The sun was just coming up over the river, giving him a lovely glimpse of his favorite waterway. At 36 Quai des Orfèvres, his taxi driver pulled up in front of the guard at the door who recognized the commandant and waved. The BC didn't get too many of their top brass arriving this early in the morning.

Mazarelle's heavy footsteps echoed across the near-empty main floor hallway and up the staircase. On the third floor, he was surprised to see the door to the main office wide open and the lights on inside. But it was just someone from the cleaning crew vacuuming. He was glad no one else was around. No need to stir up trouble. Much better to keep a low profile.

Without stopping to see who was in, or checking his mailbox, he continued up the stairs to the fourth floor with its familiar smells. His office door was closed. A light streamed out from beneath it. He didn't expect Maurice or any of their team to be in at that hour. Not yet. But someone had left Mazarelle's desk lamp burning as if he were expected back any minute. A nice touch, he thought. There was a small pile of mail for him that he planned to get to later. It could wait. What interested him now was Maurice and their team, and what they'd been up to.

From the pile of transcripts and tapes on Maurice's desk, Mazarelle concluded that they'd already interviewed a number of the suspects he'd suggested at Donovan's. But before he could examine any of the transcripts, the office door flew open. It was Maurice holding two cups of steaming coffee precariously balanced in his hands—one for himself, and the other for the next early bird to arrive—and on his face a look of utter amazement.

"When did you get back?" Maurice handed him the extra cup. "Take it. We weren't expecting you quite so soon."

"Thanks," said Mazarelle, putting his mug down. "I've got mine already."

"So when did they lift your suspension?" A concerned look flashed across Maurice's face. "They did lift your suspension, right?"

Mazarelle smiled. "Not exactly. I missed you guys. I wanted to find out what you were up to."

"I can tell you," Jeannot announced, coming in the door. "The minute you left, Cap had us working our butts off."

"It probably did you good," said Mazarelle.

Jeannot pumped his outstretched hand enthusiastically. "Glad to see you, chief. It may not have been long, but you were missed."

"Here, finish this," Mazarelle cut him off abruptly, handing him his coffee. "Don't go getting cheesy on me." He eyed the biker's getup Jeannot was wearing with a puzzled look. The sunglasses, the blue shorts, the blue helmet, the blue T-shirt with the name BELLEVIEW BLEUS BC emblazoned on it with a cheery slogan: *Allez les Bleus!*

"Another undercover job like the one we had on July fourteenth?"

"You're joking." Jeannot pointed to the name on his chest. "It's my bike club. I've got a new Ridley with a Fenix SL carbon frame."

"That's how you get to work these days?"

"Coming and going. Best of all, it keeps me in shape. And I can lock it up right downstairs in the courtyard."

Mazarelle said, "If you're not careful someone comes off the street with a pick—and your bike is gone!"

Jeannot turned to Cap. "Be right back. I've got to go downstairs to change."

Mazarelle watched him go, smiling wryly.

"Don't worry," Maurice assured him. "It's his latest girlfriend—so to speak. He doesn't let her out of his sight for more than a heartbeat."

"They last longer that way," Mazarelle said glumly. "Girlfriends can get bored. Or disappear."

He looked around the office, taking in the stacks of papers—the interviews, the murder book notes.

"So, what've you got?"

Maurice shifted uncomfortably in his chair. "Look, boss, you know how much you mean to us. But you really shouldn't be here."

Mazarelle gave him a slow grin, and said nothing. He'd let Maurice come to his decision in his own time.

Maurice shook his head.

"We can't."

Still Mazarelle kept his silence.

"I didn't work this hard to get myself fired."

"Okay, sure." Mazarelle got up to go. "By the way, did your son get that *kepi blanc*?"

Maurice had forgotten the white hat that had arrived by express Chronopost from the Legion. He couldn't keep the smile from his face.

"Oh, my god," Maurice said, "my wife wanted me to thank you for your present. She's never seen our boy so happy. Since your *kepi* arrived, he hasn't stopped marching around the house like a young recruit."

"I'm glad he likes it."

"He wouldn't go to sleep last night unless we let him wear the damn thing to bed!"

"I thought he might like to pretend he was a legionnaire."

"Loves it. Though it's not exactly the career his mother and I had in mind for him." Maurice smiled. "But thanks, boss. Nice of you to send it."

Maurice stared at his suspended boss for a long moment. Then, with a sigh of surrender, he patted Mazarelle's chair.

With a contented grin, Mazarelle sank his ample frame into the seat behind his desk.

"So give me the rundown."

Before Maurice could say anything, the door to the office slammed open, and Jeannot was back, standing in the doorway.

"We've been busting our asses," he announced with a grin.

Maurice drew himself up. "Actually, we have done quite a lot in the past few days. We've interviewed the other tenants at the Château Saint-Germain. We even called in Frank Nash, who told us you'd questioned him in Marseille. We've talked to almost everyone on the suspect list except Nico Manfredi—the racing car hotshot. Tracking him down hasn't been a picnic. He's got a long list of lady friends, drugs, you name it. But no one, including his wife, seems to know where he is."

Jeannot jumped in. "As for the husband, Lavoisier, we talked with him after the autopsy. There's nothing there. He didn't seem to be jealous about her love affairs at all. In fact, he was actually on the deed for that apartment. I guess they really did have an open marriage and . . ."

At the other end of the office, Maurice's intercom suddenly came alive.

"Captain Kalou?"

It was Coudert's assistant. Maurice walked to his desk and flipped the switch.

"Yes? Yes? What is it, Nicolas?"

"The *patron* would like to see you, Captain. Would you please stop by his office this morning at eleven?"

"*Bien sûr*. I'll be there."

The cloud hanging over Maurice's face as he walked back to his teammates only increased their anxiety. They looked at one another nervously. Noticing their concern, Maurice tried to brush it aside. "Nothing to worry about. I suppose he wants an update on our investigation. I'll take care of it."

Turning to Mazarelle, Maurice said, "He hasn't bothered us until now . . ."

"He probably just needs to be reassured. As for me, Maurice, I'd better get the hell out of here. I'm thinking I'll take the back way."

"Good idea!" said Jeannot. "I'll give you a heads-up. See if the coast is clear."

57

I t wasn't until he was outside the building, walking along the small book stalls on the banks of the Seine, that the thought hit him. In fact, it was the handwritten manuscript dangling from one stall, some kind of nineteenth-century legal document fluttering in the breeze, that reminded him. A deed of sale.

Lavoisier had told Jeannot he was the owner of Claire's apartment. But he had told Mazarelle he didn't even know it existed. So which was it? If Lavoisier really had a deed, then he probably had a copy of the key to the apartment. Which would let him in with no sign of forced entry. They needed to talk to Armand Lavoisier again. He called Jeannot on his mobile and told him to contact Claire's husband. Ask him to come in for some questions.

But Armand Lavoisier was at the Deauville Film Festival and would be there for several days, according to Emily, his housekeeper. Jeannot repeated the details of his exchange with Emily to Mazarelle. She'd reported that she herself was about to leave for a short vacation. She'd tell Monsieur Lavoisier that Lieutenant Jean Villepin of the Brigade Criminelle wanted him to call when he returned.

"When did you say that would be?" Jeannot had asked.

"Early next week. Monsieur is serving on the jury of the film festival."

"Tell him it's important."

"Don't worry, I'll be sure to say you called. Does he have your number?"

Jeannot had given her his number.

"Is this about madame's death? It was so awful. I couldn't believe it."

"Don't forget," he'd urged her. "Tell him I'm expecting his call."

That they wouldn't be able to question Claire's husband until he returned to Paris annoyed Mazarelle. He was now following two trails—the Legion and the husband. Although there was no help for it, he was painfully aware that the farther they got from the first two or three days after the murders, the colder their trails were becoming.

But thinking the matter over he realized that the husband's absence had given him an opportunity he hadn't expected. And so, later that day he parked his car not far from the Lavoisiers' house in the First Arrondissement. They lived very close to the headquarters of the Banque de France with its tapestries and *Galerie dorée*. He was amused at the proximity to the original settlement of the city of Paris. Its red-hot center, so to speak. How like Claire, Mazarelle thought. Putting herself where the money was.

Their house had a dark walnut double door that glowed as if it had been regularly polished for years. Mazarelle rang the bell. He could hear the sound tintinnabulating as it darted from room to room looking for someone to answer. He banged on the door. It didn't seem as if anyone was inside, so no problem—any more than the door itself. Checking the lovely old metalwork on the lock, he found the lock pick he needed and slipped it effortlessly into the keyhole. Mazarelle passed through the door as if it didn't exist.

The living room's parquet floor gleamed. And with the sunlight pouring in from the street, there was no trouble finding his way around. He wanted to make short work of checking the premises and getting out before he discovered the house wasn't empty. The white suits had been there, but apparently had found nothing. There was a circular staircase leading up to the floor above. Mazarelle pulled on his latex gloves and hurried upstairs.

What was it he was looking for in their bedroom? He didn't really know for sure. Anything that might be helpful. He remembered something his wife had once told him when he asked about her friend Juliette's marriage to Fabriani. She'd laughed and said, "Don't ask. Who knows about other people's marriages?" At the time he wondered if it was good advice or simply an evasion. Now it was

Claire's marriage that he was wondering about. Uncomfortably he thought maybe he was just being prurient.

In the master bedroom, the two of them shared a king-size bed that was bookended by two large walk-in closets. The first was Claire's. He'd know that delicious smell anywhere. And the bright colors. A dazzle of dresses none of which he'd ever seen her wear or would. And all her jackets and skirts hung with exquisite care. They'd been neatly arranged as if tagged and alphabetized. They'd never get lost the way he'd lost her. Lost the way Mazarelle now felt himself, as he began to have increasing doubts about why he'd come here at all.

He noticed the blue silk jacket she'd worn that first day they'd met in his office. But where was the large gold pin she had on? He opened the bottom drawer of the small bureau against the wall, and there was her emerald-colored jewelry box. Her gold sunburst with its turquoise core was on top of the trove. It had looked even more beautiful on her lapel. Mazarelle dug into Claire's treasury but there was no sign of her precious pendant—the *oiseau*. He closed the box and hurried across to her husband's closet, glancing out the window as he passed it.

Across the street, someone was looking up at the house. He had seen him before. Then he realized where. It was the bald-headed man waiting outside Coudert's office. Was he one of the *patron*'s lackeys? Was Mazarelle being followed? What did Coudert himself have to do with any of this? Clearly, his time was running out.

Inside her husband's closet the colors were dark—muted blacks, blues, and charcoal grays, with an occasional zinc white thrown in. Mazarelle's hands went instantly to Lavoisier's blue blazer, the one he'd worn the day she was murdered. His fingers sped through the pockets. At first he found nothing more than a crumpled handkerchief that might have been used to dry Lavoisier's tears. But there was one more unexpected pocket—a second inside one. Narrow. Hard to get into for someone with hands as large as his. He forced three fingers in and pulled out a sealed white envelope with no address.

Mazarelle sat down on the bed. Hesitated a moment and then ripped the envelope open.

Et voilà. Claire's *Oiseau de Paradis*! The pendant's gold clasp broken as if it had been torn from her soigné neck before it too was broken. How could anyone have done that to her, least of all her husband? Mazarelle didn't think he had the physical strength, or the cruelty, or the evil in him. Where was his love? He angrily stuffed the envelope back in Lavoisier's pocket.

Leaving the closet, he glanced quickly down at the empty street. There was no sign of the baldy. Could he have been mistaken? Either way, he was running out of time.

He hurried downstairs, hoping he had enough time to check out Lavoisier's study. Above the desk, a black-and-white blowup from a G. W. Pabst silent film *Pandora's Box*—the story of the seductive Lulu, a young woman whose raw sensuality led to tragedy—and a date with Jack the Ripper. In Pabst's film, Lulu was played by the American actress Louise Brooks, a stunner with black patent leather bangs. Henri Langlois, the French film historian, once said, "There is no Garbo, there is no Dietrich, there is only Louise Brooks." Mazarelle thought Claire, who looked a bit like Brooks, was even more beautiful.

Turning from the poster, Mazarelle gave a little shiver. Claire had ended up like Lulu. Another flower ripped out of the earth. With a sigh, he poked through the large modern desk. Its deep drawers intrigued him. Did Lavoisier keep his personal letters there or somewhere else in the house?

In the bottom drawer he found something. A small beat-up green cardboard box held together by two thick rubber bands. On its surface the message: "Tarot of Marseilles." Beneath it, "Seventy-eight cards." He immediately searched through the deck for number XII, the Hanged Man, the familiar inverted figure with his long hair hanging down. Where the hell was it? Losing patience, Mazarelle began to count the cards in the deck. There were seventy-seven and no Hanged Man. Was it missing or had he miscounted? It wasn't proof of anything, but . . .

He'd begun counting again when he heard the front doorbell shriek in alarm. He slammed the cards into their box, snapped the rubber bands around it, and tossed the deck back into the drawer. The doorbell rang again, more insistently this time. He could feel the shock through his entire body. He had to get out of there *now*.

Mazarelle fled through the living room, the dining room, the kitchen, and lucked out when he came to a door that led to the backyard. Fumbling with the lock, he finally opened it and rushed out, ran up the block, and raced around the corner to his car.

As he drove back to his apartment, Mazarelle was overwhelmed by the implications of what he'd found in Lavoisier's house. How could he have been so blind? He'd understood that Claire's husband was jealous of Frank Nash. But he couldn't imagine Lavoisier killing his wife. Yet . . .

At the next red light, Mazarelle called the office and spoke to Maurice. Told him he'd found some new evidence in the Lavoisier house in the First Arrondissement. Evidence that the white suits had missed. Told him that he thought it could help their case.

"Sounds interesting," Maurice said. "But if you bring it in, you know we can't use it."

Mazarelle chuckled. "I wasn't going to remove anything there. I'm suspended, Maurice. But you certainly can. It's all still there. Take one or two of our guys with you and get over to their house as soon as you can."

Describing the two items he wanted, Mazarelle gave Maurice specific instructions about where to find them. Then, as an afterthought, he asked him to get her husband's toothbrush from his bathroom, or any other item there that might have DNA.

"And keep it virgin until you give it to the ME. Okay, Cap?"

"Got it."

Which was when Mazarelle realized that he was almost home. He parked his car and went upstairs to pour himself a very large, very smooth snifter of Delamain XO Pale and Dry. Now he would sit back, sip his brandy, and wait to see what happened when Lavoisier returned.

58

The next day Mazarelle couldn't stay away from 36. When he got to the office early in the morning, he was surprised to find Jeannot not already there. Fixed to his computer screen as if pasted to it. "What are you doing?" Mazarelle asked him. "Have you been here all night?"

Jeannot glanced over his shoulder and crooked his finger at Mazarelle, calling him over. "Check this out, boss. You've got to see this."

The screen showed some ominous images. The shattered windows of a Jewish bakery on the edge of the city. A headline about a swastika and a late-night attack. Mazarelle leaned in for a closer look.

"No, no," said Jeannot. "Not that one. This one." His finger jabbed at the other side of the monitor.

Flashes were going off, as a *Figaro* news video tracked a chic tanned couple walking arm in arm on the red carpet waving at a crowd of smiling fans. The two of them were at opening night at the Deauville American Film Festival. The white-haired Canal+ executive, Armand Lavoisier, in black tie and tuxedo—a rosette in his buttonhole—resuming his public life as a member of the festival jury. On his arm, his new girlfriend, the stunning young Tunisian starlet Yasmine Duvall. She wore a sweeping white gown with a startling neckline that plunged to her navel. Around her throat, a single chain of gold and in her hand a bold print clutch.

Jeannot pointed to the screen. "There he is! The grieving husband not long after the tragic murder of his wife. What do you think, boss?"

Mazarelle suggested he calm down. "That's what we're here to find out."

"Look at the cleavage on that woman!"

Mazarelle laughed. "Anything else you've discovered?"

"How about the pieces of evidence you asked us to bring back from Lavoisier's house," Jeannot wondered aloud. "Will they be enough to rattle her husband?"

"I certainly hope so. If Maurice hasn't scared him off already."

Jeannot said, "He knows we're expecting him here in Paris this morning at ten. I warned him, 'Don't be late.' He didn't like that. I suppose we've cut short his time in Deauville with his new girlfriend. He complained that he'd already answered your questions once. Wasn't that enough?"

Mazarelle smiled. "I'd say he sounds a little cranky. Probably a good start for interviewing him."

Jeannot nodded. "That's what I thought."

Maurice got the call from the main office. Armand Lavoisier had just come in. He'd arrived late.

"Tell him to wait," Maurice said. He'd learned that one from his boss.

Everyone was in place and Maurice had already set up his ground rules for their interview. The recorder was on his desk. He'd be conducting the questioning himself. Anyone with something to ask was encouraged to feel free. As long as they passed their questions to him in writing. "And of course," he added, "the same goes for you, too, Commandant."

Mazarelle, sitting behind the team, nodded. He took out his meerschaum and pouch. Lighting up, he leaned back and prepared to enjoy his first pipe of the day.

Maurice checked his watch. "Okay," he said to Jeannot, "bring him up."

As Armand Lavoisier walked into the office, he seemed confused. It was as if he'd never been there before.

"Please, have a seat." Maurice pointed to the chair opposite his desk. "Thanks for coming. Sorry to pull you away from Deauville. I've heard it's wonderful at this time of year when the film festival is on. Is that why you were there?"

"That's right. I was asked to serve on the jury. But when I explained why I had to leave, the president of the jury understood. This comes first."

"That was good of him. It must have been a considerable relief for you to be at Deauville after the awful death of your wife."

"Yes, it helped a little." Lavoisier sighed heavily.

Mazarelle was struck by how subdued he sounded. He thought Lavoisier looked much better on TV in his tuxedo and black tie with Mademoiselle Duval on his arm. Now he was wearing a wrinkled shirt open at the neck with no tie, and looked as if he hadn't slept all night. He obviously hadn't shaved.

Before Lavoisier had time to settle back in his chair, Maurice began rapid-fire questioning. "Why did your wife go down to the South of France with Frank Nash?"

"They were working on an article about immigrant detention centers. That's really all I know about it. Other than that they were both interested in the subject."

"Was she doing it for her magazine?"

"That's possible. You'd have to ask Philippe Riche."

"Did you know Frank Nash?"

"Not really. Only by reputation."

"The last time you were here, you were asked about the whereabouts of the expensive present you gave your wife—the jeweled pendant she called her *Oiseau*. You said you didn't know where it was. It seemed she hadn't taken it with her on her trip south. So you told the commandant you'd check at home to see if it was there."

"Yes . . ."

"Well—did you?"

Mazarelle, who'd been admiring the pace of Maurice's questioning, eyed Lavoisier closely, eager to hear his answer. An uncomfortable silence followed.

"I did," Lavoisier finally said, "but I couldn't find it."

Maurice gave him a withering look. "Really? Well we found it in your inside jacket pocket. The blue blazer. How come?"

Her husband blanched. "In my jacket pocket? In my house? What were you doing in my house?"

Maurice brushed past his question.

"When you returned from Lyon, you said you didn't know where it was."

"That's true," he said, his words coming out in gushes. "I was so distraught—I'd just heard the news of what happened—I couldn't believe it. Claire murdered. I'd completely forgotten that she'd given her necklace to me before she left for her trip. The clasp had been broken. She asked if I'd bring it back to the jewelers to have it repaired— Van Cleef and Arpels on the Place Vendôme."

"Well—did you?" Maurice asked.

Lavoisier didn't seem to know what to say. Finally he admitted, "I forgot."

Her husband had such a woebegone look on his face that Maurice almost felt sorry that he'd asked. But not too sorry to miss another opening. "On the phone, Frank Nash told us that Madame Girard was wearing her pendant on their trip. How could she have been wearing it if the pendant was still in your house in Paris?"

Lavoisier shook his head. "He's wrong, that's all. Nash is making a mistake. My wife had all sorts of unusual necklaces he knows nothing about."

Maurice glanced at the notes on his desk. "Nash seemed to remember that it was the necklace she called her *Oiseau de Paradis*. How do you explain that?"

"I know very well how I explain that. The *Oiseau* was a precious gift I gave to my wife after a great deal of thought and care as an expression of my love for her. And I know she prized it greatly. So he might have read about that somewhere. Very likely in some fashion magazine. Or perhaps she mentioned it in passing. As for Mr. Nash, my wife and I knew very little about him and, quite candidly, he knows even less about us and Claire's jewelry."

Without pausing and with surprising sangfroid, Lavoisier said, "Let me make a suggestion, Captain. You're a busy man—as are we all here. So perhaps there are some other areas of questioning about which I might be more helpful to you in tracking down my wife's murderer."

Maurice hesitated, sorry to give up his questioning about the *Oiseau*. He exchanged glances with Mazarelle who gave him a subtle sign to get on with things.

"All right"—Maurice nodded—"how about this? As we were in your study, looking through the bottom drawer of your desk, monsieur, we came upon a deck of tarot cards. What were they doing there? What did you use them for?"

"What the hell is that supposed to mean? What were you doing there? Who gave you the right to barge into my house and go through my closets, my desk, my personal things when no one was home? Did you have any official permission to do such a thing? A *mandat de perquisition*? This isn't the Wild West, goddamn it! This is France—the twenty-first century."

Mazarelle put his pipe down and rose up. His mustache airborne, his shoulders back, he was a menacing presence. His voice was calm, his gaze fixed on their suspect. His promise of keeping quiet a thing of the past.

"You seem to forget, monsieur, this is a murder case we're dealing with here. I suggest if you want to help us get to the bottom of your wife's death that you do your best to control your emotions. Everyone in this room wants to help you." He turned to Maurice. "Since you've already mentioned the tarot cards that were found in monsieur's desk, Captain, I wonder if you'd mind my asking a few questions about them?"

"Not at all." Maurice handed over his role with obvious relief.

Striding across to where Armand Lavoisier was seated near the recorder on Maurice's desk, Mazarelle asked where he bought his tarot cards.

"As a matter of fact, I didn't. They were a present from an old friend. A gift. It came in a green box called 'Tarot of Marseilles.'"

Mazarelle pointed to the box on Maurice's desk. "It says there should be seventy-eight cards. That's a lot. Let me count them."

Sitting down, Mazarelle thumbed through the deck faceup, counting the cards with remarkable speed given the size of his fingers. "Seventy-seven," Mazarelle said. "Only one card appears to be missing. Interesting. The exact same one that I found clenched in Madame Girard's hand. The Hanged Man."

Lavoisier paled, but his voice held steady. "An odd coincidence. But I had no idea, Commandant, that you'd found a tarot card in Claire's hand. That is weird. What do you think it means?"

"Our *patron* believes we have a serial killer at work—"

"I see!" interrupted Lavoisier, as if it had come to him out of the blue. "So you're thinking it's a kind of warning—like the card on the dead body of the private investigator hanging in the canal. Was her death connected? Is that what you're telling me?" His incredulous voice squeezed an octave or more higher before it jumped out of his throat. "You can't be serious!"

Mazarelle assured him that they were quite serious. "We certainly considered that possibility. But the two murders were so different. The first one, the cool, ultraprofessional, garroting murder of Alain Berthaud, who was killed from behind, with a minimum of blood and clues; the second a crime of emotion in which your wife was killed violently, brutally, at the hands of her angry attacker, her body badly bruised by the fury of his onslaught. A crime by someone who in all likelihood was well acquainted with his victim . . . A crime, as they say, of passion."

Lavoisier's face turned the color of cement. His hands went to his forehead as he shook his head, covered his eyes. "How could any-one—?" he said, groaning. "How she must have suffered!"

"I'm afraid so, Monsieur Lavoisier. But permit me to digress. What do you know about the meaning of the Hanged Man tarot card?"

"What? I don't know . . ."

"Well, then let me tell you. The most obvious meaning, as you yourself mentioned before, was as a warning. A red flag for someone to keep his mouth shut, not turn informer for the *flics*. But another older meaning—going back to at least the fourteenth century—extends to the origin of tarot cards in northern Italy. Did you know that the cards were originally hand-painted images?"

Lavoisier raised an eyebrow, as if to say "So what?"

"Right," said Mazarelle. "They called it a *pittura infamante*—a punishment for betrayal. Often a specific kind of betrayal . . ." Maz-arelle paused. Then, gazing steadily at Lavoisier and lowering his voice, he said, "Adultery."

Lavoisier looked as if someone had dropped a noose around his neck. Taking a deep breath, he pulled himself together.

"All right, Commandant—but the card in Claire's hand. Tarot cards like that could have come from anywhere. Those decks can be bought in a thousand places in Paris. They're mass-produced."

"Of course," said Mazarelle patiently. "But, you see, our forensics division is superb. We have ways of determining exactly which of those thousands of decks this particular card came from. And your deck is a little more unusual than you may have realized." Here, he was embellishing a little. But the pale expression on Lavoisier's face told him to press on.

"Even then . . ." Lavoisier took a breath. "Even if you can tell—then someone must have stolen the card from my deck and planted it on Claire. Someone who wanted to implicate me—"

"Well—we've even considered that possibility, but think it unlikely. Much more likely that someone planted the card to divert us with the idea of a serial killer. Someone who had a much more personal motive."

"So that's what you're getting at!" Armand Lavoisier had worked himself into a fury. He jumped up, his eyes opened wide in alarm. He was shouting now. "Can you really believe that I murdered my own wife? I loved her. Do these look like the hands of a strangler?" He held up his manicured fingers high in the air to show the commandant. "That's impossible! If Claire were alive, she would have told you so herself. I don't have a jealous bone in my body. I never cared who she went out with as long as she came home to me—"

It was Mazarelle's face that turned pale now. Lavoisier's exclamation sounded amazingly like his own reaction to his wife's wanderings.

The phone on Maurice's desk suddenly came alive, its loud ringing a startling interruption. He snatched up the receiver and said, "Kalou here."

Maurice recognized the smoker's gravelly voice at the other end of the line and waved his hand at the team as if to say "keep it down."

Dr. Chardon told Maurice he'd been working around the clock with the evidence they'd brought him. The DNA from Lavoisier's toothbrush had been excellent, and when they compared that sample with the DNA they'd extracted from under the victim's fingernails— *Voila!* A match!

Clearing his throat, Chardon said, "I've already sent over a messenger with my report. You'll have it within the hour. Tell the commandant that the way things worked out in this case should be particularly satisfying to him. It's as if Madame Girard, your victim, not only put up a good fight against her killer but in the end was posthumously able to finger him for you. *Félicitations à tous!*"

Hanging up his phone, Maurice signaled to Mazarelle. The two walked to the other end of the office, where Maurice filled him in on what he'd learned. The team members and Lavoisier watched them in silence. It was impossible to tell from Mazarelle's inscrutable face what he'd heard.

The oppressively warm smoke-filled room had finally gotten to Armand Lavoisier. He kept staring at the window as if he wanted to throw it open and take a deep breath. Then he noticed Mazarelle watching him. "Can't you open a window in this place?" he cried out. "Don't you understand? I can't breathe. There's no air in here."

The commandant was tired of playing games with him. "I'm afraid you'll have to put up with it. The windows in this office stay closed. That way we don't lose any visitors."

"But it's stifling. I've got to get out of here. I can't breathe."

"Sit down." The weight of the commandant's voice fell full force on Lavoisier. He slowly sank down into his seat. "You don't seem to realize you're in serious trouble."

"Why? What?"

"You're about to be charged with a major crime, Monsieur Lavoisier. How's that for a starter?" Angrily, Mazarelle added, "It was as brutal a murder as I've seen. Will that do?"

"You're mad. You *know* I'm innocent," Lavoisier insisted, almost pleading with him to remember. "You were the one who called me in Lyon. Shocked me with the news."

Mazarelle nodded. "We also checked and found that the TGV from Lyon to Paris runs ten times a morning. Plenty of time for you to arrive, do the murder, and return before anyone missed you."

Looking at the others in the office through bloodshot eyes, Lavoisier began shouting, "I knew nothing about it. Nothing! I've never even been to her pied-à-terre at the Château Saint-Germain. Never seen the hotel," he swore, his voice cracking. "So how could I have killed anyone there, least of all my wife?"

Mazarelle watched him without a word. The tired old man fell back into his chair. He seemed to be unraveling before Mazarelle's eyes.

"Listen, Monsieur Lavoisier. We're putting you in *garde à vue*. As soon as Captain Kalou finishes typing up the transcript of your interview, we want you to read and sign it. Then the lieutenant will take you down the hall for a glass of water. Any questions?"

Lavoisier was up on his feet. "What are you trying to pull on me?" he exploded. "I'm not signing anything. *No* signing. Nothing until I talk to my lawyer."

"Yes, of course." The commandant was the epitome of reason. "But until you do you'll wait for him here in our chicken coop."

Turning to Jeannot, Mazarelle said, "Put the cuffs on him. Take him away."

As the lieutenant began trying to handcuff him, Armand Lavoisier gave him a violent shove. Caught off guard, Jeannot fell backward and went sprawling, sending his chair crashing to the floor. The prisoner looked around wild-eyed at the surprised detectives, some half out of their seats.

"Stop," he yelled. "Wait! Hear me out."

The commandant was amazed at the sudden theatrical way Lavoisier had drawn himself up, seeming to grow taller, exuding power. His voice too had now changed, darkened, deepened. It reminded Mazarelle that Claire's husband had once as a young man been an actor.

"Damnable lies!" he thundered. "Yes, it's true I threw a pearl away. But what do you really know about her death?"

Still channeling Othello, he whirled about to focus on Mazarelle. "What could I do? I had no choice. And remember this—I admit nothing."

Disgusted, the commandant told Jeannot, "Get him out of here!"

59

Coudert was feeling grouchy when he called upstairs. Maurice got on the intercom. "What the hell's going on up there?" the *patron* asked. "Are you guys having a party?"

"No party."

"Well, quit rearranging the furniture and get down here so that we can talk."

"As a matter of fact," Maurice said, "we've been questioning Armand Lavoisier."

It was as if Maurice had splashed gasoline on the *patron*'s fire. "Jesus Christ! Why are you still pestering that poor bastard with more questions? Quit it! He's just lost his wife, for god's sake!"

This was more than Maurice could handle. "Look, *patron*, it's complicated. I'm afraid I'm not the best one for this job. Why don't we let Commandant Mazarelle explain to you what's been going on here?"

"Mazarelle!" Coudert felt his jaw drop, his lungs slam into lockdown. "What the fuck is Mazarelle doing back here already? I told him to stay away from this place. Keep out of my sight. Doesn't he know he's suspended?"

Maurice realized that, like a fool, he'd let the cat out of the bag. He'd been so impressed with what his *chef* had done, and the way he'd done it, that he thought Mazarelle would be his own best advocate. "Look, *patron*, I think you should see him. Let him come down to your office. I'm sure you'll be interested in what he has to tell you."

Perhaps Maurice's guilt made him especially persuasive. Whatever it was, Coudert relented.

"Okay," he finally said, "tell him to come down. I'll see him. But I don't have all day, so step on it."

When Mazarelle appeared at Coudert's door, the mere sight of the big guy—confident as ever—was enough to make his *patron* angry.

"Well? Speak up, dammit!" Coudert demanded. "What the hell are you doing back here so soon?"

Ignoring his *patron*'s snotty tone, Mazarelle got directly to the point. "We know who murdered Claire Girard."

"What? How could you?" Coudert was astonished. "Well . . . go ahead . . . who was it?"

"The husband."

"Armand Lavoisier? Really?"

"They had an open marriage. Maybe a little too open for him in the end. He got jealous of her relationship with Nash, the American congressman. He thought she was falling for him."

At first incredulous, Coudert gradually came to terms with the news. "Hmm . . . I suppose it's possible. I've heard stranger things in my life. And the evidence?"

Mazarelle quickly summed up what he and his team had learned from their interrogation of Lavoisier. He ended with the capper. Only moments before, they'd had their suspicions confirmed by the report they'd received from the medical examiner.

"What report?" Coudert asked. "What did Dr. Chardon tell you?"

"He said that we had excellent DNA evidence of the murderer's identity," explained Mazarelle. "We'd known already that Madame Girard had tried to fight off her attacker, and that there was significant material under her fingernails. We were able to give Dr. Chardon fresh samples of Lavoisier's DNA to compare."

"And what did he say?"

"The ME told us that the two of them may not have had a marriage made in heaven, but the DNA evidence we gave him made a damn good match. It turns out," continued Mazarelle, "that Lavoisier's DNA will put him away for a long, long time."

Coudert wanted to know where Lavoisier was now.

"We've put him in *garde à vue*, of course. He's waiting to talk to his high-powered lawyer."

Looking thoughtful, Coudert nodded. He got up and paced behind his immense, immaculate desk. Two laps in, he came to a decision.

"Frankly, Mazarelle, I must admit that I was annoyed to see you here. Still, it seems that you've done some good work. So I guess—consider yourself reinstated."

Mazarelle smiled. He hadn't expected Coudert to turn around so fast. "I'm glad to be back," he said.

"No time for parties," Coudert grumbled. "There's work to do. As far as I'm concerned, your first priority is still the hanged man murder. We've got Babo sitting in jail, and the trial is due to start soon. You need to get going on that."

A small twinge of guilt stabbed Mazarelle. Poor Babo. Still innocent, still sitting in jail. All this time while he was wrapped up with Claire. He turned to head out the door.

And Coudert shot over his shoulder, "Plus I want you to take on the cop killing at the Buttes-Chaumont."

Mazarelle looked bewildered. "The Guy Danglars case? I thought you assigned that to Lieutenant Duhamel."

"Right! I did. But she's made no progress at all." Coudert shrugged. "Alice Duhamel is a good-looking woman. And a crack shot on the firing range. But, *entre nous*, as a detective she's *vraiment nulle*. The minister wants you to take the case back. I told him you were busy. But he's hoping you can do better."

"I'll do my best."

"Good. I expect no less from you."

60

Later that afternoon, when Mazarelle's team arrived at Donovan's gleaming red door, Caitlin was inside waiting for them. The pub was already crowded.

"You're late," she told Maurice, who had called to tell her they were on the way. "I had trouble saving the back room for you."

"Sorry," Maurice said. "We were held up. But this time it's going to be a *happy* happy hour. Actually, it's a party and we're feeling celebratory. The *chef* is back."

"That sounds better already. Follow me"—she waved her green fingernails—"and we'll get you caught up the Donovan way."

They started Caitlin yo-yoing back and forth toting glasses of Guinness stout and Chimay—the beers on tap. Followed next by bottles of Bass and Smithwick's Irish ale. Then ratcheting up the alcohol content of anyone still standing and ready to join their *chef* in toasts, she brought them Teeling and Paddy and Bushmills single malt Irish whiskey.

Caitlin seemed to have inexhaustible energy. She was assisted by a young fresh-faced waiter who took care of all the food.

"Did I forget anything?" he asked her nervously.

Caitlin turned to the commandant. "Anything else?"

"Nice," Mazarelle said, eyeing the spread, and went downstairs briefly to make room for another Bushmills.

When Mazarelle returned to their buoyant back room, they were all munching on spicy chicken wings, deep-fried onion rings, smoky bacon, shepherd's pies, and dumplings galore to go with their whiskeys and beer. And there too was Gilles Chardon. The medical examiner had just arrived and already had a raised glass in his hand, his first toast on the tip of his tongue.

"Here's to you, *mon ami*. And to the work you and your team have done on the murder of Claire Girard and ID'ing her killer. It's good to have you back in Paris. Welcome home."

"Couldn't have done it without your help, Gilles."

"I'm glad you realize that," the ME pointed out with an impish smile. "It makes my job so much easier."

By way of showing his appreciation, Dr. Chardon had a little present for his friend. Unwrapped, it turned out to be Turgenev's last novel—*Virgin Soil*. He hoped Mazarelle hadn't read it.

"No never."

"Wonderful. You're in for a treat. He's my favorite Russian."

Mazarelle smiled. "What's this book about?" he asked.

"Among other things," Gilles explained, "it's a novel about young love—so sweet, so sad."

Mazarelle, who had seen the doctor perform more than a few autopsies in his time, stepped back and gave his friend the once-over. "You know, *mon ami*, you surprise me. I didn't realize what a sentimentalist you really are."

Chardon took out a cigarette and lighted up, exhaling a cloud of thick gray smoke as if to conceal a blushing cheek. "I'm also a Vladimir Nabokov fan," he added, in the spirit of full disclosure. "What about you?"

Mazarelle thought it over. "I like Chekhov. His eye for detail. Maybe that's due to his medical training."

The doctor chuckled. "Another round?"

What Mazarelle felt he needed more than anything else at the moment was a few hours' sleep or he'd never be able to get up in time for their meeting tomorrow morning. As for the ME, he too had to be up at the crack of dawn. His first autopsy was at 8 a.m.

Mazarelle asked his friend, "How's chances of dropping me off on your way home?"

"A pleasure."

"What about them?" asked Caitlin. She'd been standing there taking more orders for drinks.

Chardon said, "They're much younger than we are. Give them another round and the bill."

Mazarelle went around the table, shaking hands with each one and thanking them for the boozing, the laughing, the screwing around. "It was a lovely party," he told them. "But if you're late tomorrow, it'll make me very unhappy. And you know how I get when I'm like that? Grumpy. Very grumpy. And nobody wants that, do you?"

"Hell no!" they shouted in unison.

"Good," replied Mazarelle, reminding them they'd only gotten one case done. Still two more to go. As he started toward the door with the doctor, Caitlin came running after him.

"Here, Commandant." She handed him his still half-filled bottle of whiskey. "You forgot this."

"Keep it, darling," Mazarelle insisted. "You've made my day."

She hugged him, kissed him, and ran back inside to fill their order.

As the two friends drove to Mazarelle's apartment in the doctor's Citroën, Vanessa Paradis was back on the radio, singing "Joe le Taxi." Mazarelle recalled seeing her picture on the cover of *Paris-Flash,* as he waited for Claire at her office. He tapped his foot to the music. A catchy tune. It seemed as if all that had happened a long time ago.

As they approached his building, Mazarelle was impressed with how festive the boulevard looked in the bright moonlight. Gilles pulled into the curb in front of the building's entry.

Mazarelle turned to his friend. "Care to come upstairs for a *dernier verre?*"

"After what we've already had to drink? I'm practically asleep already," said Dr. Chardon. Mazarelle smiled as the medical examiner drove off.

Punching in the code on his front lock, Mazarelle walked into the house. He waved to his concierge, Mme. Paulette, who stood at her lighted window, passed under the Moorish arch into the inner courtyard paved with black flagstones, and headed back toward the elevator. Getting out on the third floor, he pressed the button for the *minuterie,* but it didn't work. Mme. Paulette looked efficient, but she never remembered to change the bulbs. Still, he knew the braille of his floor, his apartment. In the dark, he pulled out his key and opened the door. He was relieved to see that inside his own lights were okay.

Settling comfortably into his red armchair, Mazarelle took out his meerschaum and filled it with tobacco. As he smoked, he opened his gift and began reading Turgenev. He could tell immediately that he was going to enjoy the book. But just then the concierge's intercom buzzed from downstairs.

"Messenger here with a delivery for you, *monsieur le commandant.* It looks like a present."

"Where from?"

"Fauchon. It looks quite elegant."

Mazarelle had to smile. A gift basket from Fauchon. Coudert must have been happier than he let on about his clearing the case.

"Okay. Send him up. But tell him to be careful. The *minuterie* up here isn't working again."

"I'll tell him. He's coming right up."

A few moments later, Mazarelle heard footsteps on the landing. The loud knocking on his door sounded positively jolly. He rushed over, unlocked and opened the door, ready to welcome the messenger. The light from his apartment shot across the landing, but no one was standing there. Mazarelle stepped out and peered into the shadows, trying to see if anyone was still there, waiting for a tip. Nothing. No one. No sound of footsteps on the landing. But then he saw it—a large pink and black box sitting on the floor near the top of the staircase.

Mazarelle hurried over to the Fauchon box. Bending down, he opened it and examined his gift. Inside was a spectacular array of delights: a Sicilian orange cake; a splendid chocolate Megève ganache de chez Fauchon; and, surrounding them, half a dozen cream éclairs that seemed to be decorated with cherry blossoms. The *patron* must have been really happy with his work. Mazarelle could hardly wait to carry his treat inside his apartment.

He didn't see the garrote until it was almost too late.

Out of the corner of his eye, he caught the movement, the coil, as it slipped over his head. Had he not just come from the South of France, Mazarelle would have had barely any idea of what he was up against. But in that split second, he had a chilling realization of what it had to be. Not just a garrote. *La loupe*—the double-coiled garrote, the deadly weapon used by the elite troops of the French Foreign Legion to remove enemy sentries silently.

Even as he reached up to grab at the coils, he stopped. He knew that if he tried to pull away, or yank at the ligature—the normal instinctive reaction—he'd be a dead man in less than a second. No one was strong enough to save himself that way. The edge—the leverage—was always to the attacker from behind. That's what made the garrote so deadly.

As the coils started to tighten into his neck, Mazarelle did the unexpected. Instead of trying to pull away, he rolled his shoulder, and turned right back into his attacker—slamming him in the face. The son of a bitch was almost as tall and broad as himself. He was startled, but he wouldn't let go. The two large men lurched through the darkness like drunken dancers, pounding into the wall, bouncing over toward the black railing. There the two struggled against the wooden support, each refusing to release his grasp of the other. Strength against strength. Neither yielding. The raw power of his opponent was frightening to Mazarelle.

But Mazarelle had a trick or two of his own. Dropping down, he unleashed a move learned long ago on the rugby fields of his youth—the straight elbow to the balls. Not exactly according to the rules of the game. But always a winner.

He heard his attacker cry out in some unrecognizable language—"*Da-i dracului! Dute dracului! Mânca-mi ai coaiele!*" Turning face-to-face, pummeling the wounded man in the gut, Mazarelle thought, I've got him now! But the attacker, in a burst of energy, fought back. And suddenly the two, clutching each other, went crashing into the balustrade—the wooden rail cracking and splintering. And both men, off-balance, but still locked together, went twisting, falling, hurtling down three flights toward the bushes and the black stones of the courtyard below.

Moments later, Mazarelle's motionless body lay sprawled on the ground. His head battered, with a small crimson pool expanding around it. His attacker nowhere to be seen. No signs of life in Mazarelle—just streaks on his face, his clothes.

Near him a trail of blood glinting in the moonlight led off through the stone courtyard and out to the traffic on the boulevard.

PART SIX

61

Luc was not happy about being shaken out of a sound sleep, the first he'd had in a while. He picked up the ringing telephone, ready to give hell to whoever it was. But the caller's gruff, sandpaper voice caught him by surprise. He recognized it instantly.

"It's done, Luc. The investigator is kaput. We've seen the last of him. And the rest of the plan is all set." Without waiting for an answer, the caller hung up.

Luc smiled happily, turned over on his side, and went back to sleep.

62

Every part of Mazarelle's body was falling apart. They put him on a stretcher and slid him inside the police ambulance like a loaf of bread into the oven. The main thing he recalled before they pulled away from the front of his house was the siren screaming in his ears. They told him they were going to the Hôtel-Dieu, the oldest hospital in Paris. They snapped a mask over his face that made his breathing easier. It must have been a respirator. The two attendants peered down into Mazarelle's pale face. Both of them needed a shave. He assumed that he didn't look especially good either. The next time his eyes opened, the ambulance was bouncing up onto the curb outside the hospital and into the building, and they were wheeling him into the Intensive Care Unit.

As Mazarelle slipped in and out of consciousness, he couldn't get the attack out of his mind. Each jolt of pain that shot him awake, sent him raging at the villains, whoever they were, and even more at himself and the dumb trap he'd been snared by. But through the lingering pain, one idea brightened his mind.

Something good had happened.

Sure every breath stabbed him in the side. And he had a wire or a tube plugged into every vein. But Paul Mazarelle had to smile. He had flushed the bastards. They were out in the open now. It had almost cost him his life, but the key word was "almost." He was alive. And he'd learned from years of detective work that all you had to do was survive. As long as you did, you could pick up the investigation and go on. Half comatose, he couldn't wait to get out of bed and start again.

Meanwhile Maurice, Jeannot, and Serge were in the waiting room. As protection, Maurice had insisted that they maintain a round-the-clock vigil. The attacker might return. He was not likely to fade away. As for the team, despite the doctors' gloomy expressions, Mazarelle's guys were not giving up on their chief's likelihood of surviving. They would not desert him. No more animated than gravestones, they spent the whole night in an almost completely empty hospital waiting room in silence, like figures in a late-night Hopper painting.

After midnight, Coudert stopped by. Looking around at the men on guard in the waiting room, Coudert nodded to himself. Going over to Maurice, he bent down and whispered, "I'm glad to see all of you here. As soon as your chief is moved out of intensive care, I'll post a gendarme outside his room. Then you and your men can go back to work."

Over the next week, Mazarelle went through cycles of pain. An excruciating headache that was bad in the morning but worse in the evening, body aches all day that felt as if they'd never go away. The doctors told him he was lucky to be alive. But whenever he had a bit of respite from medication, he bitterly complained about the time he was wasting. The urgent work he had to do. The assassin he had to catch. He was such a loud squeaky wheel about wanting to get back to his office, so driven to get out of there, that after ten days the medical staff was willing—even eager—to let him go home. When the nurses protested that he was a real handful, a pain in the ass, he smiled. A twinkle in his eye.

On his last day, they lined up to say goodbye. All quite glad that he was leaving. A few of his nurses stood together behind his wheelchair at the front door. When one of them came forward to help him get into Maurice's car, the commandant brushed her hand away from his arm. He needed no assistance.

Dr. Jacobus, who'd also treated him in the past, was there too, of course. He'd been especially impressed with Mazarelle's progress. He knew how much battering the commandant had already taken. His broken leg from rugby that had not been set well, the various bullet wounds he'd received, the medieval stone wall and timbers that had fallen on him in the Dordogne. And now after escaping with his life from his most recent "adventure," he was leaving them with only a concussion, a broken collarbone, and some cracked ribs—all thanks to the elaborate hedges and floral plantings that the building's gardener had recently installed in the courtyard. Dr. Jacobus doubted that Mazarelle would have survived the dangerous fall if his head had hit the flagstones instead of a bed of blossoming dahlias. As for the unknown villain who'd apparently walked away, leaving only a streak of blood, his landing had no doubt been cushioned by Mazarelle's body.

But Paul Mazarelle had the constitution of an ox. And like an ox, he was determined to keep going. The doctor's advice had been to use as much ibuprofen as necessary to keep him comfortable. If that didn't do the trick, Jacobus had something else for him.

"What's that? A billet-doux?" Mazarelle asked, taking the folded note.

"A prescription for something stronger just in case."

Mazarelle waved goodbye. He had Angelique Vasseure as his ace in the hole to keep him in *bon état de marche*. And Angelique had never failed.

63

On the way back to his apartment with Maurice driving, Mazarelle wanted details. He asked what kind of leads they had on whoever was behind the attack on him. Maurice reported they had plenty of blood for testing from the crime scene, but the PS had come up with no DNA match for it.

"It has to be the same guy," said Mazarelle.

Maurice nodded. "We're getting close, and he's getting twitchy."

"I wish we were closer."

"Well, chief, at least you're still here."

Maurice pulled the squad car up in front of Mazarelle's turn-of-the-century apartment building. The weathered stone looked good. So did his battered boss.

"Really," Maurice had to admit, "it's all thanks to your concierge."

"That old battle-ax?" Mazarelle was stunned. "What did she do?"

"Without her you might have died. She was the one who put in the call to get the ambulance here so fast. They got you to the emergency room just in time."

By way of thanks, Mazarelle decided to give all the flowers he was bringing home from the hospital to Madame Paulette. She wasn't the sweetest thing in the world, but she did her job. He recalled the list of emergency phone numbers she had hanging by tiny magnets on her refrigerator. When he knocked on her door and went in with his bouquets, she seemed flustered. She had a cat on her lap and it looked like the missing Michou.

"Where did you find her?" he asked.

"Oh no, *no!*" Madame Paulette quickly explained. "That's *my* cat. That's Fifi."

Mazarelle knew better. He hadn't lost all his brains in his fall. Her Fifi had died months ago. She was lying. But what the hell! Somehow it didn't surprise him. She was what she was. Fifi, he seemed to recall, was an orange and brown animal with white paws. But not all that colorful or well-fed. Michou was a sleek, short-haired, elegant gray— just like this little beauty. Still, the other thing about his wife's old cat—she never stayed anywhere if she didn't want to. He wondered if Madame didn't have a good nature after all.

Before going upstairs, he asked for his mail. While she went to get his letters, Mazarelle looked around the kitchen. He poked through the bookshelf behind her armchair. The books were mostly about cooking. Behind the foyer leading to her bedroom there were stacks of books that surprised him. Piles of paperback mystery stories.

And on the wall above the bookcases in the foyer was a small poster entitled *"Les Durs"*—Jean Gabin, Jean-Paul Belmondo, the villains with a heart of gold.

"I see you've got a soft spot for some of the tough guys too," he called out.

Madame Paulette hurried back with an armful of letters and pointed upstairs to the new railing on the third floor.

"Do you see that? Brand-new and freshly painted," she told him. "How do you like it?"

"Very nice. It seems to match. I'll let you know when I see it up close."

She understood. "Yes, of course. And I forgot to give you this."

He opened the familiar envelope. Was it time for the rent already, he wondered. It turned out to be an extra bill from the owner for repairs on the railing. Of course . . .

"By the way," Mazarelle said, "who was it that knocked on my door? What did he look like? The Fauchon messenger."

"He said he had a gift for you from the store."

"But what did he look like?"

She shrugged. "Tall. The one thing I remember is that he was tall and wearing a hooded sweatshirt. I only saw him for a few seconds. How should I know? He said he had a present from Fauchon. So that's why I called upstairs and told you. And you said I should warn him about the *minuterie* not working, which I did. He gave me this weird smile and went up."

"What kind of weird smile?"

"It was as if I'd told him some kind of a joke. But he wasn't laughing. Nothing like that. Maybe it was a *bad* joke? We'd been having some trouble with our hall lights."

"It was a *bad* joke," Mazarelle agreed. As he walked into the courtyard, he looked up at the third-floor balustrade and thought about the distance of the fall he'd taken. A *very* bad joke.

64

That night, his pain-wracked body didn't allow him much sleep. Popping up every few hours to take another pill. Still and all, it was good to be home. But in the morning, before he went into 36, he called Angelique to see if he could make an appointment. It turned out that she was coming in early and, according to her secretary, would be happy to see the commandant. He knew Angelique rarely came in early, but that's what friends were for. And for that, she deserved to get a washed face from him as well as a combed mustache. The way he was feeling, it was about all he could do.

Angelique's office was on the rue de l'Odéon in the Sixth. The concierge thought he was too early. She called upstairs and discovered that Commandant Mazarelle was expected. "Go right up," she apologized.

Mazarelle sat down in the empty waiting room, which always had a soothing effect on him. The walls were beige, the shelves full of healing salves, powders, salts. The vitrine against the wall displayed lacquered ebony boxes of acupuncture needles, ampules of different colored liquids, tubes with massage creams from Shanghai and Hong Kong. On one wall were two large vertical posters of the male and female human body, both outlined with Chinese diagrams and symbols.

Angelique did not keep her old friend waiting long. Her office was extremely neat and carefully arranged. The doctor herself seemed to fit right in. She wore a custom-made white linen jacket with a mandarin collar. Her blond hair tied back in an immaculate chignon. All the rooms in her office were color coded. Her private reception room was a rose pink that made her fair complexion positively bloom. She'd told Mazarelle that the French blue of the exercise room was to emphasize the calm of the atmosphere, the reason of her methods, her serenity, the trust her clients could place in her. The green of the acupuncture room heightened balance, subtly reminding her patients once again of the importance of harmony, universal love, and peace. Why not? Mazarelle thought. He glanced around at the walls, then back at her smiling face. "Lovely," he said. Leaving it open which one he was referring to.

With that, Angelique kissed him on both cheeks and asked about her friend, the soothsayer Mireille. Had she been of any help to him?

Mazarelle paused. "Well, she was . . . interesting."

Angelique smiled. "That's Madame Mireille."

"I'm not quite sure about most of what she said," Mazarelle explained. "She was a little vague. She mentioned contradictions a lot."

He was trying to be nice.

"On the other hand when it came to the Hanged Man card our friend Alain Berthaud had drawn, she was quite categorical about two things. The first was that he faced a period of grave danger. That certainly was true. Second, she added that I did as well. And I guess she was right about that too."

"There, you see! I told you she was remarkable." Angelique smiled fetchingly. "So *monsieur le commandant,* tell me, how can I help you?"

He briefly explained what had happened, beginning with the knock at the door of his apartment, the fierce struggle in the darkness on the landing, the crashing through the balustrade, the three-story fall onto the courtyard's stone floor, the ambulance, the doctors, the two weeks he'd spent in the hospital. He didn't talk too much about the strangling itself. He didn't want to shock her.

Angelique was stunned. And from the wince he gave when she touched his shoulder, it was clear how much he needed her help. She brought him into the green room and gave him a thorough examination. His ribs, his hip, his legs—each a kaleidoscope of bruised purple and yellow. Shaking her head, she couldn't believe how much damage his flesh had endured. And this was someone she cared about. It seemed to hurt her personally.

Exasperated by his wounds, as if each one was a personal insult to her, she said, "Can't you work with your mind instead of your body?"

"I do both," Mazarelle said.

"That may be. But your body can't take much more. You really need time off. A few months at least. Don't be a hero, Mazarelle."

She ran her fingers down his battered arm.

"Not everybody is worth saving. But you are."

"I'll see what I can do."

65

Even after Angelique's gentle fingers, Mazarelle was still a bundle of bruises. But he was feeling a little more like himself, and it was time to get going. The link between the murders of Alain Berthaud, Guy Danglars, and the attack he himself had suffered seemed to him inescapable. Now he had to find the man responsible. And make him answer for his crimes.

And that was why, this late summer morning, Jeannot was driving him toward the Place de la Madeleine.

"Look, it's got to be the same guy." Mazarelle grimaced as he tried to find a comfortable position in the car seat. "But we don't have his weapon—that garrote from the Legion. We don't have any ID on the DNA from the blood. All we've got is the gift box."

"Sure, I get it," Jeannot said. "Fauchon. But how do you know which one? Don't they have like thirteen shops in Paris alone?"

Mazarelle nodded. "Franchises from New York to Taiwan."

"So what kind of a lead is that?"

"If you and Maurice spent more time on the important things, then you would know." Mazarelle winced again as he turned in his seat. "Christophe Adam."

Jeannot looked over, surprised.

"It was the contents of the box," Mazarelle said, as if that made everything clear. "The Sicilian orange cake. That was special. The Megève ganache was also great—" Just remembering the attractive arrangement made Mazarelle's mouth water. Too bad he hadn't even had a few seconds to taste the cake. And too bad about the ugliness that followed. He was sorry the box had been trashed while he was in the hospital.

"But the éclairs . . . that's the key. The ones with the flowers on top.

They're called the éclairs fleuris. Inspired by the cherry blossoms of Japan."

Mazarelle followed the movements of *pâtissiers* the way sports fans followed player trades. Maurice and Jeannot could tell him all about Paris Saint-Germain's latest midfield acquisitions. But Mazarelle knew that Fauchon's pastry cook had recently come over from the Hôtel de Crillon. And anyone serious about pastry was aware of the impact of his new éclairs across the city. Éclairs only available, for now at least, at the main store of the famed market for gourmands.

Jeannot pulled the car into a handicapped spot in front of the store's black-and-white logo-patterned awnings and glass entryway. Like any Parisian, even Jeannot knew the shop on the Place de la Madeleine. Fauchon had occupied the same site since its founding in 1886. And was still just as upscale and stuffy. Not Jeannot's kind of place. Even Mazarelle rarely had occasion to go into the store. When he craved pastry, he usually shopped at one of the small *patisseries* in his own *quartier*.

Inside, the size of the bustling crowd of shoppers eyeing the displays surprised him. The pastry counter was especially busy, so Mazarelle waited impatiently for a salesperson. There were two women working the counter, one a redhead, the other a blonde, both really young girls, it seemed to him, both quite efficient. The redheaded sales clerk was a cute kid. The name on her ID was Nathalie. Mazarelle dwarfed her. Actually he dwarfed everyone. But it was Jeannot's grin that drew her over.

Hurrying across to them, the curly-haired redhead, with her best shopgirl manners, politely asked if she could help the gentlemen.

"I hope so," said Mazarelle. "I wonder if you can give me some information?"

Nathalie had a smile that lit up her display case.

"I'll try," she said.

Mazarelle described the contents of his gift box.

"Oooh—that's so surprising!" gushed the salesgirl. "It's not one of our usual ones. Actually that's a really nice combo. But I'm afraid—" Nathalie's face fell to the floor. "If you want the same today, we can't do it—"

"No," interrupted Mazarelle. "I'm wondering if it was bought here."

"Well—do you have the receipt?"

"No. It was a gift. My question is—could it have been bought here?"

"That's a little hard to answer. I know we always have those cherry éclairs available—and every other kind of éclair, too! So we can sell you that. And we have the Megève, too. But the Sicilian orange cake is a problem—"

"I should explain," said Mazarelle. "I wouldn't mind having a repeat of that box, but that's not why I'm here. I'm looking for information about whether my gift was purchased in this shop. If so, I'm wondering if anyone here might remember the guy who bought it."

"Well . . . I don't know," mumbled Nathalie. Then, suddenly, she perked up. "Look," she said excitedly, "if you know the exact date, then I can check our records to see if we had those three items for sale on that day!"

"Great," said Mazarelle, and gave Nathalie the date.

"I'll have to ask our manager—so could you wait a bit?"

"Be glad to," answered Mazarelle, already thinking that he'd fill the time by trying out one of the day's special éclairs. In fact they all tempted him, but finally, he ordered a Paris-Brest éclair. He immediately began to eat it standing up at the end of the pastry counter, careful not to drip any of the mousseline cream or the almond and hazelnut praline filling onto his shirt. There was a delightful crunchiness to the slivers of roasted hazelnuts that topped the éclair. He offered a bite to Jeannot. Utterly delicious, they agreed.

Just as they were polishing it off, a tall, thin young man materialized behind the counter. He had a serious, officious expression, holding a large volume as gingerly as if it held the company finances. He beckoned the men over.

"I believe we've found what you asked for, Inspector."

"Good," said Mazarelle, wondering how the manager knew he was a cop. Was it really so obvious?

The manager flipped the volume open.

"On the date you mentioned, we did indeed have for sale the three items you received in your gift box, so it could well have been prepared in this shop."

"Excellent. Then my next question is: Does anyone here remember putting it together for a tall guy—taller than you, and definitely much heftier."

The young man shook his head.

"I'm sorry. You see how many customers we have?"

Jeannot wasn't giving up. "You might remember his expression. They said he had a strange smile."

"A smile? Gentlemen. We're trying to help. But please . . ."

By now, the pastry counter crowd had diminished. As they spoke the blond salesgirl, no longer occupied, had come closer and was listening to their conversation.

"*Pardon*," she interrupted. "But that gift box. I think I put it together myself! There was this guy who bought it. A *méchant* type—this guy in a hoodie. He had a face like a hatchet. He seemed to be sneering at me as I prepared the gift. And he never said a word of thanks!"

Jeannot turned to Mazarelle with a grin.

"Do you have a credit card receipt?" asked Mazarelle, hopefully.

"No—he used cash. I can still see him throwing it down on the counter."

"Anything else you remember?"

"No, I don't think so. I'm sorry."

So close. But except for the Paris-Brest éclair, the trip was a bust.

"Too bad, boss," Jeannot commiserated. "I liked the story about that pastry cook."

As they turned to go, Mazarelle let his eyes run down the counter to take one last look at the latest chocolates.

"Except . . ."

The blond salesgirl was frowning.

"Well, it's not all that interesting, but . . ."

Jeannot waved his hand to prompt her. "But what?"

"Well, you know . . . the tattoo."

"Tattoo?"

"Right—it was one I've never seen before. When he lifted the box, his sweatshirt sleeve slid back. It was some kind of bird. Or maybe a dragon or something. On his forearm."

Jeannot's thanks made the salesgirl blush.

As they headed out, Mazarelle wasn't sure whether they'd learned anything useful or not. But at least he had established the store where his assailant had gotten the gift. Maybe they could do something with that tattoo . . .

66

ack at the office, Mazarelle gathered his team.

They had a suspect—a big guy with a grip like a wrench, a flair for ropes, and an ability to set a trap. And possibly someone with inside information—tracking down Mazarelle at his own home suggested that. His athleticism and his choice of the *loupe* clearly pointed to an ex–special forces type from the Legion itself.

But while the Legion connection seemed likely, the killer—his attacker—would not be easy to find. He set Maurice and Jeannot on the job of tracking down the enrollment lists from the Legion. Meanwhile Mazarelle took to the phones.

"Sergeant Delapierre, so good to hear your voice." Mazarelle grimaced as he tried to get comfortable in his office chair and imagined himself back into his role as a journalist.

"Paul Mazarelle calling. Right, right. I had such a wonderful time with you down in Aubagne. You were so kind to share that bottle of your excellent Provence wine."

"Of course, I remember you, Paul. That splendid 'stache of yours." The sergeant sounded like he might have been enjoying his fine vintage that very afternoon. "How is your article coming along?"

"Well, Sergeant, I have a favor to ask. I'm trying to track down something. A tattoo."

"A tattoo?"

"Right. Not a rose one like yours. But do you know any regiments in the French Foreign Legion that used a bird tattoo, maybe an eagle or a falcon?"

The sergeant hesitated. "No, not really. Doesn't sound like anything I know."

Mazarelle let out a frustrated sigh. "How about anything with wings. Anything at all?"

"Huh. Not really." A long pause. "Well, maybe. What about a winged dragon?"

"A dragon with wings?"

"Right. There's a regiment with that."

The salesgirl had said "maybe a dragon . . ." Mazarelle thought he might be on to something.

"Tell me about that. Is it one particular regiment?"

"Oh, yeah. And not just any regiment. That's the symbol of the Second REP—the *Régiment Étranger de Parachutistes*. A really elite unit—like one of the special forces. And it's all foreigners."

"Foreigners, *vraiment*?" Mazarelle remembered the yell of his assailant. It had sounded Eastern European. "So if I'm trying to track someone down, where do I find the enrollment lists of the regiment?"

Delapierre was accommodating, but he had reached his limit. "You must know those names are secret. They're kept secret for a reason—that's part of the gift of anonymity we offer to all our recruits. They may have troubled backgrounds. But they're trying to change their lives."

"All right, all right!" Mazarelle tried to think quickly. "How about this. Can you at least give me one name of one contact? Anyone who served in that unit that I could talk to now in Paris. Anyone at all?"

There was a long pause on the line. Mazarelle thought he had lost him. But finally, grudgingly, Delapierre sighed, and offered up a name. "Wayne Lake O'Toole. He doesn't mind talking about the past. O'Toole might be able to help you out," said Delapierre. "He's living in the Fifth these days. I'm sure you can track him down. But I can't give you any more. Good luck."

It was just a matter of a few minutes for Maurice to track down the listing, and the number. Returning to his desk, Mazarelle placed the call. And got an answering service. "I'm at work now at the Centre équestre de La Villette. If this is important, you can reach me there."

Mazarelle dialed the number. It only took a few rings.

"O'Toole here," said a high-pitched, lyrical voice. "How can I help?"

Mazarelle explained that he had gotten O'Toole's name from Delapierre. He wanted to talk about the old days in the Legion.

"Could I swing by to meet you at your workplace? It's important."

Mazarelle no longer had to pretend to be a journalist. He could have dragged the Irishman down to his office at the BC. But, as his grandmother had always said, you get more with honey than with vinegar.

And sure enough, O'Toole sounded pleased to be asked to reminisce. He'd be happy to see Mazarelle. They set up a meeting for later that day.

Arriving at the Equestrian Center in La Villette, Mazarelle gave a low whistle of appreciation for this bucolic site in the center of the city. Set among a bank of tall evergreens and white stands, red flags fluttering in the breeze. "Discover happiness on horseback!" announced the sign.

And inside the horse ring, a group of girls in red pullovers and black hats seemed to be doing just that.

Mazarelle leaned gingerly against the wooden rails to observe the scene inside the ring.

O'Toole wasn't exactly what Mazarelle had imagined from the voice. He was tall and blond and rugged. He had tanned, craquelured skin—the face of a man who spent a lot of time outdoors in the sun. A man who had seen his share of action. And right now, he looked as if he had his hands full. He was busy teaching a pretty young teenage girl how to handle the reins of her horse. O'Toole waved his hand to Mazarelle and said, "Hold on. Be with you in a minute."

It took more than a minute.

Watching O'Toole guiding the girl on the horse, his hand on her thigh, the girl smiling down at him, Mazarelle wasn't sure that if he were the girl's parents he would want her so close to that big, rough-looking guy. But it was none of his business.

Finally, the lesson done, a last pat on the horse's rump, the Irishman strolled over to Mazarelle, his arms spread wide in welcome.

"So what can I do for you, Commandant?"

Mazarelle explained his hunt for the tattoo.

"The winged dragon? That was us," O'Toole confirmed with a smile of pride. "It came from the early missions in southeast Asia. Cambodia, I believe. Here you go—"

He pulled down the neckline of his sweater, to reveal the tattoo on his shoulder. A dragon, with a ferocious snout and wings flaring. Distinctive, and dangerous looking.

"Yeah," he said, "we all got them. After a year of training, you felt you had earned it."

"What kind of unit was that?"

"The Second REP. We're a rapid intervention force. Elite. All foreigners. We've always been one of the exclusive units of the Legion."

Mazarelle thought he could work with that pride. "Sounds amazing. So where were you stationed?"

"We've parachuted in all over the world. But in my time, the early 1990s, we were in Africa."

"What part of Africa?"

"Rwanda."

The voluble O'Toole had suddenly run out of words.

"And?" Mazarelle prompted.

"And that's where we were." O'Toole exhaled. "Look, we were sent there to support the Hutu government side against the rebels. The Tutsis. They had us training youth militias."

"The militias in Rwanda?" Even the apolitical Mazarelle knew the story.

"Right." O'Toole nodded. "It was a goatfuck. We were on the wrong side of history. You know the rest." The Irishman didn't like talking about the terrible genocide in Rwanda. He sighed. "But I'm proud of my brothers. I'll always be proud. The politicians stuck us in the shit. We tried to make the best of it."

Mazarelle was interested in history. But it was time to cut to the chase.

"We're looking for one particular man. Someone with that tattoo.

And from what we can tell, more or less your age. So he might well have been in your unit in your time frame."

O'Toole really didn't look so happy now. But Mazarelle kept going.

"Tall, lean, with a strange smile. Odd, a little disturbing? Some said he was good with a garrote. Your double garrote—*la loupe.*"

The Irishman took a small step back. Even his tan seemed to fade a little.

"Sweet jaysus," O'Toole muttered.

Mazarelle nodded, and waited. Finally, O'Toole sighed.

"Listen, we had the best regiment. I want you to understand. We were all brothers. I could trust them for anything." He paused. "But there was a guy . . ."

"A guy?" Mazarelle prompted, on the edge of something now.

"I can't remember his name, but the *loupe,* that was him."

"What about him?"

"I'll never forget what he did. I mean, none of us was afraid of a little blood. But this guy . . . He loved it. He had this thing about setting snares—with ropes and knots . . ."

He paused now, warming into the story.

"So in Rwanda, out in the bush, we had this one kid. He was sneaking into our mess hall, stealing our food. A poor local kid grabbing some bread and vegetables. And this guy, he said he'd take care of it."

O'Toole hesitated to go on.

Mazarelle waited now. The story was coming. He just had to let it unroll.

"The way he took care of it?" O'Toole shook his head. "He set this trap. And he caught the kid. We thought he'd kick his ass a little, and send him home. But he gets the kid, and he straps him down to this table in the kitchen. This stainless steel table. And he gets out one of those knives . . ."

His voice faltered. And still Mazarelle waited.

"And . . . and he starts cutting. Taking little pieces of skin out of the boy. Alive! No one ever forgot that."

He gave a long sigh. "We put a stop to it, but it was too late. The kid was gone."

The story was tragic. But Mazarelle felt something else. Something more than disgust. What he was feeling was the buzz of recognition. The click inside his head. The moment he knew as a detective, when the details started to line up. The ropes. The knots. The violence. This could be his killer. His assailant. He certainly sounded twisted enough.

"So what happened to him?"

"We kicked him out of the unit when we got back home."

O'Toole closed his eyes for a long moment. And finally went on.

"You know, we saw our share of bodies there. But no one wanted to have anything to do with that guy. He liked doing that to the kid. He liked that the kid was black."

Mazarelle shook his head and said nothing for a while. Finally he asked, "So can you help me? Do you remember his name at all?"

O'Toole gave a long slow sigh. From the Irishman, it sounded almost musical.

"His French name? Well, maybe. I think it was Jacques something or other. I can't really remember. I tried to forget it."

"You didn't stay in touch? You don't have any idea where he might be?"

"You know, we have a network where we look out for each other when we get out. Help each other get jobs. But frankly, no one wanted to help him."

Mazarelle's face fell. "Really? No idea where he is?"

O'Toole gave him a once-over. "I didn't say that."

The Irishman cracked a grin. He was enjoying himself again, unveiling the story at his own pace.

"I'm pretty sure I heard he ended up working in one of the detention centers. As a security guard."

"Where?"

"Not around here. In the South of France I think."

Mazarelle was nodding now, eagerly prompting.

"Any idea which one?"

"Nice? Toulouse maybe?"

O'Toole nodded at Mazarelle. His grin faded.

"I tell you what. If you run into him, watch your ass. He's dangerous."

67

Even from a distance, Mazarelle could see the squat, ominous structure, ringed with razor wire. The government called it an "administrative detention center," but it looked like a prison. It sprawled along the highway like a giant pile of concrete spray-painted onto a Van Gogh landscape. An industrial city. And maybe a city with the resident they were looking for—a French Foreign Legion veteran who was the *ripoux*'s enforcer. Mazarelle's attacker. The man with the garrote.

Maurice and Jeannot had taken O'Toole's tip and run it through the databases of security employees at the country's immigrant detention centers. There was no shortage of men named Jacques at the camps in the south. On their trip down, they'd already seen two and eliminated both. In Toulouse, their first stop, Jacques LeBrun had turned out to be a mild-mannered, talky veteran with a cane. He enjoyed being questioned by Paris cops and hated to see them go. Jacques Tardieux at the Perpignan center, farther south, had the right angry temperament, but was short and had a beer belly.

Marseille was next on their list. The Jacques there was surnamed Vachère and listed as a security guard.

This time, Mazarelle wasn't taking any chances. He had brought Jeannot and Maurice along with him on the trip, just to be careful. And while both were snoozing now, sacked out in the car from the long drive, he felt he had evened up the odds.

Mazarelle put his foot down on the gas. The road blurred under his wheels. He could feel the momentum of the case building, moving toward its finale. It was something Mazarelle could recognize. Every investigation had its own rhythm. The slow start, the gentle coaxing of facts, and then the shot of adrenaline as each new lead came in, and the pace built with its own undeniable rhythm. And right now he hoped the end wasn't too far away. In fact, it was just around the corner . . . just beyond this curve . . .

"Oh *merde*," he muttered as the road opened onto the front of the facility.

Outside the gates, a demonstration was underway. Hundreds, perhaps thousands, of protesters ringed the metal gates, banging on the chain-link fence that surrounded the detention center. Their placards bounced up and down, poking the sky.

An earnest, bearded man, with a gray streak in his ponytail, picked up a bullhorn: "*Ici . . .*" he yelled. "*Ici!*" He jabbed the bullhorn in the direction of the wall.

"Thousands of immigrants a year. Locked up for no crime. Shackled in these secret centers. They just want to be our neighbors."

He lifted both hands to encourage the crowd.

"Shut it down! Shut it down!"

The chanting had rousted Jeannot and Maurice. Together, the three got out of the car and headed for the front gate. Mazarelle had nothing against protesters. Democracy in action, free speech. Liberty. Equality. Fraternity. All fine with him.

As long as they would get out of the way and let him do his job. But the crowd was ten rows thick in front of the gates. It didn't look like he'd be able to get in. Couldn't they have picked another day for their demonstration?

Pushing his way through the crowd, Mazarelle could see that the protesters had begun to unfurl two long banners in front of the gates. One read: STOP RISKING EUROPE, which didn't exactly mean anything as far as he could tell. The other said: AN ACCIDENT WAITING TO HAPPEN. There was no question about that one. Especially if the man with the garrote was there.

The ponytail was back on the bullhorn. "This is one of the five most dangerous facilities in France," he shouted. "A history of suspicious deaths. They call them suicides. We say it's time to crack this place open!"

Suddenly, the image of a giant crack was projected onto the side of the gray cement building. The crowd howled.

On the back side of the plant, down by the Donzère-Mondragon Canal, two black-clad figures looked up, startled at the sound of the crowd.

"Just listen to those assholes," said the short, squat one. "Hard to believe anyone could get that upset about a bunch of foreigners."

The taller one reached down to smooth out the blueprint in front of them.

"That's the way in." He nodded.

The side door was open, just as Macquart had promised.

In the pale gray corridors, they made their way to a storage closet. The short one reached into the backpack he was carrying and pulled out three capped bottles. Clear liquid sloshed inside. A toxic blend of alcohol and gasoline.

He lifted the caps off, jammed the cloth deeper into the bottles, and pulled out a lighter.

"Time for shish kebab." He grinned.

Inside the main security office, a group of uniformed guards had gathered in front of the monitors. They stared in amazement at the screens in front of them. An entire wall of monitors from the security camera feeds, and every one seemed to have bad news. The placards out front. The banners flying. And the crowds slamming up against the front gates, like waves crashing on a shore. There was no sound from the feeds. No sound in the room at all. The guards were stunned at the commotion outside. They had never seen anything like it. And now the front gates bent and bulged, and seemed as if they were about to buckle.

Striding into the room, the diminutive security manager broke the silence. "What are you waiting for?" He slammed his palm on the table. "Get out there. Everyone to the front gate now!" He turned on his heel and headed out the door.

It took a moment for their brains to catch up, but an instant later the first startled guards took off, heading to reinforce the front lines, like their ancestors at a castle siege long ago. Everyone sprinting to the gates. Everyone but Jacques Vachère.

Vachère was looking at an entirely different monitor from everyone else. A monitor all the way in the corner. The one that showed the fire starting.

Out front, Mazarelle was pushing his way toward the gates. His bulk gently shouldering the crowd aside. They meant well. They were just in the wrong place at the wrong time. In front of him.

Ever since his rugby days, Mazarelle never minded a scrum. He had the size and the strength to make his own path. The demonstrators bounced off him the way would-be tacklers had years before. He was almost there . . . And then he came to a stop. Because in front of him, a new group of demonstrators had begun to chain themselves to the metal gates, their arms stretched out and tied up. Offering themselves up like martyrs on the cross. How was he going to get through these gates now?

Inside the bowels of the detention center, Vachère came sprinting around the corner, his long strides carrying him down the grim, off-white corridors. And came to a dead stop.

There in front of him, inside the inner courtyard, a fire was burning out of control. Hard to believe there was that much flammable inside these gray concrete walls. But the flames were shooting up, catching the mattresses, the clothes, the tables.

The prisoners scattered in every direction. The yelling came in a dozen different dialects, each one pure panic. Men, women, all in the central courtyard, slammed their fists up against the bars and the plexiglass windows. Screaming louder and louder at Vachère to let them out.

He watched and thought for a long minute. Then picked up a metal shovel, and barred the inner door.

Outside, the pair from Défense Nationale watched the expanding fire with a grim satisfaction. "We wanted to send a message. Now that's a message," the taller one said. "Otherwise they'll just keep coming."

His partner grinned. "They'll get the word: they should go home."

Inside, the sound of screams, and cracking glass as the temperatures mounted.

With the fire growing, Vachère came flying back toward the control room to alert his fellow guards. But he didn't quite make it.

At the other end of the corridor stood a young couple, Algerians from the look of them, panting with exhaustion. The young man must have found his girlfriend in the chaos and dragged her out through the cracked glass. And now they were trying to escape.

Looking up in surprise and irritation, Vachère's first thoughts were in his native Romanian. *Pula mea!* he swore to himself.

He leaped up, and came sprinting, heading right at them.

"Qu'est-ce qui se passe ici?" he shouted.

The young immigrant couple didn't have time to think. They took off on a dead run.

"Stop right there!"

Fear fueled their steps. They had no idea where they were heading. They were just going as fast as they could. Around a corner. Slamming into the door. The door popping open. Outside at last. And Vachère gaining on them all the time.

"Stop!"

Now they could see the fence, and the crowd of demonstrators beyond. They put on an extra burst of speed. If they could just get to the crowd, maybe they could hide. Escape.

The gate was coming up fast. They were almost there.

BOOM—BOOM!

The twin explosions ripped the afternoon sky.

The young man lurched forward, falling onto his chest. The young woman stumbled . . . reeled . . . and toppled over.

At the fence, the crowd of demonstrators was stunned into silence. They had seen it all. The flames. The tall figure with the hatchet face. The gun in his hand. A nine millimeter semiautomatic. Two shots. Two hits. The slow pool that spread out under the young woman's head. It looked like she was resting her cheek on a crimson pillow. Just resting in the afternoon sun. But she wasn't moving. The young man rolled over, and slowly started to crawl toward the gate, dragging his shattered leg behind him. The crowd gave a low moan. They had seen it all.

Mazarelle too.

Across the pavement, Vachère looked at the two figures. He didn't seem to have much of any expression on his face. He holstered the pistol, then looked up, slowly taking in the crowd, actually noticing them for the first time, realizing that everyone had seen what he'd done.

He shook his head.

"They're illegals. They don't even belong here."

And then from the crowd, the moan changed to something else. Something darker. More primitive. And the crowd as one began to smash through the fencing. Smashing through to release the prisoners from the flames inside. Smashing through to come after him.

Vachère didn't hesitate. He had no feeling about humans. But he knew the sounds of animals. And the crowd's roar—that was the sound of danger. He understood danger. He had spent his whole life living with it. Dashing across the pavement, he jumped into his Jeep, the engine howling as he kicked it into top gear. Hurtling full speed toward the back gates, he slammed on through, the metal shattered on the ground behind him. Heading east to the one place he could count as safe. The old Legion base at Aubagne. His brothers would protect him.

68

Outside the detention center, the demonstrators and the prisoners were scattering, shouting, sprinting in all directions. They had come here today to save the world—to put their lives on the line, maybe even get arrested. But fire and gunshots? Actual bullets? That was a little too much.

The crowd spread and hurtled—banners dropped and trampled under foot, bodies slamming into each other as the protesters tried to flee the scene. It wasn't easy to save the planet when someone was shooting. Shaggy young men and earnest young women were tripping over each other as they looked for the shortest route out of the chaos.

Jeannot came running up, an astonished expression on his face. "*Putain de merde!*" he shouted. "Is that our guy?"

In the midst of the crowd in motion, Mazarelle was the one still point, a boulder in a surging ocean. Only his eyes moved, his gaze focused hard on the direction in which the shooter had run. He had never gotten a clean look at his assailant in the darkness outside his apartment. But he'd seen the way he moved. That man had moved like a leopard. Lithe, efficient, no wasted motion. Just like this guard. Mazarelle wasn't a gambling man, but he would bet big money that this was his attacker. That the hunch about the tattoo had paid off. They had tracked down the *ripoux*'s enforcer—the man with the garrote. Now they had to find him again.

Maurice was at Mazarelle's elbow.

"*Chef*—we should call it in," he said. "Get the local police here working with us."

"They'll be here soon enough," said Mazarelle, pointing at the two bodies by the fence. "We can't afford to wait for them. We've got to get going."

"Going—going where?" asked Jeannot. "Where do you think he's heading?"

"Well," said Mazarelle, tapping his nose, "I've got an idea."

He opened the door to the little rental car and, with the three of them squeezed inside, they sped off, heading east.

The highway stretched out in front of them, winding and shimmering in the summer sun. It was the A50, plowing through the heart of the Mediterranean coast, on its way to the Côte d'Azur.

As Mazarelle drove, his foot nailed to the floor, he filled Jeannot and Maurice in on his plan. If he had to guess, Jacques Vachère was heading back to the one place that had always sheltered and sustained him—the Foreign Legion headquarters.

The little Peugeot was cranked up to its top-end speed, doing one hundred miles an hour down the empty highway. They were making good time. Mazarelle felt sure they had to be gaining on Vachère. The miles flew by on the road to Aubagne.

Until suddenly, they weren't alone.

All around them, cars started to slow, and crawl. Station wagons, vans, cars piled high with suitcases and bikes, all heading to the Riviera on the A50.

"*Merde!*" fumed Jeannot. "What's going on?"

"It's August," said Maurice. "And you know what that means—"

"*Les vacances,*" the three said simultaneously.

It seemed as if the whole country was on this one road, all heading off for the beaches. The traffic had ground to a halt now—a long ribbon of metal under the Mediterranean sun. They rolled to a stop by an underpass splattered with graffiti: *Les Arabes Dehors! Immigrés Rentrez Chez Vous! Vive la Défense Nationale!*

"We don't even have our siren," Maurice muttered. "I told you we should have done it the official way and taken a squad car."

"No time for that." Mazarelle swatted the idea away like an annoying fly. "No time for this either."

Yanking the wheel over hard to the right, he pulled the little car onto the shoulder and took off at an alarming speed, slamming his hand onto the horn. Pushed back in their seats by the acceleration, Maurice and Jeannot could only watch in astonishment as the honking cleared a path in front of them.

Less than an hour later, they pulled up on the gravel driveway in front of Legion headquarters in Aubagne. Mazarelle hopped out, energized, sure that this was where Vachère's path had led.

But inside, no one had seen him.

"Why don't you try Puyloubier—the Invalides—our retirement home," recommended the guard. "It's not far. You could ask the staff sergeant there. I'll get you a map and instructions on how to find it."

"Thanks," said Mazarelle. "I've been there before. I know where it is."

On the back roads to Puyloubier, Mazarelle told his team about the retirement home—an ornate château set on five hundred acres of forest land, all for former members of the French Foreign Legion. He described the hall of heroes and the catalog of strange weapons. If Vachère was really hiding there, it would be a formidable fortress.

Their road wound through vast woods and rocky landscapes, and through the pastures leading up to the craggy Montagne Sainte-Victoire, one of Cézanne's favorite subjects. Soon, they were driving into the little town of Puyloubier, home to Saint Servin de Puyloubier, a fifth-century hermit whose claim to fame was being massacred by marauding Visigoths. The legionnaires' home was a few minutes down the road.

Pulling into the parking lot, Mazarelle asked if the guard could tell him whether Staff Sergeant Delapierre was there today.

"Yes—tell me who you are and I'll call him."

A few minutes later, the burly Delapierre was at the entrance, his one good eye gleaming, his wide smile welcoming back Mazarelle. He cast a curious look at Jeannot and Maurice.

Settled inside Delapierre's office, Mazarelle hemmed and hawed for a moment, then finally confessed: he might not have been telling the full truth the last time they talked. He and his team were actually detectives from the Brigade Criminelle in Paris.

Before Mazarelle could start his questioning, Delapierre broke in.

"So—you're no longer an ace reporter these days," he said with a laugh.

Mazarelle flashed a quick grin. "Guilty! It was an investigative necessity. But this"—he stopped to underline the point—"this is serious."

"Understood," said the staff sergeant. "So what can I do for you?"

Mazarelle explained that they were on the trail of a dangerous man, perhaps responsible for multiple homicides.

"The man we're looking for. The man we've been tracking. He's one of your own."

"Ours? What do you mean?"

"He's from the Second REP. We think his name is Jacques—Jacques Vachère."

Delapierre's face had turned somber.

"I don't know," he said.

Mazarelle waited to see if the sergeant had something else to add. He didn't.

But if Mazarelle's experience of questioning witnesses had taught him anything, it was not to give up too easily. Not to stop too soon. And also, the advantages of a sudden change of direction.

"He's here, then?"

Delapierre leaned back quickly, as if stung.

"We don't talk about our brothers," the sergeant said. "That's the code."

Jeannot had been watching the exchange quietly, deferring to his boss and mentor. But patience was never his long suit, and now he had run out.

"The code?" Jeannot blew air out of his cheeks. "That's all well and good, but we saw the guy shoot down two people in front of us. Where's the honor in that?"

Mazarelle quieted the young lieutenant with a wave of the hand, and turned back to Delapierre, focusing in hard now.

"Sergeant, is he here?"

Delapierre looked at each of the detectives in front of him in turn, and then back to Mazarelle. Seconds ticked by. He took a deep breath. And slowly shook his head.

"No, he's not here."

Maurice and Jeannot sank back in their chairs, deflated.

Not Mazarelle. He had read something else in Delapierre's expression. Something that told him a little more of the story. He leaned forward, looking harder into the staff sergeant's eyes.

"But he *was* here, right?"

Delapierre nodded. One brief nod. As if even that cost him.

Still Mazarelle prodded.

"Today?"

Delapierre sighed and nodded again.

"Just a few hours ago."

Now Mazarelle settled back in his chair, spreading his hands to Delapierre, showing him the floor was now his.

The stocky sergeant ran his fingers through his beard. And, in time, he started to talk, slowly and haltingly.

"We usually help out our brothers when they come here. But Jacques Vachère . . . ?" Delapierre shuddered. "He has a dark history."

"So, you had been hearing about him?"

"We'd heard a couple of stories. Really, more like rumors. But they were enough. That's not what the Legion is about."

"What happened when he showed up today?"

"He wanted us to shelter him." Delapierre seemed to be reliving the moment in his mind. "We refused."

"How'd he take it?"

"It wasn't pretty," said Delapierre. "He took a swing at one of the guards. And then . . . Then he just took off."

Maurice jumped in. "Took off where? Do you know where he would have gone?"

The interruption had broken the rhythm of Mazarelle's questioning. He looked over at his colleague, annoyed. Then tried to pick up the rhythm of the conversation with the now-silent Delapierre.

"That must have been hard for you—having to turn him away like that."

Delapierre wasn't the type to wallow in emotions. But he did appreciate Mazarelle's gesture.

"We protect our own."

Mazarelle nodded. And picked his way forward, slowly and carefully.

"Sergeant, we want you to understand. This is not just any soldier. This is a man who is now wanted for multiple homicides. A man who I believe attacked me. And tried to kill me. With his garrote—the *loupe*. We don't make this request lightly. But can you tell us where he might have gone?"

Now Delapierre was working his beard with both hands. He ran his fingers through the streaks of gray, twisting the hairs around between thumb and forefinger. The activity seemed to take all of his concentration. He blew out a long stream of air.

"It's possible . . ." He seemed to run out of words.

Maurice cleared his throat to jump in.

Out of Delapierre's eyeline, Mazarelle reached over to clamp his hand down on Maurice's leg and dug in his fingers. The sergeant needed to come to this in his own time.

Maurice looked over at his boss, startled. But he kept his mouth shut.

Finally, Mazarelle's instinct was borne out, when Delapierre picked up the thread again.

"It's possible . . . that he went back into the woods. Back to one of the old hiking trails. Over in the woods by the Luberon."

Delapierre seemed to have stopped again. But still Mazarelle waited.

"There's . . . there's an old abandoned campground down along the Rhône."

The sergeant nodded, almost to himself. "He might have been heading there. We've heard rumors that he was occasionally spotted around there."

Delapierre suddenly looked up, and turned to Mazarelle. "Do you remember the story of that hike from the hell week?"

"The one in the rain?"

"Yes, the cadet training session. The one where Vachère nearly died."

"I do," said Mazarelle. "It was quite a story. I could hardly forget."

"Well, that campground was where they were staged when it all happened. It seems to have some meaning to him." Abruptly, Delapierre came to a full stop. He seemed exhausted by the effort.

Mazarelle gave the moment its due. And then he reached out his hand.

"Thank you."

Delapierre took in the large meaty hand in front of him. And reached out to shake.

"Be careful. He was lethal before. Now, he's angry."

Piling back into the car, the team headed out, at first driving west toward the nature preserves of the Camargue, the marshy forest and swamp lands below Arles, where the Rhône ran down to the Mediterranean Sea. But they soon realized that they were in unlikely territory for an abandoned campground. The area was too marshy, too open. If they were looking for a hideout near the Rhône river, close to where Vachère had hiked years ago, they'd surely have to try a little farther north, where the tree line filled in.

After a half-hour drive, they reached the natural parklands known as the Alpilles. Wild and savage, it was a landscape of great craggy outcroppings of trees and jagged limestone, a rugged, Provençal terrain in the shadow of the Luberon mountains. With its dense woods, this landscape surely offered better possibilities for campsites— abandoned or otherwise. And it seemed to fit Delapierre's description. They followed a series of dirt roads that edged the forest, and soon got their first break.

There, tucked away and covered with foliage, in a small grove of pines and kermes oak trees, was a battered Jeep. Vachère's Jeep. Mazarelle pulled over alongside and parked.

"Okay," he said. "He's got to be somewhere in there. The trail starts here."

He got out of the car and looked around.

"We've got two cracks at him. One is to try to find his campground in there. The other is out here by his Jeep."

Jeannot tumbled out of the car, ready to get going. "What's the plan, *chef?*"

"I'm heading in to see if I can track him down or find where he's staying. But odds are he's most likely to come back here for his car. I need you guys to post up here by the Jeep and keep your eyes open." He handed his gun to Maurice. "Here, Cap—hold on to my SIG Sauer. It might come in handy."

"But, boss," cried Jeannot, "I have to come with you. You shouldn't go after Vachère alone!"

"No," insisted Mazarelle. "This way we'll have twice as many chances to spot him."

It wasn't the greatest reason, but he had to come up with something to keep his two men out of harm's way. There was no need for all of them to be at risk.

"You and Maurice stay here. I'll stay in touch with my mobile phone. If I need you, I'll call for you. Do you get that, Jeannot?"

"Yeah—I suppose so . . ." answered Jeannot, frowning. His face had turned magenta, and he was clenching his fists.

Mazarelle had never seen him so angry, but he knew he had to protect the impetuous young cop. And he knew what he had to do. He grabbed a flashlight from his backpack. Then, without looking back, Mazarelle strode off toward the forest, determined to track down the killer.

69

Though it had rained earlier in the day, the afternoon sun now shone fiercely as Mazarelle approached the edge of the forest. Hot and dry was how it felt. But once he'd begun penetrating deeply into the woods bordering the Rhône, searching for the abandoned campsite, there was a chill to the air. Low-hanging emerald leaves were wet and dripped pearls of rain on Mazarelle, dampening his shoulders and soaking the cap he'd been wise to take.

He passed through areas pierced by sudden rays of sunshine and then others almost as black as night. The shifts from light to dark unsettled him. He was not a natural out-of-doors guy. He'd grown up on the rue Saint-Séverin in the Fifth Arrondissement, and learned everything there was to know about the streets of Paris before he was out of secondary school. But aside from a few brief trips into the countryside for picnics and such, he'd had little to do with rural France. His short stay in the Dordogne with Martine had exposed him to another style of life but had hardly prepared him to deal with forest trekking. He found himself stumbling over roots and fallen branches, swiped by low-hanging limbs of trees, and unable to move as fast as he'd like. Soon his bad leg began to pain him, and grew worse as he dragged himself along, not knowing where he was going, or how, in this alien environment, he'd be able to find Vachère.

Back at the rental car, Jeannot sat in the passenger seat, anxiously tapping the dashboard.

"Why wouldn't he let me go with him?" he asked Maurice for the third time. "I could help him."

Maurice shot an exasperated look at the young cop. "You heard the *chef,* Jeannot. We need to sit tight and watch Vachère's car in case he doubles back."

For a long moment, Jeannot stared fiercely at Maurice. Then, suddenly, the young cop grabbed Mazarelle's gun from the dashboard; threw open the car door; and, before Maurice could stop him, raced headlong toward the forest.

Maurice watched Jeannot disappear into the woods. Then he looked at the Jeep Wrangler dumped by Vachère in the grove of trees. "*Merde.*"

The forest was dizzyingly large. As Mazarelle hiked onward, trying to find the campground Delapierre had mentioned, he began to wonder if he had been a little too trusting of the old legionnaire. Sure, a crime was a crime, murder was murder, but to a combat-hardened soldier like the sergeant, who had witnessed (and probably participated in) much worse in the field, would the word of a city cop be enough to compel him to turn on his brother? As the pain in his bad leg grew worse, Mazarelle's thoughts turned increasingly cynical. Had Delapierre sent him on a unicorn hunt in the middle of nowhere—was he trying to give Vachère a shot at escape? The old man had offered just enough detail to make it believable, but vague enough to make it almost impossible to track Vachère in a forest of this magnitude. Mazarelle could picture the old legionnaire laughing his ass off at this very moment, thinking of the squad of city cops hopelessly bumbling around the harsh terrain of the forest. If so, Mazarelle swore to himself he would make Delapierre regret it. He was counting the ways he'd do it when he spotted something that made him freeze.

Peeking out from beneath a tuft of moss on a nearby tree there seemed to be a carving of some sort. Mazarelle hobbled over to get a closer look. Kneeling down, he pulled aside the moss to fully reveal two faded letters etched into the base: *LE*. Mazarelle allowed himself a slight grin. Maybe Delapierre wasn't full of shit. Maybe this really was the old training ground for the *Légion étrangère*. The proof would be the discovery of an abandoned campsite currently occupied by Vachère. But as Mazarelle caught sight of the sun hanging low in the sky, he had the sinking feeling that he was running out of time and that his goal was still a long way off.

He had to get going. Ignoring the throb in his leg, he looked around at his surroundings. Had there been more markings he had missed? Mazarelle slowly scanned the area, his gaze stopping on the forest floor ten feet in front of him. It wasn't a Legion marking that caught his eye. Although heavily covered by leaves, that patch of ground seemed to be oddly concave. Mazarelle grabbed a long branch from the ground nearby and crawled forward, sweeping in front of him. Nothing but hard-packed dirt under the leaves as he inched closer, prodding the earth. Suddenly, his stick gave way, its entire length disappearing deep into the ground. Caught off guard, Mazarelle reeled to keep his balance, throwing his weight sideways to avoid plunging forward. Breathing hard, he pulled himself together and swept away a portion of leaves on the ground in front of him.

The last time Mazarelle had seen something like this was in one of his *école primaire* history books. The trou-de-loup, or "wolf's hole" as it was known, was a fiendish design of medieval origin—a pit six feet deep, filled with sharpened wooden spikes, and covered with wicker and leaves. The damage those spikes inflicted on advancing troops was far greater than the physical impact. Only one soldier had to fall victim for an entire battalion to be afflicted with nightmares of dying a slow death impaled on the needlelike teeth of the wolf. Though Vachère's pit was more modest, it was no less dangerous. Mazarelle shuddered at the thought, and wondered how many of these "holes" he'd had the luck to avoid thus far, and how many more lay between him and his prey. He would have to watch his step.

It had only taken Jeannot a few minutes to pick up the trail of his *chef*. Now, as he cruised deeper into the forest at a brisk jog, he felt sure he was on the right path. Mazarelle's mind may have been nimble, performing mental gymnastics on a daily basis, but his body was less so, leaving behind a wide trail of broken branches.

Jeannot knew his boss would be pissed when he caught up. He had gone against a direct order from not one but two superior officers. But when they brought down Vachère, all would be forgiven. That was what a successful arrest did for a turbulent investigation. It was the detective's holy water, washing away the sins of the past. A collar was a collar no matter how you got the results, especially in a double homicide, and Jeannot knew that whatever reprimands he faced from Mazarelle in the wake of the investigation would surely be overshadowed by the praise heaped on his unit for taking two murders off the books.

Maybe he would even be lucky enough to take Vachère down himself! He did have a gun, after all. Jeannot could almost picture himself now, standing erect as the cameras flashed, the grinning Coudert pinning a gold-starred commendation to his breast as his parents and all of Paris were there to applaud him. It would be glorious. As Maurice stood by, watching, the moment would be Jeannot's. That was how you did police work.

Jeannot grinned, picking up his jog to a sprint. To most, the uneven forest terrain would have prevented such a pace, but to a seasoned runner it was child's play. Before joining the force he had run much more religiously, every morning blazing through the Bois de Boulogne, the expansive royal hunting grounds turned park on the western edge of Paris. Most runners stuck to the trails, but for Jeannot, half the fun of running in the forest was finding your own path. Since joining the BC, his pastime had been relegated to weekends, or the odd late-night run to blow off steam, but even with only one or two times a week his body had, more or less, stayed in fighting shape. The cycling helped. He pushed onward, light on the balls of his feet, practically springing off the hard-packed earth. At this rate he would find Mazarelle in no time. He was confident of that—and yet suddenly he was falling, his foot stepping into nothing, as the ground below him gave way and the rest of his body followed.

First there was a brief moment of weightlessness as he plunged downward, rotating in the air, then pain. Burning, white-hot pain that shot up and down his right leg. A sharpened wooden spike ripped through the denim of his jeans and drove itself into the meat of his calf and out the other side. Another spike took off a chunk of his right triceps.

As Jeannot, impaled and trapped, lay at the bottom of the pit staring up at the darkening sky, he knew that this was exactly why Mazarelle had told him to hang back. How could he have been so careless? Thinking of his *chef*'s reaction to finding him, Jeannot hated himself. But this was no time for pride. He needed Mazarelle now.

"MAAAAZOOOO! Help me! For god's sake—help!" Jeannot's entire body throbbed as he screamed, the life slowly seeping out of him into the cold earth, until the darkness closed in around him and he lost consciousness.

The sun had already set, but once Mazarelle caught a scent he was like a bloodhound—three hundred million nasal receptors and all locked in on the stink of a criminal. But he wasn't rushing. Since encountering the engraved *LE* letters and the trap he had slowed down considerably, picking his way forward through the dense forest. It had already yielded dividends, as Mazarelle had found and followed two more *LE* signs, and managed to avoid a rope snare that would have easily snapped his ankle, leaving him stranded, hanging upside down. He was on Vachère's turf, and the only thing he knew for sure was that he would be a fool to take that for granted.

As he made his way forward, a new sound emerged amid the symphony of the forest's noises. A distant voice. Was it Vachère taunting him? His mind playing tricks? Still it persisted. And with a sudden shock, Mazarelle realized he recognized the sound—a timbre he had heard day in and day out since joining the BC. It was Jeannot and he was calling for help. Had the young cop followed him in? Mazarelle could stomach risking his own life, but Jeannot—goddammit! Mazarelle stood rooted to the spot, trying to figure out where the young cop might be. The call seemed to be coming from behind him. But just as abruptly as the noise started, Jeannot's pleas for help were suddenly cut short. The silence was sickening, and Mazarelle knew what he had to do. Turning back the way he had come, he headed into the darkness.

PART SEVEN

70

The air was thick with the smell of smoke and mildew. Vachère tossed another log on the fire, embers spilling out of the hearth, as he watched the flames dance. Placing the steel poker next to the roaring flames, he turned back to examine his guest. He had found the young man stuck like a pig and bleeding at the bottom of one of his many traps. A flunky of Mazarelle's, no doubt. It had only taken Vachère a minute of rummaging through the young man's pockets to confirm his suspicion—the captive he had now tied down to a large wooden table in front of him was Jean Villepin of the Brigade Criminelle. His security system had worked to perfection. Well, almost. Perfection would have meant Mazarelle tied to the table instead, but he had no problem with small victories. After all, that was how you won the war. He now knew who was chasing him and he had a hostage. And, best of all, he knew which part of the booby-trapped terrain was effective. He just needed a little more information. It was time to protect himself. It was time to protect Luc and his brothers. He had given an oath, and he intended to live by it.

Running his thumb over the gaping wound in Jeannot's calf, he gently dug in his thumbnail. The young man's eyelids exploded open, as he bucked and strained against the ropes holding him down, howling into the cloth gag that was fitted snugly into his mouth.

"Ah, there you are." Vachère smiled and gave Jeannot a playful pat on the cheek. "You really are lucky. If I hadn't found you, you'd be dead right now!"

Vachère walked over to the hearth and removed the now red-hot poker from the flames.

"First we need to do something about that hole in your leg, right? We can't have you bleeding out before we've had a chance to talk."

Jeannot's head was strapped to the table, so he didn't see the fire poker until Vachère had raised it above his wounded leg, holding it there for the young officer to appraise. Jeannot's eyes bulged. He knew what was coming next.

Vachère brought down the poker with practiced precision, the red-hot metal instantly cauterizing the exit wound of the spike—the young cop's skin sizzling like water thrown in a hot pan. The sickly sweet odor of charred flesh filled the cabin. Vachère inspected the leg, nodding to himself.

"So lucky it's a vein, not an artery. That should keep you."

He looked back to Jeannot. "And now for the other side!"

He raised the poker again.

Deep in the forest, Mazarelle was retracing his steps. He knew the pit was back this way somewhere. In the darkness, he almost fell into it. But there, flickering his flashlight over the edge, he could see what must have happened. The spikes at the bottom of the pit were still glistening. He set off, following the drag path that led away from the hole. And soon, the muffled shouts of Jeannot led him the rest of the way.

In a clearing stood the abandoned campsite, more than twenty wood cabins dilapidated and fraying with age. Once it must have housed small squads of recruits as they went through the final weeks of their rigorous four-month training. Now it was a ghost town. Roofs caved in. Doors swinging open in the evening breeze. Except for one cabin.

It seemed almost as rundown as the rest, but as Mazarelle got closer, he could see that the cracks in the logs had in fact been patched and sealed, the entire structure reinforced with dirt and mud. A window was covered with wood slats, but not completely. Lights were glimmering inside the cabin. Mazarelle crept up to the window for a closer look.

And wished he hadn't.

Inside, the killer he had fought off in his apartment building was showing a knife to his young lieutenant. The killer's expression seemed almost quizzical—as if something didn't exactly make sense. Tracing the tip along Jeannot's forearm, he carved off a tiny piece.

Mazarelle fought to keep the bile down in his stomach. Taking a deep breath to collect himself, he realized he had to do something quick if he wanted to save Jeannot. He risked a fast look back in through the window. There were only two ways into the cabin—door and window—and neither one would work. He had no way of getting inside without allowing Vachère to kill Jeannot. And Vachère didn't just have the knife. There was also a pistol on the table by his side. It was a SIG Sauer. In fact, Mazarelle realized with a start, it was *his* SIG Sauer. Mazarelle instinctively reached down to check his leg. All he had left was his small back-up gun, a Kahr K9, tucked away in an ankle holster. The last thing he needed was a shoot-out.

He had to get Vachère out of the cabin.

He spotted a stack of wood by the side wall, and had an idea.

The young cop had been harder to crack than he anticipated. For some reason he was trying to act the hero instead of simply talking. But his silence didn't matter to Vachère. He pushed back the sleeves of his black hoodie and started on Jeannot's injured leg.

"You don't need this." Vachère shook his head. "This epidural skin here, it's all dead."

He picked away a few layers of charred flesh as he tried to shake loose the information he was looking for. Prodding with the tip of his blade, Vachère made Jeannot's muscles dance unwilled before his eyes. It was crucial to establish that the cop had no control, not even of his own body.

Vachère asked him again, "How did you find me?"

Jeannot groaned, mumbling something, blood trickling down the corner of his mouth. Vachère gave him a little slap on the cheek.

"Louder."

"Delapierre."

Vachère's brow furrowed. That washed-up old fuck. He had broken the code. Legionnaire or not, the sergeant would suffer for it. He turned away and angrily paced the room for a moment. Then turning back, he asked his next question.

"How many of you are there? I know you didn't come out here alone."

Again, barely able to keep his eyes open, the young cop muttered something unintelligible, but now Vachère was angry. He grabbed Jeannot by the jaw and brought his face in close. "I said, how many."

Jeannot's eyelids fluttered open as he flashed a bloody smile.

"Surrounded. You're surrounded."

He coughed blood, speckling Vachère's face with red liquid. Vachère's expression was unflinching as his black eyes searched the young cop's face for the truth. Without breaking his stare, Vachère grabbed the Camillus and drove it through Jeannot's hand and into the wooden table below—sending the young cop howling in a fit of agony.

"Bullshit. You know how I know it's bullshit? I found you, not the other way around. I'm the hunter, not you. I'm the fucking hunter." But just as Vachère had begun to reassure himself, he heard a noise that he was not expecting—a crash of wood outside the door.

"Jacques Vachère!" came a shout. Another crash, followed by a maniacal laugh. And then another shout—"Vachère—the devil marches with you!"

Jeannot managed to mumble, "I told you."

Vachère peeked between the boards covering the front window of the cabin. It was Mazarelle, alone. Vachère smirked. Still alive. Still a fool. This idiot was taking all the fun out of the hunt. He would deal with him quickly.

Vachère moved back toward Jeannot and gave him a pinch on the cheek.

"Don't worry, Jean. It's the cavalry!" With that, he grabbed the SIG Sauer he had found on the young cop and strode outside. Out beyond the cabin, the woods were dark and silent. A tiny breeze rustled the leaves. He knew Mazarelle was out there somewhere. He just had to lure him out.

"It's time, Mazarelle."

His eyes scanned the tree line. No sign of him.

"Time for you and your boy Jean."

He was listening hard. But there was nothing.

"Aren't you worried about Jean? He's not looking good."

There on the edge of the clearing, a mere thirty feet away, Mazarelle appeared. A slow smile spread across Vachère's lips.

He put his finger on the SIG's hammer and cocked the gun. Before he could fire, Mazarelle had stepped back into the shadows.

Vachère didn't hesitate. This was his game. Closing the distance with alarming speed, he flung himself toward the woods.

Sprinting toward the tree line, he spotted Mazarelle again. The detective wasn't moving. That was strange. Leaping forward, Vachère suddenly felt the earth softening underfoot, the ground giving way, his ankle twisting, then blinding pain shooting through his foot as his body weight shifted and pushed him farther down, rooting him to the spot. The gun went flying. Vachère's gaze shot downward to find six inches of bloody wood protruding from the top of his boot. That crafty bastard. His own trap, used on him.

The pain was excruciating. He reached around. He couldn't see the SIG Sauer anywhere. Just mud and leaves, and the throbbing in his foot.

And now, there was Mazarelle, lumbering forward with a self-satisfied smirk, a small weapon in one hand, cuffs in the other.

"We're bringing you in, Vachère."

Vachère's hands fumbled in the darkness, searching frantically for the gun. It was gone. His fingers closed around something else. A rock. It would have to do.

The rock clipped Mazarelle in the cheek before he could sidestep it, sending him reeling backward, his vision blurred, his small gun slipping from his grasp.

Straining to get to his feet, Vachère calculated the odds. Mazarelle was doubled over on his knees trying to stand. Maybe if he was quick enough he could use the spike itself against him. A dazed animal was almost as easy to kill as a maimed one.

No, not enough time—he would have to go deeper in the woods and hope for another encounter. Or maybe luck would be on his side and Mazarelle would fall into one of his traps first. Either way, escape was the best scenario for survival.

Vachère quickly took two deep breaths, then grabbed the wooden spike at the base beneath his boot, and yanked his foot up hard. Grunting with pain, he appraised the wound. A euro-size hole in his boot began pooling with blood.

Mazarelle, unsteadily scrambling to his feet, was trying to regain his balance. A thin line of blood trickled down the side of his face, but it didn't feel important. In the light from the cabin, he could make out Vachère, freeing himself from the wooden spike and frantically limping away into the woods. So the plan had worked. Now to take him down!

He'd started off after Vachère, when he heard a low groan. Jeannot! How could he have forgotten? Mazarelle rushed inside the cabin and knelt by the young man's side. Jeannot was alive, but barely. Mazarelle went to work on him, ripping away chunks of cloth and quickly tying tourniquets around his bleeding appendages. He then pulled out his cell and called Maurice.

"Jeannot needs help, Maurice. Track my cell, I'm leaving it with him. Contact the nearest medical center and get Jeannot to a doctor. Stay with him overnight wherever they can treat him."

"But, boss, where are you going?"

"I'm heading after Vachère."

71

Dawn was just breaking as Mazarelle made his way through the trees that lined the rugged limestone of the Alpilles preserve. He was no tracker like Vachère, but this was a trail even he could follow—a trail of blood and trampled brush. It had taken him hours, but he knew he was close.

Emerging out of the woods, he stopped to catch his breath. His leg was really throbbing now. And his head still woozy. But the vista demanded attention. A remarkable sight—harsh, craggy, white stone, uneven and jagged, all framing a massive brown waterway.

It was the Rhône, a powerful river, churning five hundred miles from the Swiss Alps toward the Mediterranean. And even in the late Provençal summer, the river was rolling along at a flood volume—four hundred thousand cubic feet a second. The glacial snow, melting up at the riverhead, was releasing new torrents. Green and brown, the water surged past, strong enough to power electrical plants and carve through the craggy limestone that surrounded it.

In the overwhelming roar of the river, Mazarelle almost missed him.

There, coming out of the tree line, a lean, steely figure making his way south, silhouetted in the early morning light. It was Vachère—wounded, limping a little, his foot bleeding. But even at that distance, Mazarelle could tell that he was still a raw force, a coiled menace.

When Vachère heard Mazarelle's voice, he jumped and turned.

"*Vous?!*" Vachère snarled at his pursuer. "You want more?"

To Mazarelle, his fury didn't merit an answer. Instead the detective started forward, closing the distance between them.

Vachère watched him come. He stood tall on an embankment, a half dozen feet over the river, an ominous drop below. He was trapped now, between Mazarelle and the Rhône. But in his mind, it was Mazarelle who was trapped with him.

Mazarelle stopped just out of range. In the first orange rays of the morning, he could see there was no one else around but the two of them. Eyeball to eyeball, hunter and hunted. Although which was which, Mazarelle couldn't say at the moment. What he knew was that this wouldn't be easy. Facing a lethal adversary, Mazarelle's first attack wasn't physical. He went for the weak spot—his opponent's mind.

"Ready to swim, Vachère?"

Mazarelle jabbed his finger toward the banks of the Rhône.

In spite of himself, Vachère cast a quick jittery look over his shoulder. Reliving the trauma of his youth. And then steeled himself. By the time he looked back, there was no expression in his eyes at all.

Waiting, watching, he sized Mazarelle up—picking his moment.

But Mazarelle was taking his time as well. There was no need to rush. Time was on his side.

"So tell me," he said. "Why did you do it?"

Vachère just stared at him.

"Those murders in Paris. Why kill those men?"

Still no answer.

"What was the point?"

A small flicker of amusement twisted the corner of Vachère's lips. The question provoked him.

"There's no point. There's just orders."

Mazarelle nodded encouragingly. "So who sent you?"

Vachère shrugged. His mouth closed.

It wasn't much of a confession. For Vachère, it was all the same. One more coffin. And now, he seemed to be measuring Mazarelle again.

"C'mon," said Mazarelle. "This is your chance. Think about a lighter sentence. You'll never get away."

"Get away?" said Vachère. "I don't need to get away. This is my home."

For the briefest moment, something about Vachère's expression froze Mazarelle. Like a basilisk, rooting him to the spot. It wasn't the ferocity, the animal snarl. It was what came next—the odd smile.

What was this maniac grinning about? As if these were the moments that Vachère loved most. When the hunt reached its end. Well, this hunt was about to end, one way or the other.

Mazarelle swiftly moved forward to grab the killer.

But even injured as he was, Vachère was still more dangerous than Mazarelle. A slip of the hand, a flip of the wrist, and Vachère had his pursuer in a painful wristlock. Mazarelle was strong, an ox of a man. But he couldn't match the paramilitary experience of a trained special ops warrior. Inch by inch, Mazarelle was bent down by an unbearable pain in his elbow and shoulder.

Shifting his weight, he tried to wriggle his way out, to reposition his arm and shoulder in some way. Vachère gave a small chuckle, and tightened his grip. It seemed there was no way out of this one. Except—when he was engaged in hand-to-hand combat, Mazarelle did have one thing going for him. He fought dirty. Even as the pain forced him down toward the ground, he summoned one small burst of energy and drove the heel of his shoe into his opponent's bleeding foot.

Vachère's yowl of agony was deeply satisfying; his release of the armlock even more so. Mazarelle didn't hesitate. He drove forward, using his bulk to press home his advantage. But Vachère stepped back, retreating, covering. Mazarelle was frustrated at each blow. He couldn't get a punch inside. Stepping forward again, he feinted at Vachère's face, as he drove his knee into the soft flesh on the outside of the soldier's leg, right below the hip. A straight shot at the sciatic nerve. Deadening, crippling almost any leg.

Vachère seemed to buckle for a moment. But only a moment. And in almost the same instant, he reached out and grabbed at Mazarelle's shirtfront. Yanking him forward, he lined the big man up for a kill shot to the neck.

But Mazarelle didn't pull away as expected. Instead, he kept right on coming. He used the force of Vachère's tug to propel himself onward. Mazarelle's head seemed to launch forward, his forehead smashing into Vachère's face. BAM! The headbutt exploded, crashing right across the bridge of Vachère's nose. A panoply of stars detonated into a brilliant palette.

Mazarelle, unbalanced now, slipped and toppled over onto the slick stone of the embankment. Vachère, also losing his balance, reeled in the opposite direction. He spun, staggering, stumbling on the edge of the riverbank, and fell headfirst into the Rhône.

For a moment, Mazarelle lay flat on his back, stunned.

But he was back on his feet in an instant. He saw Vachère pop up like a cork, bouncing on the water's surface. The soldier struggled to reach a branch that extended over the river. It was just beyond his grasp.

"Mazarelle! I need—HELP me!" Vachère shouted. "I can't . . . ! I can't . . . !"

In the water, all Vachère's old phobias were awakened. Tormented him. Filled his mind. He sank back into the water, then popped up for a huge gasp of air.

"Help, you son of a . . . !"

It wasn't that he couldn't swim. Vachère's foot seemed to be caught. The force of the current was pushing him downstream, but his foot had gotten jammed behind him, wedged between a couple of rocks. His head would pop up to the surface, then be pushed under the current again. And with the force of the water flowing over his body, there was no way for him to work his way back upstream to free his foot. He was caught, snared in nature's own trap.

It took Mazarelle a moment to understand what was happening. Vachère would never be able to get himself loose. He saw the realization dawn in the killer's eyes. The fear. His old nemesis, this mighty river, about to claim him at last.

Mazarelle's instinct was to jump in and save the drowning swimmer. He kicked off his shoes, pulled his shirt over his head. He grabbed at his belt . . . And stopped.

Mazarelle watched Vachère's head pop up in the water again, taking a great gasping breath. He watched the bobbing head, the flowing water. He had made a career out of saving people. But not this one. Not this *salaud*. He could still see the knife marks on the arms of young Jeannot.

As if she were right behind him, he heard Angelique's warning: "Don't be a hero."

"Help!" Vachère continued to shout, as the river pounded onward. But now his voice was weaker, paler, fading.

Then all Mazarelle saw were the bubbles as Vachère disappeared beneath the Rhône's surface, the river sucking him down like a whirlpool.

72

Early the next morning, a superfast TGV from the Rhône and a very slow cab ride from the Gare de Lyon deposited the commandant back at police headquarters. He'd just sat down at his desk when the call came in. Coudert wanted him in his office to discuss the resolution of the tarot card murder.

Mazarelle wasn't sure what to expect. On the train ride back, he'd initially felt a wave of contentment. One less monster walking the earth. But the closer he got to home, the more his original satisfaction with Jacques Vachère's demise had given way to another emotion—one that felt much more like guilt. Not so much over what had happened to the murderer—who deserved every bit of his gruesome drowning—but rather that he had failed to bring him back. No arrest meant no trial. And no trial meant no evidence. No way to track down the men lurking in the background behind these murders. Because that's how Mazarelle had read Vachère's enigmatic answer. A confirmation of his own sense that, of course, there were others who gave the orders—the ones really responsible for the deaths.

"I can't say I liked the way he died—" began Mazarelle, eager to explain why and how the "accidental" death occurred.

"Listen, Mazarelle," interrupted the *patron*. "I don't need to hear the details. Neither the *directeur* nor I have any regrets. Nor should you. On the contrary, we're enormously relieved. You did well. Much better than many of us thought you'd do. Two ugly murders off the books. The tarot card murderer is gone. The newspapers are happy. The tourists are happy. And our case clearance rate is on the rise. You've saved us a ton of trouble." As Coudert spoke, he snapped shut the Berthaud-Danglars folder on his desk, as if to emphasize the end of the case.

"What happened to Babo?"

"Oh, he's been released. Had nothing to do with the case. Why was he in prison in the first place?"

Why indeed? Mazarelle gave a muffled snort. Probably because some people found it easier to look for Romani scapegoats than do the work.

"Do you think we owe him an apology?"

The *patron*'s expression was incredulous. "He's a street thug. And a Gypsy. Give him an apology, he'll want money next. Caviar. Not to mention a lawsuit."

Coudert leaned back contentedly at his desk.

"And now you can—you should—forget about the whole messy business. Take a few days off and get a little rest."

Mazarelle was astonished. He didn't mind the warm welcome, but he didn't understand what Coudert was talking about. Especially since, as far as Mazarelle was concerned, the case was far from over.

"But, *patron*," he stuttered, "that's only the killer. We don't have the people who sent him. The people behind it all."

Coudert pushed the case file to the corner of his desk and started to organize his pens and pencils, lining them up with the edge of the folder. For a while, he seemed to be ignoring Mazarelle. Finally, he sighed.

"Commandant. You caught the killer. And more than that, you avenged a cop's murder. Take the win. Wrap it up, go home."

Mazarelle reached into his pocket. And pulled out his pipe. He had no tobacco in it. It didn't matter. He was stalling for time.

"How can we call the case cleared when we don't know who was behind it? That's only half cleared. See—I have a theory."

He was surprised that Coudert had not mentioned the latest news—the arrest of Luc Fournel that morning by the *boeuf-carottes*. With a little help behind the scenes from Maurice, they had tracked the evidence, the flow of money that linked him and his Agence AB to the dirty cops. Was Coudert really unaware of the connection between the *ripoux* scandal and the murders? Or did he simply want to ignore the obvious?

Luc deserved jail time for his payoffs. But, to Mazarelle, Luc's buying and selling of salacious information, his use of bribery, his illegal offshore account in Andorra, his hacking of cops' phones—those were the least of the guy's crimes.

Mazarelle knew that Luc was also intimately tied to the murders committed by Vachère, his friend, his surrogate. Even more than that, Mazarelle was convinced that there was someone higher up, someone even more responsible for conceiving and orchestrating the tarot murders.

He cleared his throat.

"What if Luc Fournel gave the order to Vachère? And what if someone above Luc . . ."

Coudert looked up suddenly, and held up his hand. He gave Mazarelle his biggest smile, a full one hundred watts.

"Very interesting. Very interesting indeed. Did I mention, you might be in line for a commendation? Even the *Médaille d'honneur.*"

That startled Mazarelle. It was the highest honor the police bestowed.

"I've been talking with your friends at the Ministry of the Interior," Coudert went on. "They agree with me." The head of the Brigade Criminelle nodded his head sagely. "So take a rest. Take it easy. Let a few of your theories go. Come back recharged and ready for your next case."

Mazarelle was amazed. Never had a medal felt more ominous.

Tucking his pipe away, Mazarelle thanked his boss for the kind words, and left.

73

Later that afternoon, in the recovery ward of the Hôtel-Dieu hospital, Maurice had the latest issue of *L'Equipe* open. Sitting by Jeannot's bed, he was reading to the young lieutenant about the results from the most recent round of *Ligue* 1 action.

"Didn't I tell you!" Maurice chortled. "Didier! His right foot is a cannon—twenty-five meters out, and the goalkeeper never had a chance."

They both looked up as Mazarelle walked into the room.

"Please, boss." Jeannot gave a weak grin. "Save me from his mighty Elephants."

Maurice gave the bed a gentle swat with the magazine.

"Young man! You may be a hero, but don't push it."

The captain turned to Mazarelle. "His taste in teams is a tragedy."

Mazarelle shook his head.

"He's not much for listening to orders either."

Jeannot's face, a pale color, suddenly started to turn red, as he fumbled for something to say.

"But I thought you would need me. I had to help. Right?"

Mazarelle lifted an eyebrow, and gave Jeannot a little poke in his bandaged right leg.

"You tell me."

With a sharp intake of breath, the lieutenant winced, and tried to change the subject. "What about . . . what about the rest of the *ripoux*? Where are we on that?"

Maurice looked up. "Those other phone records you asked for, they came in this morning." He handed Mazarelle the envelope.

Mazarelle peered inside, then ambled over to the hospital window and looked out.

"Well," he said after a long moment, "Vachère is dead and Luc isn't talking. So we seem to be out of luck."

Maurice and Jeannot didn't know what to say.

Mazarelle finally gave them a little smile.

"But," he said, "I do have one idea."

It was a local patrolman, stationed in front of a bank in the Fourth Arrondissement, who gave him the tip he was looking for.

"Sure," said the officer. "You might want to try this bar not far from here. Chez les Jumeaux."

"*Jumeaux?*" Mazarelle was surprised by the odd name. "As in twins?"

"Exactly." The patrolman nodded. "It's his favorite after-hours hangout. Very close to the canal. It's a bit of a joint. And not easy to see your way around in there either. The lighting must have been done by Toulouse-Lautrec."

The bar was packed. Peering in the window, all Mazarelle could see was the press of bodies and a thin haze of smoke.

Inside the bar, the atmosphere was even more murky. Mazarelle tried to make out faces in the crowd. It was not easy.

But the bartenders were hard to miss. Tall. Blond. And not just one. Two. Both dressed exactly the same way. Identical red and white silk scarves. Black knit sweaters. Mazarelle chuckled to himself. So Chez les Jumeaux really was a bar run by twins.

But where was his man?

Scanning the room, Mazarelle finally spotted the tall figure in the rear booth in the corner, bent over his drink. He was alone and not looking too cheerful. I bet he'll look even less pleased, thought Mazarelle, when he sees me and guesses why I've come.

Mazarelle made his way through the crowd and approached the booth at the back. Its occupant looked up, surprised to see him.

"What the hell are you doing here?" Théo Legardère sneered. "You're ruining my happy hour!"

Mazarelle eased his bulk into the booth. And reached over to smell the scotch that Legardère was drinking.

"The Macallan twelve year?" Mazarelle asked. He turned the bottle around to take in the label, and nodded. "Sherry Oak Single Malt."

Legardère frowned and waved him away. Mazarelle ignored the gesture. He was on a roll.

"Crisp, sweet. Hints of vanilla and tropical fruits."

"Oh, please, Mazarelle. Spare me the damn Michelin Guide."

"Well, one thing any guide would tell you." Mazarelle pointed at the single-malt label on the face of Legardère's scotch. "That's a pretty pricey bottle."

"And?"

"And I didn't know you could afford to drink that on what they pay you guys. Seventy-five euros a bottle. You must have some major action on the side to be able to afford such fine scotch. Then again, I always figured you had to be pocketing something extra."

"You're dreaming!"

Legardère couldn't stand Mazarelle's snarky tone. He loved his watch, his car, his scotches. Who was this rumpled bear of a man to poke fun at him? Now three drinks in, he started to simmer, spluttering in a furious mix of alcohol and raw anger.

"I'm as clean as you are, Mazarelle, and a damn sight better cop to boot."

Mazarelle's expression made it clear he didn't share his view.

"So you can stuff that in your pipe! They should have sent me to 36," Legardère grumbled, "not you, dim bulb!"

Unfazed, Mazarelle looked slowly around the bar, all the time in the world, and turned back to Legardère with a wide-open expression, just chatting with a friend.

"You know they arrested Luc, right?"

Most people would have missed the flinch, especially in the dark corner of this bar. Mazarelle caught it.

Legardère waved his hand.

"So what does that have to do with me?"

"Two people were killed, Théo. Including one of our own. You knew Guy."

Legardère drew himself up in the booth.

"I had nothing to do with any murders. That's nothing to do with me."

Mazarelle twisted the bottle in his hands.

"What you may not know, Théo, is that Luc rolled over."

"Rolled over? I don't think so."

"Oh, yes. He told me you were in it up to your neck. The *ripoux*. You and your friends. Even if you didn't do the murder. You know something."

Legardère took a long, slow sip of his expensive scotch. And smirked.

"So what? I might have given a few tips to a couple of newspapers. Maybe I helped a few buddies out with information from time to time. Everybody does it. If they paid us anything near what we're worth, it would never happen. So what?"

Mazarelle smiled. He slowly opened his jacket to reveal the mobile phone, on and transmitting.

"So what, Théo? So what is you're going down."

Legardère looked around with a startled expression. An expression that quickly hardened into raw anger. Incensed, Legardère slammed down his glass, and stormed out of the booth, heading for the front door of the bar. Mazarelle watched as Théo flung open the door, to find Clay and Alembert, the two Internal Affairs detectives, on the sidewalk outside waiting for him. The *boeuf-carottes* had been listening to the entire conversation.

Legardère pulled up short.

"This is ridiculous," he fumed. "You'll never prove anything. There's no evidence. No one will believe you. I've got years, I've got decades on the force."

Coming up behind him at a leisurely pace, Mazarelle took in the end of his rant. Without saying a word, he reached into his pocket and pulled out Claire's thin black ledger. He held it out in front of Théo Legardère's eyes.

"Evidence?" He smiled. "We've got evidence. With your name all over it. And the payment amounts too."

Legardère stepped back, stunned. Clay clamped his hand on the lieutenant's shoulder. Alembert was reaching for the handcuffs.

"Wait," said Mazarelle.

The two *boeuf-carottes* looked over at him and nodded. They knew what Mazarelle had in mind.

"Théo. You know how this works. We need the information. Just tell us who's behind the whole operation. You can trade."

Legardère shook his head and kept his mouth shut.

"C'mon, Théo. You don't want to go down alone for this, do you? Why should you bear the weight for all your friends?"

Legardère gave a snort, and kept walking. "I'm not rolling."

But Mazarelle kept pushing. "It's Coudert, isn't it? It has to be Coudert."

That brought Legardère to a sudden stop. His head swung around. He fixed Mazarelle with a fierce expression. "Did you say Coudert?"

"Yes. The man behind the *ripoux*. Right?"

Legardère glared at Mazarelle.

"Coudert," said Mazarelle. "It has to be. He's the one who tried to sideline the investigation. The one who's high enough up to make it happen."

Legardère's grim face suddenly cracked into an open grin.

"Some detective!" He shook his head incredulously. "How did you ever make it into the BC?"

Mazarelle pushed again: "You don't have to cover for him."

Legardère chuckled. "Just amazing. It's been staring you right in the face for years. You had no idea. You still don't."

Mazarelle watched Legardère being hauled off by the *boeuf*. And as they disappeared around the corner, his quizzical expression abruptly changed to a broad smile—the satisfied smile of a winner. He had started with two suspects. Now he was down to one. The main one. And the jealous Théo hadn't even noticed.

Well, he had his target. But this was where things would get dangerous.

74

The next morning, Mazarelle awoke feeling badly rested and irritable. Still in his pajamas, he paced back and forth in his apartment, his limp worse than usual, his back in knots. Even after showering and shaving, he was still unable to settle down, unable to enjoy the morning coffee he'd just prepared.

Sure he was glad that Vachère was gone, glad that Luc and now Legardère were headed behind bars for most of the next decade. The *boeuf-carottes* and the Paris anti-fraud squad had even caught up with a handful of the low-level members of the *ripoux*. But, all through a long night's broken sleep, Mazarelle had been worrying that the one ultimately responsible for the tarot murders might not suffer any consequences. Because to take him down—that would be the biggest, riskiest proposition of all. And there didn't seem to be anyone willing to face the challenge.

Unless, thought Mazarelle, I get off my goddamn ass and do something.

Rather than waiting until he got to his office, Mazarelle placed the call from his mobile phone.

"*J'écoute,*" mumbled the man on the other end, still half asleep. "Who is this?"

Mazarelle identified himself. "I need to talk to you today."

"I didn't know you had this number. What's it about?"

"There are some loose ends in the Berthaud case. I could really use your help."

"Loose ends? I thought the case was closed. Finished."

"Not quite," said Mazarelle, surprised that the word had already spread. "Can you stop by the BC today? Or I would be glad to come to your place."

"No, no!" said the man on the other end, now wide awake. "I'm busy this morning. Here's a better idea. Why don't we meet this afternoon at my club. Six rue de Ponthieu. We can share a good cognac. Say three o'clock?"

"Perfect. See you there."

The day had started out damp. A light drizzle all morning. But by mid-afternoon Paris was sunny and steaming hot. Mazarelle, wearing one of his coolest shirts—a Cuban guayabera—took the arcade from the Champs-Élysées to the narrow rue de Ponthieu. He had overheard descriptions of the club's expensive elegance and its highly restricted members list. Mazarelle, of course, had never been invited inside until now. But he was ready for a high-stakes game.

At the door of the Aristo Club, the uniformed host looked Mazarelle up and down, narrowed his eyes, and asked for an ID. Mazarelle complied. Inside the entry hall, the host insisted on offering the commandant a selection of loaner jackets. His choice—navy or navy. Frowning, Mazarelle shook his head and without waiting strode through the doorway to the main room of the club. Claude Fabriani was already seated, smoking a cigar.

"Ah, Mazarelle," he said. "I see you're dressed in your usual high style—"

"I might say the same for you, Claude. You must have a meeting later at the commissariat."

"That's true, *mon cher*—but in this case . . ."

Fabriani gestured around them.

"The members of our club have all agreed to maintain certain standards . . . Ah—never mind! Sit down, Mazarelle. You can share some of our pleasures here."

Fabriani signaled the host, who arrived promptly with two snifters and a bottle of Rémy Martin XO Excellence. He poured a shot for each of them.

"Superb," said Mazarelle, savoring the rich taste of the brandy. Unlike the poor copies of paintings on the walls, the cognac was the real thing.

"I thought you'd like it. So what's with your loose ends? Coudert told me the case is closed."

Mazarelle raised an eyebrow. "Claude—you're an intelligent man. A man of experience. You understand how things work."

"Good of you to say." Fabriani took another sip of his cognac, a puff of cigar.

"So maybe you can help me. Do you really believe that Vachère decided all by himself to assassinate Berthaud and Guy? And if so, why?"

"Aha!—Twenty questions?"

"No, Claude." Mazarelle put his glass down. "No games—I need a serious answer."

"Okay, I'll try. Wasn't he more of a serial killer. A madman?"

"He was a killer all right. But he was following orders. He said so himself."

"But, Mazarelle—" Fabriani shrugged. "Jacques Vachère was your villain, not mine. You were the one who brought him down. You're the one who's getting the honors for it. Don't tell me you're having second thoughts about who was responsible for those murders?"

"Claude, I'll tell you exactly what I believe. I'm sure that Vachère killed Berthaud and Guy. He was brutal and efficient. But he wasn't the one who issued the orders. He was being used. When it came to those murders, he was just the tool—the weapon. Someone else picked the targets and called the shots."

Mazarelle was warming to his story.

"What personal reasons could a former paratrooper living in the South of France have had to travel to Paris to murder two people he didn't even know?"

"A coincidence?" said Fabriani, stretching and leaning back in his chair. He nodded to the host, holding up his glass.

"Will you have some more, Mazarelle?"

Mazarelle waved the bottle of cognac away. He was too focused on what came next.

"It's more than a coincidence that the two men killed were both deeply involved with matters being investigated by Internal Affairs. Matters that put the *ripoux* in danger." Mazarelle nodded emphatically. "That's not a coincidence. That's a motive."

Fabriani watched the waiter pour him a second glass, then took a contented sip.

"Okay, that's intriguing. But I don't really see how I can help you."

"Well, here's the thing, Claude. Here's how you can help."

Mazarelle took a deep breath.

"There was a lot going on in the commissariat in the Fourth. Guy Danglars and Théo Legardère both worked there. Luc Fournel used to work there too. All were members of the *ripoux*. They all worked for you. Plus you knew Luc's connection to Vachère. You were the one who told me the story."

Mazarelle fingered the mobile phone on and set to record in his pocket. It had worked once before this week. Now to bring it on home.

"There is no way all of this could have happened without your knowledge, is there?"

Fabriani took another puff on his cigar, and raised an amused eyebrow.

"All of what?"

"The *ripoux*, the murders." He tapped the table with his index finger. "You were at the center of it, weren't you?"

Fabriani gave a slow nod, as if thinking through Mazarelle's points.

"Interesting. But I don't hear any evidence. So really, it's only a theory, right?"

He didn't seem fazed. He had just been accused of masterminding a series of crimes. He would have been more upset if someone had taken away his cigar.

Mazarelle felt himself starting to simmer. He tried again.

"The Fourth is your commissariat. You're aware of everything that goes on there. Everyone knows that."

Fabriani leaned forward in his armchair with a grin.

"*Bien.* So let me play along with you in this game. Let's imagine, for example, that someone in my commissariat did somehow suggest a useful course of action to Luc Fournel—mind, I say suggested, not compelled—someone who knew about Luc's influence over that maniacal Romanian friend of his from their early days in the Legion together. And imagine that Luc then asked that friend to commit those expedient murders . . . to get rid of a few problematic people who had trouble keeping their mouths shut. Even if you did believe all that . . . even if you believed, say, that I, myself, played that supreme role in all this—"

Mazarelle could only nod. It was a brazen confession of sorts, but uttered with the ironic self-confidence of someone who knew it could never be used against him. Mazarelle's mobile phone was recording it all, but there wasn't anything usable there. Fabriani was too smart for that.

"Believed without a shred of evidence . . ."

Mazarelle raised an eyebrow.

The commissaire wasn't finished. "But why would I, for example, be involved in such a sordid scheme? What interest—financial or otherwise—would I have in any of that? You know my friends in government. You know, Mazarelle, that I'm a very rich man."

"No—I don't know that. What I do know is that it's your wife who doesn't need any further sources of income. But has she been less than generous lately?"

It was a wild guess. Mazarelle had no reason to believe that Juliette was disaffected with her husband. It was clear, however, that he'd touched a raw nerve.

"Mazarelle—please!" Fabriani snapped angrily. "You're the one with lady trouble—they all seem to die on you!"

Silence. Mazarelle sipped his cognac. Stared steadily at Fabriani. It was a low blow, and it hurt. More than he could let on. First Martine, then Claire. But it was also exactly the kind of tactic someone would use to distract him. He was closing in now. He could feel it.

"Well, Claude," he said coolly. "There is at least one piece of evidence. The phone records Maurice tracked down. The call to the crime lab—about the Mercedes? To undercut our investigation? That came from your office."

Fabriani's eyes narrowed.

"And one other thing . . ."

Mazarelle was on a roll now. "That number I called you on this morning? You were right. I never had the number to that phone. I got it here . . ."

He tossed a dog-eared phone log on the table.

"See that? Those are the records of Alain Berthaud's calls. Seems he was calling you a lot. What were the two of you talking about?"

Fabriani slammed his glass down on the table, and swiftly jumped up. "Phone calls? *Alors,* Mazarelle. Enough. This is all very amusing. But I suggest you look in some other more profitable direction. Right now I'm afraid that I must leave you. I'm expected at the Élysée Palace within the hour. The rumor is that there's a new appointment in the works."

He flashed Mazarelle his million-dollar smile.

"But please, stay as long as you like—and certainly finish your cognac."

Without waiting for a response, Fabriani was out the door.

75

Was it the cocky way Fabriani had left that made Mazarelle's blood boil? Condescending as his former boss often was, his rude exit shouldn't have been a surprise. Besides, it did provide a grim satisfaction. Now Mazarelle was more convinced than ever of Fabriani's guilt.

But proving it was another matter entirely. So many allies, so much power. The gratitude of the president in his back pocket. Mazarelle knew he'd be heading into hazardous territory.

Sitting at his desk, he started to leaf absentmindedly through the letters Juliette had given him back at the fundraiser. The stack of hate mail. He had promised to look through them for her, and had promptly forgotten. At least now they matched the mood he was in. One after another taking potshots at his old boss.

"Law-and-order crap!" the first announced. "They should lock you up." Couldn't argue with that.

A second was scrawled in big block letters: "Fascist. Die!" A little extreme, thought Mazarelle. But at least the heart was in the right place. He leafed through to a third, in computer-generated Times Roman font: "I know what you're up to," it read.

He smiled and put it down. Me too, he thought. And, just as he was about to turn away, he saw something that made him turn back.

Picking up the letter, he read the rest: "You may be shooting blanks, but I promise I'm not. You will pay now, or you'll pay later."

Mazarelle leaned back in his chair, his mouth open. He held the letter up to the light. Nothing distinctive. He put it down next to the Lucite frame. Idly turning the box with the .22 shell again, he watched as the pieces of his case began to reassemble themselves. This was the final piece of the puzzle. The motive.

It wasn't a hate letter. It was blackmail.

He had been looking at this case in entirely the wrong way—concentrating on the *ripoux*, their strong-arm tactics, and their small-time cash schemes. But what if, instead of Fabriani's greed, he focused on the commissaire's grander aspirations—his desire for political power.

Mazarelle checked the date on the envelope. July 15. One day after the Bastille Day attack, someone had sent this note. Someone who knew about the blanks. Someone who was squeezing Fabriani. Someone like Alain Berthaud.

As anyone close to Fabriani knew, the commissaire was aiming for higher office. He hoped to parlay his police credentials right into the cabinet. And as long as unrest was front and center in the public consciousness, he had a good chance of achieving his goal. In a time of fear and chaos, the president would want to appoint a law-and-order right-hand man. If the news reports were right, Chirac was about to do exactly that.

Fabriani just needed to keep that unrest simmering. Mazarelle could see how he would have set out to do it. For years, the commissaire had been quietly encouraging the *ripoux* at a deniable distance—working through cutouts like Luc Fournel and Alain Berthaud to exploit a handful of dirty cops and increase his income. But recently, his schemes were larger.

Now Alain Berthaud would have had a new use. As a member of the Défense Nationale, he could help stir up the organization's thugs, urging them to create more trouble on the streets. Alain must have been the one who recruited young Max. Probably found him in the online chat rooms, and started to groom him—at first, echoing his far right ideologies, and then, little by little, encouraging his crackpot dream of a presidential shooting.

But Fabriani and his men never wanted Max to succeed. Chirac's well-being was central to their political plans. Which is why they had switched Max's bullets for blanks. They wanted to create the mood of terror, not actually hurt anyone. It wasn't politics; it was opportunism. Fabriani was no white supremacist. He was simply ambitious.

The commissaire's scenario was working—until the free-spending Berthaud chose to cash in. Maybe to live large. Maybe to cover his alimony and childcare expenses. Alain knew Fabriani was about to hit it big. Why shouldn't he profit too? So, once the Bastille Day shooting was over, he decided that he'd earned a raise. Without telling his partner, Luc, he sent the blackmail letter. Then, one or two days later, he had followed up with a series of calls, putting pressure on the commissaire. Threatening him with exposure of his connection to all the schemes. And Alain had a lot of leverage. A lot to expose.

Luc Fournel would have known better. He would have been more patient. He understood that if he kept calm, big things were in store once the boss moved into the cabinet. All their *ripoux* income would then seem like chicken feed. So when Fabriani told Luc what his partner was up to, he would have been furious.

Fournel would know immediately what had to be done. Alain had always been too eager, too emotional, too unreliable, too caught up in his politics. If only he had kept his mouth shut. But by then it was too late.

Alain was threatening the goose and the golden eggs. And that would end only one way. With the blackmailer dead. Dangling from a canal bridge. An end to a nuisance—and a warning to the rest of their little group not to get too ambitious. As Mazarelle knew, Luc had precisely the man to take care of the problem.

76

t stuck in Mazarelle's craw to ask Coudert for help, but he thought that was the only way to go. If he laid out the evidence clearly, Coudert would have to support him.

Jumping out of his car in the parking lot at 36, Mazarelle raced up the steps to the third floor; plowed through the anteroom to Coudert's office; and, ignoring Nicolas's outstretched arms, knocked energetically on his *patron*'s door, opened it, and strode in.

"What is it?" Coudert, about to make a call, looked annoyed at the interruption. "Couldn't you at least . . . ?"

"No," said Mazarelle. "No time! This can't wait. It's about the murders and the *ripoux*—"

Coudert broke in. Held up his right hand. Sighed. "Mazarelle—I told you that case is closed. Why are you bringing it up again?"

"*Patron*, there are reasons it can't be closed—if you'll listen."

"*Eh bien*, Mazarelle—I'm a rational man. I'm always willing to listen, but I'm afraid that you're going off half-assed and making a mistake."

"I don't think so. Here's the point. We caught the murderer—but he never had a motive. So who was behind the killings? Who was running the *ripoux*? The guy at the top has not been fingered. Does not even seem to be in danger of being accused. Or even—"

"Stop—" said Coudert. "Who is it?"

Mazarelle rapped his knuckles on the desk for emphasis.

"Claude Fabriani."

"Fabriani?" Coudert's voice went up an octave. His eyes widened in alarm. "Claude Fabriani?! The head of the Fourth?"

"Yes—exactly."

"Do you know what you're saying, Mazarelle? The kind of wild accusation you're making?" Coudert's face had flamed pink, his astonishment apparent. "How can you begin to make an allegation like that?"

It was the kind of question Mazarelle loved. He opened his palms like a waiter presenting a feast.

"Do you remember what I told you about the black ledger I found in Claire's pied-à-terre? It's a record of all the payments for information. It ties all the pieces together—Luc Fournel, Théo Legardère, Guy Danglars—"

Coudert, about to cut Mazarelle off, hesitated. Closed his eyes. He didn't like to admit it, but he was curious.

"Is Fabriani actually mentioned there? Is he in Claire Girard's ledger?"

Now it was Mazarelle's turn to hesitate.

"Not exactly. He's not mentioned there—but he's the—"

"*Merde,* Mazarelle—" Coudert swallowed hard. "So you've got nothing! How many times did I tell you not to step on Fabriani's toes? Can't you understand? Besides—you don't even have a shred of evidence—"

"But there *is* evidence—" Mazarelle hurried to get back on track. "We have records of the phone calls between Alain Berthaud and Fabriani. We have this blackmail letter he got from Berthaud. That was the motive for the killing. Why they sent in Vachère."

He passed the letter across the desk to his boss, and launched right back in.

"And don't you realize how odd it is that the whole case centers around Fabriani's commissariat? The dirty cops. The murders. They all started there. Even the interference in my case—that came from his office too."

Coudert had been reading the letter as the detective talked. When he got to the end, he leaned back, and tossed it onto the desk.

"Mazarelle."

He took a deep breath. Cleared his throat nervously.

"If some of this . . ."

There was a silence. Coudert sighed and fiddled with the edges of the letter. "Even if some of this is true . . . it's all circumstantial. There's no mention of any names here. Nothing that ties anyone to anyone else. And certainly not the kind of evidence that could touch Fabriani."

This wasn't going the way Mazarelle had intended at all.

"Look," he insisted. "I know him. He's the one pulling the strings. He practically admitted it to me."

Coudert waved him off.

"Even if you had more, lots more, tons more, it wouldn't matter—"

"Just let me run with this . . . We can get Legardère to roll over."

"Mazarelle—what don't you understand?!" Coudert's cheeks now matched the burgundy of his tie. "Don't you know how highly placed he is? His connection to the president? Don't you realize he's about to be named interior minister? He'll be my boss—and yours too. At your age, you still don't know the way of the world?"

Mazarelle could see the fear in Coudert's eyes, his *patron*'s clenched fist. Nevertheless, he persisted. "*Patron*—we can't let Fabriani off. He's a goddamn criminal!"

"Forget it, Mazarelle. Do yourself a favor. You can't touch him."

"But—"

"No, Mazarelle. You can't go there. The case is closed."

"But—"

"Leave Fabriani alone. That's an order!" Coudert stood up. Walking over, he opened the door, and pointed the way out. "Please!"

Mazarelle, fuming, got up to leave.

EPILOGUE

On the stairs, heading down, Mazarelle kept replaying the conversation. That insufferable response. Can't go there. Can't touch him. Can't bring him to justice. How could that be the last word on this case? Mazarelle was so preoccupied he almost stumbled on the last step.

Back in his office, his leg hurt more than ever. He grimaced as he sat down, the pain radiating up to his hip.

Rubbing his thigh, he pushed the newspaper on his desk aside. Informed sources were confirming that Fabriani had been selected for a key position in the new administration. Probably the next minister of the interior.

That son of a bitch getting away with it all, untouched. For the first time, Mazarelle thought: Maybe it was time to retire. Maybe he was getting old. Maybe . . .

He jammed some tobacco into his pipe, and prodded it angrily. And then a little less. Until finally he struck a match.

Then again . . . maybe not.

A small grin tickled the corners of his mustache.

Outside, it was surprisingly chilly. A new weather system. In the cool air, Mazarelle, walking to his car, felt oddly refreshed.

When he got to Donovan's, it was too early for Caitlin but not for the cognac Mazarelle craved. He sat down at a table in the back. When his cognac arrived, he took a sip. That was all he needed. He was as ready as he'd ever be. Coudert might be scared. But if you lost on one front, it was time to try another. There were many different ways to win this battle.

He swung his aching leg up onto the banquette, pulled out his mobile phone, and dialed. Even the digits gave him a warm feeling. Claire's magazine, *Paris-Flash*.

"*Allô*, Philippe? Commandant Mazarelle here . . ."

He settled back into the banquette.

"Do you have your keyboard handy?"

Mazarelle picked up his glass and held it out. Not too close; not too far. He took an appreciative sniff, and nodded to himself. *La bonne distance*. He smiled.

"So, Philippe . . . Just off the record . . . About the new minister . . . Here's something that might interest you . . ."

ACKNOWLEDGMENTS

This book is a work of fiction. All of the characters in it are fictions—or, if in any way similar to actual individuals, are treated as fictions. But several of the events chronicled here actually did occur. There was an assassination attempt on Jacques Chirac at the Bastille Day parade in 2002, and he did have the good fortune to make it out unscathed. As for the story of his would-be assassin, and the way the plot evolved, they are of course inventions.

Just as Mazarelle recalls, Christophe Adam did indeed spring to culinary fame with his éclair creations, starting with the citrus éclair. From the Paris-Brest to the cherry blossoms of the éclairs fleuris, they would in time become the signature pastry of the Maison Fauchon.

There is a Deauville Film Festival—created in 1975 to honor American cinema—and it does take place at the end of the summer each year, although usually a few weeks later than attended here by Claire's husband.

The French Foreign Legion, the *Légion etrangère*, does have a museum and a long and fiercely debated history from 1831 onward—a tradition of propping up the French colonial empire, as well as fighting the war on terror. And while it has no doubt sheltered some dangerous individuals over the years, it has also offered a new start, and a new family, to recruits from more than 140 different countries . . . *Legio Patria Nostra*.

The legendary detectives of the Brigade Criminelle have been tracking down kidnappers and murderers since they began in 1924 under the name Brigade spéciale no. 1. When they moved headquarters from the Quai des Orfèvres to the rue du Bastion in 2017, they kept their mythic street number 36. And while there have certainly been instances of police corruption in the arrondissements of Paris, Commissaire Fabriani would want you to know that they are the exception, not the rule.

The rise of white nationalism and the challenges of institutionalized racism faced by the Romani and other immigrant communities over the years (from the Petite Ceinture encampment to the twenty-five migrant detention centers [the CRA]) are unfortunately all too real, and documented weekly on the pages of publications much more somber than *Paris-Flash*. The United Nations Refugee Agency, the UNHCR, has been helping them from a slightly different Paris address, away from the clutches of Legardère.

The paintings on the walls of the aristo club are quirky reproductions of famous artworks, all with different names and details. Like the club's loaner jackets, they're not the real thing but will do in a pinch.

The bars Chez les Jumeaux, and Rosebud do exist, as does the Marseille restaurant Chez Rémy (under a slightly different name), although the bouillabaisse comes from Restaurant Michel. It's worth noting that after a lot of ferocious debate through the 1980s about exactly which ingredients go into a bouillabaisse, a group of a dozen or so restauranteurs came together, put their pride aside, and agreed on a compromise—the Marseille Bouillabaisse Charter. A lesson, perhaps, for other institutions.

Thanks are owed to many people for their support through these difficult past few years.

First, thanks to you, Mazarelle's readers, for keeping him in your hearts.

To Georges, Anne, and Valerie Borchardt, our friends for years (and our new friend Cora Markowitz), for championing the novel and seeing it through to publication.

To Nan Talese, whose admiration of and advocacy for Mazarelle has been greatly appreciated. It's an honor for this novel to be among the titles in her imprint.

To Carolyn Williams at Doubleday, for shepherding the manuscript through the publication process with such grace and enthusiasm.

To Gretchen Crary, for bringing Mazarelle to the world . . . and into the Instagram age (see on Instagram: @inspector.mazarelle and @2goldbergs).

To Anne Jaconette and Rachel Molland, for spreading the word.

To Dr. Richard Meyer, Kristina Jimenez, Enrique Arencibia, Joseph Ancona, and Matt Pugliese, for keeping the corpus in working order.

To Mike Lopez, Cal Bedient, and Lynn Umlauf, for their friendship and encouragement.

To Chelsea Hughes, a light in dark times.

To Ninotchka, editor supreme.

To Karen Marmer (whom we miss dearly), Jörg-Michael Schwartz, and the ensemble Rebel, for the vitality of their music.

To Colleen Foley—whose culinary expertise is rivaled only by Madame Mazarelle—thanks for making it all possible.

To our parents and our children . . . who have taught us everything worth knowing . . .

And above all, for the great pleasure of working together as a family—Nancy Marmer, James Goldberg, Robert Goldberg, and Jerry Goldberg, still laughing, still sparkling . . .

A NOTE ABOUT THE AUTHOR

GERALD JAY is a nom de plume of novelist Gerald Jay Goldberg, writing here in collaboration with his family, Robert Goldberg, James Goldberg, and Nancy Marmer. A new Mazarelle novel is in the works.

A NOTE ABOUT THE TYPE

This book was set in Minion, a typeface produced by the Adobe Corporation specifically for the Macintosh personal computer, and released in 1990. Designed by Robert Slimbach, Minion combines the classic characteristics of old-style faces with the full complement of weights required for modern typesetting.